The Choices Series

A PRIDE AND PREJUDICE VARIATION SERIES COMPILATION

LEENIE BROWN

Leenie B Books
Halifax

Her Father's Choice

Choices Book 1

Unwittingly trapped in a compromise of her father's arranging,
Elizabeth has no choice but to accept the proposal of a man she
is not entirely sure she likes.

Prologue

OCTOBER 1811

NOT HANDSOME ENOUGH BUT with fine eyes? Mr. Bennet chuckled to himself as he tucked himself away in the corner of the drawing room at Lucas Lodge. From here he could keep an eye on his daughters and listen to various conversations as people moved from place to place. Most of them would, at one point or another, pass through the door near him to the room beyond where there was a table laid out with various forms of refreshment.

He chuckled again as he repeated Mr. Darcy's comment to Miss Bingley to himself. Fine eyes, indeed! His Lizzy possessed the most expressive eyes of any lady Mr. Bennet had ever met. One look let you know quite clearly what she was thinking.

"Fine eyes," he muttered. It was as he had suspected when he had first met Mr. Darcy — Elizabeth would make him a fine wife. It had not taken long for that reserved and well-educated gentleman to fall under the spell of a lady whose mind was just as astute as his own. Not handsome enough? The man must have been in some foul mood to have spoken so harshly and, he added with some force to himself, wrongly. Elizabeth was not Jane, but she was by no means lacking in beauty.

But that was the fly in the ointment. Elizabeth had heard the slight Mr. Darcy had made at the assembly and taken such a strong disliking to the man. Mr. Bennet sighed and shook his head. He knew that bringing the two together would be quite the under-taking — excessively difficult but utterly necessary if he wished to see Elizabeth well-matched and happy. Mr. Darcy was, in every way that Mr. Bennet could determine, the gentleman who was his daughter's equal.

"I tried to arrange a dance between them," said Sir William as he handed his long-time friend a glass of lemonade. "But, she is quite set against him, it seems."

"I saw," Mr. Bennet replied. "And then I heard him mention her fine eyes."

"Indeed?"

Bennet nodded. "Miss Bingley is quite put out by the comment. I do not envy his position of having an unhappy woman yapping at his elbow." He raised his eyebrows and smirked as he took a sip of his drink.

Sir William lifted his glass in salute. "Hear, hear. I have had it happen a time or two in the past eight and twenty years myself. There is nothing quite like the continual complaining of a dis-gruntled woman robed in supposed humour to try one's nerves."

"He is a patient one. I am sure I could not abide Miss Bingley's comments so graciously as he." Mr. Bennet shifted in his chair. "It is a good sign, for if he can tolerate Miss Bingley in a fit of pique, he should be able to handle my Lizzy."

"Aye, he should, but Lizzy's tongue and mind are a bit sharper. And her opinions are not so easily swayed." There was a hint of caution in Sir William's voice.

Mr. Bennet knew that his friend agreed with him about Mr. Darcy and Elizabeth making a fine match. That had not, however, stopped Sir William from voicing his concern, repeatedly, that Elizabeth could not be swayed from her current dislike of the gentleman.

"She will come around, although," Mr. Bennet drew out the word and lowered his voice, "that may not happen until after they are married."

Sir William laughed. "Exactly how do you propose we get her to marry him when she does not like him? Surely, you would not suggest a compromise?"

Mr. Bennet tapped his finger against the side of his glass. "I would do almost anything to assure the happiness of my Lizzy, even if it meant bearing her anger and forcing her hand."

He watched Elizabeth, who was talking intently to her dear friend, Charlotte Lucas. He smiled as she sneaked a third glance at Mr. Darcy. If Mr. Bennet was not mistaken, and he rarely was when it came to understanding Elizabeth, she was fascinated by the man from Derbyshire. It was a fascination that he was certain was foreign to her.

"I pray it does not come to it, but if a compromise is necessary, can I count on your assistance?"

Sir William studied his friend and then Elizabeth for a moment. "You are convinced she will be happy?"

"Completely."

Sir William sighed. It was a sound of resignation and the same one he always made when he was about to bow to Mr. Bennet's wishes.

"Then, my friend," he said, "I will happily assist you with whatever you need."

Chapter 1

NOVEMBER 26, 1811

THE MUSIC SWIRLED ABOUT Elizabeth as she completed the final few steps of the dance. As the last notes of the song faded into the expanse of Netherfield's ballroom, she dipped a curtsey and moved silently away from her dancing partner. The swirling feeling, however, did not die with the music.

From the corner of her eye, she could see Miss Bingley moving toward her. Speaking to anyone, let alone Miss Bingley, was not something she wished to do at present, so seeing an opportunity to slip away from the crowds, she took it. She smiled at her father as she slid behind him and out of the room into the hallway.

Assuring herself that no one had seen her escape, she hurried to the library. A need for solitude and a place to gather her thoughts and sort through the strange feelings that had her nerves all aflutter consumed her. Quietly, she clicked the door shut behind her and retrieved a book of poetry from the shelf. It was one of the books she had enjoyed reading when she had stayed here to tend to her sister.

Darcy watched Miss Elizabeth slip off her shoes and tuck her small feet under her skirts as she curled into her chair and flipped the pages of her book. His own book lay open on his lap, but not one word had entered his mind for it was filled with the lady who now presented such a charming picture before him.

This, he thought to himself, this is how an evening at home should be spent. The thought both shocked and pleased him. He shook his head and smiled, for he could not help it even in his unsettled state of mind. Thoughts of Miss Elizabeth often led him to smile. He allowed himself several moments to consider her and play again in his mind many of their interactions before he turned his mind to his book.

As fair as thou, my bonnie lass,
So deep in luve am I;
And I will love thee still, my dear,
Till a' the seas gang dry.

Darcy closed the book. *So deep in love am I.* The words of Mr. Burns' poem repeated themselves in his mind. He tipped his head to the right as he once again studied his reading companion and the truth of those words from the poem repeated themselves once again in his mind. So deep in love am I. That must be what ailed him. His disquiet, his agitation of spirit, his joy in having her near, and his torment when hearing her speak of another were not symptoms that his heart might be in danger of being engaged, as he had thought, but rather they were signs that it was already engaged and, he feared, to an unalterable extent.

Softly, he lay his book on the table next to his chair and rose to leave. He would return later to retrieve the book so that he might ponder the words and what he was to do about his heart.

Elizabeth glanced up at Darcy as he walked to the door and flipped yet another unread page. The book had not been able to capture her mind or quiet her spirit. The room still spun slowly, her heart still fluttered, and her eyes were drawn of their own accord to the man sitting across the room from her. Perhaps once he took his leave of the room, she would be able to find the peace she sought.

She turned her mind back to her book; but it was of no use, the desire to read seemed to be leaving with Mr. Darcy. So, she stood, smoothed her skirts, and slipped her feet into her slippers.

The door opened as Darcy reached it, and Elizabeth's aunt, Mrs. Philips, entered. She looked from Mr. Darcy to Elizabeth, who was still smoothing her skirts, and then peered around the room as if searching for someone or something. Her eyes grew wide, and her hand flew to her chest.

"Oh," she said. "Oh, my. Oh, Lizzy. And...and Mr. Darcy." She spun on her heels and very nearly ran from the room. "Mr. Bennet," she called. "Mr. Bennet, you are needed."

The horror of what her aunt must think washed over Elizabeth. "I must stop her," she said as she moved toward the door, but Darcy stopped her. She looked first at the hand which lay on her arm and then to the face of the owner of that hand.

"The damage has already been done," he said softly. "If you follow after her, she will only make a greater spectacle when she either scolds or questions you. It is best to await your father here." He led her back to her chair. Reluctantly, it seemed, he let go of her arm as she took a seat. "Are you well?" he asked.

"I hardly know," she replied. Thoughts of the things her aunt might be saying filled her mind. She sought a solution, an explanation that might explain her current circumstances in such a way as to repair her reputation. She knew that once her aunt spun the tale to one and all about the few seconds of what she had seen in the library, her reputation would be well and truly tarnished. Aunt Philips was the worst gossip.

She watched Mr. Darcy pace around the room and replied to his inquiries after her health each time he asked if she was well. He sat for a moment but stood again and resumed his pacing, which only stopped when her father entered. Then she noted how very rigid his stance became. She could only imagine he was just as unhappy about their current situation as she was.

"Papa," she said rising and going to him, "it is not how my aunt presented it."

Her father pulled her into his embrace.

"I have no doubt of that, but it is not about what has happened. It is about what others think has happened." He spoke gently to her as if attempting to keep the horrible reality of the situation in which she found herself from causing her too much pain. "I do not doubt your honour, but you know how the gossips work."

He released her from his arms and grasping her chin, forced her to look at him. The anguish in her eyes was nearly his undoing. "Have a seat while we discuss what can be done to save your reputation," he faltered for a moment before adding what he knew would play most heavily upon her heart, "and the reputation of our family." He clenched his jaw as he saw her eyes grow wide and fill with tears. This needed to be done. She would be happy eventually.

"There is only one option, sir." Mr. Darcy pulled Mr. Bennet's attention away from Elizabeth.

"I must marry your daughter. My reputation may be tainted slightly by a situation such as this, but the damage that would be done to Miss Elizabeth...."

He let his thought fade away and stood there, silently, waiting as Mr. Bennet gave him a sweeping glance from head to foot and back again. It was good to see he had not overestimated Mr. Darcy's honour. That would make things somewhat easier.

"I believe you have the right of it, Mr. Darcy. There seem to be few other options. I know my wife's sister is not one to keep a story such as this to herself. I fear the entirety of Mr. Bingley's guests has already come to know about this supposed compromise." He emphasized the word supposed to let both Elizabeth and Mr. Darcy know that he did not believe a compromise had actually taken place.

"No, Papa, please," she begged him. He could see the panic that gripped Elizabeth for it was etched in her expression, and it tore at his heart.

"Elizabeth, there is no other option. You will marry Mr. Darcy." His voice was gentle but firm, and he used her full name instead of Lizzy so that she would know there was no hope of his changing his mind.

"No," she said softly as she buried her face in her hands and allowed the tears she had been fighting to fall.

He put his arm around her shoulder and pulled her close and placed a kiss on her hair. "My dear daughter, it is for the best. Aunt Philips is not known for her discretion, and the story of your being alone in the library with Mr. Darcy will be circulated, and embellishments will be added. Your betrothal is all that will save your reputation. We must also think of your sisters."

Her shoulders shook as she sobbed quietly, but she nodded her head as if she understood the reality of the situation.

Mr. Bennet swallowed the lump in his throat and strengthened his resolve as he reminded himself that this was for the best, even if his heart broke at seeing her so unhappy.

"It will be a good thing, Lizzy. I know you do not see it now, but I truly believe there is no one better suited to you than Mr. Darcy." He placed a second kiss on the top of her head. "Dry your eyes." He gave her hand a squeeze as he stood to address Mr. Darcy. "I do not question your honour. I am convinced this is nothing more than an unfortunate chain of events, but the gossip will not present it as such." His conscience pricked him as he said it. Truly, it was not Darcy's honour he questioned as much as his own.

"How shall we proceed?" Darcy's voice was tight.

"It might be best if we give everyone time to adjust to the sudden circumstances," suggested Sir William, who had only moments ago, joined them in the library. "A meeting could be arranged for tomorrow."

"That is an excellent idea, I should think," Mr. Bennet agreed. A few hours to accept the reality of what was their future would make any further discussions less fraught with emotions – or so he hoped. "Do you agree, Mr. Darcy?"

Darcy nodded his acceptance before asking, "May I have a few moments with Miss Elizabeth before she leaves?"

Mr. Bennet gave him a sympathetic smile, "I think that is acceptable to allow."

The request, coupled with the look of concern on Darcy's face, eased his mind a bit. His daughter would be loved. Indeed, it appeared she already was. If only she could see past her first impression of the gentleman.

Mr. Bennet had attempted to paint Darcy in a favourable light, but no matter how hard he had tried, Elizabeth had clung to her opinion that Darcy was proud and disdained everything about her, her family, and the neighbourhood. She was wrong, of course. He had done some shooting with Darcy and Bingley and had found both gentlemen to be pleasant; although, Darcy was more reserved and thoughtful.

He pulled the door closed as he and Sir William entered the hall.

"We have done what is best, have we not?" Mr. Bennet looked to his friend for reassurance.

Sir William shrugged. "Whether it is best or not, it is done. We must trust that they will eventually be happy together." He leaned against the door frame across from Mr. Bennet. "Consider the facts. Collins was set to make an offer which would have led to a great upheaval in your household when Elizabeth refused him — for you know she would."

Mr. Bennet nodded his agreement. Elizabeth had made her dislike for the gentleman perfectly clear to everyone save to her mother and Mr. Collins.

Sir William continued, "Then, there were Miss Bingley's comments about quitting the neighbourhood. That will not happen so quickly now, which will give Jane a greater chance of being happily matched. After all, news of one wedding often leads to news of others. And," he held up his finger to highlight the point, "it would be desirable to Bingley to be closely related to Darcy. His standing would increase and the felicity between their wives would serve both men well." He shifted and crossed one leg over the other. "There is also the fact that Mr. Wickham has been showing particular attention to Elizabeth, and from rumors I have heard, he is not the sort of man a father wishes to have pay court to his daughter." He sighed. "There are no guarantees, but I do believe your choice will prove to be best...in time."

Mr. Bennet leaned his head back and closed his eyes. He prayed that he had made the right choice and that, one day, his daughter and his new son would forgive him for his interference.

Chapter 2

WITHIN THE LIBRARY, DARCY cautiously took a seat next to Miss Elizabeth. He longed to pull her to his chest and assure her all would be well, but he could not. Instead, he placed his handkerchief in her lap, giving her the only token of his care that he was allowed.

She took the piece of cloth and dried her eyes as she mumbled her thanks. Then with a slight shake of her head to gain control of her emotions, she spoke. "I am so very sorry. I should not have come in here. But the people and the noise and the..." Her control failed, and she slipped back into tears.

"It was overwhelming." Darcy grasped his knee so that he would not take her hand. Those were the very reasons he had sought refuge in the library. Those and the wish to contemplate the desire to relieve Wickham of his life which had overtaken him during his and Miss Elizabeth's dance. It was a desire he had felt once before but never with such intensity as when he considered Elizabeth being taken in by the wastrel.

She nodded. "And now you are tied to me because I allowed my desire for solace to overwhelm my good sense." She buried her face in his handkerchief. "I am so very sorry, but my family...my sisters..." The words were muffled somewhat by the cloth she held to her face.

"No, I should have made my presence known or left as soon as you entered, but I chose to stay." Colour crept up his neck. He prayed she would not ask him why he had made that choice.

She shook her head. "I knew you were there. I chose to ignore propriety. Oh, what you must think of me!" Though she had uncovered her face, her eyes were still firmly focused on the handkerchief which she wound in her hands.

"And what you must think of me." He gave her a gentle smile as she peeked up at him. "We both chose to ignore propriety."

She nodded.

"But, what concerns me more is that you find the prospect of marriage to me to be so horrible as to bring you to tears. Surely, I cannot be that bad." There was a hint of uncertainty in his voice which made the statement sound more like a question than a statement.

Elizabeth looked at her hands again. How did one tell the man you were to marry that although he stirred deep and strong emotion in you, you were not sure if you even liked him? "It is the shock of the situation, I am sure," she mumbled.

"Of course," he agreed, although she suspected he did not. They passed a very long and strained moment in silence. "You have not yet deciphered my character. You do not trust me." There was that uncertainty in his voice again though it sounded more pained than questioning this time.

"I can neither trust nor distrust you, sir," she said. For some reason, she felt a need to ease his discomfort.

"We do not need to marry immediately. How long would you like for our betrothal to be?"

She shrugged, but her mind whirled. Her mother would be unbearable and the whispering in Meryton would follow her wherever she went. While the thought of marrying a man she barely knew frightened her more than she was willing to admit even to herself, she knew that remaining in Meryton and at Longbourn would be just as unbearable.

"There are at least three readings. I see no reason to delay it beyond that. I know you are anxious to quit the neighbourhood."

"I admit that I would prefer to be in more familiar and comfortable surroundings, but I am more concerned that you be at ease."

She peeked at him once again, her brows furrowed as they had during their dance when she questioned him. He smiled. "I can see you are once again trying to read my character. I promise to answer any questions you may have, but there will be no reading of the banns. We will marry by special license."

Her eyes widened. "Why?"

"My aunt." He gave her a wry smile. "Mr. Collins' patroness," he rolled his eyes, and she caught a laugh just before it burst forth, "Lady Catherine de Bourgh is, as I am sure your cousin has made you aware, my aunt."

"And this demands a special license?" The handkerchief lay knotted but still on her lap.

"She expects me to marry her daughter. I have never had any intention of marrying my cousin, and I am not, as I am sure has been said, betrothed to her. There is no arrangement, but that does not mean my aunt will not be greatly displeased. I do not wish to give her the opportunity to cause an issue by making a statement in reply to the banns."

"You are not betrothed?"

He shook his head. "No. It is a great desire of my aunt's, but it is not mine." He sighed. "I do not like family discord. It is why I have not been more forceful in making my position known. Indeed, it is why I do not complain more frequently to Bingley regarding his sisters. I consider him as a brother. He is not family by blood, but he is family by extension."

There was a soft knock at the door.

"Our time is up, Miss Elizabeth. May I call on you when I come to Longbourn to meet with your father? Perhaps, if Bingley accompanies me, he and I could join you and your sister on a walk, and you may begin to question me." His mouth tipped up only on one side, giving him a rather playful look that startled Elizabeth in a most pleasant way.

"I would like that," she said, and she was surprised to realize just how much she actually meant it.

Mr. Bennet opened the door just as Elizabeth smiled at Mr. Darcy when he stood to leave.

"You are well?" Her father asked hopefully as he looked from her to Mr. Darcy.

"I am resigned," she said. "I know that I cannot put my wishes before my duty to my sisters. Perhaps it is as you said and will be for the best." She hugged his arm as they walked toward the door of the library. "He was exceedingly kind just now. Not at all proud."

Darcy paused in the hall as her words reached him. He hastened his steps and sought Bingley, who was just wishing Miss Bennet a good night. "I must speak with you," he said softly as he stood near his friend.

"Oh, Mr. Darcy!" Mrs. Bennet's shrill voice caused him to grimace slightly. "You are a sly one. Pretending to not like Lizzy and then proposing. It is quite surprising, I assure you. We were positively certain you disapproved of her, and I would not blame you if you did. She can be quite the outspoken sort, and her beauty is nothing compared to Jane."

Jane flinched at the comment and extended her hand to Mr. Darcy as if wishing him a good night. "I must apologize for my mother. I believe she has had a bit too much punch." She smiled that serene smile of hers, and Darcy wondered for the first time how much she might conceal behind her façade.

Gently, she guided her mother and younger sisters out the door with a quick look over her shoulder toward where Elizabeth walked with her father.

Darcy shook his head. Miss Bennet was removing her mother before a greater scene ensued. He had obviously misjudged her depths, and if he had been wrong in this, perhaps he was wrong in not perceiving her affection for Bingley.

"I will wait for you in the library."

Bingley shot him an amused look. "Have you not spent enough time in there yet tonight?"

Darcy scowled. He was in no mood for Bingley's teasing at present. The words he had just heard from Elizabeth were still stinging far too much for him to be pleasant.

"I will be there directly," Bingley said with a nod before turning to Mr. Bennet.

Darcy paced the library as he waited for Bingley. He mulled Elizabeth's words over in his mind. Not at all proud and exceedingly kind. She had seemed surprised to find him so.

"Am I proud?" he blurted as Bingley entered the room.

"Not improperly so." Bingley removed his jacket and unbuttoned his waistcoat before lowering himself into a chair with a sigh. "Of course, people have to get to know you before they realize it."

"What do you mean?" Darcy stopped in front of Bingley's chair and looked down at him.

"Your serious expression and reserve can be misunderstood as being aloof and disdainful."

Darcy pondered that for a moment. He could see how that could be. Not that being able to agree with a negative description of oneself made the description any more enjoyable to hear.

"Did you think I did not approve of Miss Elizabeth?"

Bingley laughed. "You did tell me she was not handsome enough to tempt you, a fact that, Miss Bennet assures me, her sister knows."

"I may have been wrong about her."

Bingley laughed again. "Well, I should hope so. One does not wish to find himself married to a lady who is merely tolerable and not tempting."

"No," said Darcy, shaking his head. "Miss Bennet. She quite possibly likes you." He sat in a chair and leaned his head back looking up at the ceiling. "I was wrong about Miss Elizabeth as well. She is quite handsome." He scrubbed his face. "However, she finds me proud and was surprised that I could be kind."

"That does not bode well for a marriage," said Bingley, studying his friend. It was rare to see Darcy so distraught. "So, there was no secret assignation as implied?"

Darcy groaned. "No. I read a book, and Miss Elizabeth read a book. I sat here, and she was across the room. There was nothing worthy of scandal that happened in here tonight."

"But her aunt saw you together."

"I was just leaving the room when Mrs. Philips came in in search of Miss Elizabeth. She pushed past me into the room and saw Miss Elizabeth putting on her slippers and smoothing her skirt...as any lady would do after sitting for an extended period of time." He sighed. "Before I could stop her, she was off calling for Mr. Bennet, as I am sure you and all your guests heard." He rested an arm across his eyes. "A brief discussion followed between myself and Mr. Bennet and then between Mr. Bennet and Miss Elizabeth." He drew a deep breath. "She wept at the thought of marrying me, Bingley. She wept."

Bingley could feel the pain in his friend's voice. "Do you love her?"

"I did not realize it until this evening, but yes, I believe I do love her."

"Then show her the man who is my friend. If you displayed him more often, I would not be able to claim so many angels, for they would be tripping over their slippers to be with you."

Darcy laughed lightly. Bingley always knew how best to distill a complex situation down to something dashed simple. "Are you saying you find me irresistible, Bingley?"

Bingley laughed loudly. "No! No! I am merely suggesting you could be irresistible to women if you would show your true self to them." He continued laughing. "Of course, you really only need one lady to find you irresistible."

"Yes, one lady who must marry me, but presently, I fear, does not even like me very much."

Bingley rose. "You need sleep; though, I doubt you will get much."

Darcy stood with him. "I believe you are right." He followed Bingley to the door. "I am to meet tomorrow afternoon with Mr. Bennet to discuss particulars of the marriage agreement. I have asked Miss Elizabeth to take a walk with me, and she has consented. I told her I would bring you with me so that you could keep Miss Bennet company."

Bingley turned to look at Darcy. "You agree Miss Bennet likes me?"

"I believe you could be right, but my opinion on matters feminine seems to be sadly lacking, so I would put more confidence in your own feelings than in mine."

"But you believe it is possible?"

"Yes, Bingley, I do."

"So," Bingley said as they entered the hall, "I was right, and you, the great counselor and guide, were wrong?"

"Bingley," Darcy growled, "have a care. I have had a rather trying night."

"Not as trying as mine is about to be," Bingley said as he saw his sister Caroline approaching.

"Good night. You will understand if I leave you now," Darcy said as he nodded to Caroline and took the stairs to his room two at a time before either Bingley could say anything to him.

Chapter 3

Elizabeth blew out a breath in an attempt to calm her nerves as she fastened her pelisse. There was no reason for her to be nervous about talking to Mr. Darcy. She had spoken to him on many occasions and never once had felt even the slightest amount of trepidation, but today, she was struggling to keep her nerves from running away with her sense. Last night, she had resolved, after a lengthy sisterly chat and many tears, that she would accept her fate with as much alacrity as she could contrive. However, making a decision was proving easier than holding to that decision.

"Lizzy?" Jane peeked around Elizabeth's bedroom door. "Papa and Mr. Darcy have finished their meeting, and Mr. Bingley has arrived."

Elizabeth took one more look in the glass and poked a wayward curl into her bonnet. "I am ready."

"All will be well," Jane whispered as she took Elizabeth's arm and they descended the stairs.

"I pray you are right," Elizabeth whispered back.

Jane gave her a sisterly glare. It was the nearly stern expression Jane often used when she was scolding Lizzy about something that was causing Elizabeth unease. "I know it will be well, for we shall make it so."

Elizabeth laughed at the comment. "I still do not know how you intend to do so." Jane had assured her over and over last night that all would be well. Mr. Darcy would love her, and she would love

Mr. Darcy. Theirs was to be a marriage that would rival the greatest romance in all history.

Jane pulled Elizabeth to a stop. "How can he not but love you as I do? And if he is Mr. Bingley's dearest friend, how can he be anything less than the best of men?"

She pretended to straighten Elizabeth's collar so that their stopping mid-descent would not appear so strange to those who waited below. Again, it was an action she had done often to purchase a few private moments of conversation with Elizabeth.

"Question everything, Lizzy. I should not have to tell you this as questioning is in your nature, but you have questioned very little, save his honour, since Mr. Darcy arrived." There was a sharp edge to her scolding tone.

Elizabeth felt the warmth of shame creep into her cheeks. It was true. She had not questioned any story that she had heard about Mr. Darcy. She had been willing to believe the worst about the gentleman without giving the information proper consideration.

"There." Jane gave one more small tug at Elizabeth's collar and, then taking her arm, continued down the stairs.

Elizabeth studied Mr. Darcy's expression as closely as she could. Jane had claimed there was a slight smile that softened his features when he looked at her. She did not see it.

"Miss Elizabeth, I trust you are well?" There was that puzzling uncertainty again. The same as what she had heard last night in the library.

She smiled. "I am well. And you?"

The space between Mr. Darcy's brows widened and the corners of his mouth turned up. She blinked. Was this the expression of which Jane spoke?

"I am well." He offered her his arm as they exited the house.

She glanced at him as she thought of Jane's admonition to question everything. There was no better time to begin following Jane's advice than now she supposed.

"You said I could ask questions, did you not?"

Mr. Darcy nodded and slowed his pace a bit to fall further behind Bingley and Jane.

"Just now, when you greeted me, you said you trusted I was well, but the inflection in your voice said you did not trust it to be so. Why?" She studied the ground in front of her. Her nerves were threatening to undo her again. She was certain that such an impertinent question would only increase his disapproval.

They took were three agonizingly silent steps before Mr. Darcy spoke.

"You were rather distraught last night. I worried that you were still distraught today or that your distress would make you unwell. I wanted to trust you were well, but I feared you were not."

That was not at all what she had expected him to say. It was... well... it was excessively caring. "You were worried about me?"

"It seems I must admit to another fault, Miss Elizabeth."

"Indeed?" She peeked up at him. The smile he wore took her by surprise.

"I have the propensity to torment myself by fretting...." He took a deep breath and although it looked as if it made him exceedingly uncomfortable to do so, he added, "especially about people who are of great importance to me."

She tilted her head as she studied him. Was he saying she was important to him? Surely, that could not be what he meant. They had not known each other long enough for that.

"Such as my sister, my cousin, Bingley, and you," he continued. His neck and then his ears grew red as his shoulders rose and fell pronouncedly as if breathing were difficult while his words settled into Elizabeth's mind.

"Me?" The thought was so startling that she stopped walking. He was including her as a person he though of as important. But why? What reason would he have to care for her? She could not think of anything that would prompt him to feel so. Unless... Yes, that must be it. She smiled. "Of course, I shall be your wife. It is expected."

It was his turn to cock his head and study her with confusion. But why would that make him confused? Was it not the obvious reason? What could he possibly see to find fault with in what she had said?

"I am sorry, Mr. Darcy. Did I say something amiss?"

He shook his head and gave a small laugh. "No, Miss Elizabeth, but I fear I have."

Darcy regretted his choice of words immediately as he saw the look on her face. Quickly, he attempted to correct her misunderstanding.

"I do not mean I said something amiss just now. I was referring to my comment at the assembly which seems to have left you with the mistaken notion that I could never care for you."

She had dropped his arm and now walked with her hands clasped behind her back. "I do not question your ability to fulfill your duty, Mr. Darcy."

"I am not speaking of fulfilling duty, Miss Elizabeth." He stopped in front of her.

"Then, pray tell, of what are you speaking, Mr. Darcy?"

"I am saying, Miss Elizabeth, that I have been able to think of very little else save you since that confounded assembly." He looked away from her shocked expression. "Your eyes are enchanting, and your wit is enthralling."

"But you claimed I was merely tolerable!"

"I did." He sighed. "I was in a foul mood. I did not wish to encourage my friend in his quest to find me a partner, nor did I wish to give false hope to any lady." He could tell by the lift of her eyebrow that he had said something wrong again. "I am expected to marry well. I thought the people in attendance to be beneath me."

"That was most obvious." Her tone was sharp and firm. "It is a happy thing that you did not find any in attendance to be handsome."

"I never said you were not handsome."

Her eyes were wide with surprise. "You did not?" Her tone dared him to say he had not.

He crossed his arms and glared at her and did exactly as her tone taunted him to do. "No, I did not. I said you were not handsome enough to tempt me to dance."

One eyebrow arched. "You did not say to dance."

He closed his eyes and tried to rein in his frustration. "It was implied. As I said, I was in no mood to dance that evening. You could have been Aphrodite herself, and you would not have been handsome enough to tempt me to dance, for I had no intention of dancing."

"I see." She stepped past him and began walking away.

Darcy watched her and silently cursed Bingley's idea to be more open. Explaining himself to Bingley was never this difficult. This was like trying to reason with Georgiana.

He hurried after her and had nearly reached her side when she spun toward him again.

"Why? Why did you not wish to dance?"

He flinched at the question. He knew he was going to have to broach this subject at some point, but that did not make it a topic that he welcomed having to discuss.

"Forgive me," she said. "I should not have asked."

"No, no," he hastened to assure her, "I told you that you could ask me questions to learn about my character."

He offered her his arm again and was relieved when she placed her hand on it. They walked along for a few moments in silence as he considered the best way to answer. She was to be his wife and a sister to Georgiana. It would do well for her to know what had happened, but her defense of Wickham during their dance made him uneasy.

"Before I answer your question, I must ask something of you."

When she peeked up at him, her eyes caught his and held them for a heart beat before her lips tipped up in a small, comforting smile and her hand pressed more firmly into his arm. "Of course," she said as if she knew that this topic was one which would cause him pain.

"I do not wish to offend," he began. How did one ask the lady he was promised to marry if she loved a gentleman you despised? Deciding that the answer was directly, he continued. "You spoke so passionately last night about Mr. Wickham. Has he touched your heart?" The words felt bitter. They made his stomach twist, and his heart ache. He was unsure what he would do if her answer were in the positive. Silently, he prayed that it would not be.

"Mr. Wickham?" she asked in surprise.

Darcy nodded.

"I do not understand how that has anything to do with your not wishing to dance."

"I realize it does not seem related, but I assure you it is." He looked at her and smiled softly. "I do not wish to cause you pain, although I fear I will."

She shook her head. "I have enjoyed Mr. Wickham's company, but he has not touched my heart."

Darcy released the breath that he had been holding as he had awaited her reply. "I do not know what stories Wickham has told you, although I am certain they did not paint me in a favourable light."

Elizabeth smiled sheepishly at Mr. Darcy. "They did not." A sinking feeling began to settle in her stomach. She thought of how Jane had cautioned her about believing Wickham's tales.

"He told you that he has a long connection with my family?"

She nodded. "He said his father was your father's steward."

"Indeed, he was my father's steward, as well as a good man. Did Wickham tell you that he was also my father's godson?"

"He did."

"And that my father preferred his company to mine?"

She heard the underlying pain in the question and gave him an apologetic look as she nodded.

"Did he tell you that my father left him an inheritance?"

She looked at the ground. "He said you had refused to give it to him."

She heard him draw in a breath, release it, and then draw in another. Apparently, Mr. Wickham had struck a powerful blow to Mr. Darcy with that bit of information, and Elizabeth felt her shame at having listened to the man grow deeper.

"Even though I did not see him as fit for the church, I refused him nothing at first," Mr. Darcy said calmly, though Elizabeth could feel the anger that seethed beneath. "Wickham was careful to conceal his want of principle from my father but not from me. My father, knowing nothing of Wickham's true nature and loving him as if he were a younger son, wished to see him advanced in his career as far as he was able and, to that end, my father made me promise to see his wishes fulfilled. He desired for Wickham to have a valuable family living when it became vacant and a legacy of one thousand pounds."

To Elizabeth that seemed very generous, but Wickham had neither money nor a living so if Mr. Darcy had not denied him his inheritance, then what had become of it?

"Wickham's father did not long survive my own. Not long after these events, Wickham made me aware that he had decided against taking orders and had some resolve to study the law instead. An agreement was reached wherein he resigned all rights to the living and instead accepted a settlement of three thousand pounds."

Three thousand pounds? "In addition to the one-thou-sand-pound legacy?"

"Yes."

The amount of money was not insignificant. "And you gave it to him?"

Mr. Darcy nodded. "I did not hear from him again for about three years when he petitioned me for the living that had recently become vacant. The law had not been profitable for him, his in-heritance was gone, and he had decided to take orders if I would present him with the living. I refused, and as you can well imagine, he was not pleased."

Gone? Four thousand pounds gone in three years?

Mr. Darcy stopped walking and turned to look at her. "Did Wickham tell you anything more than this?" There was an urgency in his voice.

She shook her head slowly. There was more? She was beginning to feel quite ill at the realization of how completely she had been duped. "He only told me half of what you have just now related to me."

Chapter 4

TAKING IN THE PALENESS of her face and the tears that clung to her eyelashes, Darcy sought a place for her to rest. He continued his story as he led her off the road to a stile in the hedgerows.

"My sister, Georgiana, is much younger than I. When my father died, she was placed in the care of myself and my cousin, Colonel Fitzwilliam. Earlier this year, my cousin and I removed her from school and hired a companion for her. This past summer, Georgie and her companion, Mrs. Younge, travelled to Ramsgate. Wickham followed; I suspect it was by design since we later learned Wickham had a previous connection with the lady."

He brushed whatever dust there may be from the stile before allowing Elizabeth to take a seat.

"Georgiana only remembered the kindness Wickham had shown her as a child. He, knowing she had an affectionate nature, played upon it, and soon, he convinced her that she was in love. His persuasion was such that she consented to an elopement."

Elizabeth gasped, and the tears which had threatened began to slip down her cheeks. Darcy took out his handkerchief and, stooping down, handed it to her.

"I prevented the elopement. Georgiana is well, save for an injured heart."

Elizabeth's hand rested on her heart. A small groan of what Darcy could only describe as pure grief escaped her lips.

"And this is why you did not wish to dance?" she asked.

"It is." Kneeling beside her, he longed to dry her tears for her as he had for Georgiana when she had come to realize that Wickham did not care for her as much as he cared for her money. His heart ached now as it did then.

"I had just travelled a great distance away from where my heart desired to be. My sister's unhappiness at my departure was not far from my mind."

Elizabeth's looked down at her lap where his hand covered hers. There was a comfort in his gentle touch. She shook her head at the enormity of the hurt Mr. Darcy must be carrying in his heart, and she could not fault him any longer for being disagreeable. She knew both what it was to care so for a sister and that she would not be happy to be away from Jane if she were injured.

"Why is your sister not with you?"

"She is with her aunt and taking lessons from the masters. I did not wish to interrupt her education." He smiled slightly, and there was a twinkle in his eye. It seemed out of place considering what he had just shared.

"And..." His lips twitched. "Georgiana did not wish to spend time with Miss Bingley."

Elizabeth's eyes grew wide. "But Miss Bingley led me to believe she and Miss Darcy were close."

"Miss Bingley knows how dear my sister is to me, so I believe she says it so that I will think she would make a good sister for Georgiana and, therefore, a good wife for me." He stood and extended his hand to Elizabeth. "She is mistaken if she thinks I would ever consider her as my wife."

"Because she is from trade?" Elizabeth asked as she placed her hand in his.

Darcy laughed. "No, because she is annoying and rather dull." He tucked her hand into the crook of his arm and kept it covered with his own. "I have always wished for a companion in a wife. Someone with whom I can have discussions. Someone who has read extensively and has a quick wit. I wish for my sister to have a sister who is compassionate and caring as well as intelligent and strong."

His steps faltered and then stopped.

"I believe..." he paused. "I believe I have been looking for you."

"Me?" The word had leaped from her lips before her mind had fully processed what she had just heard. Darcy stood looking at her with a look of shock on his face that matched her feelings exactly. "Surely, you could not have been looking for me."

He smiled broadly, the light of his happiness shining in his eyes. "Yes, you. I have been looking for you."

She shook her head in disbelief. The world seemed to be spinning oddly today. Indeed, it had begun to spin so last night when he had asked her to dance. Things were not as they should be. He should be pointing out her deficiency, not claiming her to be his choice for a wife. No, the choice had been removed when Aunt Philips had flown loudly down the hall in search of her father. He merely wished to see what he wanted to see.

He was still wearing that same broad smile. "You are perfect," he said softly. "Beautiful, intelligent, compassionate."

Elizabeth was sure her face had never felt so warm. "I am not perfect, nor am I beautiful." She was quite certain that Mr. Darcy was not in his right mind when a laugh bubbled out of the normally dour gentleman.

"For me, to me, you are." He squeezed her hand. "Truly, you are."

Elizabeth blinked at him and shook her head once more. "I do not see it."

"But you will."

She bristled at the sound of such assurance in his voice. She was not wrong. She knew she was not beautiful. Had not her mother said so many times? She also knew she was not perfect. She had just been presented with a glaring example of how she had been willing to believe the worst of Mr. Darcy with no more proof than the words of another agreeing with her feelings of dislike for the man. It was more than she felt she could countenance for one day, and yet the day was not more than half over. She absently rubbed the space between her brows.

"Are you well?" There was the uncertainty in his voice again, but this time she understood it.

"Merely overwhelmed, Mr. Darcy." She gave him a reassuring smile. "There is no need to fret."

They began walking again.

He laughed lightly. "Ah, but I will. I am afraid it is a well-developed fault."

Seeking to change the direction of their conversation, she asked, "Has it been a fault all your life?"

"I am afraid it has. My mother's constitution was not strong. She was often ill, and she never fully recovered from her illness after my sister was born. I believe, I was naturally prone to ponder things more than needed, but when one's mother is ill…" His voice trailed off.

Elizabeth chided herself for bringing up such painful thoughts.

"She was quite wonderful. I believe I got my love of poetry from her. Both my father and mother were avid readers, but my father's tastes tended more to the academic where my mother's were more imaginative."

The look on his face softened, and the corners of his mouth turned up slightly. Elizabeth was so taken with the expression, since it was the same he had given her this morning, that she nearly forgot to listen to what he was saying.

"She would take me up on her lap or, later, next to her in her bed, and read a poem to me and then discuss the images created with the words."

"Oh, how lovely," said Elizabeth. "The scenes that can be painted by the few words of a poet are indeed inspiring."

He smiled down at her. "The economy of words my mother called it. You would have liked her. Everyone did. Mrs. Reynolds still speaks of her with such fondness."

"Mrs. Reynolds?"

"My housekeeper at Pemberley."

A sudden jolt of panic gripped Elizabeth's heart. Her thoughts had been so tangled with her feelings or, more precisely, her lack of feelings for Mr. Darcy that she had forgotten to consider the estate of which she was to be the mistress. She was positive her knowledge of the running of an estate was not equal to the task that lay before her at Pemberley. She wrapped her free arm around her middle in an attempt to keep her insides from fluttering.

"Are you well?" There was a greater note of concern in his voice now than there had been before.

She nodded. "I had not considered Pemberley. It must certainly be very grand."

"It is larger than Netherfield."

"Much larger?" She recalled hearing he owned half of Derbyshire.

"Yes."

Oh, her heart was racing. She both needed to know and wished not to know the full extent of the responsibilities that lay before her. "And town? You came to Hertfordshire from town. I assume you have a home there as well?"

"I do. It has its own staff. Mrs. Vernon is the housekeeper there. Both she and Mrs. Reynolds are exceptional at their jobs."

She nodded. She hoped they would also be understanding and helpful.

"Your father suggested that you and your sister Mary should accompany me to town when I go to get the special license. You could meet Mrs. Vernon then and have a tour of the house. He mentioned that you would be welcomed at your aunt and uncle's house and that your aunt would be best able to assist you in selecting wedding clothes."

She gripped her stomach more firmly. The reality of all the changes about to take place in her life settled in heavily around her.

"This is absurd," she said. "My aunt and uncle live near Cheapside in Gracechurch Street. My uncle is in trade. My aunt is the daughter of a tradesman. My mother is the daughter of a tradesman. While my father is a gentleman, I am tainted by trade. This cannot be acceptable to your family. And my education is lacking. I have not the accomplishments necessary to travel in the circles in which you travel. Perhaps if I just go away quietly. . . if you could help me find a position as a companion, then all would be well for my sisters, and you would be free to find a wife who is more well-suited to the position of Mrs. Darcy." A tear slid down her cheek, carrying with it some of the frustration she felt. The breeze tugged at her bonnet and flipped the ribbons against her neck.

Darcy stopped walking. "You are overwhelmed."

"Yes, and I am unprepared."

"Both are not without remedy." Once again, he squeezed her hand where it lay beneath his on his arm. "We will remain in town for the season. You may begin by learning the running of Darcy House. It is not so grand as Pemberley and has no tenants on whom to call."

"But there will be social calls to make and soirees to attend."

He smiled at her. "You are capable. You merely fear the unknown."

She sighed resignedly. He was obviously determined not to let her escape their arrangement. "When do we leave for my aunt's house?"

"The day after tomorrow. Your father sent an express to inform your relations of your arrival."

She nodded slowly.

"Miss Elizabeth," his voice was soft but serious, "I am not unaware of the challenges before us, but you know we must marry."

Again, she nodded slowly.

"We shall face whatever challenges arise together. I have made a promise to your father that I will care for you. It is not a promise

I make lightly. Beyond that, my heart would not allow it. Can you trust me enough to believe that?"

She saw the look of concern in his eyes and heard the uncertainty in his voice. That strange feeling of needing to put him at ease washed over her again. "I shall try," she said, and then noting that his look of concern decreased only slightly, she added, "It is all I can promise right now. I shall try. I really, truly shall try."

"Very well," he said, the crease between his brows nearly disappearing. "You shall try to trust me, and I shall try to be patient."

Chapter 5

THROUGH THE FRONT WINDOW of her uncle's house in Gracechurch Street, Elizabeth watched Darcy's coach make its way through the early evening traffic. She pulled in her lip and bit it softly as she considered the man within the coach. As she had promised Jane two days ago, she had questioned everything about him. Yesterday, she had questioned him in regard to his attention to his tenants and his staff. She had asked him about his father and about his steward. She had even dared to ask about his supposed betrothal to his cousin. He had patiently borne all her inquiries.

She was beginning to run out of questions about his character, which left her in an extremely uncomfortable state, for she knew that, now, she must also examine her own character. It would not be a pleasant task since her character seemed to be wanting. How else could she have misjudged Mr. Darcy so badly? A character which had fallen easy prey to the pretty words of a charmer was not one she wished to find within herself, but there it was. She sighed.

Aunt Gardiner placed an arm around Elizabeth's shoulders. "He seems very pleasant."

"A right proper gentleman," agreed her uncle.

"Not at all as you described," added her aunt softly.

Elizabeth's shoulders lifted slightly and then dropped. How she wished she has kept her unfavourable thoughts about Mr. Darcy to herself. Then, it would not be quite so painful to be wrong, for the folly would be one which was only known privately. But that was not the case. She had written to her favourite aunt about Mr. Darcy, and now she must admit her error. "I may have misjudged him."

She turned sad eyes to her aunt. "I do not know who he is. I was so sure I knew, but I do not."

"Ah, my dear. Something tells me you know more than you will allow yourself to admit."

Aunt Gardiner turned Elizabeth away from the window. "We should get you and Mary installed in your room."

She led Elizabeth from the room and started up the stairs. "You will, of course, have to share the story about how you became betrothed to a man you were so set against. I have had your father's version, but I would like to hear yours."

She turned to the right at the top of the stairs and opened the second door on her left. "Your uncle has brought home some lovely laces and a few pieces of silk that he thought you might like. I have to say; your uncle has an excellent eye for colour. You would look lovely in all of them, so you shall have a dress from each. Mrs. Havelston has lent me her book of fashions. She knows how much you dislike spending hours in her shop choosing fabrics and patterns, and our time is limited."

Elizabeth sat heavily on the bed while Mary opened a trunk and began the task of unpacking. "It is all too much," she said.

"Are you indeed your mother's daughter?" Aunt Gardiner crossed her arms and gave Elizabeth an amused but quizzical look.

A small laugh escaped Mary. "She has been for three days now."

Elizabeth gasped.

"You have been a ball of nerves ever since the ball," Mary explained.

Not without good reason!

"I am being forced to marry a man I barely know because my aunt created a scene," Elizabeth protested. "You would not be a picture of serenity either if it were you."

Mary shrugged. "Perhaps I would be as distraught as you if I were to be forced to marry a wealthy, handsome gentleman who obviously cared for me, but I rather doubt it." Mary hung a gown in the wardrobe. "Mr. Darcy is not so awfully bad. You could have ended up marrying Mr. Collins."

"Mary!" Elizabeth shook her head not knowing what else to say to her sister.

Mary turned toward her sister and placed her hands on her hips. "Do not scold me, Lizzy. Mr. Collins had requested a meeting with Father, and he had been following you around like a lost lamb. It does not take great intelligence to know that he had selected you to be his wife. Surely, you knew." She gave Elizabeth a pointed look that said she would not believe any protest of ignorance before she returned to the trunk to continue the unpacking.

"I had my suspicions," Elizabeth admitted softly. In fact, she had looked for a means of escape every time she had seen Mr. Collins moving in her direction.

"As I see it," Mary continued, "Mr. Darcy saved you from a dire fate, and you should be grateful." She hung another dress in the wardrobe. "And I heard rumours about Mr. Wickham that would make you blush."

She turned and looked at Elizabeth with another pointed look that dared her to contradict what she had said. "I learn many things listening to conversations while I am being ignored," she added as proof that what she knew was to be believed.

"Ignored?" Shock suffused Elizabeth's face. She had never considered how little attention was paid to Mary.

"Do not mistake me. To be ignored is not a travesty to me. I much prefer to watch and listen." Mary placed a brush on the table near the mirror before joining her aunt and Elizabeth on the bed. "As I see it, you are fortunate. Mr. Darcy adores you. I know he does, for I have seen it."

"Is this true?" Aunt Gardiner asked.

"Oh, it is!" Mary assured her before Elizabeth could say anything. "Mr. Darcy watches Lizzy's every move, and the look on his face...."

She grabbed Elizabeth's hand and spoke wistfully, "It is like Jane's when she speaks about Mr. Bingley." She bounced a bit on the bed as she tucked her feet under her skirts. "And did you know he thinks you have fine eyes? Millicent heard him say it to Miss Bingley. He loves you, Lizzy. He absolutely loves you."

She turned to her aunt. "Did you not see how attentive he was today? He is that way whenever Lizzy is near."

"He certainly was attentive," Aunt Gardiner agreed.

"But what if I do not love him?" Elizabeth could feel panic at such a thought welling up in her. That was probably the thing that scared her the most about all of this. She knew Mr. Darcy cared for her, though she was not willing to call it love just yet. However, her own feelings and opinions about him were so tangled and indecipherable. What if when she finally untangled them, she discovered she could not love him?

Mary shrugged. "Then, you are a fool."

"Girls," Aunt Gardiner interrupted, "before this discussion becomes unpleasant and feelings are injured, may I suggest we allow Elizabeth to tell me what happened at the Netherfield ball."

Mary looked first at her aunt and then, her sister. "Do you wish me to leave?"

"That is entirely up to your sister."

Elizabeth shook her head. "No, you may stay."

Aunt Gardiner fluffed up the pillows, propped them against the head of the bed, and motioned for her nieces to join her in sitting with their backs resting against them.

Elizabeth smoothed her skirt over her legs. She was not sure where to begin to explain that night. "The ball was lovely, Aunt. The decorations were magnificent and the food delicious. The music was good and, of course, it was well attended. The officers were there, which made my youngest sisters deliriously giddy."

"And our mother," Mary muttered.

"Shush." Aunt Gardiner gave Mary's leg a tap.

"It is true. Mama was a happy to see the officers as Lydia was," Elizabeth said before continuing. "I danced the first two sets with Mr. Collins, and before my toes had time to recover, I was obliged to dance another with a very agreeable officer before having a moment to find Charlotte. While I was speaking with Charlotte, the strangest thing happened."

Elizabeth paused, remembering the moment Mr. Darcy had approached her. She had been shocked that he had sought her out, but there had also been a most concerning moment of pleasure. She had brushed it away quickly, for she was determined not to like him, even if she did find conversation with him to be satisfying.

"It did?" Aunt Gardiner asked, bringing Elizabeth's focus back to the conversation at hand. "And what was this strange thing?"

"Mr. Darcy asked me to dance, and I accepted."

"And this was a strange thing?" Aunt Gardiner looked at Elizabeth in confusion. "Is it not common practice for a gentleman to ask a lady for a dance at a ball?"

"Not when it is Mr. Darcy," Mary answered.

"Shush." Aunt Gardiner tapped Mary's leg again.

"It is true," said Elizabeth. "Mr. Darcy never danced with anyone outside of his own party at the assembly."

"But he did ask Lizzy to dance at Sir William's party," added Mary.

"So, this was the second time Mr. Darcy had asked our Lizzy to dance," said Aunt Gardiner with no small amount of interest.

"But only the first time she accepted," said Mary.

"I see," said Aunt Gardiner. "Why did you accept him this time and not the last?"

Elizabeth shrugged. "I was surprised by the application, I suppose."

"Does he dance well?" asked her aunt.

"Oh, very well. I have not had a more accomplished partner. However, he is a very quiet partner unless prompted to speak." Mary covered her mouth, so she would not giggle.

Elizabeth shot her a look of displeasure. "I suppose, it was not prompting so much as provoking." She grimaced slightly at the soft clucking sound her aunt made. "And, I suppose, you could say we argued." She sighed. "I think I injured him with my words at the end."

Even now she felt the sting of his cold reply and the hurt that it had transferred to her. It was not a hurt for herself but for him. It had startled her to feel anything but dislike for the gentleman. It was that moment more than even his asking her to dance that has started her world spinning.

"And then?" her aunt prompted.

"And then I sought a place to think and went to the library." She sighed again. "He was there, reading a book. I should have left and found another place, but I did not."

Her aunt nodded slowly and patted Mary's leg, a signal to remain quiet. "And why did you not leave?"

"I do not know." Elizabeth rested her head against the bed frame.

"You know," her aunt said softly. "You stayed because..."

Elizabeth closed her eyes. "I stayed because he was there," she admitted, "but I do not know why."

"I would venture to guess," her aunt said, "that it was both because your heart cared that you had injured him and because you do not dislike him."

Elizabeth nodded. She could not refute her aunt's words, but it had been more than that. She had felt an unusual peace just sitting there with him. "Then my aunt came to the door just as Mr. Darcy opened it. I was putting on my slippers and smoothing my skirts from having been sitting comfortably."

"And she assumed that more than reading had taken place?"

Elizabeth's cheeks flamed at the implication of Aunt Gardiner's words.

"Yes. Aunt Philips immediately went in search of my father. I would have gone after her, but Mr. Darcy stopped me. He told me the damage to my reputation would be far greater if I were to chase after her. So, I remained in the library until my father came."

"And Mr. Darcy, what did he do?"

"He paced the room and inquired after my health several times. Then, when my father came, he offered to marry me."

"And how has he treated you since that time?"

Elizabeth sighed. "He has been very solicitous. He has allowed me to ask him questions, and he has answered readily."

She smiled slightly as she remembered his look of patient agitation at her copious questioning. She knew that he had tired of speaking about himself well before she had finished questioning, but he had continued to answer just as he had promised her he would. Today, Mr. Darcy had willingly shared stories of his family while travelling. He had even laughed along with her and Mary when he related how, on the advice of his cousin, Richard, he had come to be standing waist deep in a cold stream making fish noises in an attempt to catch the largest fish. He was not the man she had thought him to be.

"I agree with Mary and your father," Aunt Gardiner said, climbing off the bed. "Mr. Darcy cares for you." She bent and kissed Elizabeth's forehead. "It will be a good match. I believe that confused look on your face and that fluttering of your heart..." She smiled when Elizabeth looked at her in surprise.

"I felt it myself many years ago," she explained. "It is the beginnings of love. Be brave, my dear Lizzy. Do not let those feelings frighten you, for they can lead to an incredibly happy life for you as they have for me."

She stood and straightened her skirts. "I shall bring Mrs. Havelston's book for you to look at while you rest before dinner. We can decide which design will work best with which material after you have chosen the pattern. There are four pieces of cloth, so you must choose four dresses tonight. Then, tomorrow, before we go to tour Darcy House, we can visit Mrs. Havelston so she can begin the work on your clothes." She gave Elizabeth a look that brooked no objections to her plan before she hurried out the door.

Chapter 6

DARCY PLACED HIS HAT and gloves on the table near the door before shrugging out of his coat. "I will see both you and Mrs. Vernon in my study in a quarter-hour," he said to his butler. "We will be receiving very particular guests tomorrow. It is of the utmost importance that all is in order to receive them."

Mr. Daniels's brows rose a nearly imperceivable amount, but Darcy noticed it.

"I know it is an unusual request, and I do not doubt your ability to be ready for any and all visitors, but this situation does require explanation."

"Very good, sir."

Darcy turned to go to his study.

"Sir," Daniels said, causing Darcy to stop and turn back. "Colonel Fitzwilliam is in residence, sir."

"Hiding from his father?" Darcy queried with an amused smile. His cousin often took up residence at Darcy House when he and his father were in a dispute.

"It is not for me to say, sir," Daniels replied with a slight nod of his head.

"I am sure he will tell me about it."

"I am sure he shall, sir." A slight smile and a twinkle in the elderly man's eye told Darcy that Richard had already spoken his fill to the butler.

Darcy shook his head. His cousin was not the proper son of an earl. He viewed class lines as a thing of the past and continually spoke of how the aristocracy and landowners would soon be of less significance than a skilled and shrewd tradesman. "Have him join us."

"Very good, sir." Daniels bowed slightly and went to do as requested.

Darcy entered his study and shuffled through the correspondence that lay on his desk. It was business that needed his attention, but it would have to wait. Elizabeth's visit and her acceptance in his family were far more urgent. He placed the letters he held back in the fine wooden box on the corner of his desk and took out supplies to write a note. He was just preparing to write his missive when the door to his office opened.

"Did Bingley tire of your company?" Richard asked as he took a seat in front of his cousin's desk. "Or did you tire of his sister?"

Darcy rolled his eyes at his cousin. "Neither. I have business that needs my attention."

"Does this business require particular visitors?"

"Yes." Darcy dipped his pen in the ink. "Now if you will pardon me for a moment, I have an urgent message to write."

"Urgent?" Richard stood and looked over the desk to where Darcy was writing. "Aunt Sophia?"

Darcy sighed. "I need her to be here tomorrow." He looked up from his writing. "You will understand after I have spoken to you, but this must be written first."

"Very well," said Richard taking a seat. "Particular guests and Aunt Sophia." He drummed his fingers on the arm of the chair.

"I will explain in a moment," Darcy growled, glaring at Richard's fingers, which ceased their tapping.

"It must be excessively distressing business for you to have lost what little patience you possess," Richard commented.

Darcy signed his name to the note and returned his pen to the holder. "I am getting married."

"Married?" Richard cried.

"Yes, married."

Darcy stood and motioned for his housekeeper and butler to enter and take a chair. "My betrothed is coming for a tour of the house tomorrow. That is why I needed to speak to you."

He folded his note and sealed it. "This must be delivered as soon as can be today." He lay the missive on the desk in front of Mr. Daniels. "I would like for Lady Sophia to be the first of my relatives, other than Richard, whom Miss Elizabeth meets." He glanced at his cousin. "The others can be less welcoming."

Richard laughed lightly. "Meaning she is not someone of whom my traditional father will approve?"

Darcy grimaced. There were few ladies of whom his uncle would approve, for there were few families his uncle thought good enough to be joined to his.

"I fear she is not. Her name is Elizabeth Bennet and is the daughter of a landed gentleman. However, her father is of little standing, and his wife is the daughter of a tradesman. Elizabeth is currently staying with her relations in Gracechurch Street."

"Near Cheapside?" Richard's eyebrows rose in surprise.

Darcy turned to his servants. "She will be accompanied tomorrow by her aunt, Mrs. Gardiner, and her sister, Miss Mary. They will need to be shown the entire house. Elizabeth is uneasy about the responsibilities she will be taking on as Mrs. Darcy." He could not keep the smile from his face as he said the name. "We will be remaining in town for her to become familiar with the running of Darcy House before we return to Pemberley in the spring."

Mrs. Vernon nodded. "Has she had some training?"

"She has. Her skills are only slightly lacking, but she is quick and intelligent. I am confident she will do well."

"And you say that she is fearful of the position?" Mrs. Vernon asked.

Darcy nodded. "The betrothal has come as a surprise to us both."

Richard leaned forward in his seat. "Were you finally trapped?"

"In a matter of speaking, yes, but she was as trapped as I, and she is not yet completely reconciled to the idea." He sighed as he looked at the puzzled faces before him. This would take some explaining. "Bingley had a ball. I had escaped to the library, and while I was there, Elizabeth also came in to find quiet. We read for a while, and then I decided to leave. Another aunt, who is as loud and lacking in tact as Lady Catherine, was coming in search of Elizabeth as I was leaving. She happened to see Elizabeth putting on her slippers and straightening her skirts after sitting for an extended period of time."

"So, you were trapped by her relations?" Richard asked. "And she is not pleased to be marrying you?"

"That would appear to be the case."

"She seriously does not wish to be Mrs. Darcy?" Richard could not contain his surprise.

Darcy swallowed. "She does not. In fact, she has suggested other options, none of which are feasible." He returned his attention to his housekeeper and butler. He would explain more to Richard later, but for now, only the basics needed to be shared so that the house and staff could be prepared. "I wished for you to know the complete story in case there is talk."

"She will be our mistress, and we shall treat her as such, Mr. Darcy," Daniels assured him. "And her relations shall also be received with the greatest of respect, no matter their station."

"Thank you. I expected no less, but the circumstances are of a delicate nature."

"Indeed, Mr. Darcy, they are," Mrs. Vernon said. "Is there a particular favourite we could provide in the tea service? It may help your betrothed feel welcomed."

"She has a fondness for almond cakes," Darcy said, "and Mrs. Gerard's cakes are delightful. I am sure they would not disappoint."

"They are excellent." Richard had a fondness for all things sweet.

"Will Miss Elizabeth be making changes to rooms?" Mrs. Vernon asked.

"If she would like. You may make mention of it – most particularly when you come to her suite."

"When do we expect you to take up residence, sir?" Daniels asked.

"The evening of the sixteenth of December," Darcy replied. There was not much time to get everything ready, but he knew his staff was capable.

"I will speak to Mrs. Gerard about a special meal to welcome our new mistress. Perhaps you could find out a few more of her preferences?"

Darcy smiled. "I can."

"Will there be anything else, sir?" Mr. Daniels took the note from the desk.

"No, that will be all."

Richard waited until the door closed behind Mr. Daniels. "It appears you are not displeased with this arrangement."

Darcy shook his head in wonder at the fact that he was not. Indeed, the idea of marrying Elizabeth had not given him more than a moment of pause before he had suggested the solution to Mr. Bennet. It was her response which caused his disquiet.

"I wish Elizabeth were more comfortable with the idea, but no, I am not displeased. She is just what I need in a wife and what Georgie needs in a sister. And I need both you and Aunt Sophia to support me in this should your father be difficult."

"Ah, so, that is why you have sent for her." Richard steepled his fingers in front of him as his elbows rested on the arms of the chair.

"It is. Aunt Sophia will love her." He knew it to be true, for he and his aunt rarely disagreed on anything. Therefore, if he loved Elizabeth, and he did, his aunt would also love her. Darcy could tell by the broad smile on Richard's face that he was not unaware of this fact either.

"Wickham has joined the militia. He is in Meryton."

The smile faded from his cousin's face.

"He befriended Miss Elizabeth."

"And you will marry someone who is friends with Wickham?" A deep scowl had replaced his former grin.

"She knows about Wickham's treachery. I told her about it."

"About Georgie?"

"She will be part of our family and sister to Georgiana; she had to be told. Besides, she had believed his stories about my ill-treatment of him." He could see her sitting on that stile, tears staining her face, and his heart ached to have been the cause of them – no matter how necessary it had been. "She was shocked and understandably disturbed by the information."

Richard tipped his head and studied Darcy for a moment before nodding. "If you trust her, then I must too. You do not often err in choosing whom you trust."

"Thank you." Darcy stood and went to the window. "I only hope Elizabeth comes to that same conclusion soon."

"She does not trust you?"

Darcy's shoulders sagged under the truth of that statement. "I did not make the best first impression, but we have had some good discussions. I believe she is changing her opinion of me." He sighed. "I pray she is," he added softly. He had always considered being in a loveless marriage to be the worst fate, but now, he knew that it would not be. A marriage of unequal affections would be far worse.

"You realize my mother and father will insist on meeting her as soon as they know."

Darcy turned and leaned against the frame of the window. "I am aware of that." He groaned. "I forgot to inform Mrs.Vernon that I will be hosting a dinner for your parents and Miss Elizabeth's relations."

He smirked at Richard. "I prefer to be in the position to throw people from my house rather than being removed myself. Now, tell me why you are here."

"My father has been in discussions again with Lord Beacham. I feared a trap, so I am here. And he will still not hear of selling my commission and refuses me entrance to the workshop. Your staff is much more obliging in that regard."

"You still wish to retire and craft furniture?" His cousin had always loved to make things with his hands, but his father would hear of no other occupation save the army. His sons, he said, would serve their king as he had. "How much longer before you have completed the required term?"

"A year."

"Does that mean I can expect you to be hiding out in my workshop for the next year?"

"Quite possibly, unless some miracle of grace occurs, and my father becomes less rigid." Both laughed at the idea. Lord Matlock was known for his firm and unalterable stance. No opponent had ever shifted him from his position.

"You are welcome to stay for as long as you need, of course," said Darcy, moving towards the door. "Now, while I search for Mrs. Vernon to tell her of the dinner party that needs to be planned, you can tell me how Georgie gets on with her new companion."

Chapter 7

LADY SOPHIA'S TOE TAPPED an impatient rhythm as she waited in the sitting room with Georgiana at Darcy House. She had been shocked to receive the letter she had received yesterday from Darcy. She had hoped that one day, he would finally find a lady to marry. However, she had expected his courtship of said lady to be one which was lengthy and extremely proper. His letter seemed to suggest he was marrying a lady he had only just met, and such a rushed arrangement did not speak of anything proper. To say she was curious was to make a grave understatement. Yet, she was not one to jump to conclusions. Her own son had found himself in a bit of a scandal that was not of his own making, and then, there were her own siblings with their secrets. She shook her head. She knew very well that things were not always what they appeared to be.

She glanced at the clock near the door. "Your brother should expect me to be early. I always am." She straightened her sleeve. "I am anxious to meet the lady who has finally captured your brother."

"Captured would be the proper word for it," Richard said as he entered the room. He gave each lady's cheek a kiss. "I did not realize you were coming today, Georgiana."

Georgiana pursed her lips and looked at her aunt. "I was not supposed to come."

Truth be told, it had taken very little persuasion to get Georgiana to accompany her – far less than Lady Sophia had thought she might need to employ. As was natural, Georgiana was just as curious as her aunt to know about the lady her brother was marrying. The girl was just less comfortable with doing something that might cause Fitzwilliam discomfort or displeasure. Lady Sophia had no qualms about either of those things.

"I am sure it was simply an omission made in error on your brother's invitation."

Georgiana looked at her aunt doubtfully. "My brother does not make errors of omission. He is the most fastidious correspondent."

"Ah, well, that may be in most circumstances. However, your brother does not get married every day."

"That is true." Georgiana's tone was not one of a person who was utterly convinced of the truth of a matter. Her nerves were most certainly on edge.

Lady Sophia gave her niece a soft smile. "He will see his error just as soon as I have explained it to him." She patted Georgiana's hand reassuringly before turning to Richard. "Now, tell me why captured is the proper word. Was he trapped?"

"It seems –" Richard began.

"That I am the topic of gossip within my own home," Darcy finished as he entered the room and gave Richard a stern look before turning to his sister.

"Georgiana! It is a surprise to see you." He placed a kiss on his sister's cheek while giving a questioning look to his aunt.

Lady Sophia tilted her cheek upwards for his kiss as she explained. "Georgiana is to have a new sister, and it is far better for her to meet her before my brother and his wife." That was the truth of it. That had been her entire reason for insisting on Georgiana's attendance at this meeting today.

"But I do not wish to have Miss Elizabeth overwhelmed on her first visit either," Darcy cautioned. His tone was gentle. Lady Sophia knew he was being the excellent brother he had always been and attempting to question his aunt without causing unease for his sister.

"Georgiana is incapable of overwhelming anyone," she stated.

"Yes," said Darcy with a smile, "but I fear just your presence alone will be enough to overwhelm."

Georgiana giggled while Lady Sophia huffed.

"Such insolence," she chided.

It would have seemed rather a stern scolding had it not been for the smile that was broad enough to make her eyes crinkle slightly. Darcy knew that his aunt was not even mildly offended by his comment.

"I am a bit much at times, am I not?" she said. "It is why my brother has never quite known what to do with me, especially now that I have an establishment of my own and the money left to me by my husband. But then, I suppose that is exactly why you wish for me to meet this young lady before your uncle does."

Darcy tipped his head in acknowledgment of that fact.

"My guess is that she is not..." Lady Sophia tapped her lip. "How shall we say it? Am I to assume that your betrothed does not meet with Lord Matlock's exacting standards in some way?"

Again, Darcy inclined his head in acknowledgment.

"However —" she held her finger in the air, "Miss Elizabeth is someone of whom I will approve, and you wish for me to give her my support."

"Precisely." Darcy took a seat near his aunt. "We must marry. There is no other option, so it is imperative that you give both of us your support."

Lady Sophia's brows rose quite high. "Must marry? I admit I suspected that there was a reason for the rapidity of your betrothal, but I had hoped it was due to some innocent reason such as being madly in love, but you say you must marry? Why?"

Darcy felt his face warm to what he suspected was a lovely shade of embarrassment. There was no overly gracious way to answer his aunt's question. "We were found in a compromising situation."

Richard laughed. "He makes it sound worse than it is. According to what I have heard, they were reading in the library without the presence of a chaperone, and the young lady had removed her slippers."

"Reading?" Lady Sophia crossed her arms and gave Darcy a skeptical look.

"At a ball," Richard inserted in a loud whisper.

"You were in a library during a ball with a young woman and no chaperone, but you were reading?"

Darcy knew that in town, a rendezvous between a lady and gentleman in a library during a soiree was not for the purpose of perusing the contents of the library's shelves. "I found myself in need of a reprieve from the festivities, as did Miss Elizabeth. I assure you, most sincerely, that we were reading just before we were discovered. Unfortunately, I was just leaving, and Miss Elizabeth was putting on her slippers as her aunt entered."

"Indeed?" One finger tapped her arm as she waited for further explanation.

Darcy rubbed the space between his eyes. He had known she might have some difficulty believing such a story, and he had expected a small amount of questioning, but he had not expected to have to defend both his honour and that of Miss Elizabeth with his sister present.

"Would it help you to believe me if I told you that she does not wish to marry me?" He tried not to grimace at the confession but failed. How he wished Elizabeth were as happy to marry him as she was to marry her.

Shock suffused his aunt's face. "You are marrying someone who does not wish to be Mrs. Fitzwilliam Darcy? I had not thought that possible." She collapsed backward in her chair as if overwhelmed by the thought.

"I did not make a good first impression when I arrived in Hertfordshire. I was in a foul mood, and I said something which I should not have said, although it was not meant as it was heard."

He cast a sidelong glance at his cousin and hurried on with his explanation before his aunt could ask him about what he had said. "That is not the only reason Miss Elizabeth held for her dislike of me. There were also disparaging stories that she heard from a former acquaintance of mine. Things have been made right as much as I am able, but I cannot force her to like me."

Lady Sophia studied him through slightly narrowed eyes. Her finger tapped softly on the arm of her chair and silence reigned in the room beyond that sound and the ticking of the clock for a moment. Then, she sat forward. "Do you wish for her to like you?"

Darcy attempted to shrug as if the question were unimportant. He did not wish to expose his heart to his aunt or his sister. "We are to marry. It would be best." He knew from the raised eyebrow and the small smirk on his aunt's face that his attempts at hiding his true feelings had been unsuccessful.

"Very well. We will do our best to convince her of your worth, will we not, Georgiana?"

"Of course, Aunt."

Darcy sighed. He had known they would both support him in this. However...

"I appreciate your willingness to take up my cause, but I fear the weight of proving myself must fall squarely on my shoulders. She will trust me less than she does now if she suspects I have given you the task of convincing her of my worth."

His aunt's eyes narrowed slightly again as she held his gaze. "Am I to believe then that this Miss Elizabeth is someone of whom I will not only approve but is also someone whom I will find hard not to love?"

Darcy heard the true question behind her words. "Yes," he said, acknowledging both to his aunt and to himself, once again, that he did indeed love Elizabeth Bennet.

Lady Sophia's eyes and smile softened. "I see," she said, and he knew she did. She had always been excessively perceptive to what he was truly saying. "Then, I am even more eager to meet her and to lend my support to you both, no matter the objections my brother shall raise."

Darcy shifted slightly in his chair. He knew he had to disclose how Miss Elizabeth fell short of his uncle's expectations, but it was not something he wanted to do. Now that he had wrestled those reasons away and had allowed himself to love her, it was unsettling, to say the least, to point out any perceivable flaw. Yet, it had to be done. It was best if his aunt knew exactly what objections Lord Matlock would raise.

"You know how my uncle does not approve of my friendship with Bingley, do you not?"

"Is Miss Elizabeth from trade?" Georgiana asked.

"No. She is not a tradesman's daughter. However, her mother is, and one uncle is in trade, while another is a country solicitor."

Concern etched Georgiana's features. She had heard many of the discussions he had had with Lord Matlock about Bingley not being a proper friend due to his father being a tradesman. It did not matter how wealthy the elder Mr. Bingley had been. A tradesman was a tradesman to his uncle, and tradesmen were a class with whom Lord Matlock did not associate himself unless ordering work to be done.

"Miss Elizabeth's father is a gentleman but of little standing." That was another class of people for whom Lord Matlock had no time. "She brings little by way of wealth or position to the marriage."

Darcy had, by this time, risen and was pacing in front of his aunt and sister. The thought of his uncle's condemnations made him unusually furious. He had endured Lord Matlock's pompous blustering with as much fortitude as he could muster when his uncle disparaged Bingley. But, at the moment, imagining him saying such things about Elizabeth left a twisting, knotting feeling in his stomach and a fire in his veins that spread to his heart.

"A person's worth does not come from social position or wealth, but from character," Georgiana repeated one of the arguments her brother had used on many occasions with her uncle when discussing Bingley. She smiled when Darcy looked at her in surprise. "I would not say so to our uncle, for I am not so brave as you, but I believe it is true."

"As do I," Richard agreed.

"Ah, young, revolutionary ideas," Lady Sophia teased.

"And yet these young, revolutionary ideas are one which, I believe, we learned from you," Richard retorted.

She shrugged and chuckled softly. "Perhaps, but I believe you possessed the intelligence to discover such truths on your own. Therefore, I would rather like to think that I merely assisted you in your discovery."

Darcy could not help but laugh at her reply. She was always twisting things to make her approach to life seem as if it was the most practical way – which, other than being forcefully thrust upon those for whom she cared, was probably quite accurate. To Darcy, her thoughts about how things were and should be were, for the most part, logical.

"Has tea been arranged?" she asked, glancing at the clock.

"It has." Darcy gave a look of caution to his sister. "Almond cakes are one of Miss Elizabeth's favourites."

Georgiana giggled. "I promise not to eat them all."

She held her hand out to him, and he took it.

"I am glad you have found someone to love," she whispered.

"I did not say –" He stopped when she shook her head.

"Yes, Fitzwilliam, you did." She squeezed his hand. "And I am happy for it."

His eyes held hers. Was it so bad to have her aware of his feelings for Elizabeth? Richard and Lady Sophia already knew. His pain would be no greater nor any less if she knew. It was what it was. He nodded his head and whispered a thank you before releasing her hand and pacing to the window to watch for his carriage.

Chapter 8

ELIZABETH'S EYES GREW WIDE as the carriage Darcy had sent for them drew to a stop in front of a very grand townhouse. "Half of Derbyshire and a good portion of London," she muttered in amazement.

"It is most certainly a fine house," Mrs. Gardiner agreed. "But it is just a house. One with finer furnishings and more staff, to be sure, but a house nonetheless. I imagine it runs quite well now and will continue to do so once you have gotten your feet under you." She placed a hand on Elizabeth's arm. "Your intelligence will aid you in learning the management of this and any other establishment Mr. Darcy owns, but it is your heart that will make it a home."

Elizabeth smiled at her aunt. How many times since last night's discussion had her aunt encouraged her to consider her heart and what it was saying about Mr. Darcy? She had even listened patiently and, if truth be told, with a greater interest than she had ever had before as her sister read to her about love from Paul's first epistle to the Corinthians. She had spent several hours considering what both her aunt and sister had said, and in the late hours of the night, she had come to realize that perhaps the feeling of the tilting and swirling of the earth under her feet was as her aunt had suggested — she did care for Mr. Darcy.

She drew a deep breath and then, covering her aunt's hand with her own, she said, "I believe both my heart and my courage are ready for the challenge."

The door of the carriage opened, and the steps were put in place.

"Though," she whispered as she prepared to descend the steps, "my legs are trembling at the thought."

Mrs. Gardiner followed her nieces out of the carriage and took Elizabeth's arm as they ascended the steps to Darcy House, while Mary walked behind them. Before Elizabeth had time to even pause for a moment in front of the door, it opened, and they were ushered in.

Elizabeth took in the grandeur of the entry.

"It is beautiful," Mary whispered.

Elizabeth could not disagree. The ceilings were high, and the floor shone. The furnishings were elegant but not overly ornate. This lovely, but unfamiliar, house was to be her home. The thought almost overwhelmed her determination to keep her courage high.

She smiled in relief when she saw Mr. Darcy step out of what she assumed was the sitting room to greet them. He was not utterly unfamiliar. In fact, he was a welcome sight. How strange a heart was to so easily flit from thinking of someone as an unwelcome acquaintance to being delighted to see them.

"I hope you do not find it overwhelming, but I asked my aunt, Lady Sophia, to join us today," he said.

His aunt. She could do this. She was good at meeting people.

"Not at all," Elizabeth replied. "I shall have to meet my new relatives eventually, shall I not?"

Darcy chuckled. "Indeed. Lady Sophia insisted upon bringing my sister, and my cousin has taken up residence for a few days." He noted how she pulled her lip between her teeth as she had on their walks whenever something had concerned her.

"You have nothing to fear," he said softly. "I have told them the details surrounding our betrothal, and they are the most agreeable of my relatives. Their support will be invaluable when you meet my less agreeable relations."

She squeezed his arm where her hand lay on it. "I trust you."

Her cheeks coloured slightly at the admission, while his heart leapt at the hope those words gave him.

"Truly?"

She smiled at him impertinently. It was a smile that he had not seen since before the ball at Netherfield.

"Did I not tell you that I would try?" She shrugged slightly. "When I put my mind to a task, Mr. Darcy, I quite often am successful in accomplishing it."

He caught the eye of his butler and tipped his head toward the sitting room. The servant gave him a nod and said to Mrs. Gardiner and Mary, "If you will follow me."

Darcy stopped Elizabeth when she moved to follow her aunt and sister. "You will pardon my surprise, but it was not many days ago when you did not trust me."

She smiled up at him. "I have done a great deal of thinking, and I find no reason not to trust you."

"I am glad of it," Darcy said as he led her into the sitting room.

After they had eaten almond cakes, drank tea, and had all the usual conversations and inquiries one would have when meeting a new acquaintance, Darcy was pleased to have Elizabeth at his side with her hand on his arm to begin the tour of the house.

"Every room in the house is open to your viewing. Nothing is to be omitted."

She lifted an impertinent brow at him. There was a hint of trepidation in her eyes, but only a hint. She had seemed to take to his aunt and his aunt to her with alacrity. He had suspected they would get on well.

THE CHOICES SERIES

"It is a good thing then," she said, "that I have a fondness for walking, or this could be a very tiring excursion."

He laughed lightly. "I assure you, Miss Elizabeth, it is not that large a house."

She gave him a disbelieving look. "And just when I thought I could trust you," she teased. "I assure you, sir, that this is indeed a large house. Remember to what I have to compare it. Longbourn is modest in size, and my uncle's house in Gracechurch could fit into this one, two, if not three, times over."

"And remember, Miss Elizabeth, to what I have to compare it. I assure you that compared to Pemberley, this house is not large."

"Do you mean to frighten me, sir?"

He smiled at her. How he enjoyed her teasing banter. "I merely wish to prepare you."

Mrs. Vernon shared an amused look with his aunt. It was not the thing to be done, of course, but Mrs. Vernon had over the years developed a sort of friendship with Lady Sophia.

"Shall we begin above or below stairs, sir?"

"Below," Richard replied. "Since I am sure it is the most frightening."

Darcy glared at him. Elizabeth's teasing he relished. Richard's taunts he could do without. "You do not need to accompany us."

"I promise to desert you shortly as I plan to spend some time in the workshop."

"But," Lady Sophia inserted, "you wish a few more treats before you do."

Richard laughed. "You are correct, and for that reason, I suggest we begin with the kitchen so that Darcy can be rid of my presence as quickly as possible."

"Very well," Mrs. Vernon said, "If the lady does not object, we shall begin in the kitchen."

Elizabeth nodded her assent, and the tour began below stairs. Richard, true to his word, left them after pinching a few treats in the kitchen.

"How are you finding things?" Darcy asked as they climbed the stairs to the public rooms of the house. He had been watching her closely for he remembered how worried she had been when they had first spoken about the size of his homes.

"Surprisingly reassuring," she replied with an easy smile that spoke of how at ease she was at present. "The running of the house is on a grander scale than that of Longbourn. The kitchen is larger, and the storerooms and servants are greater in number, but it is as my aunt has said, the operations are remarkably similar. For all that my mother flutters about and chatters, she knows how to manage a household and has passed on much of her knowledge to me."

"I am happy to hear that, and do you like everything you have seen?"

"I do."

He smiled, and it lit his eyes in a way that Elizabeth had noted earlier when she told him she trusted him, and just like then, a small tendril of pleasure wrapped itself around her heart as she once again realized that her good opinion was important to him.

They circulated through the public rooms, followed by the guest rooms, and, finally, the private family living quarters. Elizabeth peeked into each room. They were all tastefully furnished, and the decor was very much to her liking.

As they moved from room to room, ascended stairs, and passed through corridors, she still found the idea of Pemberley to be daunting, but she felt more and more at ease with this part of her duties as Mrs. Darcy. That is, she felt at ease until they began touring the family bed chambers. Then, her courage wanted to hide, and her nerves began to flutter.

"And these are my rooms," Georgiana said, opening the door to the next room along the hall they were walking down. "This is the sitting room. Over there," she motioned to her right, "is my dressing room and here," she opened a door that led off the sitting room to the left, "this is my bedroom."

"It is beautiful," Elizabeth said. The room was decorated in soft shades of blue with accents of cream and yellow. "It is very like a garden on a spring morning."

Georgiana smiled. "It reminds me of a meadow at Pemberley that is always dotted with white and yellow flowers. It is one of my favourite places."

"You shall have to show it to me. Will the flowers be in bloom when we arrive?" She looked to Darcy.

"They will be," he assured her and offered her his arm again as they proceeded out of Georgiana's room and moved on to the master suite.

"This is Mr. Darcy's room," Mrs. Vernon was saying as she opened the door.

This was the room that caused her nerves to bloom in all their glory for it was such a private, intimate space. "It is very dignified," she said, feeling she must compliment it in some way. It was a very beautiful room. Indeed, it looked a lot like Mr. Darcy. Well-ordered, subdued, and yet, noble.

"Brown is my brother's favourite colour," Georgiana said.

"One of them," Darcy corrected. "There are many colours I favour, but brown is very calming."

"And boring," Georgiana said, earning her a scowl from her brother.

"I think that a colour is only boring if it is not complemented with other shades of that colour or set off by some other colour," Mary said.

"Indeed," Elizabeth agreed, wishing for the conversation surrounding the decor of that particular room to be at an end. "I believe brown is very adaptable as it can complement many other colours. Besides," she said as she moved toward the next door where Mrs. Vernon stood, "both chocolate and gingerbread are brown. I am sure a colour cannot be truly boring if such lovely treats are that colour."

She now stood inside what was being explained to her was a sitting room that was shared by the master and mistress of the house. Knowing that this was to be a room used by both her and Mr. Darcy did nothing to decrease the feeling of unease in her stomach.

"It is lovely," she said, for it was. She could not fault any of the décor nor the arrangement. If she had been given such a room to decorate, she would have chosen many of the same things. She particularly liked the shelves of books near the fireplace where two comfortable chairs stood.

"You can change whatever you wish," Darcy said. There was that unease again. The unease she had learned about on their first walk after Mr. Bingley's ball. He was worried about her.

She shook her head. "There is nothing I would change," she assured him. "I like it just as it is. In fact, I am sure it cannot be improved upon save for a few fresh flowers in season."

"Through here," Mrs. Vernon said, "is your bedroom and dressing room."

"I had this room redone just a year ago," Darcy said, "but it is yours to do with as you would like."

"You chose these things?" asked Elizabeth in amazement. This room was so different from his bedroom. The furnishings were still elegant, but the design was delicate.

"Lady Sophia helped." There was that hint of nervousness in his voice.

"You have done very well," Mrs. Gardiner said. "Very well, indeed. This is lovely."

Mary ran her hand over the back of a chair which sat near the fire. "Do you not love it, Lizzy? It is as if you had done it yourself."

"It is," Elizabeth agreed. She turned to Georgiana. "Lavender is my favourite colour."

"You like it then?" asked Darcy.

"Yes. Very much."

The smile on her face let him know that she was indeed pleased, and he felt the knot that had been forming in between his shoulders begin to melt. She would be happy here. He was mostly certain of it, and at present, he was only allowing himself to focus on the mostly certain thoughts. She trusted him. She got on well with both his favourite aunt and sister. And she seemed at ease in his home – their home. Certainly, things between the two of them could grow into a wonderful something, could they not?

"I like her very much," said Lady Sophia, sometime later, just after Elizabeth had left. "You may not have selected her in the traditional way of choosing a bride, Fitzwilliam, but you could not have done better. A gem is what she is."

He watched his carriage moving away from his house. "I believe, Aunt," he said, "that I would have selected her if given time and the opportunity; however, I fear she would not have accepted me." How strange that he should feel so content about being trapped into marriage. "And because of that," he said turning from the window, "I find myself oddly grateful for her aunt's lack of discretion."

Chapter 9

TWO DAYS LATER, DARCY was in his study working through some matters of business when Richard entered the study with a paper in his hand and a piece of wood under his arm.

Darcy looked up briefly from his papers. "Did you lose your way to the workshop?" he teased.

Richard took a seat in front of Darcy's desk and placed the diagram of a jewelry box on top of the papers Darcy was reviewing. "Will she like it?"

"It is lovely." But then everything his cousin created out of wood was exquisite. Richard truly had a gift for what he did.

"Yes, I know. I try not to design anything hideous," Richard said dryly. "What I need to know is will Miss Elizabeth like it?" He pointed to the design to be carved in the top. "Is this a flower she would appreciate?"

Darcy shrugged. "I cannot be certain, but it does seem to be something she would like. I have never thought to ask her which flowers she prefers."

Richard drummed his fingers on the desktop and hummed as he tipped his head one way and then the other. It was obvious that this gift for Elizabeth was of great importance to his cousin.

"She will like anything you make her."

Richard scowled. Apparently, he did not want her to like just anything he made. He wanted to make something that was liked above everything else.

Suddenly, a thought occurred to Darcy. "When we toured the house, Elizabeth said her room was decorated as if she had done it herself. There are some pieces of yours in there. Remember?"

"Quite right!" Richard stood and snatched the diagram from Darcy. "Do you mind if I borrow one? I can follow the pattern from before but add a few distinguishing features." He was nearly at the door before Darcy could reply that the idea was excellent.

The door opened as Richard reached for the handle.

"Father." Richard nodded to the gentleman who stood behind Mr. Daniels.

Lord Matlock glanced at the wood Richard held under his arm and then, with a raised brow and a pointed look, said, "Colonel."

"For another year, my lord, and not a day longer," Richard said as he pushed past his father.

Peeking quickly at the clock on the mantel, Darcy rose to greet his uncle. He knew that in less than an hour, his aunt, who had insisted on being seen in town with Elizabeth, would be arriving for tea, and Georgiana, Elizabeth, and Mary would be with her. He did not wish for his uncle to still be here when they arrived. However, he doubted that any interview would be short in duration.

"Are you still allowing my son to use your workshop?" Lord Matlock waved the butler away.

No, this was not going to be short or pleasant. "I am."

"I do wish you would not encourage his foolish notions." He waved a hand as if brushing something of insignificance away as he said foolish notions.

Darcy waited for his uncle to be seated before taking his own. He truly despised how Lord Matlock could belittle his own son as he did.

"Perhaps I encourage it because I do not see it as a foolish notion. Women stitch and net. I do not see why a gentleman cannot carve and join wood."

"It is not done is why. And to compare a man's pursuits to that of a lady?" He shook his head and clucked his tongue as well as any old biddy might. "Preposterous! It is utterly and completely preposterous! But I am not here about that foolishness. I am here about a completely separate but equally concerning piece of news that I have had from my sister, Sophia."

Darcy waited uneasily for him to continue, which Lord Matlock did after taking a moment to straighten his jacket so that all the fastenings were in a perfectly straight row.

"She has informed me that you are to be married, but I cannot believe this to be true since I have not had word from Kent proclaiming the event."

"Lady Sophia is not mistaken. I am to be wed, but as I have said many times, I will not be marrying my cousin Anne."

"But you have a duty –"

"Yes," Darcy interrupted. He was unwilling to give his uncle the upper hand in this conversation. "I have a duty to see to the proper management of my estate and to see that my sister is well-cared for. These are things which I have not and will not neglect."

Lord Matlock clucked his tongue again and lifted his chin a bit higher, so that he could look down his nose at Darcy. "You forget –"

Darcy did not let him continue. "I forget nothing, my lord. Both Pemberley and my sister shall be well-cared for, and if the good Lord so deigns, I shall have an heir to take my place when I am gone. No duty shall go undone."

Lord Matlock leaned forward and placed both hands on the edge of the desk. "You are forgetting your duty to family position. With your wealth and land holdings, you could have made a very advantageous match."

"I believe I have." Darcy knew, without a shadow of a doubt, that there was far more advantage to having Elizabeth for a wife rather than some lady of the ton — no matter the lady's connections in parliament or the size of her dowry. With Elizabeth as his wife, he would be happy. Georgiana would have a sister of sense, and his estate would flourish with Elizabeth's intelligence and dedication.

Lord Matlock snorted. "Miss Elizabeth Bennet," he said with disdain. "She is nothing. I have inquired about her. Ties to trade. A father of no significance, and extraordinarily little to add to your coffers."

Darcy felt anger welling up and fought to control it. His uncle often brought on this battle to keep his emotions regulated. However, hearing uncle's oft-spouted vitriol directed at Elizabeth made it a much harder battel to win.

"Elizabeth is to be my wife." He knew his tone was harsher than normal by the way his uncle lifted one imperious brow. "I will not discuss your opinion of her," Darcy continued. "If that is what your purpose was in coming here today, I fear you have wasted your time." He stood and moved toward the door.

"I have not finished," Lord Matlock said.

Darcy stopped and folded his arms across his chest. "I believe you have, for I will not listen to any disparagement of Miss Bennet. My promise has been made, and it will not be withdrawn. Elizabeth Bennet will be my wife."

Lord Matlock's lips curled up in disgust. "She will not be accepted by..." He paused. "Society," he concluded.

Darcy heard the underlying threat. His uncle was not above spreading rumours if needed to sway the opinion of the ton to manipulate someone to support him. The thought that his uncle would purposefully attempt to harm Elizabeth's reputation allowed Darcy's anger to gain the upper hand, and his voice turned hard and menacing.

"A breach, my lord, would be most unadvantageous. Most unadvantageous, indeed. I may not have a seat in the House of Lords, but I will remind you that I am not without influence." He skewered his uncle with a pointed glare. "Do I need to refresh your memory about my father's reaction to your father's attempts to keep him from the woman he loved?"

The momentary look of concern which passed across Lord Matlock's face let Darcy know that his uncle did remember the pressure, both societally and politically, that his father had been able to apply through his sphere of influence. There were people who held strong and long ties to the Darcy family.

Darcy pulled open the study door, indicating that this interview was assuredly at an end.

"Are you saying, then, that you love her?" His uncle stood in front of him, nearly in the doorway but still inside the room.

"Most ardently," Darcy said firmly.

"Love does very little to build an estate, my boy."

"You are mistaken, my lord. My father's estate was strengthened by love — love for his wife, love for his children, and love for his land, as well as love for his servants and his tenants." Darcy shook his head. His uncle's way of thinking was so foolish!

"You have only to compare Pemberley to Matlock to see how love has improved one while the other falters." He saw anger spark in his uncle's eye, but truthfully, he did not care. He knew he was not wrong in this. He had a point to carry and carry it he would.

"How many of your peers have estates teetering on the brink of ruin?" He shook his head again. "Many. Perhaps, if they had married for love instead of position, they would spend more time tending to their estate and less time and money on cards, drinking, and mistresses. It is not love which has destroyed their estates and families but rather a lack of it. Such will not be my lot."

Darcy could tell by the clenching of his uncle's jaw and the narrowing of his eyes that he wished to debate the point. However, Darcy had no interest in arguing the topic further. Some people refused to ever see things logically. Lord Matlock was one of them.

"My invitation for dinner should reach Matlock House later today. I was just approving the menu before you arrived. The dinner is being held in honour of my betrothed. Her relations will attend with her."

He stepped a little closer to his uncle and lowered his voice. "Do not accept the invitation unless you come with a welcome on your lips. I will not abide any disparagement of either Elizabeth or her relations. I am not above having you forcefully, and not quietly, removed from my home if you are anything less than welcoming. Do I make myself clear?"

Lord Matlock's face was a brilliant red, but his voice was cool. He was livid, and that thought caused Darcy's lips to curl upward, ever so slightly, into a faint pleased smile.

"Do not cry to me when you have realized the error of your choice," Lord Matlock said.

"I have no intention of doing so, for I have not made an error." Darcy stepped back and bowed slightly. "Good day, Uncle."

Darcy watched his uncle leave. Aside from the anger at his uncle that lingered, that interview had not gone as badly as it could have, and it had been much shorter than Darcy had expected. Hearing a loud "I take no leave of you" and the door to Darcy House closing, Darcy turned back to his study, satisfied that his uncle was gone, and returned to his desk to attempt to finish the work he had started.

Chapter 10

ELIZABETH WANDERED THE ROOM, looking at one sculpture and then another. The detail of each was exquisite. It was as if the men and women had merely turned to stone.

Mary sat with Georgiana on a bench nearby. Both had their sketchbooks in hand and were busy drawing while Elizabeth was happy to just be looking at the exhibits. Drawing was not a talent she possessed, and the act of drawing was more of a frustration for her than it was for Mary, who found pleasure in the exercise.

She smiled. It was a lovely feeling to be affording an opportunity for her sister to experience drawing amongst the Townley collection. It was one of many opportunities she might be allowed to offer her sisters as a result of being Mrs. Darcy. She paused as the name passed through her mind. Strange how it was starting to sound familiar and not unwelcomed.

"You appear happy," Lady Sophia said.

"I am. I have wanted to visit the museum for a long time, but I have not had the opportunity until now. It is filled with so many wonderful things about which I have only read. It is utterly delightful."

"Are you a lover of learning?" Lady Sophia had already guessed it to be true. In fact, it was why she had suggested the outing to the museum.

The main purpose, of course, had been a public show of support for Elizabeth, but she also wished to find a place where she could begin to form a bond with her. She knew that Elizabeth's acceptance in society and even by Darcy's relations would be difficult. Elizabeth would need someone to help her through such trying times. And as lovely as she thought Mrs. Gardiner was, Lady Sophia knew that Elizabeth's aunt was not as familiar with the ins and outs of the ton as she herself was.

Elizabeth gave a little shrug and ducked her head as if embarrassed. "I am, and my mother bemoans the fact on a regular basis. It is not the thing for a lady."

"Oh, I disagree," Lady Sophia said. "But, then again, I disagree with a great many things that are the thing." She linked her arm with Elizabeth's as they walked. "I am a lover of learning, as was my husband. It is a glorious thing when a lady can find a gentleman who not only tolerates but encourages his wife to learn —not just as most ladies do but as a capable, rational human being should."

She paused in front of a statue. "My nephew is such a man. You are a fortunate lady." She pretended to admire the figure for a moment. "I love my nephew as if he were my own son, and I know he will love and protect you with every fiber of his being. It is his way."

She turned to face Elizabeth. "But he is not a lady, and sometimes a lady needs advice from another lady. I am familiar with the ways of the society in which you will be moving, and I would be excessively pleased if I could stand beside you this season as you make your debut."

Elizabeth felt a mixture of apprehension and delight mingle in the depths of her stomach. The thought of being introduced to London society was not something to which she looked forward, but to have Darcy's aunt, the sister of an earl and a countess in her own right, at her side made it seem more manageable. "I would be most grateful for the guidance."

Lady Sophia gave her an approving smile. "I like you, Miss Bennet. And not just because you are to marry my nephew and likely irritate my brother and his wife, but I feel a kinship of spirit."

"But we have only just met," Elizabeth protested.

"One does not always need to know another person for an extended period of time before knowing these things."

They were strolling amongst the sculptures again.

"I would dare say Darcy knew you were perfect for him from the moment you met. He is much like me in that regard."

Elizabeth laughed. "I am not so certain. We spent much time arguing, and his first comments about me were not exactly complimentary."

"My nephew was rude? To a lady?"

"He was not so purposefully. I believe he was distracted by much weightier matters than the suitability of a dancing partner."

"Ah," Lady Sophia said. "I was concerned that the whole nasty business with his sister had addled his brain. It seems my fears were not unfounded."

"I can understand how the concern for a sister could occupy one's mind." Elizabeth felt a strange need to defend him.

Lady Sophia smiled. She had hoped to be able to talk about the events surrounding Darcy and Elizabeth's betrothal. "It is why you agreed to marry him, is it not?"

A bit of colour crept up Elizabeth's neck and onto her cheeks. "It is. I could not bear to be the cause of disappointment for any of my sisters."

"But, you did not like him?" Lady Sophia suspected that such was no longer the case but wished to hear her suspicions confirmed.

Elizabeth's face grew warm. She looked around, but there were few visitors and the ones that were present were a good distance away from them. "I did not know him."

Lady Sophia nodded her understanding. "And now that you are becoming familiar with him, how do you find him?"

"He is most surprising and not at all as I imagined him to be." She covered her mouth with her fingers.

"You have not misspoken, Miss Bennet. He was rude, so you expected a boor. It is only natural."

"Natural or not, it was ungenerous to come to such a conclusion based on one comment."

"Perhaps, but it is still a very natural response to bad behaviour." Lady Sophia leaned a bit closer to Elizabeth's ear and whispered. It was not so much that the information she had to tell Elizabeth needed to be guarded any more than what they had already shared, but she had seen a couple of well-known gossips watching her. It would do well for them to think that she was sharing a great confidence with Elizabeth.

"Fitzwilliam grumbles and snaps when he is distressed. He has all his life. I know he tries not to do so, but his restraint only stretches so far." She saw one of the ladies who had been watching them whisper something to her friend and then both glanced in her direction. "Come. We are expected for tea, and I am always early. If I am not early, he will worry that something has become of me."

Elizabeth laughed, causing the two gossips to look once again in Lady Sophia's direction. "He does fret excessively, does he not?"

"Indeed, he does." She motioned to Georgiana, who spoke briefly to Mary.

"I believe," she said to Elizabeth, "that you are about to become the talk of the town. Believe only half of what these ladies say. The more dramatic and sensational a piece of news, the better they like it."

"Much like my aunt," Elizabeth said softly.

"And my sister." Lady Sophia winked at Elizabeth before turning to greet the two ladies who were approaching.

"Miss Ivison, Miss Pearce, may I present my soon-to-be niece, Miss Bennet. Miss Bennet, this is Miss Ivison." She motioned to the slightly plump lady who was wearing a deep shade of green and had a rather large feather accenting her bonnet. "And this," she motioned to the shorter of the two ladies who was wearing a lovely shade of blue, "is Miss Pearce."

"It is true then?" Miss Pearce asked. "Mr. Darcy is to marry?"

"He is indeed," said Lady Sophia. "And I, for one, am exceedingly pleased."

Miss Ivison gave Miss Elizabeth an appraising look. "You are from Hertfordshire?" She did not wait for Elizabeth to answer. "Near Netherfield, I understand."

Elizabeth opened her mouth to reply, but Miss Ivison was not planning to let her speak.

"I have had the full story from Miss Bingley. I must say I was surprised that Mr. Darcy would fall for someone of such low standing — not that there is anything wrong with being of a lower station, it is merely the idea of a higher rank and a lower rank being united that is a bit shocking. However, I can see why he would be tempted to leave his realm. You are very pretty, Miss Bennet." She gave Elizabeth another appraising look. "Very pretty," she mumbled.

Elizabeth smiled to hide her displeasure. "I thank you for the compliment," she said. "But I assure you I am not so pretty as my sister Jane. Did Miss Bingley mention her, too? I would be surprised if she did not, for her brother appears to be quite fond of my sister. Which I suppose, if things go well, might result in another lower rank being joined with a higher rank. A fortunate circumstance for Mr. Bingley," she paused, "and his sisters."

Lady Sophia smiled to herself. Standing at Elizabeth's side during the season could be a delightful experience. She had a quick wit and sharp tongue.

"I understand," Miss Ivison said, "that you are fond of libraries."

There was no mistaking the insinuation in her voice. Lady Sophia thought to put an end to Miss Ivison's meddling, but before she could utter a word, Elizabeth had replied.

"I admit I do find a certain enjoyment," she paused again, "in reading." She leaned a bit toward the women and spoke in a hushed voice. "I suppose it really ought not to be done so often as I do it, but books are such great sources of pleasure, are they not?" She did not allow either lady to reply. "I regret that I will be in town for so short a period of time and with all that needs to be done, I am not able to receive callers. However, you must call on me at Darcy House after the new year."

She smiled at Lady Sophia. "You will have to pardon us, but we are late. Mr. Darcy expects us for tea, and I would hate to disappoint him or cause him to worry needlessly by being tardy." She dipped a curtsey. "It has been a pleasure."

"Indeed," Lady Sophia said. It had been a pleasure to watch Elizabeth handle the situation so effectively.

"Well done," she whispered to Elizabeth as they joined Mary and Georgiana.

"Who are your fine feathered friends?" Mary asked Elizabeth.

A small burst of laughter escaped Lady Sophia. "They do rather look like a couple of preening parrots, do they not?" Her eyes twinkled with amusement. "Miss Ivison is in the green, and Miss Pearce is in the blue. They are two of the ton's best gossips."

"And apparently friends of Miss Bingley," said Elizabeth. "They have had news from her."

Mary rolled her eyes.

"You do not like Miss Bingley?" Georgiana asked.

"I do not like her behaviour," Mary said very primly. "She is always trying to elevate herself by lowering others. It is not right."

"No," agreed Lady Sophia, "putting another down to raise yourself up is not right and often ends in embarrassment and disappointment. Unfortunately, it is a common trait within the ton, and a disappointed lady with such a fault in character can be very cunning and cruel."

Georgiana smiled at Elizabeth. "I imagine Miss Bingley is very disappointed since she can no longer claim my brother for herself."

"As are Miss Ivison and Miss Pearce," Lady Sophia said. "I fear you will have to face several jealous ladies, my dear."

Elizabeth sighed.

"Do not fear, Miss Bennet. You have already given a strong signal to the ton that you are not weak."

Elizabeth's brows pulled together in question.

"You rose to your own defense and that of your intended. News of your defense will circulate. Those two cannot keep a bit of news to themselves even if it does show them in a poor light." She noted the look of shock on Elizabeth's face. "It is a strange world which you have entered."

Elizabeth agreed. She was not unfamiliar with such behaviour. It was, after all, the work of gossip which found her now betrothed to Mr. Darcy. Gossip spread by her aunt, someone who did not consider the effects the gossip might have on her niece.

She shook her head. "I believe it is the nonsensical nature of gossip which continues to surprise me."

"That, my dear, is because you possess what they do not — sense. And," she continued as she climbed into the carriage, "it is why I am so pleased that you are marrying my nephew. He cannot abide the nonsensical and needs a woman of sense which he will now have." She pulled her skirts in to allow Elizabeth to sit next to her. "I am beyond happy to have you as a niece, my dear. Beyond happy."

Elizabeth settled into the seat and attempted to listen to the conversation around her, but her mind kept wandering back to the exchange with Miss Ivison and Miss Pearce. She had felt a need to defend herself, but it was not what truly inspired her to speak as she had. What was it about Mr. Darcy that made her feel a need to see that he was well and that his name was not harmed?

"Oh!" Her hand flew to her mouth and her eyes grew wide as understanding dawned on her.

"Are you well?" Lady Sophia asked.

Elizabeth smiled brightly. "I am well. I was merely woolgathering." She now saw her dislike for those two women and Miss Bingley for what it was. Mr. Darcy had touched her heart, and she was jealous.

Mary looked at her doubtfully. "Are you sure you are well, Lizzy?"

Elizabeth nodded. "I am well. Very, very well." And, she added to herself, quite possibly in love with the man she was going to marry.

Chapter 11

DARCY HAPPILY SETTLED INTO a chair near the hearth in the library. The fire snapped and popped sending a spray of sparks floating upward as the flames danced below. Warmth radiated out from the pleasant site and wrapped itself around Darcy. There was such comfort in home and hearth, especially today.

Despite the unpleasant visit with his uncle, the day had been a good one. He had accomplished the work he had set out to do, and he had had a most agreeable visit with Elizabeth. While he was a person given to judging his success by the number of tasks accomplished, he suspected that had his work remained undone, he would have still considered this a good day simply because of Elizabeth's visit.

She had seemed pleased to see him today, and he dared to hope that it was an indication that her opinion of him was changing. Perhaps, just perhaps, she had come to like him. He would not yet venture a thought to consider she could love him. He was not that daring, nor was he about to give up his present contentment just to long for something yet to come. For now, he was satisfied to reflect on her smiles and gentle teasing. He smiled and shook his head at himself. When had he become such a mooncalf?

"You look pleased," Richard, who sat in the chair across from him, said.

"I am." Darcy broke the seal on his letter from Bingley.

"Is there a particular reason?"

Darcy nodded. "Miss Elizabeth seems more accepting of our situation." He unfolded the letter and smoothed the creases. "I do wish Bingley would learn to write more neatly. So many blots."

Richard laughed and opened the book on his lap. "I shall assist you in deciphering if you should require it."

Darcy chuckled and began reading. There was every likelihood that such assistance might be needed. Bingley truly wrote the least tidy letters Darcy had ever seen, but he also knew that it was because Bingley's thoughts flowed as rapidly as a river rushing to the sea after a season of rain.

Darcy,

You know I am not excessively fond of writing correspondence, and since I do not feel the need to impress you with my skills, I shall refrain from discussing the pleasantries of the weather and how the neighbours get on.

I will not, of course, refrain from the pleasantry of mentioning Miss Bennet. She is as lovely as ever, and you were indeed wrong about her, my friend. She likes me well enough to consent to a courtship, a step I thought I should not skip, although those who are considered my betters might deem it unnecessary. I believe I have startled my sister with the laughter I could not contain at my jesting.

Darcy shook his head and chuckled silently. He was certain that Bingley was never going to let him forget that night of the ball at Netherfield, and truthfully, Darcy did not care if he did or not. The results were currently proving to be happy.

Caroline is still unhappy...

Of course, she was.

...and I fear she shall remain so until I can find another of equal or greater standing to take your place. It would be much nicer if she would seek to marry for love instead of advantage, but as you know there is little reasoning with her at times. I shall be glad to pass her care and fickle temperament on to another. Of course, I care for her, and I will always do my duty to her, but I do not always enjoy it.

Darcy did not envy his friend's position in caring for a sister like Miss Bingley. Caring for Georgiana had brought its share of troubles, and not all of them were small, but she was a delight, especially when he compared her to Caroline.

Thoughts of my sister bring to mind the purpose for writing — aside from the desire to tell you of my success with Miss Bennet.

Caroline has heard some whispers regarding the night of the ball. It seems, from what she has heard — and I only know this from listening to her relate the details to Louisa — she has not spoken to me directly (and I have no intention of asking her about it) — that you and Miss Elizabeth may have indeed been trapped.

Darcy's left brow arched. He had been trapped?

The facts which I have been able to catch are that Mrs. Philips was asked to find Miss Elizabeth, and then as Mrs. Philips was looking for her niece, Sir William pointed her in the direction of the library. Afterward, Sir William and Mr. Bennet retired to the card tables but did not play. They merely partook of some punch and conversed until Mrs. Philips came through the rooms searching for them at a very loud volume.

I fear, my dear friend, that your compromise was arranged by Mr. Bennet.

Darcy blinked and read that sentence again. He had been trapped by Mr. Bennet?

Miss Elizabeth, as far as I can tell and your tale of her distress confirms, had no part in it.

That, Darcy could believe.

I have come to enjoy Mr. Bennet's company, and though he may not care for his family as he ought, he does care for his daughters and particularly for both Miss Bennet and Miss Elizabeth. Therefore, I am entirely convinced that he would only do what is right for them, and knowing this, I believe he chose you for Miss Elizabeth because he genuinely believes there could be no better match for her.

It is only my trust in your character, which I know would not cause Miss Elizabeth to suffer due to the actions of her father, that allows me to write of these things with any measure of composure. You must know however that I considered carefully whether I should write to you on this or not, for I did not wish to bring you pain or incite your anger. Be that as it may, yesterday, I saw my sisters having a conversation of what appeared to be a profoundly serious nature with Miss Bennet. I fear how they may have presented this information to Miss Bennet and knowing how close Miss Bennet and Miss Elizabeth are, I would expect the information to be carried to Miss Elizabeth with the next post.

Do write to let me know how you will proceed. I shall worry about whether my decision to write to you was wise or not until I have heard.

God bless,

CB

Darcy dropped the letter into his lap, furrowed his brow, picked the letter up, and read it once again. He should be horrified by the news it related to him. His ire should be bubbling at his having been used in such a fashion, and yet, it was not. Strangely, he was filled with gratitude, though he could not quite put his finger on why.

He held the letter out to Richard. "It seems you were right. I was, indeed, trapped."

Richard took the letter from his cousin and made short work of reading it. As he finished his perusal, he looked to Darcy with raised brows. "How will you proceed?"

"I will have the license and marriage papers in my possession by the end of the week. We will endure an evening with Lord and Lady Matlock if they choose to accept my invitation. And after that, we shall return to Hertfordshire and be married as planned."

"So, in other words, you will not change your plans."

"Exactly. I see no need to change them." He took his letter back from Richard and folded it before slipping it into his pocket. "I am happy to be marrying Elizabeth."

"But her father duped you."

Darcy shook his head as the reason for his odd feelings after reading the letter took focus. "No, he did not dupe me. He helped me. You must remember that Elizabeth did not wish to marry me while I had begun to suspect that I very much wished to marry her. Her father merely made sure she could not refuse me." His brows furrowed as a rather disturbing thought came to mind.

He blew out a breath. "I suppose she may not be as complacent with the news as I am." He scrubbed his face with his hands.

That thought filled him with apprehension. His only hope to avoid having to convince Elizabeth that they still must marry was the way she had welcomed him today. Perhaps she liked him enough to follow through with marrying him.

He yawned and stretched as the day caught up with him and the warmth of the fire worked its relaxing magic.

"She may attempt to cry off."

"But you will not allow that, will you?"

Richard's tone seemed to say he knew the answer Darcy would give, and that he would not accept any other. It was one of the things Darcy appreciated the most about his cousin. Richard always sought what was best for those about whom he cared deeply. Darcy was happy to be one of those people.

He shook his head as he rose to retire for the night. "No, I will not allow that. I cannot. Not only because of the situation in which it would place both her and her family but also because my heart would not survive it. I love her, Richard. I do not know how, in such a short acquaintance, I have come to love her as much as I do, but I do love her."

Richard caught him by the arm as he moved past Richard's chair. "Let me know if I can do anything to assist you. Anything."

"I will." He stood next to Richard for a moment. Then, he placed his hand on Richard's shoulder and said, "Pray that your assistance is not needed," before leaving the library in search of his bed.

Chapter 12

ELIZABETH LOOKED ONCE AGAIN at the letter Jane had written. It could not be true. It simply could not be. Her father had arranged the compromise in the library at Netherfield? A tumult of emotions cascaded through her as she read.

...Miss Bingley assures me she has spoken to no one else on the matter. She has not even spoken to her brother, for she fears he will tell Mr. Darcy, who she claims despises all forms of deception and should he hear of our father's scheming, is likely to demand that you release him from his promise. She said — and I cannot believe I did not laugh as she said it — that she was worried how such an occurrence might harm you.

We both know, dear Lizzy, that she has very little care for you — a fact she has made quite evident, since you have been gone, with small disparities here and there. They have all been said, of course, with a feigned air of concern for you, but she does not fool me. I must warn you. Because of Miss Bingley's comments, Mama has begun to grow concerned that you will not be a credit to Mr. Darcy with your education as it is now and has been petitioning Father for a longer engagement period so that she can instruct you more fully.

Do not fret, my dear sister. Miss Bingley is simply jealous. I would not place any confidence in what she has said. Indeed, I would believe the exact opposite to be true. I would advise you to lay before Mr. Darcy the details of our father's meddling. I believe him to be an honourable man and am fully certain he would do right by you.

If possible, please write to me, for I am anxious to hear how you get on and am not certain I can abide waiting until you return.

Yours, etc.

Jane

Oh, if she had not seen Miss Ivison and Miss Pearce today, she might be able to believe that Miss Bingley had not spoken to anyone on the matter! But she had seen Miss Ivison and Miss Pearce, and they had claimed to have had the whole of the story about her and Mr. Darcy from Miss Bingley. There really was no way for them to know about what had transpired at Netherfield except for Miss Bingley to have shared it. She doubted that such delicious information as her father's involvement in the compromise would be kept a secret and not shared.

Her stomach churned, and her heart raced. She did not know how Mr. Darcy would respond to this information, but she knew that she was angry at her father, as well as Miss Ivison, Miss Pearce, and Miss Bingley.

"How could he?" She tossed the letter on the bed. "Father knew I did not like — nay, despised — Mr. Darcy, and yet he would subject me to marriage to him?"

Mary took up the letter.

"There." Elizabeth pointed to the section containing the news of her father's involvement in the events at the ball. "And this." She pointed to what Jane had said about Miss Bingley.

Mary pulled the letter away and moved out of her reach while she read it. When she had finished, she folded it and placed it on the bed near Elizabeth, but she moved no closer. "You should thank Papa."

Elizabeth gasped. "Thank him? For forcing me to marry a man I do not like?"

"*Did* not like," corrected Mary. "You like him quite well now, do you not?" She did not wait for a response. Instead, she marched across the room, pulled Elizabeth's green muslin from the wardrobe, and tossed it at her. "You have an appointment with Mrs. Havelston."

"For the fitting of a wedding dress which may not be needed," Elizabeth said as she began to lift the dress over her head with Mary's assistance.

"The wedding dress shall be needed."

"But what if Mr. Darcy is angry?" Elizabeth's voice was somewhat muffled by the fabric as it lowered over her face. "How can I marry a man who has been forced to marry me and is angry about it?" It was not possible. She could not do that for it would lead to a most miserable existence.

Mary, who had begun to work on the fastening of Elizabeth's dress, spun her around and place one hand firmly on each of her sister's shoulders.

"Do you care for Mr. Darcy?" she demanded.

Elizabeth, somewhat taken aback by Mary's harsh tone, nodded.

"Do you think he is honourable?"

Elizabeth blinked. "I do."

"Has he not been solicitous of your feelings?"

Elizabeth nodded. How often had she heard the uncertainty in his voice as he worried about her?

"Does he care for you?"

Elizabeth's lip trembled slightly as she nodded once again. She hoped he still did.

Mary softened her tone. "Do you believe him capable of ever treating you ill?"

Elizabeth shook her head. He had not even treated Mr. Wickham ill after the abominable thing he had done. Mr. Darcy was as noble as any man could ever be. But was that not also the problem?

Mary turned her around again and continued working on the fastenings. "Will you be content to part ways with him?"

Elizabeth's heart pinched. The thought of never seeing Mr. Darcy again brought tears to her eyes and her real fear to her lips. "But what if," she said softly as a tear slid down her cheek, "what if, when he learns about Papa's actions, he wishes to part ways with me?" Several more tears joined that first tear in racing down Elizabeth's cheeks. The thought of him sending her away broke her heart in a way it had never been torn before.

Mary wrapped her arms around Elizabeth from behind. "I am not as wise or as serene as Jane, and I have not her experience of years. However, I have spent time learning and have concentrated that learning on books which, I have every confidence, contain truth for living as I ought."

Elizabeth covered Mary's hands where they were clasped on her chest with her own. Once again, she was struck by how often she had given Mary no notice. Mary did not have an older sister or a younger sister to whom she could look for guidance or solace.

"Is that why you chose to read sermons?"

"Sermons and the family Bible," Mary corrected. "I sought truth, and Father did not seem inclined to teach me what I wished to know." She squeezed Elizabeth more tightly. "And I repeated what I had read aloud so that I could retain it more fully."

Elizabeth giggled. "I thought you did that to torture us, especially Kitty and Lydia, by pointing out our errors."

"Well, there is that," Mary said with a laugh as she released Elizabeth from her embrace. "It may not be right of me to say or think. However, as I see things, our younger sisters' behaviour borders on the utterly ridiculous, and it is they – well, Lydia, to be precise – who will be the ruin of us all if her behaviour is left unchecked."

Elizabeth could not disagree with that. Lydia was the most forward and flirtatious of them all. It was not difficult to imagine her making some foolish mistake and plunging herself and her family into ruin. Elizabeth made a few last adjustments to her dress and then, turned to assist her sister.

"What have you learned from all your reading that would apply to my current situation?" she asked.

Mary's brow furrowed. "I would say that it is a child's duty, no matter her age, to honour her parents, but I am not sure that applies when the parent has been deceptive."

Mary looked as if she was seriously contemplating what her response should be, so Elizabeth waited patiently and silently while she finished fastening Mary's dress.

"I suppose," Mary finally said, "that I should remind you to forgive those who have wrongfully used you. Then, I should admonish you to rejoice with those who rejoice — did not Jane share her joy at having accepted a courtship with Mr. Bingley? And finally, I think I should tell you to consider the story of Joseph. He would not have chosen his lot in life, but God used the nefarious scheming of his brothers to work good for a nation. If the Almighty can do that, can He not also use the scheming of a well-meaning father to bring blessing to you and your family?"

She sat down in front of the mirror as she finished speaking and began working the clasp of her necklace.

Elizabeth's mouth hung agape for a moment. Mary, for all her moralizing and reciting of scripture and sermons, was not so foolish as her father had implied. In fact, she was likely to be the wisest of her sisters. Guilt pricked Elizabeth's conscience. She had neglected Jane's happy news by choosing rather to focus on that which pertained to herself.

Mary turned to look at her. "Do you remember the comments Miss Bingley made days before the ball about longing to return to town?"

"I do." Miss Bingley had mentioned a soon return if her brother could be persuaded to change his plans.

"If Mr. Bingley had left," Mary continued, "would Jane have found such happiness?" She shrugged in reply to her own question before expanding on it further. "If you and Mr. Darcy were not planning to wed, I dare say Miss Bingley would have had her way and her brother would have departed from Netherfield, and our sister's heart would have been injured. As I see it, your situation has already brought blessing to our family, and it shall only continue to do so." She rose and wrapped her shawl around her shoulders, which she drew up and back. "We have an appointment. Are you ready?"

Elizabeth nodded. "I am."

She hoped with all that was in her that the appointment would not be for naught. Her fear must have been etched on her face, for Mary gave her one last quick hug and said, "Mr. Darcy will not wish to part ways with you, Elizabeth. His eyes say he loves you far too much for that."

"Thank you," Elizabeth whispered before following her sister from the room.

Chapter 13

DARCY WATCHED ELIZABETH ALIGHT from the carriage. Happiness and dread mingled within him. He would have to talk to her today about what he had learned from Bingley. He had decided, last night as he lay in his bed, that it was best to just deal with the matter directly instead of hiding it and waiting until she discovered it some other way. He was not a supporter of prevarication, especially on things as important as marriage.

"She is here," he announced to his cousin as he tugged at his cravat and straightened his jacket. He had felt unusually fidgety today. Sitting or standing still for any amount of time had been torture.

"And our aunt?" Richard asked and laughed as Darcy returned to the window to see if his aunt had also arrived. "You are not yourself today."

That was true. Darcy felt unlike himself. He smiled wryly. "If she has had word from her sister..." He did not finish as he heard Daniels opening the door and greeting their guests.

His happy future hung in the balance today. He would do his best to convince Elizabeth not to give him up, but he could not force her to keep her promise to marry him. He blew out a deep breath and sat next to the chair in which Elizabeth had chosen to sit on her first visit to Darcy House, but he had only just gotten seated when he popped back out of his chair to greet the ladies.

Lady Sophia was the first to enter the room. She greeted both Darcy and Richard with a kiss before taking a seat near Richard. "Is he well?" she whispered.

"A bit on edge is all," Richard replied. "He has had some news from Bingley."

Her brows furrowed. That was interesting for that made two individuals in this room who should be resplendent with happiness who were anything but. "Miss Elizabeth worried her handkerchief throughout the entire carriage ride."

Richard grimaced. "Then, I suspect, she has heard the news as well."

"Is this news disastrous?"

"It could be, or it might just be a small bump in the road to their happiness. Only time will tell."

"Does that mean that some scheming to allow them time alone is in order?" she questioned.

Richard nodded. "It would be best."

"Well, then," she said. "It is not very much of a scheme but here goes." She shifted forward in her seat and looked pointedly at Georgiana. "Did you not wish to show Miss Mary your new piece of music? I am certain I heard you say something about it earlier."

"I did," she replied with some excitement. "Could I do that now?"

Lady Sophia smiled. She could always count on Georgiana to be eager to play the piano. "I think it would be wise if you wish to have ample time to practice."

She waited until Mary and Georgiana had left the room, which did not take long since Mary seemed as eager to be gone to the music room as Georgiana. It was a fine friendship that was forming between the two. Mary was quite to Lady Sophia's liking. But her thoughts about Mary and her niece would have to wait. At present, there was another relation and a lovely young woman who needed her attention and direction.

"Now, Darcy," she said with a smile. "I am absolutely positive that Miss Elizabeth would rather take a tour of the library with you than sit here while I knit, and your cousin tells me about his latest creation. I guarantee that it will be rather dull."

Darcy gave her a questioning look.

She shook her head. If only he were as obliging as his sister when it came to taking a suggestion. She would just have to be direct with him.

"You have been fidgeting, and Miss Bennet has nearly destroyed a well-embroidered handkerchief on the way here today. I do not know what it is all about, but if you need to go to the library or some other room in this house to discuss it, then you need to go." She made a sweeping motion toward the door. "However, if you prefer to sit here and have me question you about it, then you may remain, but I do promise to be most infuriatingly curious."

Darcy gave both his aunt and his cousin, who was barely containing his laughter, a look of displeasure before standing and offering his arm to Elizabeth. He knew full well that as soon as he and Elizabeth left the room, his aunt would have the full story from Richard.

"I do apologize for my aunt's lack of discretion," he said. "However, she is correct in that I would like a few moments of private conversation."

He attempted to smile at Elizabeth reassuringly, but from the way she was biting her lip, he was not sure it was effective. Nevertheless, she rose with what appeared to be alacrity and placed her hand on his arm.

"Could we go, perhaps, to the blue sitting room adjacent to the library?" she asked as they moved toward the door to the drawing room.

He was pleased that she remembered that room. It was one of his favourites for sitting in with Georgiana and Richard.

"We may go to whichever room you please."

"Then, I select the blue sitting room, for it seemed a lovely room for having a conversation."

"I have always found it so," he assured her as they passed down the corridor to the grand staircase. "The last time I saw you, you mentioned that you had an appointment with the modiste. Was it a successful visit?"

"Indeed, it was," Elizabeth replied as they began to ascend the stairs. "I assure you that I possessed no concern that the work would be excellent, for Mrs. Havelston's work always is, but I was somewhat fearful that my order was too large while the time in which she would have to complete it was too small. However, she had all the gowns ready to make final adjustments before adding embellishments. Those which are necessary will be ready before we leave for Hertfordshire, and the others she will have delivered."

"I will make sure Mrs. Vernon and Mr. Daniels know to expect them." He had thought his reply would help put her at ease, but it seemed to do just the opposite. She had once again pulled her lip between her teeth.

"Mr. Darcy," she began as they entered the blue sitting room, and she dropped his arm. "Some information has come to light which may alter your opinion on if we should marry."

"Ah, I take it you have heard from your sister."

She looked at him in astonishment. "I have, but how did you know?"

"Bingley wrote to me. I received his letter just yesterday," he said as he stepped towards her.

"Mr. Bingley?" A deep crease formed between her enchanting eyes. "But Jane said that Miss Bingley had not spoken to him."

"She did not," Darcy said. "Bingley only reported to me what he overheard of his sisters' conversation."

"Oh." Her gaze dropped to the floor.

"My wishes have not changed."

"But my father..." she said, looking up at him.

"Your father is, in my opinion, a tremendously wise man." He led her to the settee near the window which overlooked the street.

"You do not wish for me to call off the wedding because of his scheming?"

He shook his head, but then, seeing her eyes fill with tears, he took her hand as his heart seemed to climb to his throat and yet knock soundly against his ribs at the same time. "I am sorry if you were hoping for another answer."

"You truly do not wish to part ways with me?" A smile lit her face though a tear did escape her eye and slid down her cheek.

"Never," he said softly.

"Oh." She sighed in relief. Her shoulders sank as her posture relaxed. "I was so afraid you would."

Hope poked at him, but he pushed it away. He would rather know the truth than to just hope for what he wished for to be true. He pulled out his handkerchief and blotted the tears which were sliding down her cheeks. "Are you saying you wish to marry me?"

She covered his hand with her free one and held it against her cheek where he had been drying her tears. He looked first at her hand holding his and then at her eyes. What he saw there filled his heart with joy even before she spoke.

"I do." She bit her lip and was about to continue speaking when Daniels came to the door.

"Pardon me, sir, but the lady's uncle has come on a matter of great importance."

"My uncle Gardiner?" Elizabeth asked in surprise.

"Yes, ma'am. He is in the drawing room with my lady and the colonel. I have already summoned Miss Mary."

Elizabeth hurried from the room and down the stairs to the drawing room with Darcy following close behind. She stopped at the entry to the room, her hand flew to her heart. In front of them, her uncle was embracing Mary, who was weeping. Whatever news Mr. Gardiner brought it was not good.

"Uncle?" Elizabeth said as she entered.

He turned tear-filled eyes to her. "You must return to Longbourn as soon as can be. Your father has fallen ill."

"Papa?" The word came out as someone's breath might when an opponent had punched them in the stomach.

"Yes."

"Is... Is he alive?" The question was no more than a whisper.

Darcy saw her sway and, wrapping his arm around her waist, pulled her firmly to his side. He knew all too well how shocking news such as this could be. His heart clenched at the possibility of Elizabeth's losing her father as if her pain were his own.

"I do not know," Mr. Gardiner said. "The message said his condition was grave and all haste must be made. I am sorry."

Chapter 14

MARY'S HEAD RESTED AGAINST Elizabeth's shoulder as Darcy's coach bounced along the road towards Longbourn. Elizabeth looked out the window once again at the darkness of the night. The curtains were not drawn. They were, instead, tied out of the way so that the light of the moon, mingled with the light from the carriage's lamps, could illuminate the interior of the carriage.

Mr. Darcy's coach was bedecked with lanterns enough to make the journey, but Elizabeth was happy to have the extra light of the nearly full moon to make travelling just that much safer and faster. She had not wished to spend even a moment longer than absolutely necessary in London, but she would have been far less calm about the journey if the night had been a moonless one.

She peeked across the coach at Mr. Darcy. His head rested against the well-cushioned back of the coach and his eyes were closed. However, she doubted he was asleep, for his legs kept moving slightly as if sitting still were a trial.

He had been in constant motion from the moment he had heard about her father. His travelling coach had been ordered. He had seen Elizabeth and Mary back to their uncle's home and inquired after anything that either they or the Gardiners might need to prepare for her and Mary to be made ready to travel. Then, he had departed for Darcy House, only to return in an hour and a half to gather them.

He had to be tired, but she imagined that the circumstances in which she and Mary found themselves were not unfamiliar to him. He had, after all, lost both of his parents. Elizabeth drew in a shaky breath as quietly as she could while dabbing at her eyes. How had he born this sort of pain on his own? She was certain she could not have done it. She was not so strong as some might think. She was courageous, to be sure, but courage only existed in the presence of fear, did it not?

Mary shifted and leaned against the wall of the coach instead of against her sister. Elizabeth watched Mary to see if she was going to stay situated. Satisfied that her sister was indeed going to stay positioned as she was, Elizabeth slipped across the coach to sit on the bench next to Mr. Darcy, whose eyes immediately flew open, letting her know that her assessment of his lack of sleep was indeed accurate.

"Can I sit here for a moment?" she asked.

"You may sit here as long as you wish," he said. There was a hint of grogginess to his voice, assuring her that she had also been correct in guessing that he was tired – likely exhausted.

"I wanted to thank you." Elizabeth placed her hand on top of his. "You knew exactly what needed to be done to have us travelling as soon as possible."

He turned his hand over where it lay under hers and twined his fingers with hers. "I understand the urgency of such a trip as this," he said softly.

She nodded, unable to speak for a moment as tears once again threatened. She tightened her grasp on his hand, finding comfort in his strength. "Thank you," she whispered once again, "for caring for me."

He turned his face toward her. "I will always care for you."

She smiled at him through her tears. "I know, and I will always care for you."

She looked down at where their hands lay joined. "I have been foolish. My father tried to convince me to consider you. He was extremely impressed with your character and told me, more than once, that I was wrong to think of you as anything less than a fine gentleman." She drew a shuddering breath. "I thought I knew better. My foolish, injured pride refused to allow me to see you for who you are."

He reached over and pressed her head lightly against his shoulder. "Shh...rest, my love," he whispered.

She tipped her head to look up at him. "He was right. There is no one who is better suited to me than you."

He stroked her cheek and brushed a thumb over her lips before bending to place a gentle kiss on her forehead. "I love you," he whispered.

She smiled at him again. "And I love you." The admission still made her heart flutter, but not in an uneasy fashion. It was rather a happy sort of fluttering – even now, when things were anything but happy.

His thumb brushed her lips once again. "May I..." He darted a quick look at Mary, who was still sleeping, "May I kiss you?"

He waited only long enough to get a partial nod before bending to place a gentle kiss on her lips. The happy fluttering in Elizabeth's heart increased, and she sighed softly as she leaned into him, pressing her lips more firmly against his while her hand found its way to his cheek and his moved to the back of her head.

Across the carriage, Mary stirred, and Elizabeth jumped, breaking the delicious kiss she had been sharing with Mr. Darcy and began to move to return to her seat. Mr. Darcy, however, seemed unwilling to have her leave his side and refused to let go of her.

"Stay," he said, "for just a while longer."

She wanted to stay right where she was but not just for a little while, forever. She hoped she would have the chance to thank her father for his interference.

Elizabeth glanced at Mary. It would not be the thing for Mary to find her so cozily arranged with Mr. Darcy.

"Stay," he whispered one more time, and Elizabeth settled back onto the seat and lay her cheek on his shoulder again. The warmth of his person and the fragrance that was him wrapped its comfort around her, stilling her thoughts and calming her heart. She breathed deeply, and he did the same as he squeezed her hand tight.

She awoke sometime later when the coach began to slow as they approached Longbourn. Mary tapped Elizabeth's foot, and with eyebrows raised, gave her a disapproving look before closing her eyes again as Darcy began to stir. Elizabeth gently removed her fingers from his loose grasp and then rising to move, placed a soft kiss on his cheek before taking her seat next to her sister.

Mr. Darcy opened his eyes at the contact of her lips on his cheek and smiled at her. The soft happiness that shone in that smile and his eyes passed from him to her. What lay ahead of her was no doubt going to be challenging, but she knew that she did not have to face it alone. "I love you," she mouthed, causing his smile to grow.

Then, as soon as she was settled back in her place next to Mary, he stretched, and, when the carriage came to a stop, exited first before handing both Elizabeth and Mary out of the carriage.

The door to Longbourn flew open, and Jane hurried down the steps to greet her sisters. "I am so glad you are both here," she said as she embraced them.

"How is Papa?" asked Elizabeth.

"He has his moments of wakefulness, but he is not strong. We must prepare ourselves, for his heart grows weak." She looked at Mr. Darcy. "He has also been asking for you. I have told him that you would come and to rest while he waited, but he said he cannot rest until he has seen you." She began to move them toward the house. "Do you remember the slight cough he had after he got wet while out shooting just before the Netherfield Ball?"

"I do," Mr. Darcy said.

Elizabeth and her sisters looked at him in surprise.

"Bingley and I were with him on that hunting trip. He was not the only one who got wet."

"Yes, Mr. Bingley mentioned that you and he had also gotten wet," Jane continued. "Two days ago, Papa's cough, which refused to go away, settled into his lungs and was accompanied by a fever. The fever broke this afternoon, just before Mr. Bingley's physician arrived, but it has done its damage."

"But he could recover," Mary said.

"It is unlikely," Jane said.

"But he could," Mary whispered.

Jane placed an arm around her shoulders. "Come, Mary. You shall see him first. Lizzy," she tilted her head toward the sitting room, "Mama."

Elizabeth drew a deep breath and released it as she turned toward the door to the sitting room. "Are you sure you wish to stay, Mr. Darcy? My mother can be trying when she is well, but she can be even more taxing when she is not."

"Your father wishes to see me, and I wish to see him," Darcy said, taking her hand and placing it on his arm. "And I do not wish to leave you to face any of this on your own."

It was just as she had thought. He would stand beside her through whatever came. The fledgling love she felt for him deepened further, causing her to marvel at how quickly one could fall deeply in love once one allowed it to happen. Then, drawing on the strength his presence provided to her, she whispered a thank you to him and allowed him to lead her into the sitting room to sit with her mother and younger sisters.

Half an hour later, Jane returned to tell Elizabeth that their father wished to speak to her and Mr. Darcy. Mary had gone to her room but promised to be down soon to see her mother.

"Is she well?" Elizabeth whispered to Jane.

"She will be," Jane replied. "At least as well as can be expected."

Out of the corner of her eye, Elizabeth saw Mr. Darcy rubbed his temples. Between the late hour and her mother's incessant chatter for the past half hour, his head must be hurting. She offered him her hand and with a small smile, he took it.

"You have done very well," he said when they entered the hallway. "I do not think anyone but I saw your tears."

"You saw my tears?" She had known he was watching her. She had seen him, but she had not thought that he had watched her so closely.

"I did." He wrapped her arm around his and pulled her close to his side as they ascended the stairs. "I dare say you were just what your mother and sisters needed."

The pride in his voice warmed her and made the strain of the last hour and a half feel just a little less heavy. She rested her head on his shoulder as they walked the short distance down the hall to her father's room.

"Shall I wait here?" Mr. Darcy asked when they stood came to her father's door. "Would you like some time with him alone first?"

She shook her head and pushed the door open. She wanted him with her. Always.

Chapter 15

"Ah, at last, my Lizzy," Mr. Bennet said. He lifted himself up higher on his pillows until a coughing fit gripped him.

Elizabeth removed her hand from Mr. Darcy's arm and hurried to his side. The closeness of the two did what remained of his heart good to see. Hopefully, that closeness would remain after he made his confession.

He reclined comfortably on the pillows Elizabeth had propped behind him. Taking a cup from the nightstand, she held it to his lips when the coughing had subsided. He disliked seeing her as worried as she was, but there was nothing he could do about that, except pray that her worry was for naught.

He took a sip and then wiped his mouth with the back of his hand. "I am so glad to see you. Did you have a successful trip to town? Are all the gowns in the kingdom to be deposited at Mr. Darcy's door?"

She smiled at his teasing. "I have been forced to stand for more fittings than is my preference, but I do believe there are ample gowns left for the other ladies. Uncle Gardiner had selected four fabrics before I arrived, so I shall have four new dresses soon. Would you like for me to describe the lace to you?"

Mr. Bennet raised his hands slightly and coughed twice before replying, "Please do not tell me about lace or bonnets." He smiled and patted her hand. "I know without hearing a word about them that you shall look lovely in each one. Will she not, Mr. Darcy?"

"Of course, sir," Mr. Darcy said. "And I am afraid she will have to endure a few more fittings once my aunt begins her plotting to show her off to one and all in society."

Mr. Bennet chuckled along with Mr. Darcy as Elizabeth groaned. Kitty or Lydia would be delighted to stand for fittings and pick fabrics, lace, and trims, but Elizabeth was more like Mary in not liking to be fussed over. Jane was too pleasant to either like or not like being fussed over. He was happy for her presence these past few days. He knew that her calm demeanor and ability to take charge of a situation had been a godsend to her mother and through her mother to him.

Hopefully, what he was about to say would not need to draw on Jane's fortitude to calm things. She had endured much already.

"Now," Mr. Bennet began, smoothing his blankets and watching his hands do it, "this betrothal…"

"We know, Papa," interrupted Elizabeth.

He lifted his eyes to see Elizabeth's face before darting a look at Darcy. "You know about my part in the arranging of events?"

Elizabeth nodded. "Miss Bingley figured it out and told Jane about it. And Jane, of course, told me."

Miss Bingley? Oh, that was not good. A disappointed lady was rarely a kind lady – especially if she tended to be haughty like Miss Bingley was.

"And you told Mr. Darcy?" He looked between the two faces which bore no sign of displeasure. Could he be so blessed that they were not put out with him?

"No, Bingley told me."

"Well," Mr. Bennet said in surprise, "if so many know, I am surprised my wife has not congratulated me on my scheming."

"I am certain few in Meryton know of the events other than how my aunt has shared them. The number in town who have been informed may be larger," said Elizabeth. "While at the museum with Lady Sophia, who is Mr. Darcy's aunt, I met two of Miss

Bingley's friends. They hinted at knowing about how my betrothal came about."

"I am sorry," said Mr. Bennet. He had not considered that his scheming might make her new life more challenging. However, he was not certain if knowing that at the time of setting things into motion would have stopped him. He looked from his daughter to Mr. Darcy and back. "I knew that Mr. Bingley was considering leaving the area," he explained, "and I knew that with him would go not only Jane's chance at happiness but yours as well."

He shook his head and rolled his eyes, for remembering Mr. Collins always made him shake his head and roll his eyes. That man was such a buffoon! "And then, when Collins requested two dances with you and a meeting with me and knowing your mother as I do and having had no success in changing your opinion of Mr. Darcy, I saw no option other than to arrange things as I knew they should go."

"You were right, Papa," said Elizabeth, holding out her hand to Darcy, who took it as he came to stand next to her. "There is no one more well-suited to me than Mr. Darcy, but I was too blinded by my pride to see it."

"Does this mean that you are happy and that I am forgiven?"

"Yes, I am very happy." Elizabeth looked up at Darcy with a smile that spoke of the truth of her words and eased Mr. Bennet's mind. The way the gentleman replied to Elizabeth with a smile of his own, eased Mr. Bennet's mind further.

He rubbed his chest and attempted to hide a grimace. "Then, I shall rest more easily." He leaned back more fully into his pillows. "I assume by your presence at my side that they have told you my condition is not good?"

Elizabeth's free hand covered her father's. "They have."

"They may be right, or they may be wrong. No one, not even Bingley's doctor, is all-knowing." He coughed as he attempted to take a less shallow breath. "However, in the event that I fail in proving the doctor wrong, there are some things which I must ask of you." He looked at Darcy. "Bring a chair. No need to stand for the full interview, my boy. Bring it over next to Lizzy, so you may continue to hold her hand."

Elizabeth clung to Darcy's hand for a moment as he began to move to do as instructed before their fingers parted. Ah, the felicity between the two delighted Mr. Bennet. He would be glad to tell Sir William that he had been correct in predicting his daughter's happiness.

"Now," he said as Darcy took his seat, "about your sisters, Lizzy. Your mother will not be penniless, but her funds will be diminished after Collins receives his inheritance. Do not allow her to force any of my daughters to marry that man. He is utterly without sense as his father was, and I would prefer the entail to die with him. But even a man without sense appears a good option to many ladies when he has an estate."

A bout of coughing followed his firm statements, and Elizabeth once again offered him a drink, which he readily accepted. "I have told Mary already that I forbid her to marry that man. I have told your mother of my wishes as well, but when she is in a fit of nerves, she remembers very little and can only look for an escape."

He tightened his grip on Elizabeth's hand and looked at Darcy. "Mr. Bingley has declared his intention to eventually marry Jane. Do not let Collins attempt to dissuade him or deny him. Do not let Collins have any say over my daughters' futures. He may inherit my estate — what is it but stuff and money — but I shall not hand over to him those things which are of highest importance. Do I ask too much of you and Mr. Bingley to see to their care and futures?"

Mr. Darcy's expression was serious, but his eyes were kind. He was just as fine a gentleman as Mr. Bennet had thought him to be. He proved it further when he replied.

"I cannot speak for Mr. Bingley, though I suspect he will be in agreement with me in saying that it would be an honour to serve you in this way."

Mr. Bennet sighed for a heavy weight had been lifted from him. "I shall have Mr. Philips show you the papers tomorrow, and you will see that with proper management there are ample funds to maintain a modest establishment for my wife whether here near her sister or in town near her brother. She does not have to intrude upon your homes, though she might insist it is absolutely necessary." He chuckled and then coughed.

"You should rest, Papa," Elizabeth said as she returned the cup to the nightstand after she had seen him take another sip from it. "Mr. Darcy and I shall see to the care of my sisters and my mother. Jane shall be happy with Mr. Bingley, and I shall be happy with Mr. Darcy. And you shall grow strong and disappoint Mr. Collins with your obstinate refusal to allow him his inheritance." She leaned forward and kissed him on the forehead. "I love you."

"And I, you, Lizzy." Tears gathered as he wrapped her in his embrace for a moment before kissing her cheek and letting her rise to leave. He caught her hand before she could escape. "Tell your sisters of my love for them and my pride in having been their father. Tell them often, for I have not told them enough." He dropped her hand and settled down into his pillows.

"Until the morning," she said, giving him one more kiss.

Elizabeth wrapped her robe tightly around herself and took the candle from the stand next to her bed. She had tried to sleep, but she had not succeeded. The sound of coughing that she heard as she slipped into the hallway reassured her that her father was still alive, but it also meant he was not sleeping – at least, not as he should.

She crept down the stairs as quietly as she could, taking care to avoid the squeaky seventh step but forgetting that the third one creaked slightly as well. She stood still and listened to see if she had caused anyone to rise to investigate the sound. Satisfied that she had not disturbed anyone, she continued on her way to her father's study.

She paused as she noticed a faint glow of light under the door. She pushed the door open. Mary sat in her father's chair, wrapping a wisp of hair around her finger, and studying the books and curiosities that lined the shelves.

"I wanted to sit with him, but I dared not disturb him if he was asleep," she explained as Elizabeth drew near. "I cannot sleep knowing..."

"Neither could I." Elizabeth placed her candle on the desk and motioned for Mary to slide over so that they could both sit in the large chair. She wrapped an arm around her sister as she snuggled in next to her. "He is coughing, which I will take as a good sign."

"Do you remember when he planted that ivy and placed it up on the very top shelf?" asked Mary.

"I do," said Elizabeth. "Mama was not pleased to have it there. She claimed it would not survive, and then she complained loudly that it was too high to be properly tended, which is why there is now a ladder in here."

"This room is so filled with memories," Mary whispered. "I have always loved this room; though, I never spent as much time in here as you did."

Elizabeth squeezed her tight. "He would have allowed you to spend time in here, too, if you had asked."

"I know," said Mary. "I wish I had."

They sat for a moment, each lost in her own thoughts.

"What do you suppose will become of all these memories when Mr. Collins takes possession?" Mary asked.

Elizabeth sighed. "If we are fortunate, they will be boxed up and given to us, but if we are not fortunate, well, I do not like to think of that." She stroked Mary's hair. "I will ask Mr. Darcy to speak to Mr. Collins. I think our cousin will listen to Lady Catherine's nephew."

Mary giggled softly. "He is overly fond of his patroness, is he not?"

"Mmm hmm," Elizabeth agreed. "Some people are enamoured by wealth and position."

"What will become of us?" The question was barely a whisper.

"I will marry Mr. Darcy, and Jane will marry Mr. Bingley. And you will come to stay with me, and I will put you in the way of many fine gentlemen, and you will find your own happiness."

"And what of Mama and Kitty and Lydia?"

"Oh, we shall find them a small house with servants enough to tend them, and then once you are settled, we shall both assist Kitty, but Lydia may need to rely on Mr. Bingley, for I believe he has a greater tolerance for loud and demanding sisters than Mr. Darcy does."

Mary giggled again. "How is it, Lizzy, that you can find laughter at a time such as this? I can find only gloom, but you, you bring brightness."

Elizabeth rested her chin on top of Mary's hair. "If I did not seek laughter, I would be consumed by the gloom. It is not that I do not feel it. I just am not strong enough to endure it, so I push it away with a laugh when it becomes too enveloping."

Some while later, Elizabeth stirred when she felt a kiss on her cheek.

"Sleep," Mr. Darcy whispered. "Your father is resting well, and it will soon be morning when you may take my place at his side."

"You have been sitting with him?" she asked drowsily, her eyes refusing to stay open.

"I have, except for when I heard a creak on the stairs and saw you were here," he said as he tucked a blanket, which he must have brought with him, around her. "Rest, my love." He kissed her cheek once more and then lit a low flame in a lamp before snuffing out her candle and leaving the room.

Chapter 16

FIVE DAYS LATER, ELIZABETH leaned her head back against the wing of the chair next to her father's bed and closed her eyes. The book she had been attempting to read lay discarded on her lap. Her father was breathing evenly, if still shallowly. His colour was beginning to return even if he could not move very much or draw a full breath without coughing. Still, his small improvements were enough for her to allow her heart to hope that he would recover, contrary to what the doctor said.

Behind her, the door nicked open and stocking-clad feet padded softly across the room. She smiled for she knew who it was without looking. Mr. Darcy had insisted on removing his boots and wearing slippers around Longbourn when he called so that he could easily slip out of them when he entered Mr. Bennet's room. His ways of helping to care for her father were so gentle and considerate. He had made certain that Mr. Bennet had everything he might need for his comfort and treatment, and if there had remained any part of Elizabeth's heart that had not already been his, Mr. Darcy's care for her father had claimed it. She knew without a flicker of a doubt that her heart was now, and would always remain, completely his. He was, as Jane had proclaimed him nearly three weeks ago, the best of men.

Darcy took the book from her lap and placed her ribbon between the pages before closing it and laying it softly on the nightstand. Then, taking her hand and after placing a kiss on it, he drew her to her feet. "Come, my love," he whispered. "Let your father sleep. Sally will call us if we are needed."

It was then that Elizabeth noticed the maid, whom he had sent for from London, taking up a place near the window where she would best be able to see the stitching she was doing.

Elizabeth turned her attention back to her father and saw his eyes snap shut. It was not the first time that she had caught him peeking at her and Mr. Darcy when she thought he was sleeping. His expression now – the small smile on his lips and the absence of any worried lines – was one of peaceful happiness just as it had been on each other occasion.

She placed her hand on his, gave it a little squeeze, and whispered, "Rest. All will be well," before leaving the room with Mr. Darcy.

Upon reaching the hallway, Mr. Darcy slid his feet into his slippers and then, with a look up and down the hallway, drew Elizabeth to him, wrapping her in his arms tightly and kissing her.

"Your father seems to improve daily," he said as he released her. "He may indeed prove the doctor wrong."

"But there is no guarantee until the cough leaves, and he is able to get out of bed," she said as they began to descend the stairs.

"There is no guarantee even then," he cautioned.

Hearing that uncertain tone in his voice which meant he was fretting about her, she said, "Do not worry. I am fully aware that my father may leave us at any time. I just prefer to look for the glimmer of hope because, without it, the gloom of melancholy is too easily all-consuming."

"Indeed, it is," he agreed, and then, drew her to a stop as a loud and unfriendly voice reached them. "My dear, do you remember that I said I have relatives who will be less welcoming and how I wished to be married by special license because of my aunt Lady Catherine?"

Elizabeth nodded.

"I believe I hear my aunt in the sitting room."

"I said I must see my nephew," the voice of Lady Catherine carried to the hallway.

He grimaced. "I am sorry. It will be unpleasant."

Despite how her heart was beating wildly, Elizabeth gave him a small smile that she hoped was reassuring. There was no need to cause him further distress by allowing her nerves to be put on display. He looked concerned enough without adding her anxiety to his.

Gathering her courage on behalf of both herself and him, she said softly, "I will still love you."

He smiled at that, and the furrow between his eyes disappeared.

"You are no more in control of what your relations do or say than I am of mine. Come," she tugged on his arm, "we shall face this together."

"This is a very small room," Lady Catherine was saying as they entered the sitting room.

"Aunt Catherine," Darcy greeted with a small bow. "This is an unexpected and poorly timed surprise." He led Elizabeth to a settee and took a seat next to her. "Forgive me if I repeat something you have already been told, but, the gentleman of the house, Mr. Bennet is ill, and visitors are being limited." His tone was as cool as a frosty autumn morning.

Lady Catherine huffed, and Elizabeth wondered at the near incivility that Darcy showed her.

"I have no intention of staying for long," she replied in a tone that was even colder than the one Darcy had used, "but I must speak with you."

"If that is the case, allow me to tell you what you wish to know so that you can be on your way without delay. I am getting married, but it is not to Anne."

"It is true?" She looked down her nose at Elizabeth, assessing and appraising her with a sweep of her eyes, before returning her haughty glare back to Mr. Darcy. "My brother told me you would not do your duty to your family. Of course, I did not believe him, but now that I see you with my own eyes, I can say I am as shocked and disappointed as he."

His aunt was as Mr. Darcy had said – unpleasant. Next to her, Mr. Darcy sighed as if utterly exasperated, and likely he was if this was how his aunt always behaved.

"I will tell you what I told him. I am not forgetting my duty. My estate is not forgotten, my sister is well-cared for, and my family name is respected within society and will remain so."

Lady Catherine drew herself up a bit straighter in her chair. "Am I to understand then that you insist on marrying beneath you?"

Darcy took Elizabeth's hand, and she gave it a supportive squeeze. While she did not relish being thought of as beneath anyone, she knew that there were those who would consider he as such. Were not Miss Bingley and her friends proof of that?

"I do not marry beneath me. Miss Elizabeth is a gentleman's daughter, and I am a gentleman's son. In this, we are equal."

Indignation at being contradicted seemed to radiate from Lady Catherine. "But what of her mother?" she scoffed.

Mrs. Bennet gave a small gasp. Elizabeth glanced in her direction. Anger flickered in her mother's eyes.

"Do not think me ignorant of who her mother's father is," Lady Catherine continued in the same ridiculing tone.

"And do not think me ignorant of who your true father is," Mrs. Bennet snapped.

All eyes turned toward her.

"I have heard the stories," she explained. "There is some question regarding the legitimacy of the previous Lord Matlock's children. A tradesman for a father is far superior to a groomsman, is it not?"

Darcy blinked, and his mouth hung open. He had not heard the story of those rumours for years and had thought them forgotten.

Mrs. Bennet shrugged and smiled cunningly, causing Darcy to re-evaluate his first impressions of her. Apparently, the matron of the Bennet family was more than just flighty thoughts about parties and seeing her daughters married well. At present, her expression reminded him of Miss Bingley when she was about to be catty towards some unsuspecting lady.

"A certain groomsman came to work for my father after he was dismissed from his position at Matlock," she said with a frigid sort of calm that was somewhat frightening to a fellow like Darcy who had not thought her capable of such.

"Until today," she continued, "I had thought the stories I heard about why he was dismissed to be fanciful tales. However..."

Her smile turned from cunning to something more cutting. It was the sort of smile that hid social death behind a veneer of friendliness. Darcy was certain he had not seen any lady of the ton wear that expression better than his future mother-in-law.

"I must say that your colouring is much more like his than it is like the previous Lord Matlock's." She rose from her seat, standing about two inches taller than Darcy had seen her stand before, and called for tea. "It seems, my lady, that we have both risen above where we started our lives."

This was followed by a flutter of lashes and a sympathetic look for Lady Catherine.

"You would do better to find the son of a peer or even the second son of a peer to marry your daughter. Oh, Mr. Darcy is rich enough to be sure, and I do not doubt he has well-respected connections. However, as any good mother knows, if you truly wish to purge the taint of lineage from your family and your daughter, there is no better way to do it than to mix her blood with the blood of a peer." Having rung the bell for tea, she had returned to her seat.

Lady Catherine sputtered. "There is no truth to the rumours. My father was Lord Matlock."

"Oh, my lady," Mrs. Bennet cajoled, "there is truth to the story. Do you remember from the stories that were passed around that there was a particular object which was given to the young groomsman by your mother? I know that detail was not reported in any papers, but that does not mean I have not seen this object or heard the story behind it from the man himself. I have even seen the accompanying note, written in your mother's hand. So, unless you wish to have this particular part of the story circulated once again and with such evidence as I know there is to support it, I suggest you rethink your objection to my daughter marrying your nephew."

Neither Darcy nor Elizabeth nor any other occupant of the room said a word. The composed and calculating woman who stood and began to pour tea was not the woman any of them had come to know as Mrs. Bennet. And it seemed she was not yet done defending her daughter, for she looked at Lady Catherine and asked, "Do you prefer your tea with one sugar and no milk as your mother did or with milk and no sugar as your true father did?"

Lady Catherine's eyes grew wide and her face blanched. "I do not have time for tea. I must continue on to London before the day is too far gone." She rose with more haste than was her usual habit and began to make her way to the door.

"Allow me to see you out," Darcy offered.

She waved him away. "I am capable of seeing myself to my coach. You stay and take tea with your new family. I shall expect to see you in the spring as always, and you may bring your wife." And with a small nod of her head to Elizabeth and to Mrs. Bennet, she was gone.

Mrs. Bennet stared at the door for some time after it closed; then, turning to the still silent room, she said excitedly, "Oh, my, a real lady and in my sitting room. I never thought I would see the day that that would happen."

She continued to pour tea. "Of course, the meeting did not go as I would have thought it should, but a lady can only abide so much disparagement of her home and family before she rises to their defense."

She handed a cup of tea to Elizabeth.

"I do hope you will forgive me for speaking to your aunt so," she said to Darcy before taking her seat, "but it really was outside of enough."

"It really was," Darcy agreed, lifting his cup in salute to her, which made her titter.

Silently, Mrs. Bennet sipped her tea and then studied her cup for a few moments before rising to quit the room. "I shall check on your father," she said as she placed her cup on the tea tray.

"He is probably sleeping, Mama," Elizabeth said.

"Then, I shall watch him sleep," she said, pulling the door closed behind her.

Chapter 17

"SHALL THE REST OF us take a walk?" Darcy asked when he had finished his tea.

"Oh, yes," Lydia said. "I have had enough of sitting and watching and waiting for horrible news. A walk would be most welcome, would it not, Kitty?"

"We mustn't go far," Kitty replied quietly.

She appeared to be the more sensitive of the two youngest Bennets. Or, perhaps, Darcy amended, she just showed it in a softer fashion than Miss Lydia. Either way, he knew that a change of scenery was just what was needed. As Miss Lydia had said, just sitting and waiting for horrible news was dreadful.

"We will stay close to the house," Darcy assured her. "A short stroll down the lane or a meander through the garden should satisfy, but the fresh air will be beneficial."

Miss Bennet readily agreed and instructed her sisters to get their things. "I will bring your pelisse, Lizzy. I would not wish for you to abandon Mr. Darcy altogether." She was just about to leave the room when something caught her eye through the window. "I shall be but a moment," she said as she darted out of the door.

Darcy chuckled as he saw Bingley riding up the lane. "Do you know that at one time I thought your sister did not care for him?"

Elizabeth looked surprised at the confession. "Did you indeed? I had thought it obvious from their first meeting that she adored him."

Darcy shrugged. "I also thought you liked me well before you did. Therefore, it seems when it comes to Bennet ladies, my skills of observation are of little use." He stood and offered her a hand to assist her from her seat.

"It would appear that way, sir, but I do hope your skills improve upon acquaintance with us."

"I believe they have." They walked to the hall to await Jane, but she was already hurrying down the stairs, calling over her shoulder to the others to be quick.

"Papa will no longer be sleeping with noise such as that," Elizabeth scolded as she took her pelisse from Jane.

"I was not so very loud," Jane protested. "And the house will be as still as a church on a Monday just as soon as we are out of doors." She stood at the bottom of the stairs, tapping her toe impatiently.

"I am afraid you have discovered our family's most guarded secret. Jane is not always the picture of serenity," Elizabeth whispered to Darcy, who had been watching the proceeding with amusement while he put on his boots.

Miss Bennet gave a small huff and glared at Elizabeth. "If Mr. Darcy were not here, you would be as impatient as I am." She smiled and surprised Darcy with an impertinent look. "At least, now that she likes you that is."

Darcy laughed softly. "I imagine Miss Elizabeth used to be just as impatient as you are now while she waited for me to leave. However did you abide those days at Netherfield, my dear?"

"It was not easy," Elizabeth said with a laugh.

"Ah," Darcy said. "That is why you were so often in the library. You were seeking solace." He noted how she bit her lip as she agreed. "Forgive me for mentioning that particular room," he whispered.

"It is not that," she whispered in reply. Then, she took his arm and moved toward the door. "We shall wait for you outside, Jane," she said as she opened the door. "Mr. Bingley, it is good to see you."

She pulled Darcy out the door and away from the house, and though he was confused and curious, he willingly followed.

"I have come to realize something," she said when she finally stopped and turned toward him. "My father may say many nonsensical things because they are fun to say, but he also says some things which are very wise."

"Such as?" Darcy was unsure of where this conversation was leading, but his curiosity was most certainly aroused more now than it had been when she pulled him from the house.

"He has often told me 'Your feet will take you where your heart leads even if your head does not know it.'"

Darcy's brow furrowed in confusion which caused her smile to broaden.

"For instance," she continued, "if I am upset and begin wandering while thinking, my feet will inevitably take me to a favourite vista or a place where I can find what my heart needs to make sense of whatever it is which is troubling it."

While one of Darcy's eyebrows arched of its own accord as the meaning of her father's saying started to become clear, a faint blush crept onto her cheeks.

"My heart was leading me to the library because that is where it would find you. It is as you said on our first walk. I was searching for you."

She took his arm and began walking as her sisters and Mr. Bingley exited the house. "I thought it a strange thing for you to have said at the time. How could someone look for someone whom they did not know existed? But then, I was reminded of what my father said, and it began to make sense."

He glanced over his shoulder to where the others walked. "And where do your feet and heart desire to take you today?"

"Here. Right here with you, and in a week's time they will happily go with you to London. They shall endure the balls and soirees, as well as the disapproving relations. My heart shall be happy as long as it is with you." She smiled up at him impertinently. "Although, it may occasionally require a respite in a quiet library."

"It is then an incredibly happy fact that I have two such libraries." He lifted her hand and kissed it.

At that moment, as they rounded a bend in the lane, a gentleman on horseback called out to Darcy, causing him to sigh.

"It seems that today is the day for unexpected visits from my family." He nodded in the direction of the horse and rider who approached. "My cousin, the Earl Rycroft."

"Is he friendly?" Elizabeth asked.

Darcy chuckled. Rycroft would be shocked to be thought of as anything but amiable.

"Rycroft is nothing like Lady Catherine or Lord Matlock. He is Lady Sophia's son, and yes, he is very friendly." He drew her just a little closer as he remembered his cousin's flirtatious bent. "Perhaps too friendly."

"Darcy, I am happy to have found you," Rycroft said as he swung down from his horse. "My mother told me about your betrothal, and I wished to congratulate you in person."

Darcy raised a brow in question. "You have come from town to congratulate me?"

"No, no," he said, tossing the reins for his horse to the groom who accompanied him. "I have not yet reached town. I was on my way there but decided to stop at Bingley's new place before continuing on to town." He bowed to Elizabeth. "You must be Miss Bennet."

"I am one Miss Bennet." She motioned to the others who had not yet joined them but were drawing near. "There are four others."

His eyes grew wide, and Darcy watched Elizabeth bite back a smile at his cousin's shocked expression. "Five Miss Bennets?"

"Indeed," said Darcy. "The one on Bingley's arm is Miss Jane Bennet, the eldest. Next, there is Miss Elizabeth, my betrothed. And then Miss Mary, Miss Kitty, and Miss Lydia. In that order."

"Which is which?" Rycroft asked.

"Mary has flowers on her bonnet and is walking by herself, while Kitty and Lydia both favour ribbons on their bonnets. Lydia is the one who is talking," Elizabeth explained. "We are only walking a bit farther before returning to the house. Would you care to join us, my lord?"

"Mr. Bennet is ill," Darcy inserted before Rycroft could accept Elizabeth's invitation. He was unsure if he wished to have another member of his family impose upon the Bennet home while Mr. Bennet was still so unwell. He was also not particularly fond of the idea of his cousin, who was known for his charm, spending time with Elizabeth's sisters, though he was certain Miss Lydia would enjoy it.

"Is Bingley staying for a visit?" Rycroft asked. "I only ask because I stopped at Netherfield before coming here. It is only his sisters and Hurst who are there, and I did not wish to spend my time with his sisters."

Again, Darcy saw Elizabeth bite back a smile as she saw the look on Lord Rycroft's face, for he looked as if he had bitten an apple that was not quite ripe. To Darcy, it was a fitting expression of how unpleasant being fawned over by Miss Bingley could be.

"He is, but..." He let the rest of his thought hang in the air. He was certain his cousin knew what the rest would be by the smile the curled his lips and the laughter that danced in his eyes.

"Do not worry, Darcy," Rycroft said, proving that he did indeed understand what Darcy had not said. "Your lovely lady is safe from my charms. I shall be pleasant and civil, but I shall refrain from being my devilishly charming self in her presence." He winked at Elizabeth.

"And her sisters?" Darcy's tone held a warning that his cousin would not and did not miss.

"Two seem quite young," he said, "and one is smitten by Bingley, but there is the middle sister..." he added in a teasing tone.

He held up his hands when Darcy glared at him. "I jest. She is much too studious in appearance to be of interest to me. Much too serious."

Darcy saw Miss Mary stop and look in their direction before walking away quickly. Elizabeth must have seen it too, for she looked at him with a pained expression and said, "I am not sure what the issue is with the gentlemen in your family, Mr. Darcy, but it seems they have a propensity for insulting the ladies in mine."

Lord Rycroft looked first at Elizabeth and then at Miss Mary. "It was a jest!" He cried, clearly dismayed by what had just transpired. "Darcy knows how I have been teased all my life because I am not as quick at learning as he is. I promise you that it was not a disparagement of your sister."

"You may wish to explain that to her," Elizabeth said. "However, she may not be easily convinced of your innocence for she has always been teased about being too studious." She excused herself from them and hurried toward Mary.

Rycroft removed his hat and ran his hand through his hair. "I have not had a formal introduction, or I would run after her and explain."

And Darcy knew he would. Rycroft was not one to allow misunderstandings to fester if he was the cause of them.

"If I could give you some advice." Darcy placed an arm around his cousin's shoulders. "Your charm will not work on Miss Mary like it would on many of the ladies in town. Miss Mary is serious and sensible, Georgiana's friend, and a favourite of your mother."

Rycroft groaned, and Darcy knew he was likely imagining his poorly chosen words being repeated to Lady Sophia. "Miss Mary has met my mother?"

Darcy nodded and removed his arm from his cousin's shoulders. "Both she and Miss Elizabeth have. They accompanied me to London for a week before their father fell ill and they were called home."

"Is he gravely ill?"

"He is improving, but yes. He has made his last wishes known to me."

Rycroft blew out a breath. "Perhaps I should take my chances with Bingley's sisters."

"No," Darcy said, "an angry Miss Bennet is still better company than a happy Miss Bingley."

Rycroft laughed loudly at the comment, causing all to stop and look at him.

"Come," Darcy said. "I will introduce you to my new family. But please, try to make a better impression than Lady Catherine did earlier today."

"Aunt Catherine was here?"

"She was."

"I suppose she is displeased that you are not marrying Anne?"

"You could say that."

Darcy watched Elizabeth link arms with Mary and hand her a handkerchief. It was not a good start to his cousin's visit.

"Allow me to tell you about our aunt's visit."

And he did.

He related to his cousin the full content of the conversation in the Bennets' sitting room and then proceeded to tell him about the opinion of Lord Matlock to his betrothal, as well as his reply to his uncle. Although his cousin joked about being the lesser intelligent man of the two of them, Darcy knew that he was anything but unintelligent and would hear the caution in the tale. Elizabeth and, by extension, her family were of great importance to him, and any disparagement would not be tolerated.

Rycroft nodded and clapped Darcy on the shoulder. "Point taken, Darcy. I shall be on my best behaviour. I promise."

Chapter 18

THE NEXT WEEK PASSED with all the flitting and fluttering one would expect when a wedding breakfast worthy of a man of Darcy's consequence was being planned by a woman such as Mrs. Bennet. Elizabeth escaped from her mother as often as she could to walk with Mr. Darcy or to sit with her father, who steadily improved. Still, by the morning of her wedding, she was quite ready for the ordeal to be done.

The service, on the morning of the delightful day when Elizabeth Bennet took on the new name of Mrs. Darcy, was solemn and sweet as is proper and expected. Her father had insisted upon attending her to the church and doing his part. He valiantly tried to refrain from tears but had on one occasion found it necessary to cough into his handkerchief in such a way as to catch an errant tear.

Now, with the ceremony behind them, Darcy guided Elizabeth down the hall and away from the throngs of people gathered in Netherfield's ballroom, which had been decorated to host the wedding breakfast. Mrs. Bennet would not hear of not having a wedding breakfast when Elizabeth had insisted that the preparations would be too much for her father and that she would be satisfied to have just a small family gathering. Mr. Bingley had stepped into the breach and proposed a compromise when the discussion had entered its second half-hour. And so, Netherfield's ballroom was now filled with family and friends eager to celebrate the union of Darcy and Elizabeth while the happy couple sought a few moments of solace in the place where they tended to find such relief from the busyness of a soiree.

Theirs was not to be an easy escape, however.

"Darcy," Lord Matlock said, impeding their progress down the hall outside of the ballroom.

"'My lord, I had not expected you to journey to Hertfordshire for my wedding breakfast." He tucked Elizabeth's arm close to his side and covered her hand with his. She understood his actions as those meant to protect her, and she loved him for it. Lord Matlock had declined Mr. Darcy's invitation to meet her, and she knew that he was one of her new husband's most contrary relations.

"I would not have — it is not customary, you know. However, my sister insisted on putting forth a show of support. She said something about a unified family having a stronger position in the ton." He took a sip of his drink and gave it a questioning look.

Apparently, the beverage was not up to his standards, though it was, according to Uncle Gardiner, some of the best that could be had.

"Not at all like the way things are done in true society," he muttered before cocking his head to the side and examining Elizabeth. One brow was raised slightly, and his lips formed a bit of a scowl. "So, you are Miss Bennet?"

She glanced briefly at Darcy with an amused look on her face. She wanted for no one's approval other than that of the handsome man holding her close to her side. She would not allow his uncle – her new uncle – no matter his station, to intimidate her or cause her to feel less than she was.

"I am sorry, but I am not." She saw her husband's lips twitch in amusement before she turned her attention back to Lord Matlock, whose brow was furrowed and whose scowl had deepened.

"You are not?" His tone was filled with ridicule.

"No, my lord, I am not. I cannot rightly say how things are done in true society, but in this society, when a lady joins her hand with a gentleman in marriage, she leaves her name behind and takes his. So, although, I was Miss Bennet earlier this morning, I am no longer she. I believe I am now Mrs. Darcy."

His eyes narrowed slightly. "You are very impertinent," he said.

"So I have been told, my lord, but I assure you that I am only so when the offending party has fired the first shot, as it were."

"Offending party!" he sputtered.

Elizabeth smiled at him. "Yes, my lord. I have not yet had a formal introduction to you, and you have already told me that you are here against your wishes and that the proceedings which have been carefully arranged to my preference and that of Mr. Darcy do not meet your standard for true society. Thus," she held up a finger as he opened his mouth to speak, "indicating that you feel all in attendance, including myself and my husband, to be beneath your notice. These things are considered offensive in this society."

Lady Sophia, who had come to stand behind her brother, chuckled softly. "Well-spoken, Mrs. Darcy." She lifted her glass in salute. "Darcy, have you not introduced your wife to your uncle?"

"I have not had the opportunity, Aunt Sophia."

Lady Sophia stepped forward and gave first Elizabeth a kiss and then Darcy. "You look lovely, Mrs. Darcy, and contrary to the opinion of some, I find the breakfast to be well-done. I know a few in my acquaintance who would be green with envy to see how excellent everything is."

She stepped back and motioned for Darcy to do his duty in making introductions, which he did.

Although Lord Matlock only deigned to give a small bow and mumble a word of greeting, Elizabeth performed a proper curtsey and assured him of the pleasure it was to meet him. Her behavior would be above reproach even if his was lacking.

Lady Sophia winked at Darcy. "I believe you were whisking your lady away somewhere when my brother stopped you, were you not?"

Darcy's ears felt warm. He had hoped to sneak Elizabeth away without being noticed. "I was," he said. "I had a gift for my bride that I wished for her to have during the breakfast."

"Well," his aunt said as she slipped her arm through her brother's, "do not let us detain you." She pulled her brother toward the ballroom. "Come, and do try to be civilized and polite."

"Civilized?" Lord Matlock sputtered. "Of all the impertinent things! I am always civilized."

"While that may be true," Lady Sophia said, "you are not always polite." And then, she continued to scold him as they walked down the hall.

Elizabeth giggled softly behind her hand. "She is very bold."

"She is much like you." Darcy drew her down the hall toward the library once again. "Just like you she is a beautiful woman with a strong mind..."

"And an impertinent nature?" she asked as he closed the door behind them.

He nodded. "I have always liked that about my aunt, and while I am not as fond of the trait in my sister, I find it beguiling in you." He pulled her to him and kissed her softly. Then, he took her hand and led her to the chair she had been sitting in on the night of the Netherfield ball – that fateful night which had brought about this wonderful day.

"As I said, I have a gift for you. One of many actually." He moved to the shelf that was home to works of poetry and retrieved the parcel he had stashed there this morning.

"Oh, I do like presents," she said excitedly, causing him to laugh. He loved her light and lively spirit.

"This is the first. Another awaits you in the carriage, and if my message was received and my directions followed, there are a few awaiting you when we get to London." He placed a small velvet bag in her hands.

He waited as patiently as he was able while she untied the ribbon that held the bag closed and then widened the opening so she could retrieve his gift.

"Oh, these are lovely," she exclaimed as she drew out two lavender shoe roses that had a few clear glass beads sewn to the edges of the petals.

"I asked Mary to assist me with making sure they would attach properly to the buttons on your shoes today." He knelt at her feet. "May I?"

She lifted the edge of her skirt and allowed him to replace the roses on her slippers. "Do you always remove your slippers when reading?" he asked.

She laughed. "Not always, but nearly so."

"I remember seeing your slippers under your chair a few times when you were reading during your sister's illness." He leaned back on his heels and admired the roses. They suited her. "I dare say your father is aware of your habit, is he not?"

She nodded. "I am sure he is as he has tripped over my slippers in his study more than once." She gasped as what Darcy was hinting at bloomed into understanding in her mind.

"He knew that my aunt would see me without slippers and would embellish the tale of us being alone. Oh, he is most devious!"

While her words were those which might be uttered harshly, they were not spoken with anything more than a hint of laughter. There was no longer any doubt in Darcy's mind that she was happy with how the events in the library that night had turned out – not that the process to get here had been utterly enjoyable. He could still remember her tears as she cried at the thought of being forced to marry him. However, her smile as she twisted her foot one way and then another admiring how the beads sparkled in the light was the memory which he would tuck away in his heart and recall whenever he entered a library, whether here at Netherfield or elsewhere. Elizabeth was his, and she was happy to be so.

"They are beautiful." Her eyes lifted from her toes to him.

"Nearly as beautiful as the lady who wears them." He took her hands and drew from her chair. "We must return before we are missed. I would not wish your aunt to have more stories to share about us."

She giggled as he pulled her into his arms.

"Let them talk. For what can they say that is not true? I love my husband and libraries."

"And I love my wife," he replied before placing a kiss on her lips and exiting the library.

Chapter 19

"Oh, Lizzy!" Mrs. Bennet took her by the arm as she and Darcy entered the room. "Mrs. Long has been looking for you to congratulate you as has been Lady Lucas."

Elizabeth gave her mother a skeptical look. "They have been looking, or you have been looking so that you can remind them of your good fortune?"

Mrs. Bennet chuckled. "Well, I dare say I have reason to do so. They have forever been saying how much trouble I would have marrying off five daughters. Be that as it may, I have one who is married and another who is well on her way, for we know Mr. Bingley will not be able to resist Jane's charms forever. Indeed, he has already made his intentions known by courting her."

She paused to look around the room. "Oh, there they are." She pulled Elizabeth toward a group of ladies who were chattering in the corner. "You know neither Mrs. Long nor Lady Lucas has a daughter attached to any gentleman. One married and another as good as, and they each only have one daughter and still have not done so well as I."

Elizabeth fought the urge to roll her eyes.

"It was clever of me to have Jane become ill. I dare say, your time at Netherfield is when Mr. Darcy began to change his mind about you."

Elizabeth shared a look with Darcy, who only shrugged and smiled.

"Yes, yes," she continued to herself, "that must be it, for when else would he have come to know you well enough." She drew Darcy and Elizabeth into the circle of ladies and preened as the ladies gave their congratulations and wishes for health and joy.

As they left the group of ladies, Darcy leaned close to Elizabeth's ear. "One hour, my love, and then we shall need to leave if we wish to reach town in time for Mrs. Vernon's dinner."

"Mrs. Bennet," Lady Sophia said as she took Mrs. Bennet's arm. "This is a fine fete. One of the best I have attended, and I am not given to meaningless flattery."

Together, the two ladies walked toward the far end of the room where the piano had been placed. Georgiana and Mary were seated comfortably at it, taking turns playing.

"My niece will no doubt be returning to her brother's home as soon as he and Mrs. Darcy are settled, and I shall be quite alone."

"But do you not have a son?" Mrs. Bennet asked.

"I do." A son she would like to see married. "However, he is often gone to our estate, and when he is in town, he has his friends and clubs. He is not inattentive, mind you, but he is not the sort to sit and stitch with his mother."

"I would be surprised if any gentleman were the sort to do so," Mrs. Bennet's voice was filled with surprise.

"Precisely," Lady Sophia agreed as she watched Mary turn the pages for Georgiana. Theirs was a friendship she was glad to see and wished to nurture for the sake of both young ladies. With that in mind, she turned her attention back to Mrs. Bennet.

"I was wondering if I could be so bold as to ask that you allow me the company of one of your daughters. I have the means by which to sponsor a young lady for a season, and Miss Mary is such a delight."

"Mary?" Mrs. Bennet looked at Mary as if never having seen the girl before. "Mary is a delight?"

"Indeed, I find her so, but I am not typical."

"You would like to give my Mary a season in town?" The excitement was building in Mrs. Bennet's voice.

"Yes, Mrs. Bennet, I would, and as a countess and the mother of the Earl Rycroft, I can guarantee she would be given the greatest opportunities to meet and mingle with many eligible young gentlemen." She smiled and whispered, "You may find yourself with three married daughters before any of the others have even one. Although I cannot guarantee it will happen," at least not with great certainty, "I do think with a bit of specific training — which I can arrange — she will take quite well. You may even find she has more than one offer from a worthy gentleman."

"Oh, my lady, you do us a great honor. I would be delighted to allow Mary to stay with you for the season." Mrs. Bennet's fan fluttered with the excitement of it all.

"And I am elated to know I shall have such excellent company."

Mary had not meant to be listening, but, being close to where her mother and Lady Sophia were talking, she had heard the majority of the conversation. She was to go to town for the season?

"Oh, Mary," Georgiana whispered, "I shall be so glad to have you near. Is it not exciting?"

Mary nodded. A sense of freedom welled within her.

"Of what are we conversing about in whispers, dear cousin?" Lord Rycroft drew a chair near them.

Mary lifted a brow in disapproval. "It is not polite to ask about another's private conversations."

"I do apologize, Miss Mary, but you both looked so delighted, I found myself overcome by curiosity." It was not the first apology he had offered her, and he suspected it would not be the last. He had offended her, and true to what Darcy had said, a Bennet lady did not forgive an offense readily. She had said she accepted the apology, but her manners still said otherwise.

"Would it be impolite of me to request that you play that last song once again? I rather enjoyed it."

She gave him a wary look. "Some might find it repetitive to listen to the same piece twice in a row." She took her music from the instrument. "I shall play it, but not until after I have had a moment to walk around and partake of a glass of punch." She rose and dipped a quick curtsey. "If you will excuse me."

"Did you offend her?" Georgiana asked, turning toward her cousin.

"Why do you ask?" He said, stretching his legs out in front of him.

"Because she was rather cross." Georgiana crossed her arms and scowled at him.

"I may have said something as a jest that she found offensive, but I have apologized. She is just unwilling to forgive."

"Hmph," huffed Georgiana. She spread her music out on the piano and began to play. "Since you have driven her away, you will need to pay attention so that you can turn the pages for me."

Darcy watched Mary cross the room. "I see your sister is still not on friendly terms with Rycroft."

Elizabeth laughed lightly. "She is not." She leaned a bit closer to Darcy. "She says he smiles too much to be trustworthy."

Darcy chuckled. "He seems intent upon having her forgive him. I have not seen him so persistent in trying to obtain a pardon from anyone — gentleman or lady. Of course, he has not offended a family member in some time, and she is now family."

"Very true," Elizabeth agreed. "She will forgive him in time... probably, but then again, how much will she be in company with him? It is not like he will have reason to travel to Hertfordshire, and Papa does not go to town."

"She will visit us, and it is likely he will visit as well. There shall be times when they will be in company," Darcy said. "Rycroft does not visit so often as Richard, but he is not an unfamiliar guest in my study."

Elizabeth sighed. "In that case, we shall just have to hope all is well by then."

"Bennet." Sir William handed his friend a cup of tea and joined him in sitting in a small alcove that afforded him a view of the room but kept him removed from any draft.

Mr. Bennet had had a difficult time convincing any of his family to allow him to journey to Netherfield to observe the festivities. But this was not a day he would miss.

"They appear happy, and it has happened before they were married," Sir William said.

"They are happy. I have spent many hours in bed watching them as they sat with me." Mr. Bennet smiled and sipped the warm tea. He watched Darcy talking to Elizabeth, and then as something had obviously concerned her, for she had sighed, he had watched Darcy wink at her and lift her hand to his lips. "It is a very good match."

"And Jane's happiness is also nearly secured." Sir William nodded to where Bingley and Jane stood quietly conversing together.

"And Collins is gone." Mr. Bennet sighed. "But he shall return. He insists on mending fences, which is something that cannot be done without the entail being broken, but he does not see that." They sat in silence for some minutes, each drinking their tea.

"I have heard from my wife that you are planning a journey to the seaside after the winter," commented Sir William.

Mr. Bennet nodded. "If I tarry." He pulled in a less shallow breath. "I do wish to see all my daughters so happy as Lizzy, but I fear my heart may expire before then."

Sir William gave him a sympathetic smile. "Well, then, Mary is next. Who shall we select for her?" He rubbed his hands together.

Mr. Bennet chuckled softly. "I shall not be selecting any other husbands, but, do not fear, Mary's future is well in hand." He nodded to where his wife stood with Lady Sophia. "I believe she will be having a season if Darcy's aunt has her way. It seems the lady has taken a liking to my Mary."

"She is a sweet girl."

"That she is. A bit fond of sermons, but sweet and good. I have no doubt she will shine away from her sisters."

"Papa." Elizabeth did not wish to interrupt her father's conversation, but it was time to take her leave and the longer she waited, the more difficult the idea was becoming.

"Ah, my Lizzy, is it time?" He looked to Darcy, who was standing behind Elizabeth.

"I am afraid it is, sir."

"Very good," Mr. Bennet said as he began to push up from his chair.

"No, Papa."

"I shall stand and give my daughter a hug and see her to the door." He stood slowly. Sir William stood at his elbow ready to assist him if he should need it. "Come, give me a hug and make it a good one as it shall have to serve me well until the spring."

"I love you, Papa," Elizabeth whispered as she squeezed him tightly.

"And I, you, my dear Lizzy." He kissed her cheek and then placed her hand in Darcy's. "I know you will care for her well."

"I will, sir. Thank you." Darcy took Elizabeth's hand, tucked in the crook of his elbow, and held it there.

Mr. Bennet took up his walking stick and placed a hand on his friend's arm. "I shall follow you to the door, Lizzy, but it may take me a while. I do not move so quickly as I once did." He coughed lightly into his handkerchief.

Darcy walked slowly toward the door with Elizabeth on his arm. A few from the room had moved into the hall to farewell the newlyweds, but all stood to the side and allowed Mr. Bennet to pass.

Jane and Bingley stood at the door with Mrs. Bennet. Elizabeth paused to give her mother and sister a hug, and then waited for her father to reach the door, so that she could give him one more brief hug before descending the stairs to the waiting carriage. She turned as she entered it and gave a final wave to those who were waiting.

"Are you well, my love?" Darcy asked as he took his seat next to her and wrapped his arms around her.

"I am." She snuggled into his embrace. "He chose well." She smiled up at him.

"He did indeed." He stroked her cheek and brushed a thumb across her lips before bending to kiss them. She sighed and pressed her lips more firmly against his as she had done the first time he kissed her.

He had intended to give her the book he had requested from Bingley — the one she had been reading when the compromise had occurred — and perhaps he would give it to her in a while. But for now, he was content to revel in the privilege of holding her and kissing her as no other man had.

And as her hands slid up his chest and around his neck, he said a word of thanks for having been fortunate enough to be her father's choice.

No Other Choice

CHOICES BOOK 2

At first, all Lord Rycroft wanted was Mary's forgiveness. Now, he wants her to be his countess.

Chapter 1

December 18, 1811

Samuel Rycroft, Earl Rycroft, blinked and looked at his mother, Lady Sophia, as if he was unable to understand what she had said. To be honest, he was not entirely certain he was capable of understanding her at this time of the morning.

What did she mean they were not leaving yet? She was always early. She never departed for anything at a normally expected hour or, heaven forbid, late! Was that not why he had risen half an hour earlier than he wished to do – so he could be on time for his mother? And now she said they must wait?

He took off his hat and placed it on the table in the entryway at Netherfield. "Pardon me?"

Perhaps he had not heard what he thought he had heard. Why did they need to wait for Miss Mary Bennet before they could leave for town?

"I said we will depart for town when Miss Mary arrives." His mother made her way back into the sitting room and peered out the window. "There is no need to fear," she called to him as he entered the room behind her. "Miss Mary knows I am always early."

"I still do not understand why we must wait for Miss Mary."

He unbuttoned his greatcoat and began to shrug out of it. He had hoped to be in the carriage by now and on his way to town

– not only because he had risen early and he hoped that effort was not a waste, but also because Miss Bingley was growing insufferable in her pursuit of his title. If he did not leave soon, he would likely say something he should not, or, more precisely, he would say something his mother thought he should not say. What he said would be perfectly acceptable to himself, but his mother's tolerance for rudeness was set to a fine gauge that he knew would not allow for him venting his spleen about grasping harpies.

"Good morning, Georgiana," his mother said as his cousin, who would be travelling with them, entered the sitting room. "Did you have something to eat, my dear?"

"Yes, thank you." Georgiana laid her outerwear on the settee with her aunt's things and took a seat near the window so that she could see the drive. "I cannot wait for Miss Mary to arrive. I will be ever so pleased to have her company."

"Company?" Rycroft's brows drew together. "Surely, we must not wait for you to finish a visit before leaving." He had things to do in town and a sister of Bingley's to avoid. Added to that, he had risen early! Early! He definitely did not have time for a social call.

Georgiana laughed. "A visit? At this time of the morning? I think not, Cousin. Miss Mary is to travel with us."

Lady Sophia sighed at her son's still puzzled expression, but what other expression was he to wear when no one seemed willing to clarify for him why he was out of bed before he needed to be and what Miss Mary had to do with it?

"Miss Mary is coming to stay with me," his mother explained. "Georgiana will soon be able to return to her brother, and I do not wish to be lonely." She smoothed her skirt over her legs. It was an action she often did when caught in the midst of some scheme.

With her eyes lowered as they were, he knew she could not see his expression, which was most likely her intent, but she could see his toe start to tap as the silence in the room grew. Yes, that did it. She looked up at him with a smile but then, turned to look out the window.

"A project, Mother?" It was not unlike his mother to take on a less fortunate lady and help her to find a husband.

"No, no." She shook her head. "Miss Mary is not a project. She is a friend." She turned back to look at him. "As you know, I like to have companionship of the female sort, and if my companion happens to be a young lady of marriageable age and in need of some assistance..." She shrugged as if it was the most natural thing in the world to take in stray young women and match them with an eligible gentleman.

"It makes me feel useful," she continued. "It has been all arranged. Miss Mary will travel with us today and stay the week. We will visit the shops and arrange for her orders; then, she will return with her aunt and uncle to Longbourn for Christmas. She will rejoin us in the new year to participate in the season."

"A project." He ran his hands through his hair and shook his head. "And I am supposed to pay for this project?"

Lady Sophia crossed her arms. "Miss Mary is not a project. She is a friend and a guest of mine."

And a project. No matter how much his mother protested it, Miss Mary was Lady Sophia's next project.

"Aunt," Georgiana said softly.

Rycroft shook his head and sighed as he resigned himself to his mother's plans. "I suppose that you will require me to attend all of the functions you select?"

"Well," Lady Sophia said, ignoring Georgiana's second soft call just as she had ignored the first one, "we will need an escort, and you need to attend anyway if we ever expect to find you a wife."

"We do not need to find me a wife. I can do that on my own."

He hated being reminded of his duty to the title and his need to marry. He had been looking, but there were not any young ladies who interested him. They were all so agreeable, so biddable, so boring. Who wanted a boring wife? Not him. He would much rather have a lady at his side who interested him and even argued with him at times – much like his mother was arguing with him now. Life was too short to surround oneself with nothing but smooth waters and clear skies. A few waves and clouds added to the interest of a day. Not that he wanted to live in a storm with some harridan either. But there must be a balance of calm and challenge. That is what they should teach at those schools that ladies attended rather than how to paint a scene. A lively, sharp mind far surpassed the ability to converse in three languages – unless, of course, she could argue in all three.

"You have done a poor job of it thus far, my son." Lady Sophia cocked her head to the side and gave him a stern look. "If you will remember, I gave you until this season to sort it out for yourself. Now, I will assist you. The deadline has passed for you to continue on without my interference."

His eyes narrowed and his jaw clenched slightly. Perhaps his wife should be a trifle less argumentative and demanding than his mother, for his mother was currently insufferably disagreeable.

"If it will please my lady, I shall trot about with you and your project, Miss Mary. However, I will make my own decision about whom I will marry or even consider marrying." He stiffened as he heard a gasp from the doorway behind him.

"Miss Mary," Georgiana greeted Mary as excitedly as she could, probably in an effort to counteract his words.

He had done it again. He had offended Miss Mary without meaning to do so. All the effort he had put in thus far to make reparations for the last time his words had caused him trouble with her were now of no use. He would have to begin again – and with her under his roof in town.

"I have been anxiously awaiting your arrival," Georgiana continued.

Miss Mary smiled as Rycroft had seen her do when her mother or younger sisters had said something insulting. Rycroft hated that he was to be placed among those whom she had to tolerate because of their carelessness. Yet, here he was, heading the list of unthinking insulters.

"Good morning, Miss Darcy, Lady Sophia, Lord Rycroft. My things are on their way with the carriage you sent, my lady."

Rycroft noted not only how her lips smiled in a practiced fashion, but also how her eyes held an ample amount of displeasure when she looked at him — which she did only briefly. Her words may have been pleasant, but he was certain her thoughts were not.

"Ah, Miss Mary, it is delightful to see you." Lady Sophia crossed the room to her. Placing an arm about Mary's shoulders, she said, "Please ignore my son. I am not sure where he gets his deplorable manners, for both his father and I did try to instill good ones in him."

She cast a displeased look at Rycroft. "He likes to refer to any lady that I have taken under my care as a project. He thinks I am only interested in the hunt for a husband for the young lady, but I assure you, I am also interested in gaining many young friends and excellent connections for myself."

Rycroft scowled at his mother. It was not entirely his fault that Miss Mary had been offended. It was his mother who had provoked him to say what he had said.

"Perhaps, my lady, he needs to spend more time at church, so that he can learn to respect his parent, even if she is just a mother." This time, she did not attempt to veil the look of displeasure she gave him. "Or a bit of reading, perhaps, at night might suffice. I can give you recommendations if you wish." The smile returned to her lips, though this time there was some actual amusement in it, and her left brow rose just slightly.

The taunting woman! She and his mother would get on fabulously – what a dreadful thought!

"I do not need your recommendations, Miss Mary. And I will have you know that I do attend church regularly." He pulled on his coat as his mother began to move toward the door with Mary. "And I do not appreciate being thought of as a man who does not respect his mother."

Mary halted and turned toward him. "Then, my lord, you should strive to make your actions match your beliefs, for at present they are quite contradictory."

"Quite right," his mother agreed.

Rycroft drew in a deep breath and released it, attempting to tamp down his irritation, as Georgiana took his arm. She looked up at him with a brow raised and a scolding look. "Do not," he said.

"Do not what?" She fluttered her lashes and smiled sweetly.

"You know very well, but since I must clarify, do not chide me. I know I have insulted her once again and must apologize, although I doubt that she will forgive me." And that bothered him for some inexplicable reason.

Georgiana hugged his arm tightly. "She will if you are sincere. Miss Mary is quite agreeable and sweet."

Rycroft gave a soft, short burst of laughter, unable to believe Georgiana's description of Mary. He had only seen her as scolding and scowling. However, he admitted to himself, he had not precisely given her reason to treat him well. He had, after all, said she was too studious in appearance and too serious to be of interest to him. And that was before he had even met her. Of course, he had not meant for the words to be a disparagement of her. He had been, in fact, disparaging himself.

Although he was not precisely a slow learner, he had always been compared to his excessively diligent cousin, Fitzwilliam Darcy, and so the tease was meant to give Darcy a reason to chuckle at his cousin's expense. However, it had not gone as planned. Mary had heard his comment and taken offense, which in turn earned him a slight scolding from her sister, Elizabeth, and a lecture disguised as a story from Darcy.

For the past week and two days, he had done his best to mind his words and actions. He had even attempted to engage Mary in cordial conversation but to no avail. Although she had readily accepted his apology, she seemed determined to avoid him whenever possible, and when that was not within the realm of possibilities, she often found an opportunity to correct him for some small blunder.

She really was a most frustrating young lady, and now he was to be in her company for the entirety of the season as her escort. He sighed. Perhaps his mother would magically transform the scolding and serious Miss Bennet into something more agreeable.

If it were up to him, he would start by lightening the colours she wore and loosening that knot of hair on her head. It really did make her look entirely too studious and old, or at least older than he suspected she was. Indeed, dressed as she was, it was more likely that some gentleman in town would offer her the position of governess to his youngsters rather than some young buck offering for her hand in marriage. Of course, she was not his project even if he could squint his eyes, as he stood here in Netherfield's entrance hall, and see the great potential in her looks. Her transformation was up to his mother.

Chapter 2

LORD RYCROFT'S MORNING WAS to be one of frustration and inconvenience which was determined to try his patience at every turn, from the moment he turned down his covers earlier than wished, to the turn that had taken place in his plans, to the lady who turned from the grand staircase to join her brother in the hall to say their farewells. And with Caroline Bingley's arrival at her brother's side, Lord Rycroft's hope that his mother's plan to leave "quite early" would have given him the opportunity to depart from Netherfield without speaking to Bingley's younger sister vanished into the confining air around him.

Miss Bingley was just the sort of lady he always tried to avoid. She was both cunning and simpering at the same time. He shook his head. It was beyond his understanding how any gentleman could be so easily taken in by the flutter of eyes and the strategic display of assets by ladies like her. Did they not realize that there needed to be a woman of substance behind the pretty face and tempting figure?

That was not to say, however, that he had not enjoyed more than one tempting figure in his seasons. That thought brought a smile to his lips and kept him from rolling his eyes at Caroline Bingley's profusion of pleasantries to his mother. It did not escape his notice nor, he suspected, that of his mother, that she kept peeking in his direction to see if he was noticing the care she was paying to his mother. She was not the first lady to use such tactics. Perhaps if the good wishes and praise were sincere, it would have warmed his heart instead of causing him to wish to be elsewhere, but he doubted very much that there was any more affection in the lady's actions than what was necessary to draw his notice.

He chuckled silently to himself. He would not be the only one experiencing disappointment this morning. And with that thought helping to cheer him, he turned his eyes to where Bingley and Mary were speaking quietly.

"Mr. Bingley," Mary was saying, "should my father — "

"I will send word to Darcy and Rycroft immediately if there is any danger," Bingley assured her as he smiled and grasped Mary's hand, the one that was not dabbing her eyes with her handkerchief.

Her tears reproved Rycroft most forcefully for his ill-spoken words from moments ago. What sort of cad insulted a lady who was experiencing such a trying time as Mary was with her father being ill? Him. He was the sort. Not that it was purposefully done, but it had been done.

Mary's lips trembled slightly as she accepted Bingley's promise. "Thank you. I would not leave him, but he insisted. He kept saying that he wished for me to go seek my happiness."

Bingley's face took on a serious expression, one which Rycroft had only seen on a few occasions. "He wishes to see his family secure. My father was the same when he became ill."

Mary nodded. "I know. He is thinking of when — " The handkerchief was once again near her eyes, and instead of continuing, she shrugged.

Rycroft knew intimately how hard it was to talk about a beloved parent's death. It was one of the curses of having a title, since the title was only bestowed on an heir after the passing of the previous lord. Titles, such as his, were excessively costly things.

Bingley's expression returned to his engaging smile. "He is thinking if, not when. We must always hope."

Mary murmured another thank you and a final goodbye before moving toward the door.

"You will take care of her, will you not, Rycroft?" Bingley asked as he watched Mary standing at the door, waiting for the rest.

"There is no need to fear. My mother will have her well in hand, my friend."

Bingley drew Rycroft away from Georgiana and Caroline. "Lady Sophia will be able to help her with most things, but you have seen the betting books and heard the talk in clubs. I would hate to see her put upon by some schemer."

Rycroft knew well of schemers, for he had been one at one time. "I have already been informed that it is my duty to escort my mother and Miss Mary to whatever events my mother chooses this season."

"I am pleased to hear that, and I know Darcy will do his best to be of service to her. However..."

Rycroft laughed. "Yes, he will likely be too occupied with his new wife to be present at many of his clubs."

Bingley smiled knowingly. "As will I, if things go well."

"So then, am I to be completely alone in my misery this season?"

"No, I will still have to escort my sister, unless you would care to take her on as well?" Bingley laughed and slapped him on the shoulder.

Rycroft narrowed his eyes. "I do not have the patience of my cousin."

He was unsure how Darcy had endured the fawning of Bingley's sister for all these years. She had been very persistent in making her desire to marry Darcy known. While Darcy seemed to take it in stride and rarely diverted his plans to avoid the lady, Rycroft did his best to limit his exposure to her by insisting on meeting with Bingley only at a club or Rycroft Place.

"Few have Darcy's patience," Bingley agreed. "I have told her she has no hope of snaring you, but she will not listen. I told her the same thing about Darcy, and you have witnessed how useless my cautions were. I may as well have been shouting into the wind at nothing."

Instead of agreeing heartily with Bingley that the man's sister was impossible, Rycroft sighed and rolled his eyes as Caroline came to where her brother was standing.

"Lord Rycroft," she began extending a hand to him.

He took it briefly and mumbled a hasty thank you and farewell before turning once again toward Bingley. "You will come around when you return to town, will you not?"

Bingley bit back a smile that Rycroft was positive was due to his amusement at the displeased look on Caroline's face. "Certainly. You know I am not one to forego an opportunity to visit with friends."

"Very good. Then, I will expect you." Rycroft placed his hat on his head and gave a bow of his head to both Bingley and Caroline before walking to the door where he offered Mary his arm.

Mary lifted a brow, and he gave her his best pleading look to which she rolled her eyes and placed her hand on his arm.

"I am sorry," he whispered as they walked down the steps to the carriage.

She nodded what he hoped was an acceptance of his apology. He made to hand her into the carriage, but she shook her head.

"Your mother should be first," she said.

He inclined his head. "Of course."

He turned and offered his hand to his mother and then to Georgiana and finally to Mary before climbing into the carriage to take his place next to his mother.

He leaned his head against the back of the carriage as it began to roll down the drive. Georgiana took out a small book and a pencil and began to draw. His mother took out a book and opened it to read. Mary also pulled out a book, but only held it on her lap under her hand which still clutched her handkerchief as she looked out the window. He saw her dab at her eyes and considered for the first time how difficult this trip to town must be for her.

She was not travelling for the pleasure of the trip. She was simply doing what her father and his mother wished for her to do. Hopefully, the shops and amusements in town would do something to ease her pain. He glanced out the window but quickly returned his eyes to her.

Her lips pressed together to keep from trembling. Her eyes blinked rapidly, and that handkerchief dabbed and dabbed, while her book remained unopened. She must have noticed his observation, for her cheeks coloured slightly. It was a lovely shade of pink.

"I may be an oaf," he said, which caused her to smile quickly, "but I do understand the difficulty of not knowing..." His voice trailed off and his eyes sought the lull of the countryside passing outside the window as he remembered having to return to school for his final term while his father was ill. He had been fortunate to have been able to return and spend time with his father before he died. It had been both a pleasure and sheer torture to be reminded and instructed about the responsibilities attached to the title he now wore by the father he loved and knew was about to leave him.

And then, he had spent the next three years attempting to hide from the weight of that responsibility. He had tended to all the business involved, but he had spent an equal or greater amount of energy trying to lift the weight of the responsibilities by pursuing pleasure, a pursuit that had led to his seclusion at his estate for the past six months while the gossip which had driven him from town swirled and finally died.

When he returned his attention back to Mary, she was watching him closely with what he would label fascination. The expression in her eyes was like that of one who was seeing something for the first time. She smiled when he gave her a small shrug and a half-smile.

"Do you miss him?" she whispered.

"Every day," he said with a nod. It was hard not to think of his father every day when he rose from his bed in the room that had been his father's and sat at the desk that had been his father's and heard himself called Lord Rycroft, a name which had been his father's.

She held his gaze for the span of three heartbeats. Then, her lips twitched as if somewhat amused. In his opinion, it was a far better thing to see than the trembling those lips had been doing earlier even if he did not understand what about missing a parent could be humorous.

"Perhaps you are not a complete oaf," she declared as she opened her book.

Ah, yes, that explained the lip twitch, Rycroft thought as he laughed softly to himself. It was, he figured, the closest he was going to get to a statement of forgiveness. The cloud of regret for the sorrow he had caused her lifted somewhat. It was not all gone. He still felt his error and would continue to feel it for some time. He would also continue to work at proving himself worthy of being dubbed a partial oaf by Mary. Mayhap, one day, he might remove even that partial stain from his record. Until then, however, he would content himself with this small bit of progress.

He tucked his blanket more securely around his legs, and then, tipping his hat to cover his eyes, he leaned his head against the back of the carriage and prepared to hasten the journey by drifting off to sleep.

Chapter 3

MARY SIGHED AND FLIPPED another page of the book she held in her lap. She had been through it twice already and still was as far from making a decision, if not further from it, than she had been when her Aunt Gardiner had delivered Mrs. Havelston's book of patterns to her earlier today. Mrs. Havelston did not lend her patterns to everyone, but Uncle Gardiner supplied her with some very fine fabrics, and since he also referred several customers to her, including his nieces, she was willing to lend the book to Mrs. Gardiner for an evening when needed.

Tomorrow, she would need to return this book to Mrs. Havelston and place her order for the most important dresses of her life – the ones she would wear in the ballrooms and drawing rooms of London as she made her debut in high society with the hope of finding a husband. She really needed to get this right.

"These are all so lovely that I simply do not know what to choose."

"Surely, it cannot be so difficult." Lord Rycroft took the book from Mary and placed it on the table where he had been playing cards with his mother while Georgiana and Mary had been looking at patterns. He motioned for her to join him at the table.

"I believe you said your uncle had sent some pieces of material with the book. May I see them?"

Mary placed several swatches of silk, satin, and muslin on the table before sitting down next to Lord Rycroft.

Lord Rycroft ran a hand over the fabrics before pinching them and rubbing them each between his thumb and finger. Then, he picked up first one and then another of the samples and held them up in her direction as if studying them and her at the same time.

"Your uncle has a good eye. These will all go quite nicely with your complexion, I dare say."

His words and the accompanying smile felt wonderful to Mary. She knew he was not saying she was beautiful, but he had implied she would look nice in these colours, had he not?

She watched as he flipped through the book. His head tipped this way and that. A brow would arch now and then, and the page would be turned quickly; or a smile would tip his lips, and he would place a piece of fabric between the pages before moving on.

"How many patterns are you to pick for this order? Six was it?" He peered up from the page at her.

"Yes, six."

"Very good," he said, turning his eyes back to the book. "You will need gowns for driving, balls, and calls. You have a few acceptable day dresses now, do you not?" Again, he peered up at her.

Mary bit back a smile as she nodded. She had not seen another gentleman so interested in ladies' fashion besides her uncle, although, she suspected their interest in fashion was for very different reasons. Her uncle wanted to purchase and resell the best fabrics, ones which would be sought after by many. She knew that Lord Rycroft had no interest in selling fabrics. She suspected he just liked how the fabrics looked on the ladies he met.

"There. That is six. You will be among the best dressed of the season." He closed the book. "Now, could we please have one more hand before we retire for the night?"

He picked up the cards and began shuffling them.

"Oh!" He lay the cards down and picked up the book again. "Do you ride?"

"A little."

He tilted his head to the side and raised a brow. "Georgie, we will have to improve that. All proper ladies must know how to ride." He flipped a few pages and scrutinized a few patterns before placing his finger on a picture. "That. In..." He studied her with eyes narrowed for a moment. "Green," he said at last. "Yes, a dark green. It will set off the auburn tones in your hair and the touch of gold in your eyes."

The thought that he had noticed her hair and eyes in such detail was startling to Mary. She looked at the book. The patterns he had chosen were very similar to what she might have chosen herself once she was forced to just pick something, although, she had to say, that the ones he had chosen were a bit more daring than she would have considered.

She smiled and thanked him as she closed the book.

A bit of daring was good. She was in town to find a husband and to experience the freedom of not being pushed around by her mother and called upon to serve her younger sisters. She was not here to be the same old Mary, sitting by the wall and hidden in the background. No, she was here to see and be seen. The idea both thrilled and terrified her. But she was determined to be successful. She would not leave this season without either a husband or a glorious tale to tell to her nieces when she reached her spinsterhood.

She picked up her cards and arranged them in her hand. "You have a very keen eye for ladies' fashion, my lord."

Georgiana giggled. "He has a keen eye for ladies," she whispered.

Rycroft's eyes narrowed, and his lips curved downward in a scowl. It was a most intimidating look.

"I appreciate beauty and have an eye for quality." He lay his cards down on the table.

"It is not the quality ladies whom I worry about," Lady Sophia said.

A small hint of colour crept up Lord Rycroft's neck. "I am not the same man, Mother."

Lady Sophia patted his hand and smiled at him. "Time will tell, my son. I do not doubt your resolve. I just know the temptations."

He closed his eyes, and that hint of colour from before deepened. "I would rather not discuss temptations at present."

"One must not forget about them or the misery to which they can lead," Lady Sophia said.

"I do not think it is possible for me to forget that, Mother." His tone was on the edge of sharp. His discomfort was palpable.

"I believe it is your turn, Georgiana," said Mary. She gave Rycroft a little smile when he peeked at her.

"Thank you," he mouthed, and she gave him a slight nod of her head in acknowledgement.

Mary watched the play circle the table and come back to her. She was not sure why she had provided a way for Lord Rycroft to avoid the lecture she was sure his mother was about to give him, one she was certain he deserved. Perhaps it was because she knew what it was to have a mother embarrass her with a scolding remark.

She played her turn.

Perhaps it was because she felt she owed him a favour since he had saved her from the task of making a decision about fashion. She did not mind speaking about fashion or admiring it, but she had very little knowledge on how to dress herself to advantage. Or, she sighed, perhaps it was because she had determined in the carriage ride from Hertfordshire that she would give him a chance to improve in her opinion.

"Lord Brownlow and Mr. Blackmoore are here to see you, my lord. Are you home?" Mr. Morledge, Rycroft House's butler, stood at the door to the drawing room.

"They are calling at this hour?" Rycroft placed his cards face down on the table. His hand did not look like a winning hand so he was happy for the interruption, but it was an unusual time for his friends to call.

"It appears so, my lord." There was a hint of disapproval in the austere butler's tone.

"Very well. I suppose it would be the height of rudeness to send them away." One of his eyebrows rose, and his lips curled into a small smirk as he contemplated sending them away.

"If you are certain, my lord." Morledge held his place.

"Yes, yes, show them in. Either I shall scold them for their calling at such an inappropriate time, or my mother shall." He winked at Mary. "Unless, of course, Miss Bennet, you would care to do the service?"

Mary's eyes narrowed, and then that one critical eyebrow on the left rose a slight bit. "I am quite certain, my lord, that scolding is not how a lady makes a good first impression."

"Especially when the gentlemen are of the marriageable sort and very eligible, my dear. Brownlow has a title, but Blackmoore is not without his advantages. I have heard that he is quite plump in the pocket." Lady Sophia gathered the cards and stacked them. "Georgiana, ring for tea. We will put on a good show."

"Mother," cautioned Rycroft, "they have come to see me, not Miss Mary."

"Of course, they are here for you and not Miss Mary. How can they be here for someone they have not met?" She smiled sweetly, but he knew that look. Perhaps he should be pitying Miss Mary more than himself for having to endure a season of his mother's scheming and matchmaking.

Chapter 4

"Lord Brownlow and Mr. Blackmoore," Morledge announced.

Behind him stood two of Rycroft's good friends.

Rycroft noticed how Miss Mary studied his friends and scowled. His mother's selected friend-to-see-married looked rather eager to begin her search. He straightened his spine and lifted his chin. These two might be the same age as him and employ his tailor, but neither of them was as tall as he was. In fact, they were both two to three inches shorter than he.

"Brownlow. Blackmoore." Rycroft greeted them.

"Rycroft." Lord Brownlow, Rycroft's friend with sandy hair and sparkling eyes that ladies claimed made him irresistibly charming, extended his greeting first. "We know it is late, but when Blackmoore and I did not see you at our club this evening, we thought we should come here to welcome you back. It has been an age since we last saw you." Then, as if recognizing for the first time that there were others in the room, he bowed. "Lady Sophia, I trust you and Miss Darcy are well."

"We are quite well, Lord Brownlow. I thank you." She motioned toward some seats. "Please do sit down. I have sent for tea." She cocked her head slightly and gave them a smile. "Although I suspect, if you have been at your club all evening, you would do better with some coffee. However, it is too late; the tea has been called, and we must make do." She raised a brow. "One must never waste tea. It is much too precious."

"Indeed, my lady," Brownlow said as he and Blackmoore each took a seat. "We had not intended to intrude on your evening, of course." He glanced at Miss Mary, who was sitting quietly observing the conversation.

"It is a pleasant intrusion. We were merely playing cards and discussing fashion. I am certain my son is happy for the disruption." She looked at Rycroft and gave a tip of her head toward Mary.

"Yes, I fear I was about to lose," Rycroft said with a chuckle. "And Miss Bennet is off to the modiste tomorrow, fashion catalogue in hand, so selections had to be made." He took a seat. "Miss Mary, this is Lord Brownlow and Mr. Blackmoore. Gentlemen, this is Miss Mary Bennet of Hertfordshire. She is my mother's guest for the season."

"It is a pleasure to meet you, Lord Brownlow, Mr. Blackmoore." Mary smiled and nodded her greeting very properly and without so much as a critical eyebrow twitching. Rycroft scowled once again.

"Bennet?" It was the first word Blackmoore had spoken, and Mary smile grew as though she quite liked the way her name fell from his lips. Rycroft was not so fond of it. Apparently, the promise he had made to Bingley had worked its way into his head a little deeper than he had expected it to and was clouding his vision of his friends.

"Miss Darcy," Blackmoore continued, "did not your brother marry a Miss Bennet?"

"He did. He married Miss Mary's sister, Miss Elizabeth."

"Ah, a sister," Blackmoore said while nodding his head. "And you are from Hertfordshire?" He turned his attention to Mary.

Rycroft cocked an eyebrow. Had he not just said that?

"I am," Miss Mary replied, surprising Rycroft with her demure tone and a light blush that graced her cheeks. She was not the first young lady he had seen respond to Blackmoore in such a fashion. He had heard more than one lady describe his friend with deep brown hair and only slightly lighter eyes as dark and dashing. However, Rycroft had not expected Miss Mary to be so affected by Blackmoore, nor was he particularly pleased by it.

"Her father owns the estate that neighbours the one Bingley has leased," Rycroft explained.

Mr. Blackmoore nodded again. "I hear Bingley has also found a potential bride."

"Another sister," Mary said. "My eldest sister, Jane. I also have two more sisters who are younger than I. And no, I do not have a brother. It is what everyone asks," she added when Blackmoore's brows rose at her direct reply.

"That is a lot of ladies in one house," Blackmoore said.

"It is, indeed."

"And is it only your sister, Mrs. Darcy, who is married?"

"Yes, for now."

Thankfully, at least to Rycroft, the tea arrived at that moment, and the subject of sisters and brides was forgotten, as talk turned toward the weather and the happenings in town. And when a proper amount of time had passed, and their teacups were empty, his mother – bless her! – stood and excused herself, as well as Miss Mary and Georgiana, citing Mary's early appointment with the modiste and the return of Georgiana's companion and the continuation of her lessons.

"She will take well," Blackmoore said after the ladies had departed. "That is why your mother has invited her to stay, is it not? Miss Bennet is Lady Sophia's latest project."

Rycroft cringed. "That is what I called Miss Mary, but my mother has assured me it is not true. Miss Mary is a friend and companion, not a project. And I advise you not to use that term within her hearing."

Brownlow laughed. "She scolded you, did she?"

"Not as thoroughly as Miss Bennet did."

Brownlow's laughter increased. "Surely you did not call Miss Bennet a project in front of Miss Bennet?"

Rycroft shrugged. "I did not know I had, but yes, I did." He could still hear her gasp and feel her glare of displeasure. And, to be honest, he had deserved her censure.

"Is she a scolding sort of young lady?" Blackmoore asked.

Rycroft shook his head. "Not if you speak to Georgiana or Bingley or my mother or Darcy or, apparently, anyone but me. To them, Miss Mary is all sweetness, if a bit too serious, but to me, she is more of a governess. I have been on the receiving end of more than one lecture."

There was a small gasp from behind him. He closed his eyes and grimaced as he realized that the door had not opened to allow entrance to a servant to gather the tea tray. Turning, he saw Mary standing near the card table, the book of fashions in hand. Her cheeks were rosy, and her eyes were looking at the floor.

"I am sorry for the intrusion, my lord." He could feel the undertones of embarrassment and pain in her voice. "I forgot my book, and your mother insisted that I return to get it."

"Very good," said Rycroft. "I... we..." He sought to find the right words to explain what she might have heard.

"There is no need to explain, my lord." She lifted her eyes to him. There was fire in them. Well-deserved fire.

She turned away from him and towards his friends with a smile and a curtsey – all that was proper. "Good night."

She moved toward the door but stopped just before exiting and turned toward Rycroft. "I never lecture, my lord, unless there is a want of learning." She curtseyed once again and left the room, closing the door firmly behind her.

Mary clasped the book tightly against her chest and took a few deep, calming breaths. Then, having gained control of her emotions, she headed toward her room. Her resolve to give him that second chance crumbled with every step she took. Her anger at having been the subject of conversation, and in such a light, grew. By the time she had reached her room, her emotions were no longer under regulation, and the hurt she had felt at his words had been replaced by anger.

"Are you well?" Georgiana sat on Mary's bed, waiting for her.

Mary placed the book on the bed and closed the door. "No. Your cousin is a dolt." She flopped on the bed. "When I entered the drawing room, he was telling his friends that I am given to lecturing him." She sat up. "How will I be able to find a husband if he is labeling me a shrew? I would have a better chance of finding a husband with my mother standing next to me, pointing out my sisters' accomplishments and my lack of them." She flopped back on the bed again.

Georgiana flipped open the book and began paging through it. "He selected some very nice gowns."

Mary covered her face with her hands. "I cannot wear them."

"Why ever not? They are lovely and would complement you very well."

"But to wear what he selected? I will be constantly reminded of what he thinks of me."

"I apologize, Mary, but I do not see how the two things are connected."

Mary uncovered her face. "I suppose you are right. They really are not related except for the fact that what he said was said by him and they were chosen by him."

"So, my cousin is the connection?" She looked at Mary, who nodded.

"But could you not use that connection to prove him wrong?" Mary lifted onto her elbows, interested to hear what Georgiana had to say.

"What if you wore them and were the most unshrew-like lady ever? Would that not just prove to him that while he may have known what would look best on you, he knew nothing of who you were beneath the dress? You shall wear the gowns he chose and charm all the gentlemen with your sweetness, and Samuel will have to admit he was entirely wrong about you, which he is, of course. Men are not the brightest of creatures, you know. At least, that is what Aunt Sophia says."

"That is simply brilliant!" Mary sat up and pulled the book closer so that both she and Georgiana could look at the pages. "This one is very lovely."

"And you shall be the belle of the ball in it." Georgiana lowered her voice. "Do you think Mr. Blackmoore will ask for a dance? He is very dashing, is he not?"

Mary sighed. "Very."

"Oh," Georgiana's hand covered her mouth, and her eyes sparkled. "That would be the very best way to prove my cousin wrong! You must convince his friends that he is wrong." She clapped her hands in excitement. "I so wish I could go to all the soirees with you. It is going to be so much fun."

Mary laughed. Lightness and hope filled her. "I believe you are right, Georgiana. This could be a very entertaining project."

Chapter 5

LORD RYCROFT RUBBED HIS neck and then stretched. He had been bent over his account books for far too long. He needed a distraction. The letters and numbers were beginning to jumble themselves together. He pushed the account books away and stored his pen. Perhaps stretching his legs would be beneficial.

The rain that beat against the window told him that his ramble would have to be confined to the house, and so he followed the notes of a lovely song to the music room, planning to slip into the room and sit quietly at the back while Georgiana practised. He was at the door with his hand on the handle when the voices from inside made him pause.

"No, no," a strict voice chided. "The right foot, not the left one. Again. Watch Miss Bennet."

The music began once again, and Rycroft pushed the door open just a bit to see Miss Mary and Georgiana standing up to dance with each other.

"You know they could progress much more quickly if they had proper partners." Lady Sophia's whisper, which had come from directly behind him, caused him to jump and rattle the door.

How had she managed to sneak up on him? Her eyes were filled with amusement when he turned to her.

"There is only one of me and two of them," he retorted.

"You are one and the dancing master is another. That makes two. The perfect number of partners needed." She pushed the door to the music room open and held it while she waited for him to enter. "It will not do you any harm to polish your steps before you begin your quest to dance your way into some young lady's heart."

Oh, she was intent upon his marrying, was she not? He sighed. A wife would have to be found at some point, and dancing was not a horrible activity. Indeed, it was one he quite liked.

Within the room into which he looked, the music had stopped, and the occupants of the room were not waiting patiently for the disruption at the door to come to an end. Each one wore a differing amount of irritation on their faces. Neither protesting his mother's desire to see him married nor slipping quietly away to some other room could be accomplished with any amount of grace. Therefore, he stepped across the threshold as Lady Sophia announced that he was there to be of assistance.

The dancing master gave him an appraising look. "Do you dance well?" he queried.

"I would like to think I do," Rycroft replied. He had never damaged any toes, and he had been complimented by more than one matron and her charge for his dancing ability.

Of course, he could have broken some debutante's toes, and he still would have been complimented for his skill. A gentleman with a title and a fortune did not have to possess exceptional skill at anything for it to be said he did. It was a frustrating fact, but it was a fact. Some liked to fawn and flatter. Some titled gentlemen liked that sort of thing. He was not one of them. He would rather be spoken to and about honestly.

"Would you be able to execute a cotillion?" the dancing master asked.

"Of course."

"Very well," the instructor said with one last appraising look. Apparently, to this man, a title did not equate excellence in all things. He would require Rycroft to prove himself.

"Stand up opposite Miss Bennet," the man continued. "I shall stand with Miss Darcy. She is struggling to know her left foot from her right foot at the moment, but Miss Bennet only wants practice to refine her steps." He bestowed a nod and a smile on Mary.

"So, you dance well?" Rycroft took his place across from Mary and bowed. She must if a man as exacting as this master appeared to be seemed pleased with her performance.

"I would like to think I do." She curtseyed, looking very much like she wished to laugh at her repetition of his answer.

She had not scolded him once today. She had not even glared at him once today. She had been everything that was pleasant at breakfast and when he had seen her before she, his mother, and Georgiana had left the house for their appointment with Mrs. Havelston. He had been sure there would be some repercussions for his blunder last night. Truth be told, he would presently feel better if she had scolded him. However, she had not and did not look as if she were willing to perform her duty to reprimand him now, either. And that left him feeling just as foolish now as he had last evening, as well as a bit nervous because he did not know if she would at some moment feel the need to chastise him.

She looked expectantly to the musician seated at the piano. That was another thing! Her eyes had only met his when absolutely necessary today. It was as if she were attempting to avoid him even when he was present.

"Do you like to dance?" Rycroft asked, feeling a need to fill the void her silence created. Moreover, if he could get her to speak to him, perhaps he would soon be given the reprimand he deserved, and the gnawing of his conscience would subside.

She smiled at him. Her eyes met his, and an eyebrow raised a bit in amusement. "I do," was all she said, and then, her eyes were once again averted.

"Do you dance often?" He attempted again.

She pressed her lips together for a moment before saying, "Not as often as I would like."

Her eyes never left their observation of the musician who had just finished spreading her music on the instrument in preparation for the dance that the instructor had requested.

Averted eyes, no effort to extend a conversation, the constant flicker of amusement in her features – she was attempting to avoid him even when he was present, and she was, quite annoyingly, delighting in her success.

He tipped his head to the side and cocked an eyebrow in challenge. "I see what you are doing."

She fluttered her eyelashes and smiled sweetly at him. It was not a look with which he was unfamiliar, for it was the practiced look of a devious lady playing the part of an innocent. There were many who played at that game in a ballroom.

"I assure you I am not doing anything," she said.

"You are angry, so you are refusing to speak to me."

"I am sure I have not refused to speak to you. I believe I have answered all your questions." The music began, and she took his hand and curtseyed as he bowed before taking Georgiana's hand and beginning to circle.

When she had crossed over and back toward him, he said, "But your answers have been abrupt, and you seem averse to conversation." And she had not denied that she was angry just now.

She crossed over and back to him. "My answers were concise because I am intent upon my lesson. Now, if you would be so kind as to allow me to concentrate on my steps and the music…" She gave a small nod of her head as if thanking him for his compliance as they parted and came back together again.

The frustrating woman! Dismissing him with a fabricated reason. How was he to get what he needed if he was not able to talk to and provoke her? He blew out a breath and he decided to bide his time.

Thankfully, as he progressed through the steps of the dance in silence, his stiff muscles relaxed, and the activity brought alertness to his mind. And dancing, as he was, in silence gave that more-alert mind time to observe Miss Mary. Her steps were precise and soft; her movements were graceful; and if he was not mistaken, he heard her softly humming the tune. While her skills told him that she had danced often, the joy on her face gave evidence beyond her sweet humming that she did indeed enjoy dancing. It was a delightful picture, one that brought a smile to his lips. Eventually, the music slowed and came to an end.

"That was much improved, Miss Darcy," the dancing master said.

"You can return in two days, can you not?" Lady Sophia asked. "Miss Mary's time to prepare for the season is limited."

The gentleman inclined his head. A smile crinkled the skin around his eyes. "I would return every day to dance with Miss Bennet. However, I have other students, so I shall have to be content to wait two days before I return." He turned to Rycroft. "It would do well if the ladies had an opportunity to practice once between now and our next lesson." He cocked his head to the side, and both brows rose as he waited for Rycroft to respond.

"I have business—" he began, but a small cough from his mother stopped him. "However, I am certain I can find a few moments to be of assistance."

The instructor turned to Miss Darcy. "Do you have the music for the dances we did today?"

"I do."

"Then perhaps you could play for Miss Bennet and Lord Rycroft, and then Miss Bennet — you do play, Miss Bennet, do you not?" He waited for her assurance that she did play before continuing. "Then you must play for Miss Darcy and Lord Rycroft." He gave a sharp nod of his head, indicating that the plan was good and the discussion at an end. Then, with a scold to the musician to be quick, he donned his hat and coat and took up his walking stick.

Chapter 6

"You dance so very well," Georgiana said to Miss Mary once the dancing master and his pianist had quit the music room at Rycroft Place. "I wish I could dance as well as you do."

Miss Mary put an arm around Georgiana's shoulders, and they started moving towards the piano. Rycroft followed.

"You will," Miss Mary assured Georgiana. "I started dancing when Jane and Elizabeth were first learning. I have had more practice is all."

Georgiana shook her head. "My feet do not always follow my head."

"That is the problem," Rycroft said. "You must not dance in your head." He smiled as Mary rolled her eyes. Finally, he had gotten a response that was not prim or proper as all her others had been today. "Do you not believe me, Miss Mary?"

He kept his tone teasing and waited expectantly for her to reply with an *I most certainly do not*.

She paused and glanced at him warily as if afraid of what he might do. Then, her expression shifted to a sweet smile, and she said, "I await your explanations, sir."

One of his brows arched, and his mouth became a displeased line. Whether she would admit it or not, she was definitely playing at something. He had just handed her a perfect opportunity to instruct him on the need to know the dance in one's head before it could become a learned pattern for the body, but instead of taking it, she had deferred to him. And now, he needed to explain something he was not sure he could explain.

"Of course, the steps must first be known by the head." He glanced at the pianoforte and remembered how Georgiana seemed to flow along the keys with the music. The music never came from her head. It, rather, came from her heart. Each song seemed to pour out from her soul. A smile tipped his lips on one side. That was it.

"While the head is the beginning of learning a piece of music, it is the heart which must be engaged for the performance to be more than a plunking of keys in a set pattern. Do you count the notes and timing?"

She shook her head. "I did at first, but I no longer do."

"Ah." He smiled as he saw Mary's eyes narrow. He was certain she had hoped he would not have an explanation, and until a moment ago, he had thought she would get her wish. "If you do not count, how is it that you can play a piece as it is written?"

A smile spread across Georgiana's face. "My heart and body feel it."

"Just so." He tapped her on the nose. "Would you agree, Miss Mary?"

Her eyes narrowed just a bit more, and he smiled just a bit more broadly.

"I would." She moved toward the instrument. "However, sometimes, fingers and feet do not learn at the same rate. One may require more practice than the other." She took up a piece of music which lay on a bench near the pianoforte.

"If you will excuse me." She looked at him and then toward the door. "My fingers do not learn as readily as my feet."

Did she think to send him away when he had not yet gotten what he craved? It was a pity for her that he was not more obliging, and instead of leaving as she had clearly signaled she wanted him to do, he pulled a chair close to where she took her seat at the instrument.

"You may require assistance with the pages," he explained when she looked up at him with brows drawn close in question.

Her shoulders drooped a bit. He was close to breaking through her game. He could hear it in her frustrated sigh.

"I would not wish to keep you from your business," she protested – politely.

He waved the idea way with at flick of his wrist. "My business can wait. I have worked at it all morning and desire some time away from it." He leaned back in his chair. "Was your trip to the modiste a success?"

"It was. Mrs. Havelston was impressed with your selections."

"Did you tell her they were mine?"

"Yes. She complimented me on my fashion sense, but it was not my sense that deserved it. It was yours." She placed her fingers above the keys and gave him a tight smile. "Now, if you would be so kind as to allow me to concentrate on my music."

He nodded. She was a most unusual lady. Most every lady he had met in town during his seasons would have simply said thank you for the compliment and allowed their modiste or whomever else chose to compliment them on their taste in fashion to believe that it was their taste and theirs alone. But not Miss Mary. She did like to make sure things were done properly.

Her fingers began working their way through the song as his cousin joined her companion, Mrs. Annesley, near the window to work on a sampler, and his mother took a seat near him. She was likely concerned he might behave inappropriately, and he could not blame her for her concern. He had done an exemplary job of offending Miss Mary at every turn since meeting her.

"You think too much," Lord Rycroft whispered as he moved a page.

"Shush." Mary shook her head and huffed as if annoyed with herself and not just him.

"You do," he whispered again, trying to push open that small chink in her armour and reveal the Miss Mary she was hiding. The one that, for some incomprehensible reason, he needed to see.

Her hands stopped, and she let the notes fade into the air before turning to Rycroft. "This is a new piece, and I cannot learn it properly if I do not think about what I am doing. And I cannot think about what I am doing if you insist on speaking to me."

It was not a scold, but it was an explanation, which was close to a lecture. Yes, the wall behind which she was hiding was beginning to crumble. Therefore, he snatched a sheet of her music, and took up the argument he knew she did not want to have.

"This is not entirely new. You played it when we were in Hertfordshire. I remember it." He settled back in his chair with a rather smug look upon his face. "And, I believe, my cousin spoke to you while you played."

"And I stumbled." Exasperation was in her tone. "I do not wish to stumble when called upon to exhibit during the season." She held out her hand for the sheet of music he held. "I must begin again."

He shook his head. "You do not need this." He placed the sheet on the floor next to his chair.

"Very well, I shall practice later." She began to rise from her seat.

"I will not return it to you until you have attempted the song without it."

Mary's mouth hung open for a moment.

"You have only to sit and play badly to prove to me that you do not know the piece."

She sat once again and held her hands over the keys.

"Have you not embarrassed me enough?" she asked softly. "Must you insist on continuing to do so?"

She began to play. She stumbled once, and it was not fluid, but she managed to complete the portion of music he held ransom.

It was neither a lecture nor a scold, but it was what he had sought, an acknowledgment that he had hurt her. And as her soft words twisted in his heart, he had no idea why he had felt so compelled to hear it.

"You did well." He placed the page of music he had taken in line with the others and stood to leave. "I have deserved every one of your lectures and more." He gave her half a smile and hoped she heard the depth of sincerity in his apology. "Remember, I am an oaf."

"Not a complete one," she replied with a small smile of her own. His Mary had returned, and they could move forward as friends. Or so he hoped.

He gave a bow and left the room. However, instead of returning directly to his study, he stood with the door open just enough so that he could see Mary. Her eyes were closed, and her face wore the same smile of pleasure it had during their dance. Then, she placed her fingers on the keys and began to play. This time, the music seemed to dance with her as she played, gracefully moving from one key to another.

Rycroft had meant to spend only a moment watching. However, the fascination of seeing the emotions play across Mary's face and seeing her body rise and fall with the notes held him in his place for so long that the final note was fading as he hurried to close the door softly so she would not discover him watching her.

He shook his head, baffled by his response to her. She drew things from him that no one else could. He would have never pursued anyone else until they chastised him. No one else but her. It made no sense. None whatsoever.

The music began again, and he looked at the door that separated him from Mary. He wanted to push that door open once more so he could watch her. However, instead of doing what he wished to do, he removed his hand from the door handle and returned to his study.

Chapter 7

KNOWING THAT LORD RYCROFT had mentioned the previous evening that he would be riding in the morning, Mary entered the breakfast room, confidently assured of a quiet meal that would be free of Lord Rycroft's unsettling presence.

Yesterday, she had managed a full day without once giving in to her desire to lecture him about anything, and he had seemed rather contrite in all his actions toward her after he left the music room. It was as if he were trying to prove to her that he was not the oaf he continually claimed to be. It was quite disconcerting to have him behaving so well. It made it difficult for her to maintain her resolve to avoid him, for he truly was pleasant company.

Relieved that the breakfast room was as she had expected it to be – empty – she filled her cup with tea and prepared to toast her bread. She had only just begun warming it when her good luck was dashed.

"Ah, good," Rycroft said as he entered the room. "Is Georgiana awake?"

"Are you not riding?" Why was he not out on his horse somewhere other than here? Mary turned her bread, trying to focus on it rather than the man who was disturbing her quiet breakfast.

"I have, and I will." He took a piece of bread and placed it on a toasting fork before joining her at the hearth. "You said you did not ride well. We should remedy that."

"Today?" Mary's eyes grew wide in surprise, and she nearly forgot to turn her bread again.

He nodded. "Did you have other plans?" He cast a wary, sidelong look at her as if he were trying to determine if he had done something wrong or not.

"Georgiana and I are going to the museum to draw this afternoon. However, I had no plans other than to practice or read this morning." And she had planned on avoiding him again today.

"Good." He placed his bread near hers. "Now, do you know if Georgiana is awake?"

Mary sighed and turned her bread one last time. "She is." And when Mary had left her, she was just getting dressed for the day. "But I do not have a riding habit yet. We have only just placed my order with Mrs. Havelston. Therefore, I am afraid we will not be able to ride today."

"I thought of that."

He had?

"I have borrowed one from Brownlow's sister."

"You did what?" Mary pulled her bread from the fire and slid it off onto a plate. Apparently, avoidance of his lordship was not going to be an option today.

"I borrowed a habit."

"From a lady I have never met?" She hoped beyond hope that he had not painted her as a project in need of assistance.

"Is this a problem?" His brows were drawn together. "Lady Serena was happy to help."

Mary's knife stopped with the sweet cream only half spread on her toast. A knot formed in her stomach. "What did you tell her?"

"I said that my mother had a guest staying with her and that the lady would like to ride but, unfortunately, did not have a habit with her." He joined her at the table, his toast looking, in her opinion, a bit too sickly white to be proper. "I did not say anything that would embarrass you."

"Are you certain?"

He paused and his brows drew together again as he thought. Then, he nodded his head. "Yes, I believe everything I said was acceptable."

Relief washed over her as she cut her bread into small triangles. "Then, I thank you."

He blinked as if her response had startled him. He truly did think of her as a lady who lectured, did he not? She shook her head.

"Is Lady Serena a particular friend of yours or merely the sister of a friend?"

He was still staring at her as she asked the question and then lifted her piece of toast and took a bite, but his gaze quickly shifted to his plate as the tip of her tongue flicked out and caught a small bit of jam that remained on her lips.

"Merely the sister of a friend. She is all but betrothed to Lord Bowthorpe. It is expected to be the match of the season, or so her mother says." He peeked up at her just as she kissed a bit of something from the tip of her finger. He expelled a breath and returned his attention to his own toast. "I believe, however, that your sister's conquest of my cousin may eclipse it for a time."

At that, Mary giggled. The thought of her sister Elizabeth being the talk of the ton was strange.

"If I had to choose a sister to be the topic of gossip, I would not have chosen Elizabeth." She shrugged when he looked at her. "Kitty, possibly. Lydia," she sighed, "more than likely."

"And you?" His eyes remained on her as if trying to reason something out. A small smile curved his lips most becomingly.

"It is not one of my goals," she replied with a laugh. "But if the gossip were for a good reason, which it rarely is, I would not be averse to being a small topic of conversation."

"And what would you say is a good reason?" He filled his cup with tea and added some milk.

"I do not know. Something noble. Something of significance to help another."

He laid his spoon on his saucer and, lifting his cup, stared at some object across the room. "Even when an act is done for all the right reasons, the gossips have a way of twisting it around to make it scandalous. They do not want to hear of good or noble acts." He shook his head. "Nor do they deal in the imparting of truth or kindness." There was a hint of bitterness in his voice. "And they enjoy nothing better than to ruin the life of any young lady who makes an error." He took a sip of his tea and fell silent.

Mary enjoyed the quiet as she finished eating her toast, washing the final bite down with the last of her tea.

"That is what happened to you," she said softly.

He turned to her in surprise. "You heard?"

She lifted one shoulder an let it drop. "Papa read the news, Lydia read the *on dit*, and I listened."

She stood to leave. "Do not fear. I will not ask. You may be a partial oaf, but I do not believe you are what the gossips portrayed. The gentleman whom I have met does not match the gentleman in that article." Lord Rycroft's heart was too good. He might be given to insulting her, but his grief at having done so shone in his eyes, revealing his true nature. That is what made him only a partial oaf and not a complete one in her mind.

Lord Rycroft grabbed her hand as she moved to leave. "You do not wish to know?"

She smiled at him. "I did not say that. I said I would not ask." She wanted to know. She very badly wanted to know.

He dropped her hand. "Thank you. That you, an acquaintance of short duration and a lady of principle, would not label me as they do means a great deal, and for you to do so without knowing the full story means even more."

She waited for him to continue, for he looked as if he would.

"I was actually very much like the man the gossips portrayed me to be. Reckless. Seeking pleasure. Shirking responsibility. But never to anyone's harm but my own."

Mary lay her hand on his. "As you told your mother, you are that man no longer."

He smiled and nodded. "That is what I said, and I hope it is true."

She held his gaze. "You must not hope, my lord. You must believe."

She turned and walked to the door, but stopped before exiting the breakfast room. "The riding habit you borrowed from Lady Serena, is it in my room?"

"It is." He was still staring at that spot across the room. "Have Georgie join us in three-quarters of an hour."

He glanced toward her, and she curtseyed quickly. "As you wish, my lord."

"Forgive me. I should have asked, not ordered," he said before she could duck out of the room.

"I am not offended," she said as a smile formed on her lips of its own accord.

"Am I forgiven?"

"For this."

His laughter followed her down the hall. Perhaps he was not so bad as she had thought. He might not even be a partial oaf. He had taken it upon himself to help her in learning to ride, had he not?

As she ascended the stairs, she replayed his comments about the scandal that had driven him out of town. The emotions that had played across his face and found their way into his tone spoke of a man with more depth than she had considered.

She had said she would not ask about the scandal, but oh how she still wanted to! She remembered the story. She had looked for it in the stack of papers in her father's study after she had met him. Having matched him to the Lord R of Essex mentioned in the paper, she had read the information several times.

Lord R of Essex has made himself scarce from town after being found in the company of Miss F when he was known to have been courting Lady S. It is said that the jilted lady's brother, a close friend of Lord R, has broken ties with him.

She stopped as she pushed open the door to her room and her gaze fell on the beautiful blue riding habit that lay on her bed. Lady S! Lady Serena?

She turned and looked back down the stairs. He had said Lady Serena was merely the sister of a friend – a friend who had looked nothing but pleased to see Lord Rycroft when he had come to visit that evening.

She walked to the bed and ran her hand over the fabric of the habit. Even when an act is done for all the right reasons, he had said. As she moved to the bell pull, Mary considered what right reasons there could be for jilting a lady, especially one who was presumably a friend. How she wished she had not made the promise to not ask him about the scandal!

Chapter 8

MARY HAD JUST RUNG the bell to have a maid help her into her riding habit and had just begun to unfasten her day dress when she remembered that she was supposed to tell Georgiana to be ready in three-quarters of an hour. She left her door open and hurried down the hall as she refastened the bib of her dress.

"Miss Darcy," she called as she knocked on Georgiana's door. Then, she turned so she could watch for her maid. Thankfully, Georgiana was quick in opening the door. "We are to go riding with Lord Rycroft in three-quarters of an hour."

Mary looked over her shoulder and saw the maid just reaching her room. "Oh, I must go. I forgot that I was to tell you of the riding until after I pulled the bell for the maid to help me with my riding habit. Well, actually, it is not my habit, it is borrowed."

Georgiana followed her. "Borrowed?"

"Yes," Mary said as she reached her room and made quick work of undoing her gown. "Lord Rycroft borrowed it from Lord Brownlow's sister."

Georgiana's eyes grew wide. "Lady Serena?"

Mary nodded.

Georgiana sat on the bed. "I would not think she would lend him anything after what happened."

Mary stepped out of her day gown. "Then, she is the Lady S who was jilted?"

Georgiana nodded. "I did not think it strange that her brother would visit my cousin since his sister is now attached to an equally worthy gentleman – Lord Bowthorpe – who from all appearances is loved by Lady Serena and who loves her in return. Such a good match is just the happy balm needed to heal a breach such as that."

She rose from the bed as Mary was being helped into her borrowed gown. "But then, men are such fickle creatures at times. They most certainly seem able to forgive each other more easily than some ladies do. And that is just it."

She stood at the window looking out across the garden. "How does a lady who has been so injured recover from such a thing so fully and in such a short time?" She shook her head. "I am sure I could not."

"I imagine it is because love heals," Mary said. "You did say that Lady Serena loves Lord Bowthorpe, and he loves her, so that must be it. Love has made it possible for her to move forward."

"I suppose that must be it." Georgiana turned toward Mary. "Oh, Miss Mary! You look lovely."

Mary fastened the closures on the jacket. "It is a beautiful dress, and it fits so well." Surprisingly well! It was almost as if the dress had been made for her. She and Lady Serena must be the same size.

"That it does," said Georgiana motioning for Mary to turn in a circle. "You will not have to ride well to be noticed in this dress. You will most certainly be turning heads."

She grabbed Mary's hand. "Come. Bring your hat. I will have my maid adjust your hair once I am dressed." Georgiana pulled her down the hall towards her room. "You must explain more of what you meant by love healing while I am dressing, Miss Mary."

Mary entered Georgiana's room. "Could you call me just Mary?"

Georgiana smiled. "If you will call me either Georgiana or Georgie."

"I would like that." Mary sat on the bed. "Georgiana is a beautiful name."

"Thank you. I have always liked it."

Georgiana's maid, who had just finished helping her dress when Mary had arrived to tell Georgiana they would be riding, had laid out her mistress's riding habit and set about helping her change as soon as the door had been closed.

"Now, that thing about love healing."

Mary cocked her head to the side and studied Georgiana. She seemed very anxious to hear this. Her expression was one of eager anticipation.

"My theory," Mary said, "and it is only a theory because I do not know the full story, is that there was either no attachment or a false attachment. Perhaps there was an infatuation between Lord Rycroft and Lady Serena. Such sentiments are easily replaced by true and steady affection, which is a healing balm that wraps itself around your heart until the cracks and pain gradually fade away, and its steadfastness frees your heart to trust once again." At least, that is what she hoped true love would do.

"What a beautiful thought," said Georgiana with a sigh. "Have you ever felt you were in love only to discover that your heart had tricked you?"

Mary smiled. "What young girl has not?" Even Jane had been infatuated with others before meeting Mr. Bingley, and none of those infatuations had proven to be more than a passing fancy.

Georgiana, fully gowned in her habit, motioned for Mary to sit in front of the mirror. "Have you ever considered doing something very foolish because of those feelings?"

Mary noted the hint of pink that crept into Georgiana's cheeks. Ah! Was that what was behind Georgiana's need to know that love could heal? She could understand that need. It was why she held to her theory so strongly.

"I have," she answered, "but I was prevented."

Georgiana's maid had removed the pins from Mary's hair, and it tumbled down her back nearly to her waist. She brushed it and divided it into three parts.

"I was to meet a young gentleman alone." Mary looked in the mirror at Georgiana and then the maid. She had never told anyone this before. It was her most shameful secret. She would hate to have the story spread to others – especially Lord Rycroft or Lady Sophia!

"Oh, Sarah is very discreet," Georgiana said. "She will not share what she hears."

"No, miss. What I hear stays with me, miss." She had very deftly plaited Mary's hair and was beginning to pin it up securely in loops.

"Very well. I shall trust you. I have never told anyone this." She gave Sarah a smile in the mirror. "It happened when I was fifteen and our neighbour's cousins came for the summer. They were both older than me.

"One cousin in particular – Roger – was of interest to me. He had just passed his eighteenth birthday. He was tall and had lovely blond hair that curled around his ears, at his neck, and on his forehead." She sighed. "He was so very handsome, and instead of paying any attention to my sisters Jane or Elizabeth, he chose to spend his time with me." It had been such a lovely thing to be noticed ahead of anyone else.

As Sarah pinned her hat in place, Mary turned so that she could see Georgiana. "I had never had the attention of such a gentleman before Roger." Nor had she had the attention of one since. "Roger was amiable and charming. He was all that I thought a young man should be, but he was not as he appeared." She stood and allowed Georgiana to take her turn at the mirror.

"He read me poems and said very pretty things, and soon I fancied myself in love with him. I was so convinced of my feelings that I agreed to meet him privately on a walk. He had often whispered his desire to hold my hand and to kiss me.

"I blush to say that his constant attentions, his small brushes of his hand against my arm or the tucking of a stray strand of hair behind my ear, had left me desiring his kisses. I slipped out of the house on the day we were to meet a few moments earlier than necessary. I have never been given to tardiness, and it is that habit which saved me. For as I approached the gate where we were to meet, I saw a bonnet duck behind a bush. I followed. He had been waiting for me with another. I saw them embracing. His hands were roaming over her back and..." Her cheeks coloured, and she dropped her eyes, "lower."

Georgiana's eyes grew wide with understanding. "How dreadful!"

Mary nodded. "I felt like the biggest fool ever for having fallen for such a man."

Georgiana stood with her hands on her hips. "But he was a deceiver! You could not have known."

Mary shook her head. "I should have known when he chose me over my sisters," she said quietly.

"Why?"

Mary smiled sadly at Georgiana. How did one explain one's lack of beauty?

"Oh, no!" Georgiana cried as understanding dawned in her expression. "No, no, no. Stand here." She pointed to a spot in front of the mirror. "I do not know what you looked like then, but look at yourself now. You are beautiful. Your cheeks are perfectly rosy. Your nose is small. Your eyes shine with your emotions, and your mouth is lovely — neither too thick nor too thin. And your figure..." Georgiana studied Mary for a moment. "Although you are not tall, your height is by no means deficient, and you have — oh, I do not know how to say it politely — you have softness in all the proper places. You will find many gentlemen to admire you this season, and one of them may possess that healing love of which you spoke."

Mary's cheeks were glowing quite rosy, and she had to blink against the tears that had formed in her eyes. "Thank you," she whispered. "I have never before heard myself described as anything so pleasant."

Georgiana wrapped her arms around Mary from behind. "You are everything that is pleasant. Is she not, Sarah?"

"That she is, Miss. Always polite and very pretty." She ducked her head a bit. "I should not say it, but I heard it mentioned by a footman or two that you were pretty. They did not say it in an improper way, mind you. It was merely a comment made in passing about your arrival."

Mary smiled at Sarah, who was looking uneasy about having shared so much. "Thank you. That is very nice to hear."

Sarah dipped a curtsey before turning to Georgiana. "Did you require anything else, Miss Darcy?"

Georgiana looked at her reflection in the mirror. "No. You have done an excellent job. I dare say we are both very well-turned-out." She took Mary by the arm. "Shall we go present ourselves to our escort and instructor?"

Mary took a last look in the mirror, turning just a bit to inspect her complete outfit. It did fit well, and the style Sarah had created for her hair gave a softness to her features that she quite enjoyed. She smiled at her reflection and nodded her head. She was ready.

Chapter 9

RYCROFT STOOD AT THE foot of the steps to Darcy House. The knocker was not on the door, just as he had suspected it would not be. However, that did not matter, for knocker or no knocker, he was going to seek admission. To that end, he mounted the steps and gave a good loud rap on the door. Taking a step backwards, he waited for a count of ten before stepping forward and rapping once again. Another count of ten passed, and again, he knocked. Finally, the door opened.

"Good day, Mr. Daniels, before you tell me that my cousin is not home to callers and close the door in my face — treatment that I know I well deserve since I have come to call so soon after his wedding — let me assure you that I would not have called if I were not in dire need of his assistance." He put up his hand to stop the butler from replying. "A paper and pen would suffice. If I could just leave a message?"

Darcy House's butler gave Rycroft a most disapproving look but stepped to the side. "Please wait here, my lord. Mr. Darcy is currently in a meeting. I shall see if he is willing to speak with you after he has finished."

Rycroft's eyebrows rose. "A meeting?" That was interesting.

"Yes," Daniels replied. "It seems you are not the only person to ignore propriety today."

Rycroft shifted from foot to foot as he waited for Daniels to return. He was not even sure why he was here. He just knew he needed to speak to someone about that riding lesson. He shook his head to clear the images of Mary in her borrowed riding habit from his mind. He did not remember Lady Serena ever looking so enticing when wearing that gown.

He had judged correctly that Lady Serena and Mary might be the same size, but... he swallowed... Mary's curves were apparently somewhat more voluptuous, and unfortunately, he was not the only gentleman to notice how lovely she looked.

He ran a hand through his hair. What was he going to do when Mary had a full wardrobe of gowns designed to show her off to best advantage? How was he to manage a full season of escorting the alluring Miss Bennet from soiree to soiree? Without calling out every gentleman who smiled at her? Today had been tormenting enough.

During their ride, they had been stopped by several of his acquaintances. Each gentleman had made a show of welcoming Rycroft back to town, but from the way their eyes wandered to Mary, he knew their real intent in approaching was not to see him but rather to gain an introduction to the beauty next to him.

Rycroft had been particularly put out when Brownlow and Blackmoore had joined them, for both Mary and Georgiana had found the company of Blackmoore to be to their liking. He had even seen Mary ducking her head and blushing for the fool! He smacked his hat on his leg. The anger that bubbled even now in his chest as he remembered the events in the park was most disconcerting. Blackmoore was a friend. So why had he wished – nay, not had wished – the desire had not left him. Why did he still wish to run the man off?

"The master will see you."

Rycroft followed Daniels to Darcy's study. He had not seen anyone leave the room. He smiled to himself. Perhaps the meeting had been with Mrs. Darcy?

He stepped into the room as Daniels announced him. Mrs. Darcy sat in one of the chairs in front of Darcy's desk while Bingley sat in the other.

"Bingley!" Rycroft crossed the room and shook Bingley's hand. "You said you would call when you returned to town. Should I expect you later?"

Bingley laughed. "You should."

Rycroft looked at the faces of each of the room's occupants. "It is not dire news that you bring, is it?"

"No, no. My news is of the best sort. Miss Bennet has agreed to marry me. I have written to my solicitor about the license and papers, and I am in town for a few days as I finalize things. Miss Bennet has come to stay with her aunt and uncle, so I am here to let Mrs. Darcy know about her sister's arrival and to invite her and her husband to join us for the wedding." Bingley's smile grew as he spoke. "How is Miss Mary?"

"Miss Mary?" Darcy parroted, looking first towards Bingley and then, Rycroft.

"She is well." Rycroft felt a bit of heat beginning to creep up his neck. It was an odd reaction. He had not blushed in years. "I have been compelled by my mother to assist Miss Mary and Georgiana with their dancing lessons."

"Mary is taking dancing lessons with Georgiana?" Elizabeth looked at Rycroft in confusion.

"Forgive me," he said. "My mother has arranged for Miss Mary to join her for the season. Your sister is to stay with us until the end of the week. Then, she will return to Longbourn for Christmas before coming back to Rycroft Place after the new year."

"And I suppose you are to escort them to all their soirees?" Darcy asked.

"I am, but it is not as if I would not be required to attend all the functions anyway," Rycroft said with a sigh. "My mother is intent upon finding me a bride this season, so I have no choice but to attend."

Bingley laughed as he stood. "I hope you are as successful as Darcy and I have been." He bowed to Elizabeth. "It has been a pleasure to see you, Mrs. Darcy."

"Thank you for letting me know that Jane is in town," Mrs. Darcy said. "When you see her, let her know I will see her before she returns to Hertfordshire."

"I most certainly will tell her. Darcy," Bingley said with a nod of parting.

As Bingley moved toward the door, Darcy shifted in his seat so that he was facing Rycroft.

"What can I do for you, Rycroft? I had not intended to spend the whole of my day in my study."

Rycroft nearly laughed as he saw Elizabeth, her cheeks glowing rosy, duck her head and smile.

"Yes, I am sorry to intrude," he apologized, "but I needed some advice."

"And it could not wait or be obtained from any other source?"

Rycroft shook his head. "I am afraid not."

"Very well," Darcy motioned to the chair Bingley had just vacated. "We will be in Hertfordshire the day before Christmas, Bingley," he called to Bingley before the man could close the study door.

Bingley gave a nod of his head. "Your rooms shall be waiting."

"Now, Rycroft, about your business..."

Rycroft cast an uneasy glance in Elizabeth's direction. "It is of a private nature," he said softly as that infernal blush deepened.

"I am not home to visitors because I am spending my day with my wife." Darcy smiled as he said the word *wife*, and for a fleeting moment, Rycroft felt a small jolt of envy, which surprised him nearly as much as his anger had earlier today.

"If you wish to speak to me," Darcy continued, "you must also speak to Mrs. Darcy."

Rycroft shifted uneasily in his chair. "It involves a lady." His ears were now burning so greatly that he wished to cover them with his hands to cool them.

"Very good." Darcy sat back in his chair with a look of enjoyment on his face. "My wife is a lady. She may be of assistance."

"I mean no disrespect, but I do not think so."

Darcy's brows rose, and his smile grew. He was most assuredly enjoying this. "Then, we have an impasse, for I shall not be parted from my wife today."

Rycroft blew out a breath. "Very well, if you insist."

He shifted again in his chair, trying to dispel some of the unease he felt. It was of no use. Nothing at present was going to make what he needed to discuss easier to broach.

"There is a lady of my acquaintance who seems to have a very peculiar and disturbing effect on me."

From the corner of his eye, he saw Elizabeth motion toward the door with her head, but Darcy shook his, and she remained seated.

"I find myself seeking out opportunities to be in her presence," Rycroft continued, "even when I know she is going to disagree with me or wishes for me to leave. And today, when we were out riding, I wanted to run off a friend because she seemed to favour his attentions. And," he swallowed and spoke softly, "her figure..." He raised his eyebrows but did not finish. There were limits to what he would admit in the presence of a lady – especially when that lady was the sister of the lady who was causing him so much distress.

"Why? Why do I feel as I do? What is wrong with me and how do I fix it?"

Darcy's smile had grown quite wide, and Rycroft had to be glad that Mrs. Darcy was present since it was likely only her presence that was keeping Darcy from teasing him as he suspected his cousin might do if they were alone.

"What if someone were to threaten this lady of yours?" Darcy asked and then chuckled. "You do not need to tell me. I can tell by your look of horror that you would do whatever you needed to protect her. Am I correct?"

Rycroft nodded. "What do I do?"

Darcy looked at Elizabeth. "You marry her."

Chapter 10

RYCROFT WAS SURE HIS heart had stopped beating at his cousin's statement. Perhaps Mrs. Darcy's presence was not enough to keep Darcy from teasing him. "Marry her?" Surely, Darcy was teasing.

"It sounds to me as if you are in love with this lady, and I find myself a great proponent of matrimony these days."

Rycroft had risen and was pacing the room. How could he sit still with such shocking thoughts being hurled at him? "In love?"

How could he be in love with Mary? He had not even thought to think about her as someone he could love. A gentleman did not fall in love in such an unsuspecting fashion, did he? Surely not!

"Yes, Cousin, in love. It is not such a horrible place to be."

Maybe it was not to someone who wished to be there. Rycroft shook his head. "No, I have simply been out of town for too long." That was all it was.

Darcy laughed. "There were no ladies in the country?"

Rycroft shot him a look of displeasure. "None to my liking. Very grasping."

"Ah, so very unlike the ladies of the ton."

Rycroft did not miss the note of sarcasm in Darcy's voice. "I cannot marry her."

"And why is that? Is she of inferior standing?"

Rycroft rolled his eyes. "She is not titled, but she is a gentleman's daughter – not that standing is of great importance to me, as you well know. Indeed, she would make a fine countess."

"Is she married?"

"No."

"Betrothed?"

"No."

"Has she been so tainted by scandal that your standing would suffer?"

"No."

"Then, I really do not see a reason why you cannot marry her," Darcy said.

Rycroft huffed and folded his arms across his chest. "I cannot marry her because she does not like me."

Elizabeth laughed. "May I suggest that you employ the use of a library at a ball and a loud aunt who loves to gossip? Then, your lady shall have to marry you whether she likes you or not."

Rycroft looked at Elizabeth in horror. Trap Mary? He shook his head.

"I jest at my husband's expense, my lord," Elizabeth explained. "He has told you of our betrothal, has he not?"

Rycroft nodded. There had been some scandal about missing slippers and reading alone in a library, but the pair before him were obviously smitten with one another. "But you like him."

"Yes, now, I do, but at that time, I thought I did not like him." She rose and walked behind the desk to stand at Darcy's side. "Fortunately, my opinion of him has improved."

Darcy put an arm around her and pulled her close to him. "Yes, fortunately," he muttered. "Perhaps if Elizabeth met her —"

"No!"

The word was said so quickly and with so much force that it startled both Darcy and Elizabeth.

"Not that there is anything wrong with Mrs. Darcy, of course." Rycroft moved toward the door. "I am not ... it would not be ... I cannot," he stammered and shook his head.

He stopped with his hand on the door handle. "I shall let you return to your day. I do apologize once again for the inconvenience."

The door was nearly closed when he popped his head back into the room. "Thank you."

He pulled the door closed and stood in front of it for a moment. He likely wore an expression that was just as perplexed as both Darcys had worn at his stumbling and hasty exit, but who could blame him for being so out of sorts? Love and marriage, as it pertained to himself, had been nowhere near his mind when he had entered, and now that both words had been thrust at him in relation to Mary, he was not sure what to do with himself.

"My lord," Daniels said with a bow as he opened the door for Rycroft.

Rycroft placed his hat on his head and drew in a deep breath, filling his lungs with the crisp December air. Hopefully, the coolness of the day and exercise of riding home would give him time to turn himself right way around.

Two hours later, freshly dressed and having had a small beverage to fortify his still topsy-turvy emotions, Rycroft stood outside the door to the sitting room at his home, ready to escort his mother, his cousin, and Miss Mary to the museum. Or, at least, he felt as if he was ready until he heard what sounded to be Blackmoore's voice coming from inside the sitting room.

Rycroft stood for a moment, listening to the conversation. Perhaps it was at an end, and Blackmoore would be leaving. His brows rose as he heard Blackmoore mention a desire to visit the museum with the ladies.

"Samuel is to escort us," Lady Sophia said, "but he might enjoy your company."

No, Samuel would not enjoy Blackmoore's company. However, it seemed that at least a few minutes of it could not be avoided. Therefore, Rycroft straightened the sleeves of his jacket, took a deep breath, and entered the room. "Whose company might I enjoy, Mother?" He bent to kiss her cheek.

"Blackmoore's." His mother watched him carefully as if she expected him to object.

He would not. No matter how much he wanted to do just that. Carefully, he schooled his face to remain expressionless. His mother smiled as if she saw something he did not want to be seen. She was crafty like that. Always had been.

"Mr. Blackmoore expressed an interest in attending the museum with us," she said, "and I thought, since your cousin and Miss Bennet will be drawing, you might find it less tiring to wait for us if you had a companion. The two of you could get lost in the exhibits for an hour or so while Mary and Georgiana draw, and then afterwards, you could show us some of the exhibits you found particularly interesting."

"An excellent idea, Mother." That was a lie. An excellent idea would be for Blackmoore to leave town and not return for the remainder of the season. But it would not do to say that, now, would it? Rycroft smiled. "What say you, Blackmoore? Care to traipse about the museum with me? Or shall we bring our drawing pads and join the ladies?"

Blackmoore laughed. "And have my drawings stand beside yours? I think not."

"You draw?" Miss Mary's voice held not a little surprise, and her question drew his attention and meant that he could no longer, politely, avoid looking at her.

The dress she currently wore was not as fetching as that riding habit had been, yet still, she was alluring, and what had been seen this morning could not be unseen. It seemed that this morning's ride, coupled with Darcy's advice, were determined to colour everything about Miss Mary today.

Her brow furrowed. Right! She had asked if he drew.

"I draw some. Mostly diagrams, maps, and those sorts of things."

"No sculptures or nature?"

"I am afraid not any longer." He gave her a sad smile. Sketching was a pastime he had enjoyed as a young man.

"I would be very sad to have to give up drawing things of beauty," Georgiana said.

Rycroft cocked his head to the side and gave his cousin a lopsided grin. "Are you saying that a diagram cannot be a thing of beauty?"

"That is not what I meant," Georgiana protested. "I meant I would hate to give up drawing objects whose very purpose is to be beautiful."

"Such as a flower?" He raised an eyebrow.

"Yes. No." Georgiana huffed. "I know what you will do. You will tell me that although a flower is a thing of beauty, it may also have a purpose such as to produce fruit and, therefore, food." She turned to Miss Mary. "It is what he constantly does to me. He twists my words. He says he does it to make me consider them more carefully."

Mary's left brow rose most enchantingly, or so Rycroft thought. "I would have to agree that to consider one's words is a most important skill."

He held her gaze for a moment. He knew what she implied with her agreement. "Only an oaf would not," he said with a tip of his head in acknowledgment that he knew the true meaning of her words.

"Or a partial one," she added with a smile.

"Very true." He could not help the smile that he wore. Indeed, he wished to chuckle, but instead, he made a sweeping motion toward the door and said, "Shall we?" He only grimaced slightly when Blackmoore offered his arm to Mary.

"I trust your ride was refreshing," his mother said as she took his arm.

His eyes shifted from where they were watching Mary and Blackmoore to his mother. Her eyes were dancing as if she knew that he was displeased with Mary being on Blackmoore's arm.

"Yes, most refreshing." He said the words she expected to hear, but in truth, he was anything but refreshed. His ride, which had included that visit to Darcy, had left him with more perplexing things to ponder than it had relieved.

However, he had come to a determination on his ride. He would fulfill his duties as an escort for his mother and her charges, but, when he was not needed, he simply would bury himself in his work for the next three days until Mary had left. Then, he would take his ease until she returned.

He hoped that when she left, his unruly mind would finally be able to set itself to right. It was merely the presence of an attractive female in his home which had him at sixes and sevens. Surely it was nothing more. With the return of Mary and the beginning of the season with its numerous debutantes and other hopefuls, he would find his attentions drawn to various ladies, and this feeling of one's entire existence being dependent on the acceptance of one lady would be just an unsettling memory.

He averted his eyes from Mary once again as Blackmoore handed her into the carriage. He dared not watch, for the overwhelming urge to remove the man from her presence was once again growing, as it had earlier, during their ride.

Three days. Just three days, he reminded himself. In three days, Mary would be safely away from Blackmoore's attentions, and Rycroft's own heart would be safely returned to the calm state of being securely under his regulation once again.

Chapter 11

MARY TIPPED HER HEAD and studied the statue before beginning the work of completing the fine details of her drawing. The museum was wonderful. She had never seen so many interesting things all in one place before, and if the exhibits were not fascinating enough, there were always people, dressed in the latest fashions, to watch. She glanced at her drawing and then back to the statue before adding a few lines of detail she had missed.

"Mr. Blackmoore is very handsome," Georgiana, who was seated next to her, whispered. "And I do believe he has taken a fancy to you." There was a great deal of excitement in her voice. It was a sentiment Mary shared. It was a delightful feeling to be preferred by a gentleman.

"I would not be disappointed if you were correct." She began shading her drawing, giving it depth. "He is handsome and seems polite, but I know very little about his character." She held her pencil still and looked at Georgiana. "And, as I have learned, a gentleman's character is of far greater importance than his pleasant features and flattering words." She sighed. "It is not impossible for the two to coexist, for I believe they do in both your brother and Mr. Bingley, but I admit to remaining wary when it is my heart which is in danger of being hurt again."

"I cannot fault you for being cautious," Georgiana said. "I think it is actually very wise to not rush forward. You must not risk a second injury. That being said, Mr. Blackmoore is my cousin's friend. Surely there is something to be said in his favour because of that. And he is truly a friend and not just a former one like..." She looked right and left before whispering, "like Mr. Wickham was."

Mary considered that for a moment while she drew. She was not certain that a fact such as being friends with Lord Rycroft was a mark in favour of Mr. Blackmoore's character.

"I do not wish to offend," she finally said when Georgiana had looked up at Mary from her work for a third time, "for I know Lord Rycroft is a beloved cousin, but it is my understanding that before he journeyed to the country, he was considered..." She paused and looked around the room quickly as Georgiana had done a moment ago. "Somewhat of a rake," she whispered. Her cheeks flushed slightly at having spoken such a thing. "He has proclaimed he is not the same man, and I believe him, but does that not cause you to wonder about his friends?"

Georgiana laid her pencil down. "I had not thought about that, but surely one man is not guilty of all his friends have done just because he is their friend, is he?"

"I believe a person must be careful not to condemn another based only on supposition, but I also believe a person must be prudent about whom they associate with, since not all are so judicious in their casting of condemnation." She sighed deeply. Discerning good character from poor character while not becoming shrewish or lackadaisical about accepting new friends, confidants, or possible suitors was no simple task.

"*By their fruits you will know them*. That is what the Good Book says." And it was the principle she had taken to heart and attempted to put into practice ever since she had been deceived those years ago. "We must watch a gentleman's actions and deeds," she continued. "How does he treat his mother, his sister, a friend, or even his servants and animals? If he is harsh with them, you can know he will also be harsh with you. If he is too liberal with them, he may also be too liberal with his finances and the direction of his children, both of which could lead to ruin."

Lord Rycroft was none of those things. He treated others well – except when he was speaking without thinking or attempting to provoke her purposefully. Even then, he did not do it without conscience.

"In addition to that, one must consider whose interests does the gentleman you are considering place first? Are they always his own?" She did not know that about Lord Rycroft yet, but she did see how he bent his will to that of others at times. "If they are, he will also place them before your interests and needs. There really is so much to consider when accepting the attentions of a gentleman. It is quite daunting, but our lives and happiness depend upon careful consideration of all things."

She smiled at Georgiana, who, Mary had to admit, was looking overwhelmed by the gravity of what was involved in finding a good match. "I do apologize. I am given to moralizing. It is something about which my sisters have often chided me."

Georgiana shook her head. "I do not see anything wrong with your instruction. Indeed, I am thankful for it. Even if there is a lot of it."

Mary laughed. "You are only thankful because you have not been subjected to my admonishments as frequently as my sisters have. However, I am attempting to learn to lecture only when necessary, but I do find it hard not to state my opinion when provoked."

Lady Sophia, who, along with Mrs. Annesley, had joined them, chuckled. "I would venture to guess that such is the struggle of all intelligent females. What are we discussing?"

"The many things which need to be considered when accepting the attentions of a gentleman," Georgiana answered.

"Indeed?" Lady Sophia's brows rose in surprise. "I had not thought you would be discussing something so serious, but I am happy for it. May I ask what is on your list of considerations?"

"Character demonstrated through actions." Georgiana beamed like a pupil who had been called upon and knew the correct answer, causing Mary to chuckle softly to herself. None of her sisters had ever looked so happy about one of her lectures on propriety.

"Again, I am impressed with the serious nature of your discussion." And Lady Sophia looked it as she favoured Mary with a pleased look. "Are you not also delighted?" she asked Georgiana's companion.

"Most certainly, my lady. I am sorry to have missed the discussion."

"Mrs. Annesley and I have been admiring the exhibits," Lady Sophia said. "There is a fine collection of jewelry that might be of interest when you have completed your drawings, and we will not keep you from completing your task. We only wished to check your progress and share our hope of viewing the jewelry with you." The pair of older ladies left the younger ones.

While Mrs. Annesley and Lady Sophia took another turn around the room, Mary and Georgiana continued their work. However, they had only been working for a short period of time when they were once again interrupted.

"Oh, Miss Darcy! It is a pleasure to see you." Caroline Bingley, followed by two other ladies, stopped in front of where Georgiana and Mary were drawing.

"Miss Bingley." Georgiana's tone was polite but not overly warm. "I did not know you were in town."

Miss Bingley waved the comment away. "My brother had some business, and I just could not bear to spend even a few days alone in the country."

"Were your sister and her husband not there?" Georgiana asked in surprise.

"Yes, yes, Louisa and Hurst actually chose to remain in the country, although I do not know why." She glanced at Mary, giving her a brief nod of acknowledgment, and then turned back to

Georgiana. "I missed my friends ever so much. There is so very little to do in the country."

"I look forward each year to when I can return to the country," Georgiana said. "Indeed, I prefer it to town. Solitude pleases me."

"Oh, to be sure, seclusion in such a place as Pemberley must be refreshing, but Netherfield and the surrounding area are so unrefined."

"I did not find it to be so." Georgiana gathered her things and rose. "Miss Mary and I were about to take a stroll around the exhibits."

"As were we," one of Miss Bingley's friends said. "What fun it would be to view them together."

"Such a large group?" asked the other of Miss Bingley's friends.

"Yes," said the first lady, giving her friend a nudge with her elbow.

"You know that does sound rather pleasant," the second lady agreed.

Mary fought the urge to roll her eyes.

"Do forgive me, Miss Darcy," Miss Bingley said. "These are my friends, Miss Ivison and Miss Pearce." She turned to her friends. "I am sure you likely feel as if you know Miss Darcy since I have spoken of her so often." Miss Bingley gave Mary a look that said she found Mary's company not to her liking. "And this is Miss Bennet."

Both Miss Bingley's friends gave Mary an assessing look and then turned away from her. The rude creatures!

"Is your brother in town for long, Miss Bingley?" Mary asked.

"Unfortunately, he is only here for three days. He has some documents to gather from his solicitor," she added the last part with a wave of her hand as if whatever her brother needed to do was of little importance. "Why his papers could not wait until after the new year, I do not know."

"But if he had waited, would that not mean you would have missed this opportunity to visit with your friends?" Mary linked arms with Georgiana.

Miss Bingley did not answer, but she slipped her arm through Georgiana's other arm. "Miss Darcy, when you have your come out, you will then understand more fully the attractions of town. The balls and soirees are so diverting. It is fortunate that Hurst and Louisa insist upon returning for the season. I would simply perish if I were forced to spend the season in the country."

"Yes, we understand you have an aversion to the country," Mary muttered.

"You would not know the pleasures of a season in town, Miss Mary." Miss Bingley's tone was cool. "If it were not for the charity of your sister's new relations, I dare say you would never have had the pleasure."

Mary felt the sting of the comment. "I am grateful for the invitation to join Lady Sophia for the season. Whether it proves a pleasure or not remains to be seen. What one person deems enjoyment may not be to another's liking, and as you have already mentioned, I have not experienced a season in town, so I can neither agree nor disagree with your assessment of its pleasures." Mary gave Georgiana's arm a squeeze and whispered her desire to admire a particular statue as she removed her arm and walked away from the group.

"A season will be of little pleasure for one of her standing," Miss Ivison whispered rather loudly to Miss Pearce, who tittered in response. "I wonder if she likes libraries as much as her sister?"

Chapter 12

MARY BLINKED AGAINST THE tears that gathered in her eyes as she moved away from Georgiana and toward the statue she had feigned a desire to see. If these were the sorts of ladies with whom she would have to contend in town and an example of what was going to be said about her and her sister, she was certain that her season would be anything but a pleasure.

"Are you well?" Lord Rycroft asked as he came to stand beside her.

She glanced at him and then looked around. It was just the two of them standing in front of this statue that Mary cared not one whit about seeing.

"Blackmoore is not far behind me," Lord Rycroft said. "He stopped to speak with some acquaintances. I promise you I did not abandon him."

She looked at him in surprise.

"I thought I should tell you that so you would not feel the need to instruct me on my duty to a friend."

Mary opened her mouth to retort but closed it again as she saw the lopsided grin he wore.

"Forgive me. I had hoped to take your mind off whatever or whoever has upset you. Perhaps my choice of topic was not the best, but what can one expect from an oaf?" He offered her his arm.

"Partial oaf, my lord." She placed her hand on his arm. "And I am well." She sighed. She must learn to deal more effectively with ladies such as Miss Bingley and her friends. Was there a master for such lessons as there was for dancing, drawing, and singing?

"If you wish for a lie to be convincing, you may wish to refrain from sighing next time," Lord Rycroft said softly. "Those three are not worth the discomposure, I assure you."

She glanced up at him. He most certainly was a caring sort of gentleman and not the sort she had cautioned Georgiana against. She could lay her concern in front of him, could she not?

"They are low-quality ladies," he added. "All three of them."

She decided to trust him. "But how does one bear their barbs with composure?" As she said it, the answer came to her, and she shook her head at her own lack of thought, for it was an obvious answer. "There is no need for you to answer. I know how."

"You do? So quickly and without my assistance?"

She nodded. "I will simply pretend they are my mother or my aunt or my younger sister. I have endured their comments for years. I shall smile and attempt to ignore them."

"Your mother and sister? They have been unkind to you?" His voice was suffused with incredulity.

"Surely you noticed their treatment of me."

His brow furrowed, and he was silent for a moment. Apparently, he was thinking back on his time in Hertfordshire.

"I suppose I did," he finally said. "Are they like that all the time – demanding you do things and pushing your ideas to the side?"

She nodded. "Please, do not misunderstand me. I love them, but they do not think before they speak."

"And they ignore you."

She laughed. "When I am so fortunate."

"Still," he said softly, "I am sorry you have been treated so." It was the same tone he had used in the music room that day when he had apologized. It was a tone that made her feel as if he shared her pain and wished to take it away as his own.

"Thank you." She smiled at him, and he responded with one of his own.

"Did you complete your drawing?" he asked.

She shook her head. "No. Miss Bingley arrived."

"Do you wish to finish it? I can sit with you." His smile held a bit of something wicked in it. "That would certainly make Miss Bingley and her squawking friends displeased."

Mary chuckled. "While it might be enjoyable to vex her, it might provoke her more than displease her."

"Very well, then, we shall continue our tour and try not to provoke the ire of Miss Bingley or her friends."

It proved impossible, however, to accomplish such a feat. Miss Bingley, as well as Miss Ivison and Miss Pearce, conveyed very well through their mannerisms and slighting comments just what they thought of Mary, and it was not difficult to read the displeasure in their eyes when both Lord Rycroft and Mr. Blackmoore paid greater attention to Mary than to any of them.

Therefore, when it was time to leave and after they had said their goodbyes to Mr. Blackmoore, Mary sank with relief onto the carriage seat.

"It becomes easier," Lady Sophia said gently. "Not all women in the ton are so small-minded as those three."

"How do they ever expect to get husbands?" Georgiana asked in surprise.

Lord Rycroft laughed. "They are not painful to look upon, and they do each have a fortune. There are men who require little else."

"If I were a man," Georgiana said in indignation, "I am certain there would not be a fortune large enough nor a figure fine enough to tempt into marriage with a woman like that!"

Lord Rycroft smirked. "If you were a man in need of fortune and an heir, you might indeed find yourself tempted." He put up a hand to stop her from retorting. "However, I agree. They offer nothing that would induce me to consider them either."

Georgiana crossed her arms and gave him a hard look. "And your friends? Do they agree with your way of thinking?"

Lord Rycroft's eyes darted toward Mary. "I assume you are inquiring after Blackmoore."

Mary's cheeks grew warm.

"I cannot speak for the motivations of my friends – not even Blackmoore – but I have never heard them mention any of those ladies in a favourable light. As far as I know, none of my friends needs a fortune, though all will need an heir, and a few need to make a connection that will be acceptable to their fathers."

"Acceptable in what way?" Georgiana asked.

"That depends on the father, and it is not my place to say."

"If you cannot say, then how am I to know what a man finds acceptable in a woman?" Georgiana asked. "How does a lady secure a worthy husband if she does not know what men, such as your friends, find acceptable? Your friends are honourable, are they not?"

"As honourable as any man of failings can be." Rycroft shifted uncomfortably in his seat. "I cannot speak to what all men want in a wife, for each man is as unique as each woman."

"Then, tell me what you will be looking for in a wife," Georgiana persisted.

"Yes," Lady Sophia agreed eagerly, "I would like to know what you consider necessary so that I can help you find such a wife."

Mary had to admit that she was also eager to hear Lord Rycroft's thoughts.

He, however, did not seem eager to share them, for he groaned and rubbed his brow. "It is not an easy thing to put in a list."

"Try," his mother said.

Lord Rycroft scowled, but despite his obvious desire to do anything but what his mother asked, he obliged her, as he often did.

"Very well," he said, "but I warn you it will sound trite."

"We will not judge you," his mother assured him.

To Mary, it did not look like Lord Rycroft believed that. Still, he proceeded.

"I wish for a companion. That is all. I wish for a lady who is more than a lover and the mother of my children. I want someone who understands me and can converse with me. She should be someone who shares my beliefs and opinions and is not afraid to challenge me when we disagree. However, she must do so with grace and kindness."

There was nothing trite about such a lovely desire in Mary's mind. It was similar to what she wanted in a gentleman. Oh, how delightful it would be to have someone who loved her and understood her!

"What about her features?" Georgiana asked.

Lord Rycroft ran a finger around his cravat and looked excessively uneasy. "I think that is likely inappropriate to discuss."

"I find it perfectly acceptable in a lesson situation such as this. Do you not agree, Mrs. Annesley?" Lady Sophia said.

"Indeed."

Lord Rycroft darted a look toward Mary.

Did he want to know if she approved? Did she? She shrugged. She was curious about his answer, but she was not going to press him to give it.

He blew out a breath. "I would, of course, wish for a wife who is fair of face – pretty, if not beautiful. But truly, as much as this sounds like an answer given to placate, it is the character of the lady which shines through her words and actions that is most attractive. Be that as it may, I do not wish to marry someone who is old and fat with warts and poor hygiene." He smiled. "Whatever other physical attributes I prefer, I shall not disclose." Again, his eyes nervously darted toward Mary.

Did he truly care what she thought of his reply? It was, as his other had been, perfect. Simply, utterly perfect. Some lady would be very fortunate to have him for a husband someday. She smiled her warmest smile at him, hoping he would understand that she was more than pleased with his answers and be put at ease. Oddly, however, her smile seemed to have exactly the opposite effect.

Chapter 13

FOR THE NEXT THREE days, Rycroft attempted to keep to his study, but although his mind told him to focus on his business and to avoid his mother and her charge, his feet refused to obey. More often than not, he found himself sitting in the music room, listening to Mary play, or in the sitting room, reading a book and chuckling softly at her grumbles while she worked on some stitch that was trying her patience.

On top of the times when he seemed unable to keep himself away from Miss Mary, there were also the required dance practices and two more rides in the park to improve her riding abilities which had thrust him into her presence.

Overall, however, it had been a most enjoyable three days. It was only the constant twisting of his heart and his ever-present growing dislike for Blackmoore, who had come to call at Rycroft Place on each and every one of those days, that coloured the past three days with anything disagreeable.

Today, it was Bingley who had brought unpleasantness into Rycroft's life, for at present, Bingley stood at the door to Rycroft Place, instructing how Miss Mary's things were to be transported. This was the day to which Rycroft had been looking, the day on which his thoughts were supposed to start righting themselves. However, they were doing anything but ordering themselves. Indeed, they were a jumbled mess, to put it none too gently.

Rycroft stood to Bingley's side, watching the proceedings at the carriage, and listening to the conversation in the sitting room across the hall where Kitty was telling Georgiana about the gowns Jane had ordered and the new one that she had been allowed to have made. He knew that Mary's order of dresses would be arriving soon and that the two that had arrived yesterday were safely packed into her trunk, for Georgiana had insisted that they be taken to Meryton and worn. Oddly, he was unhappy about that, for he wanted for some incomprehensible reason to be among the first to see her in the designs he had selected.

"I think everything is secured," Bingley said, pulling Rycroft's attention away from wondering how lovely Miss Mary would look in the new gowns and back to what was happening.

"We are set to start our journey," Bingley added.

The unsettled feeling that had begun this morning when Rycroft saw Mary's trunk waiting near the door began to grow, and he thought for a moment he might cast up his accounts. It was just another of the baffling things he had endured in the past week. Taking Bingley by the arm, he led him down the hall a short distance.

"Your sister," he began.

Bingley smiled broadly. "Would you like to offer for her?"

"No," he said quickly and with a great deal of force to emphasize his dislike of Miss Bingley.

Bingley chuckled, but then sobered. "Then, is it her behaviour that has caused an issue?"

"Not today," Rycroft replied, "but the other day at the museum, she and her friends were quite unpleasant to Miss Mary."

Bingley sighed. "If you are worried that it will continue, I can assure you it will, for it does not matter what punishments I put in place. Caroline will do what she wishes to do."

Rycroft just barely refrained from shifting uneasily. "I understand you cannot control her actions, but they caused Miss Mary to be distraught, and if you could perhaps just..." he paused and dropped his gaze to the floor "...perhaps just make sure she is not made too uncomfortable during your journey?"

"Miss Mary?" There was no mistaking the surprise in Bingley's voice, and Rycroft could not blame him for it. The unshakeable need to make the request was just another one of the strange things swirling around in the vicinity of Rycroft's heart which could not be explained.

However, he did feel like he owed Bingley some sort of explanation. Therefore, he put into words the reason he was attempting to make himself believe. Not that he was going an exemplary job of believing it. "She is a friend, and I am concerned for her. It is nothing more."

"Of course." Bingley's smile and tone let Rycroft know that he was not convinced that Miss Mary's being a friend was the reason. "She will have her sisters, as well as mine. All will be well."

"Right. I should have thought of that." Truthfully, he *had* thought of that, but the information did nothing to relieve his growing unease. Despite his ever-increasing disquiet, he let the matter drop as he followed Bingley into the sitting room and made what he hoped was a good show of being delighted to have his home just a little less filled with ladies.

"Thank you," Miss Mary said as she left the room. "You have been a very patient and gracious host."

He smiled. "Mostly. I did have a rough start."

"But you have improved."

Her commendation brought a genuine smile to his face. "Do you not fear that I will fall back into my oafish ways without your influence?"

She laughed and assured him that she would return soon to correct any habits that insisted upon returning. She would soon return. There was unexpected comfort in those words.

He took her hand and tucked it into the crook of his arm to escort her to the carriage. It was only after they had reached the door and began to descend to the street that he remembered to remove his hand from covering hers, and then, he had wished he had not remembered.

Soon, all too soon, she was safely ensconced inside Bingley's carriage between her sisters, and the door was closed, separating her from him. He stood on the walkway for a good five minutes after the carriage had pulled away from the house. Then, giving himself a bit of a shake, he asked for his horse to be readied. He needed a ride, for he most certainly could not go back into his house where she would not be, but her memory would be. That would definitely not help him turn his mind right side up.

As expected, after an hour of riding, he was beginning to feel more steady. That did not mean, however, that he was ready to go home, for he feared he was not so well rid of his topsy-turvy existence as to face memories of and conversations about Miss Mary. So, he sought out one of his clubs. A drink, a game, and some time in discussion with acquaintances seemed a good diversion.

"Rycroft," a gentleman in a fine blue jacket called to him as he entered the inner sanctum of his club. "We've not seen you in an age. Come back for another go at the marriage mart?" The man's golden curls bounced as he laughed. "I dare say you'll not have an easy go of it. The mamas will be wary of you."

"Endicott." Rycroft clapped the man on the shoulder before taking a seat across from him. "I am still an earl. There will be many who will turn a blind eye to many things if it means their daughter could become a countess." He thanked the server and took a long draw of his ale. "Not that I wish to be ensnared by a fortune hunter."

Endicott laughed again. "Not many do. However, if they are of the upstanding variety, Blackmoore is looking. Heard he has been courting some chit from the country who is in town for the season and staying with someone." He drummed his fingers on the table. "Never been good with names," he muttered.

Rycroft took another long draw from his tankard. "I believe the name for which you are searching is Lady Sophia Rycroft."

Endicott snapped his fingers. "That's it precisely. Well, then I guess I do not need to tell you about it." He leaned towards Rycroft. "Blackmoore says she is rather pretty. On the opposite side of tall but with a pleasing womanly figure." He winked at Rycroft.

Rycroft took one breath and then another as he reminded himself that it was not Endicott, but Blackmoore, who had been looking at Mary's figure. He knew that such a description was only the beginning of what Blackmoore would have said because Blackmoore was not one for speaking with decorum when amongst his friends. It was something which had not bothered Rycroft until this moment.

He placed his mug on the table and turned the handle a quarter turn towards himself. There was no reason for the action other than to keep his hands occupied. "He is not wrong."

"And she is staying with you?"

"With my mother and my cousin, Darcy's sister."

"Ah, heard Darcy got married." It was obvious that the beverage which Endicott was now enjoying was not his first.

"He did. It is his wife's sister who is staying with my mother."

Endicott's brows rose, and he pursed his lips as he nodded his head. "Makes sense then."

"What makes sense?" Rycroft felt a strange foreboding. He was almost certain that what he was about to hear was not something he wished to know, but rather something he needed to know. He waved to the server and motioned to his mug. Another drink might be needed.

"Blackmoore has been blubbering these past three months about his inheritance being held for ransom. His father fears he will run the estate into the ground with his entertainments."

Rycroft's brows rose. "Entertainments?"

"Shortly after the whole incident with Brownlow that sent you running, Blackmoore took up with an actress who fancies herself an excellent faro player, which she is not."

"I was not running from Brownlow. I was travelling with a friend."

Endicott laughed. "Of course, and the friend just happened to be a very pretty young woman."

"She needed a ride. Ask Brownlow. Things were not as they were reported. Surely, you know how facts get manipulated to create a story." Rycroft finished his first drink. Endicott was a pleasant fellow, but he was not in possession of a quick wit when not drinking. When drink was involved, his ability to reason decreased even further.

"Yes, yes, Brownlow said he was not calling you out and that you had done him a favour by leaving." He motioned to the server, but Rycroft pulled his hand down and called for tea.

"You are foxed, my friend," he said as Endicott began to complain. "Now, you were saying about Blackmoore?"

Chapter 14

A TRAY WITH A pot of tea, two cups, a few biscuits, and all the accompanying necessities, such as milk, arrived quickly, and Rycroft poured a cup of tea for his inebriated friend. Then, he sat back with his tankard of ale and looked at Endicott. The man's brow furrowed as he lowered his cup to the table. Yes, the man had most certainly had more than a wise allotment of libation.

"Blackmoore," Rycroft prompted.

"Ah, yes, Blackmoore. That was it." Endicott took another sip of his tea. "Blackmoore claims he loves this actress and wishes to marry her. His father is not in favour of such a union."

"Understandably. Draining the family coffers is not something a father should condone. Both the subsequent lowering of financial standing and the union with someone from a lower level of society would be a blight on the family reputation that would be hard to overcome, and Blackmoore has a younger sister who will be coming out this year."

Endicott nodded and attempted to put his finger on his nose, but it landed on his cheek. "Just so. Which is why his father had his will redrawn and threatened to cut Blackmoore off completely unless he marries a lady who meets his father's approval. And a connection to Darcy would be extremely acceptable to Blackmoore's father."

The sense of foreboding had grown to one of dread. "Are you telling me then that Blackmoore cares nothing for the lady he is courting?"

Rycroft could hear the disgust in Endicott's laugh. It was answer enough, but Rycroft waited to hear what else might be revealed.

"She is a means to an end," Endicott said. "If Blackmoore can secure her, he will have his father's money, a pretty chit to bear him an heir, and a mistress to occupy him when his wife is unavailable." He gave an angry huff. "The love of a woman can turn a man. I would have never expected such from him." He lapsed into a thoughtful silence as he sipped his tea and ate the biscuits Rycroft had ordered for him.

Rycroft also drank in silence, pondering what he should do. He knew what he wanted to do. However, running Blackmoore through was likely not the best option.

"Have you seen Brownlow today?" He needed to ask Brownlow about these facts. It was not that he did not believe Endicott. No, he was certain that what Endicott had related was true. What he needed to know was if Brownlow also knew about Blackmoore's scheme and if Brownlow would stand with him when he confronted Blackmoore about it.

Endicott shook his head. "No. Just you and Beaumont."

Rycroft drained his mug. "I had hoped to see him here, but it seems I will have to go in search of him."

Endicott waved him away. "Go. I will find my way out of here soon.

Rycroft stepped into the deepening shadows of a December afternoon. He mounted his horse and pulled his jacket a bit tighter as he made his way toward Brownlow's townhome. However, as he rode past Darcy House and saw the knocker on Darcy's door, he altered his plans.

"If you will wait here," Daniels said, showing Rycroft into the sitting room.

Rycroft took a seat in a chair with a high back and allowed his head to drop back against it. He rubbed his face and then covered his eyes with his hands. It was not late, but he suddenly felt very tired. He was more weary than he could ever remember feeling. His promise to Bingley to keep Mary safe from schemers kept repeating itself in his mind. Not only had he not succeeded, but he had also been the one to introduce the man to her. He sighed deeply. Blackmoore had been a good friend, and, although rather rakish, he had never before dallied with any proper lady's emotions.

"Are you well?" Elizabeth's question startled him.

He removed his hands from his eyes and rose to greet her. "A bit tired is all."

Elizabeth gave him a concerned look. "I find the shortness of the days at this time of year affects me, as does the desire to curl up before a warm fire on a cool day." She took a seat. "My husband will not be long."

"Do you travel to Hertfordshire on the morrow?"

Elizabeth smiled. "We do. I admit to being anxious to see my father."

He looked out the window. "Bingley left today."

"Yes," Elizabeth said. "I had a visit from Jane this morning. It was unfortunate that their departure was delayed so that they will have to travel in the darker part of the day. However, one cannot get married by special license without a license, so it could not be prevented."

"Bingley mentioned the delay when he arrived to collect Miss Mary." Rycroft lapsed into silence.

Upon entering the room, Darcy gave Elizabeth's cheek a kiss and cast a wary look at Rycroft, who was still staring out the window. "Is he well?" he whispered.

Elizabeth shook her head. "He says he is merely tired, but I fear it is more."

Rycroft pretended not to hear. Mrs. Darcy was perceptive.

"Rycroft," Darcy said.

Rycroft rose and clasped Darcy's outstretched hand.

"Do you wish to speak here or in my study?"

Rycroft looked at Darcy and then Elizabeth and shook his head. "You both should know." He returned to his seat. "Mr. Blackmoore has been calling on Miss Mary this past week."

"Is he an eligible gentleman?" Elizabeth asked.

"So he appears." Rycroft attempted to keep the bitterness he felt out of his voice, but he was unsuccessful. He swallowed and held Darcy's gaze. "I have just, moments ago, learned something about him that has left me at odds with myself. He has always been a friend, tried and true, and, despite his eager pursuit of pleasure, he has been honourable. I thought nothing of his attentions to Miss Mary. I did not doubt his intentions until now."

Darcy leaned forward. "What has happened?"

"Nothing yet." Rycroft shook his head. "But his intentions are not honourable."

"How do you know this?" Darcy asked.

"While at my club just now, Endicott related to me how Blackmoore took up with an actress shortly after my departure from town. It is not a connection his father wishes to see move forward and, accordingly, strictures have been placed upon Blackmoore's inheritance." He drew a deep breath and expelled it. "He must marry someone who is acceptable to his father, and who could be more acceptable than a gentleman's daughter who has connections to you?" Again, he shook his head. "The marriage would only be to please his father. He has no intention of giving up the actress."

Elizabeth gasped.

"I am sorry," Rycroft said. "I promised Bingley I would protect her from schemers, and yet, it is I who has brought this schemer to her." His jaw and fists clenched.

"And you wish to do harm to him," Darcy said quietly. "However, he is a friend, and it feels wrong to think of harming him."

Rycroft nodded. "But what he has planned…"

"Is reprehensible. I understand far more than you know," Darcy said. "You may remember that I was once friends with Wickham."

Again, Rycroft nodded. "I know I must deal with Blackmoore, but what about Mary?"

"I will speak to her," Elizabeth offered. "Perhaps her affections have not been engaged."

Rycroft's shoulders relaxed somewhat. It felt as if a small weight had been lifted. He prayed that Mary's heart had not been touched and would not be damaged when she learned what sort of gentleman Blackmoore truly was.

"You have not failed her."

Rycroft looked at Darcy in surprise.

Darcy gave him a wry smile. "As I said, I understand far more than you know. You have kept your promise to Bingley. Did you not hear of a scheme and take immediate steps to prevent harm?"

Darcy stood and Rycroft followed.

"Go home, Rycroft. Mary will be well. The direst circumstances have been avoided."

Elizabeth took Rycroft's hat from the table and handed it to him as he reached the door. "Thank you," she said.

"For what?" he asked in surprise. For bringing a schemer into her sister's life and possibly causing heartache?

"For caring for my sister." She smiled at him. "You do care for her, do you not?"

Rycroft turned his hat in his hands. "Very much," he admitted. There was no denying it any longer. Mary had left, and instead of feeling relieved and his mind clearing and righting itself, he found that his world seemed to be lying at his feet in pieces, and he knew that it would never be right again without her in it.

Elizabeth laid a hand on his arm. "A library, an aunt, and a ball."

He chuckled despite his gloom. "If it becomes necessary, Mrs. Darcy. If it becomes necessary."

Chapter 15

MARY OPENED HER TRUNK and shook out one dress and then another before hanging them in her wardrobe. It had been only a week since she had left home, but it felt strange to be in her room listening to the chatter created by her mother and sisters. She sighed. She had not missed it. She preferred the quiet of Rycroft Place.

She saw the handkerchief Georgiana had attempted to tuck into her trunk as a surprise. She had embroidered a dark blue M on one corner and had put small yellow flowers on the other corners. Flowers she said Mary would have to see one day when she visited her at Pemberley. Mary ran a finger over the flowers. Georgiana was one of the many delights of Rycroft Place she was going to miss, for shortly after Mary returned to London, Georgiana was to return to her brother. Oh, she would not be happy to see that day come, for she had enjoyed their discussions. Some had gone far into the night.

She tucked the handkerchief into her pocket and went back to her unpacking. She had nearly finished when her door was flung open, and Lydia skipped across the room and flopped on the bed.

"Was it very grand?" Lydia asked.

"Was what grand?"

"Rycroft Place, silly." Lydia clutched her hands to her heart dramatically. "Did you meet any gentlemen that made you swoon?"

"May I come in?" Kitty stood at the doorway.

"Of course, you may come in," Lydia said before Mary could say a word.

Kitty looked to Mary, who nodded. "What was town like?" she asked softly.

Mary joined her sisters on the bed. She knew that she would not have a moment's peace if she did not answer Lydia's questions, although she doubted Lydia would be satisfied with any of her answers.

"Rycroft Place is very grand. It has many maids and footmen. The floors where you enter shine, and you would be able to stand four ladies side by side on the steps. There are three sitting rooms... not all on the same floor... and several bedrooms, a music room, a dining room, a library..."

"Is there a ballroom?" Lydia asked, turning onto her stomach.

"Yes."

Lydia sighed. "I should so love to have a ballroom. Then, I could dance and dance. Did you dance in it?"

"No," Mary said with a laugh, "but I did dance in the music room since it is where Miss Darcy has her lessons."

Lydia expelled a loud sigh of longing. "I should love to have dancing lessons."

"I would, too," added Kitty.

"Was the dancing master horrible? Did he smell funny and have rotten teeth?"

Mary laughed again. "No, he was a gentleman of about five and forty. He had a funny way of speaking because he was not born in England. He was very direct, but he was pleasant." She was certain her youngest sister would not appreciate his directness, but Mary did.

"Did you dance with him?" Kitty asked.

"I did twice. The other times, I danced with Lord Rycroft, so that the dancing master could help Miss Darcy through the new steps."

This time, Lydia's sigh was wistful. "Lord Rycroft is handsome, is he not?"

"Most handsome," Kitty agreed with a sigh of her own.

Mary simply nodded. She could not deny that she found him attractive. Quite.

Lydia propped herself up on her elbows. "I have heard he is a rake." There was excitement in her tone.

Mary shook her head. "He may have been, but he is not any longer. He is a very fine gentleman."

Lydia pouted. "So, he did not try to kiss you?"

"Kiss me?" Mary cried in surprise. "Why ever should he do that?"

"Because he is a rake and that is what rakes do. They kiss ladies."

"I told you," Mary said in a rather stern voice, "he is not a rake. He did nothing improper."

"Well, that is not at all amusing."

"Impropriety is not amusing. It is dangerous and can lead to your ruin and that of your family."

Lydia rolled her eyes. "Did you go anywhere?"

"I went riding and to the museum. And there were a few trips to the modiste with Aunt and Lady Sophia."

"Lady Sophia. How I would love to have such a name."

Mary shook her head at Lydia's tone of longing. "Perhaps if you learn to be proper, you might catch the eye of a peer." She doubted that a peer would ever consider someone of their standing, but she knew the idea might induce her sister to at least attempt to learn propriety.

She stood. "I would like a cup of tea before I retire."

She wished to end the discussion before she had to admit to being called on each day by Mr. Blackmoore. She knew, without a doubt, that soon Lydia would want to know if she had met any gentlemen, and Mary would have to either tell her that she had or lie and say she had not.

What would she tell her sister about Mr. Blackmoore? He was handsome and had called on her every day for nearly a week. However, despite having enjoyed his company and attention, she did not miss him. Truly, until this moment she had not thought much about him. Her thoughts since before she had left Rycroft Place had been filled with sorrow over being parted from Georgiana, Lady Sophia, and, most startlingly, Lord Rycroft. What was to be made of that, she did not know.

The following day, as Mary waited outside the milliner's shop for her younger sisters to conclude their shopping, she drew in a deep breath of air and shivered. She prayed her sisters would be quick as she stamped her feet to warm them. Shopping had never been a great pleasure of hers, but it was even less of one when her sisters squabbled over this lace and that ribbon. Therefore, she had chosen to endure the cold December air rather than remain in the store with Kitty and Lydia.

"Is there no room in the shop?"

Mary spun toward the familiar voice. "Colonel Fitzwilliam, what a delightful surprise! What brings you to Meryton?"

He shrugged. "My men."

Mary blinked. "Your men? This regiment is your regiment?"

He nodded. "I do not quarter with them in the winter, but I do check on them sporadically. I may detest my profession, but I will not disgrace it, nor will I have it disgrace me." His jaw was firmly set in displeasure.

"Have some of the men attempted to disgrace you?" She could not imagine anyone not wanting to please the colonel. He was a very agreeable fellow. Of course, she was not a soldier who had to take orders from him. He might not be as agreeable then.

"No more than expected." He looked toward the shop. "Why are you standing here instead of inside where it is warm?"

"My sisters," Mary said with a sigh. "More precisely, Lydia. Kitty is not an issue, but Lydia lacks decorum. I came out here to find some peace."

Richard laughed. "The busy street is more peaceful than a shop with your sister inside?"

Mary nodded slowly as a small smile curled her lips. "You have not met Lydia. She can fill a village with noise even if she is the only one in it." She could see her sisters moving toward the door as she spoke. "I do believe you are about to have the privilege of meeting my youngest sister."

Richard continued to chuckle as the door to the shop opened. His laughter soon faded as Lydia did as Lydia always did. She launched into a litany of descriptions of the embellishments she had purchased for her bonnet without so much as a moment to notice her surroundings. That was how she often was – completely absorbed in her own affairs.

"Lydia," Mary said in a cajoling tone about the time she suspected the colonel was sorry to have stopped to speak to her, "I am positively certain that you have made the most excellent choices in embellishments."

It was only then that Lydia noticed that there was someone standing next to Mary and smiled and fluttered her lashes. It was the response she often gave a redcoat. Colonel Fitzwilliam's lips twitched with amusement, and Mary breathed a sigh of relief that he was not immediately offended by her sister's obvious flirtatious nature.

"Colonel Fitzwilliam, these are my sisters, Lydia, and Kitty..."

"Katherine," said Kitty softly.

Mary gave her a questioning look but corrected herself. "My sisters Lydia and Katherine, whom we call Kitty. Kitty, Lydia, this is Mr. Darcy's cousin, Colonel Fitzwilliam. It is his regiment that is quartered here for the winter."

"Miss Katherine, Miss Lydia, it is a pleasure to meet you." He tipped his head to each of them as they curtseyed.

"Your regiment." There was awe in Lydia's tone. "Mr. Darcy did not tell us that this was your regiment. Oh!" She covered her mouth with her fingers. "Wickham did not mention you either."

"I imagine Lieutenant Wickham would rather forget me." His lips curled wickedly.

"Why ever would he wish to forget you?"

"Lydia," Mary scolded. She was certain the question had popped from Lydia's mouth without an even minuscule amount of thought.

"It is a fair question, Miss Lydia." He smiled reassuringly at Mary. "Lieutenant Wickham has been assigned to my unit at my request, for he owes me a particular debt of honour, and I shall most easily see it paid with him under my charge."

"Oh, my, a debt of honour?" Lydia's hand rested on her heart, and for a moment, Mary thought she might swoon.

"His charms belie his character, Miss Lydia. I would be cautious in my dealings with him."

The colonel's smile had faded from his face and a hardness had appeared in its place. Mary could see now that he might be a demanding superior that some men, such as Lieutenant Wickham, might wish to discredit, though to her way of thinking that seemed a foolish thing to do.

"He is particularly not to be trusted with pretty young ladies such as yourself," Colonel Fitzwilliam continued.

"Is he a rake?"

Again, Mary cringed at Lydia's inappropriate comment, but the colonel did not seem to be shocked by it.

"The word, Miss Lydia, is too good for him. Deceiver, seducer, and blackguard are all more fitting."

Lydia's eyes grew wide. "Indeed?" She looked at her sisters. "This is very shocking. He seemed so obliging." She lifted her chin. "I for one shall not speak to him again, except perhaps to offer a greeting.

It would be unspeakably rude not to at least greet him on meeting, would it not?" She turned her full attention on Mary.

Was Lydia actually asking for her opinion on this? That was surprising.

"We should be kind even to our enemies," Mary instructed. "Kindness does not mean turning a blind eye to their characters, however. You would do well to be cautious."

Lydia nodded and spoke not a word. It was a reaction that stunned Mary. Lydia was not one to accept instruction so readily.

Mary turned her attention back to the colonel. "We were about to walk home, Colonel. Did you wish to join us to meet our father?"

"I would indeed," replied the Colonel, offering her his arm. "I would like very much to meet him."

Chapter 16

MARY TAPPED SOFTLY ON the door to her father's study and waited for his call before pushing open the door. "Papa, we have a guest."

Her father peered over his spectacles at Colonel Fitzwilliam and motioned to the chairs in front of his desk. "I would stand to greet you, sir, but I fear if I did so, you may be required to pick me up off the floor when I toppled over." There was a lightness to his voice and a twinkle in his eye that did Mary's heart good.

"Papa," chided Mary softly. "You are not so ill as that, are you?"

He chuckled. "No, but it did sound better than admitting I am too tired to stand." He gave her a wink as she bent to kiss his cheek. "And who is your friend, Mary?"

"This is Colonel Fitzwilliam. It is his regiment which is stationed in Hertfordshire, and he is Mr. Darcy's cousin." Mary stood beside her father as Richard stuck out his hand in greeting and waited until the colonel had been offered and taken a seat.

"Do you wish for tea, Papa?"

He tipped his head toward the cabinet on the right side of the study. "Port," he said. "Will you join me, Colonel?"

The colonel acknowledged he would, and Mary took the port and two glasses from her father's cabinet.

"Did you have much trouble making your way through my home while wearing such a fetching jacket?" Mr. Bennet tucked his blanket around his legs more tightly and leaned back in his chair. His book lay open on the desk in front of him.

Mary poured a small amount of beverage into the first glass.

"There was a bit of a flutter." Colonel Fitzwilliam chuckled while accepting his glass from Mary with a nod of thanks.

Mary filled her father's glass and placed it on his desk near his right hand.

"A red coat can be a distraction with the ladies." Mr. Bennet smiled widely.

Especially her mother and youngest sisters, Mary thought.

"I spent a few years in one myself as many young men do," her father continued after taking a sip of his port. "However, I cannot say I enjoyed it, aside from the attention from the ladies and the opportunity to travel to another part of our great country." He steepled his fingers on his chest and rested his chin on them. "It also kept me away from my cousin. I was not so fortunate as you, Colonel. My cousin lacked a great deal of sense."

"I am fortunate in that way, I suppose," the colonel replied. "Speaking of my cousin, we expect his company at Netherfield this evening."

Mr. Bennet grinned and took a sip of his drink. "Not one to be housed with your men?"

Colonel Fitzwilliam shrugged. "Not when there is a more comfortable arrangement to be had."

"Smart man," Mr. Bennet said.

"Do you need anything else, Papa?" Mary asked.

"No, no. I am quite content. A good drink and a good conversation," he lifted his glass and tipped it toward the colonel, "what more could be required?"

It felt lovely to have been the source of a pleasant diversion for her father. "Then, I shall return to Mama and my sisters."

"Ah, she is a good girl," she heard her father say as she closed the door. She stood for a moment in the hall, leaning against the wall and smiling.

"Are you well?" Jane asked as she approached Mary in the hall-way.

"Papa said I was a good girl," Mary whispered.

"And you are."

"But he has never said so before."

"You have not heard him say it," Jane said, "but I have. He gives praise sparsely."

"Save for you and Lizzy." Their father was liberal with his approbation for his two eldest daughters, but when it came to Mary, Kitty, and Lydia, he was more likely to tease than commend.

Jane allowed it to be true, but she assured Mary that it was beyond her understanding as to why it was. Mary noted the letters Jane held in her hand.

"Are those for Papa?"

"One is." Jane held up the second letter. "This one is for you."

"For me?" Mary took the letter. Her brows furrowed. "I do not recognize the hand." Who could possibly be writing to her?

Jane did not knock on her father's door but waited as Mary broke the seal.

"Oh!" Mary's eyes grew wide as she scanned the message for the signature. "It is from Mr. Blackmoore." She folded it and handed it back to Jane. "I cannot accept this. It would be improper." Why would he write to her without being given permission to do so? The wonderful feeling from a moment ago when she had heard her father's words fled.

"What did it say?"

"I did not read it. I should not even have it." Mary shook her head and wrapped her arms around her middle. A feeling of unease had begun to wash over her as she wondered if Mr. Blackmoore was another gentleman who would prove to have a character far less attractive than his features. Why must any handsome man who paid attention to her be less than honourable? What was it about her that attracted such gentlemen?

"We are not betrothed. We are not even courting. He is merely a gentleman who is a friend and has called while I was in town. I have not given him leave to write to me." She looked at Jane with wide eyes, hoping that her sister might have some explanation for Mr. Blackmoore's behaviour that was not as condemning as what she suspected. "Please, when you give the letter to Papa, let him know that I did not read it. I cannot be forced to marry Mr. Blackmoore."

"He seemed amiable."

"You are right. He was, but a gentleman who writes a letter to a lady to whom he is not betrothed or courting shows very little care for the lady's reputation. Marriage to such a man would be a misery, I am certain of it." Mary brushed at the tears that slid down her cheeks, dashing them away.

"Come." Jane took her by the hand and led her into her father's study. "Forgive me for my intrusion, Papa, but it is a matter of some urgency." She placed the letters on his desk and stood beside it with an arm around Mary's shoulders.

"What is this? Is it dreadful news?" Mr. Bennet picked up the letters and noted the one that was opened.

Mary nodded. Whatever Mr. Blackmoore had to say could not be anything less than dreadful, for he had presented himself to her in a most unacceptable fashion.

"I did not read it, Papa." Her voice quivered just a bit. "I only looked at the signature."

Mr. Bennet's eyebrows furrowed as he saw the signature. "Mr. Blackmoore?" He lifted his eyes to Mary. "Do you know a Mr. Blackmoore?"

Mary nodded. "He called on me at Lady Sophia's house. He is a friend of Lord Rycroft."

"Ah," he placed the letter, unread, on the desk and picked up the second one. "I assume this is also from the gentleman." He broke the seal. "Is there anything I should know about him before I read this?" He peered over his glasses at his daughter who shook her head.

"I have told you all there is to tell, but I shall not have him. I shall not be tied to a man who thinks so little of a lady's reputation as to send her a letter without permission."

"May I intrude on this matter?" Colonel Fitzwilliam asked. "I know we have just met, sir, but I would agree with Miss Mary's conclusion."

"Do you know this Mr. Blackmoore?" Her father unfolded his letter as he looked at the colonel.

"Some, and what I know, while not utterly defamatory, is not flattering."

Mr. Bennet nodded and began to read the letter.

Mary twisted her fingers together as she waited to hear what her father would say.

"I assume," he said as he placed the letter on the desk after he had finished reading, "that the one addressed to you, Mary, is to ask you for a courtship. He has requested a meeting with me if I should be agreeable to it."

He quickly skimmed the letter addressed to Mary. "It is as I suspected. He would like to court you. I must say he certainly writes a pretty letter."

He held it out to Mary, who shook her head in refusal. She had no desire to even touch that piece of paper. Why must it only be unsavoury sorts of gentlemen who chose to pay court to her?

"Am I agreeable to a meeting?" Her father asked.

"No, please, Papa."

"Jane, is anyone else aware of the letters?"

"Hill, but no one else."

"Very good, then, I shall consign them to the fire and write my refusal of the young man's request." He looked once again at Mary. "Is this what you wish?"

"Yes, very much so." Her head bobbed up and down to emphasize the point.

"Very well. It shall be done. Now, Jane, I think it best if you take Mary to her room and allow her to recover." He raised a brow. "You must not let your mother know of this," he cautioned.

"We shall take the servants' stairs," Jane assured him with a smile.

Mr. Bennet held his hand out to Mary, and she took it.

"Go with your sister and know that all will be well. I will do my best to see that it is." He smiled at her. He squeezed her hand, gave a nod of his head in approval, and sent her on her way.

Chapter 17

Lord Rycroft sat in the sitting room at Rycroft Place with his mother and Georgiana. What passed for bright morning light in mid-December spilled in through the window and across the book that lay open on his lap. His fingers of his right hand drummed a steady pattern on one page as he stared out the window.

He had stopped at Brownlow's house after his conversation with Darcy two days ago, but the man had been out at a dinner party. He had left a message for Brownlow to call first thing in the morning. However, his friend had sent his regrets saying he would not be able to return Rycroft's call until the following morning. This morning. The one that was ticking away with no callers. Rycroft checked the clock on the mantle again and watched it for a moment to ensure that the hands were moving, for time seemed to be standing still.

"You seem anxious," his mother said.

He gave her a small smile and lifted his brows as he tipped his head to the side and shrugged slightly. She knew it was his way of saying she was right, but he was not willing to talk about it. How could he not be anxious? He might lose a second friend today, and then, there was Mary.

"It is rather dull without Mary," Georgiana said.

Silently, Rycroft agreed. How he wished Mary were here so that he could see that she was well. He would even welcome her lecturing him about the importance of choosing friends wisely if

it meant she could forgive him for being the source of her introduction to a scoundrel like Blackmoore.

"I wonder what she is doing," Georgiana continued. "It must
never be dull to live with so many sisters."

"Sisters can be pleasant, but they can also pose problems," Lady
Sophia cautioned. "We must be content with what we have. I have
asked your brother and new sister..." She gave Georgiana a pointed
look that made Rycroft smile, for he knew that look well. "...to
stop here on their way out of town this morning. Mary's first
ball gown has arrived, and she absolutely must have it for the ball
Bingley is planning."

Georgiana sighed. "It is so beautiful. I do wish I could see her in
it."

"You will," her aunt assured her, "just not now."

Georgiana sighed once more and went back to her stitching.

Rycroft placed his book on the table and moved to the window.
He also wished with all his heart that he could see Mary in that
gown. He leaned against the window frame and fixed his gaze on
the chair that Mary had occupied every morning for the last five
days she was at Rycroft place as she would stitch beside Georgiana.
A sigh escaped him before he could catch it, drawing his mother's
attention and causing him to turn once again toward the street.

Finally, he saw Brownlow mounting the steps to his front door.

He straightened both his jacket and his posture. "I would like to
see Darcy when he arrives," he said to his mother. "I will be in my
study with Brownlow."

"Do you wish for tea?" his mother asked as he was about to exit
the room.

"No, no. I have what we need."

She raised a disapproving eyebrow.

"It will be a short meeting and will require only a small drink." It
was not as if he was known for drinking. He could not remember
the last time he had imbibed so much that he had suffered any
painful or embarrassing consequences. He might like to have a

good time, but he had his limits. And drinking to excess was not inside those limits.

Her eyebrow lowered, but she still wore a scowl.

"Truly, Mother," he assured her before stepping into the hall. "Brownlow." He motioned for his friend to follow him to his study.

"Your reply to my message yesterday sounded most urgent," Brownlow said as he took a seat and nodded his acceptance of a drink Rycroft was about to pour.

It was urgent. He had hoped to know all he could about Blackmoore before the Darcys left town so that Elizabeth would have all the facts necessary to help her protect Mary's heart. He rolled his eyes to look at the ceiling as he drew a calming breath.

"I had an enlightening conversation with Endicott about Blackmoore." Rycroft handed a glass to his friend and turned to pour himself a glass. "What do you know about his keeping an actress in funds for gaming?"

Brownlow sipped his drink and glanced warily at Rycroft, as well he should. All Rycroft's closest friends knew that he was not the sort of gentleman to thwart propriety in some areas or run roughshod through his inheritance. He, Brownlow, and Blackmoore were known to have a good game with Endicott from time to time, but it was always low stakes. Whatever money Rycroft might lose in the name of pleasure was not going to sink him, his title, or his estate.

Although everyone thought Rycroft to be a notorious rake, Brownlow knew better than most that Rycroft was actually the most responsible of their lot. He rarely got foxed; he refused to enter a gaming hell; and, though he flirted with nearly every lady he met, he rarely dallied beyond a few kisses. He was not the sort of fellow who was going to have illegitimate offspring dotting the country and drawing on his coffers. That was why Brownlow had trusted him to play the part of a suitor for his sister when the gentleman to whom she was now betrothed needed encouragement to come up to scratch.

"He was to end it before the beginning of the season," Brownlow said.

Rycroft sat behind his desk. "So it is true?"

"That he has taken up with an actress? Yes." Brownlow swirled his drink, a sign he was not being forthcoming.

Rycroft placed his glass on the desk and leaned forward. "Endicott said that he had no intention of ending his relationship with this actress. In fact, according to Endicott, Blackmoore intends to marry a lady of sense and solid connections to appease his father and continue to keep the actress. Is this true?"

Brownlow nodded slowly.

Rycroft rose from his seat and paced to the window and back. "And is Miss Mary who he has chosen to pay such a price?" He placed his hands on his desk and leaned towards Brownlow. "No lady deserves such treatment."

Brownlow swallowed and nodded. "I know. I had hoped Blackmoore would truly be taken with Miss Bennet, and he would come to his senses. However, he has not." He drained his glass and placed it on the desk. "There is more, but you must believe me when I say I have only just learned of this last evening."

"Go on."

Brownlow wiped his hands on his pants as if nervous, and Rycroft's heart picked up its pace. Whatever Brownlow knew was not something he wanted to hear.

"Blackmoore has written to both Miss Bennet and her father requesting a meeting with her father and proposing a courtship to Miss Bennet."

Rycroft dropped into his chair, his heart sinking with him. His suspicion had been correct. It was not something he wanted to hear. "When? When did he write?"

"It was sent express yesterday."

Rycroft dropped his head into his hands. "I was entrusted with her protection from schemers."

"I had hoped..." Brownlow's voice trailed off as Rycroft lifted his head.

"I would have hoped the same," he assured his friend. The thought that Blackmoore had become someone he despised was unsettling, to put it gently. "One does not expect his friend to take such a turn."

He rose. While discovering a friend was not what he thought was disturbing, it was not as bad as the thought of losing Mary. He shook his head. "To lose her is one thing, but to have her so injured and nearly at my own hands." It was more than he could allow his mind to consider at the moment.

"Lose her?" Understanding began to dawn in Brownlow's eyes. "Ah, that is why you looked like you wished to call him out when we were riding the other day."

The other day and every day since.

At that moment, Darcy entered the study. "Your mother said you wished to see me."

Rycroft motioned to the chair by his desk, but instead of joining Darcy and Brownlow there, he stuck his head into the hall and called for Morledge. "Have a bag packed quickly." He turned to Darcy. "You are at Netherfield for how many days?"

"The wedding is to be Tuesday next, and if the weather holds, we will return then."

"Pack enough for a week," he said to Morledge before turning his attention to Darcy and Brownlow. "Tell him about the letters," he said to Brownlow. "I must prepare to travel."

He stuck his head back into the hallway. "My horse," he called to a footman. "Have my horse readied." He turned back to Darcy. "My bag and my man, may they travel with you?"

Darcy shrugged and nodded, looking very much as if he was lost in the darkest part of the woods.

"Tell him about the letters," Rycroft repeated to Brownlow as he set about sorting paper and correspondence on his desk. He was almost positive there was nothing that could not wait a week to be seen to, but he wanted to make certain.

Brownlow did as Rycroft had said and told Darcy about the letters that had been sent the previous day. "And Rycroft, here, does not wish to either hurt or lose her," he concluded.

Darcy's brows rose. "So my wife was correct. He cares for Mary."

"Loves her, actually," Rycroft said as he closed his account book and put it on the shelf behind his desk.

Brownlow rose. "Since that is the case and though he has not asked it, I believe I must go warn Blackmoore of this development. I trust he is wise enough to know to step down, for if he does not, I fear he is risking far more than his inheritance."

Darcy chuckled and rubbed his jaw. "Not even I am willing to challenge Rycroft." He rose from his place just as Rycroft clapped his hands once and rubbed them together.

Everything was done here, and his bag would be nearly packed. All that was left to do was change, say goodbye to his mother and Georgie, and be on his way. "I will ride on ahead, Darcy, for she must not accept him." He spun and left the room.

Darcy and Brownlow followed.

"You must at least give a word of greeting to Lady Sophia, Brownlow," he heard Darcy say, "and I believe you have not had the very good fortune of meeting my wife. Both of whom will find the reason for delaying my trip most diverting."

Chapter 18

Mrs. Philips entered Longbourn's drawing room and greeted her sister and nieces before settling into a chair near Mrs. Bennet and beginning to share what she considered to be the best items of news from the village. Amongst the top stories was the fact that the butcher had been seen speaking with the baker, and this was just after the butcher's son had been seen walking with the baker's daughter. He had even offered her a ride on Sunday last. Surely, a wedding was in the offing. It was a most pleasant prospect.

However, on the other side of things, the parson's nose had been uncommonly red last Tuesday, and he had not been sneezing or sniffling. Lady Lucas was certain he had been indulging in spirits, and Aunt Philips concurred. Mrs. Bennet gasped and declared it could not be, only to be assured by her sister once again that prayers were needed on their parson's behalf. And so, it continued for some time.

Mary did her best to ignore what was being said and applied herself to the dress she was mending. A low branch had caught her skirt on her walk this morning. It was naught but a small tear and easily repaired.

"There is one thing that will be of particular interest to you, Sister."

Mary peeked surreptitiously at her aunt and mother and saw her aunt look at her with a curious expression.

"I dare not believe it is true, but, when she told it to me this morning before I came here, Mrs. Long insisted that she has had it from a most reliable source, though she would not tell me from whom she heard it. Yet, she insists it is true. You know how her husband is always at the tavern and hears the best things."

"Oh, indeed, I do," Mrs. Bennet said.

"Mrs. Long and I agree that you must know what is being said."

"Me?"

"Yes, you, for it is about one of your daughters."

Mary's mother gasped, and again, Aunt Philips looked at Mary with that same curious expression she had worn before.

"Mrs. Long said that she heard that Mary has been receiving letters from a gentleman and must be secretly betrothed."

Mary kept her eyes on her needle, not daring to look at her mother or aunt as her stomach twisted in a most nauseating fashion and her heart raced. She would not be forced to marry Mr. Blackmoore. She simply would not be!

"Oh, it is true," Lydia said. "I heard Hill say there was a letter for Miss Mary. It came express." She leaned toward her aunt and whispered loudly, "From London."

"Well, that explains it then. I would wager that Mr. Long heard it from the express man himself. You know they do like to stop at the tavern."

Mary's face flushed while her head spun.

"Is this true?" Mrs. Bennet asked in a shrill voice.

Mary looked first at Jane and then her mother. "Is what true?" she asked cautiously.

"Are you secretly betrothed?"

"No."

Aunt Philips sucked in a sharp breath. "Are you receiving letters from a gentleman to whom you are not even betrothed?" She shook her head and clucked her tongue. "First, Lizzy and now, Mary. Sister, I am surprised you have not taught them better."

Mary watched her mother's eyes narrow and her cheeks become pink.

"It is not as it appears, Aunt," she said before her mother could begin to have a spell of nerves. "A gentleman has written to Papa requesting a courtship, but it has been denied. I could not tie myself to a man who would so blatantly snub propriety by writing to me without some sort of understanding. It would not be right, would it, Mama?"

Mrs. Bennet's mouth snapped shut, but she continued to look at Mary with surprise. "It most definitely would not." She tilted her head, and her brows drew together as she considered Mary as if she were a stranger.

Kitty turned from the window and her contemplation of the garden. "You refused him?"

Mary gave her a pleading look, hoping that she would not ask any further questions. "I did."

"Do you know who he is, Kitty?" her aunt asked eagerly.

Kitty's eyes grew wide as she realized what she had begun. She shook her head. "I do not know who has written to Mary." She bit her lip and ducked her head. "I only know she has had potential suitors call on her while in town." She peeked at Mary. "I could not begin to imagine who might have written with such a short acquaintance."

She gave Mary a sly smile and a wink. "But, with her new dresses and the hair style that Miss Darcy's maid has given her, not to mention the connections Lady Sophia must have, it would certainly be foolish for Mary to consider an offer so soon. Why," her voice rose to a level of excitement to match that of Lydia when presented with the news that the militia was to arrive in Meryton, "being the sister of a man such as Mr. Darcy and the particular friend of Lady Sophia and her son, Lord Rycroft, I would not be surprised in the least if Mary had several offers and perhaps even one from a peer."

Mary breathed a sigh of relief. Her mother and aunt seemed to be enthralled with such an idea and immediately began planning a wedding breakfast fit for a lord.

Kitty crossed the room, extended her hand to Mary, and nodded toward the door. "I think a stroll before the sun sinks any lower would be most beneficial."

Mary gladly accepted the means of escape and, taking her sister's hand, hurried from the room.

"Was it Mr. Blackmoore?" Kitty asked when they got to the back entry and took their wraps that hung there from their hooks. "I shall not tell a soul. I swear."

"It would not be right to say," Mary said, though she gave a small nod of her head.

"He is very handsome and wealthy."

"He is," Mary agreed as she fastened her wrap around her shoulders. "However, we seemed to have very little in the way of common interests, and it appears his character is wanting." Most seriously.

"How do you do it?" Kitty snuggled close to Mary's arm and shivered.

The air was decidedly cool, but the emptiness of the garden afforded the only real privacy to discuss such things as they were discussing. It also was a heavenly retreat away from their mother and aunt.

"What do you mean? How do I do what?"

"How do you make them like you?" Kitty shivered once more. "Mr. Blackmoore, Lord Rycroft, Colonel Fitzwilliam. They all seem to be taken with you, yet you never bat your lashes or drop your gaze when you smile."

Mary was shocked to have such a question put to her. She had enjoyed the company of the three gentlemen mentioned, but other than Mr. Blackmoore's nearly fawning attention, she had never suspected any to have been interested in her as anything more than a person with whom to have a conversation. In fact, she was quite certain that Lord Rycroft found her presence to be somewhat of an inconvenience at best and a trial at worst.

"I believe you are mistaken. They are friends, nothing more."

"Friends? Only friends?" Kitty cried in disbelief. "I have seen the way Lord Rycroft watches you, and though I know only a little about men, I do not believe his look expressed mere friendship. He looked decidedly jealous of Mr. Blackmoore."

Mary laughed. "It is not possible."

"Why?" Kitty stopped walking and turned to face Mary. "How is it impossible for him to like you?"

Mary smiled tightly. Why must she be required to explain this? Was it not obvious? "I am not the sort of lady whom a man desires. I am bookish and opinionated, and I have very little to recommend me by way of looks."

Kitty's mouth hung open for a moment before she closed it and gave a shake of her head. "I own that you are excessively opinionated, but little in the way of looks?" Again, she shook her head, as if she could not believe that it was even a question that needed to be addressed. "That is a falsehood of the highest order. You may not put it on display very often, but you, my dear sister, are beautiful."

She snuggled in again next to Mary as the wind tugged at her wrap and caused her to shiver once more. "False modesty is just as much a sin as vanity, is it not?" She laughed at Mary's small sound of shock. "I listen. Not always, but sometimes," she explained. "You are beautiful, and your beauty is the sort that you have admonished Lydia and I to find, for it is a beauty based not solely on the physical appearance but the lasting attractiveness of a lovely character." She sighed. "I wish I knew how to be like you. How do I find that beauty that inspires men to notice me?"

"Oh, no! You should not try to be like me. You should be like you."

"But I am not interesting," Kitty protested

Mary laughed. "Neither am I, and yet you think there are three gentlemen who admire me."

"But you are smart."

"And you are talented," Mary assured her younger sister. "Your sketches are excellent, and your eye for detail will make you a marvelous hostess." She rubbed her hand up and down Kitty's arm that was twined with hers. "We should return before you catch a chill."

Kitty suffered easily from chills and headaches. They were rarely serious, but feeling ill was not pleasant, and so Mary did not wish to place Kitty in danger.

"Do you," Kitty began as they turned back toward the house, "do you..." She took a breath and then spoke the rest of her question quickly, "find Colonel Fitzwilliam attractive?"

Ah! That was what all this was about. Her sister must be interested in the colonel.

"He is handsome," Mary said, "but he is merely a friend." She leaned a bit closer as they were nearing the house, and she wished to keep her voice soft. "Do you find him attractive?"

Kitty nodded.

"I am glad," said Mary. "It would be a fine match for you. However, you must remember that he is a younger son, and his inheritance is still under his father's control. Therefore, I must caution you to guard your heart."

Kitty nodded again.

"From what I understand, he only has a year remaining before his father will release some of what will come to him," Mary said. "Patience may be required."

Kitty pulled Mary to a stop. "You will not tell anyone that I prefer him?"

"No." Mary attempted to move toward the house once more, but Kitty held her in place.

"You have refused Mr. Blackmoore, and Colonel Fitzwilliam has not touched your heart. But what about Lord Rycroft?"

Mary sighed. "I do not know. He is good and kind and solicitous of my needs." She felt her cheeks warming despite the cold. "And he is very handsome."

Kitty smiled. "And he has come to call." She pointed toward the drive.

Mary looked to where her sister had pointed. There, hat in hand, brushing off his coat, was Lord Rycroft. He, looking up at just that moment and catching her eye, smiled as he tilted his hat towards her before replacing it on his head and moving toward the front door.

Chapter 19

Mr. Hill handed Rycroft's outerwear to a maid, and then, with a bow, said, "If you would follow me, my lord, I am certain the master would be pleased to see you."

Rycroft gave a nod of acceptance and then, when the man had turned away from him, drew a deep breath before following Longbourn's senior servant down the hall to Mr. Bennet's study.

On his way from London, Rycroft had attempted to plan how he was going to present what he knew to Mary's father. His horse and any creature that might have been listening knew all about Blackmoore. Not all his sentiments had been polite, so he had been thankful that his audience was unable to repeat what had been said while he was spewing it. However, at present, he almost wished his horse could speak, for all his well-thought-out ideas had flown from his head when Mary had smiled at him and lifted her hand to give him a small wave as if she were glad to see him. Desperately, he attempted to gather a few well-worded sentiments as he was introduced and stepped into Mr. Bennet's study.

"Lord Rycroft." Mr. Bennet rose from his chair with some difficulty and gave his guest a small bow. It was obvious that the gentleman was still weak.

Lord Rycroft returned the bow but waited until Mr. Bennet took his seat before sitting down himself. He remembered how his father had tried to continue on with life when he became ill.

Most times he succeeded in doing what he wished. However, on occasion, there had been a need for some subtle help.

"What brings you to call on me today?" There was a twinkle in Mr. Bennet's eye. "I am sure you were not just in the neighbourhood, unless your sense of time and direction is sorely lacking."

Rycroft chuckled. The man's sharp wit was not ailing. "My sense of time and direction is normally accurate, so you are correct that I have come with a purpose. I have been made aware of some unsettling information concerning a friend of mine and your daughter."

Mr. Bennet's brows rose.

"I assure you most heartily that it is only my friend who is at fault." He paused. He had come to the end of the few thoughts that remained nicely composed in his mind. "I do not know how to best tell you the details."

"I prefer the straightforward approach."

That was excellent since being direct was likely going to be easier than being delicate. It would, however, still be a challenge to not let his anger bubble through too greatly.

"Then, I will not shroud this in anything to soften the details."

Mr. Bennet made a small motion with his hand for Rycroft to proceed.

"It has come to my attention that my friend, Mr. Blackmoore, has picked up some unsavoury habits while I was out of town. His father is not pleased about his activities and has threatened to remove his inheritance unless he marries a lady who is acceptable to his father."

"Ah, that explains his letter wishing to court Mary."

Rycroft's jaw clenched and his head turned ever so slightly as he swallowed the colourful names for his friend that sprang to mind.

"Blackmoore." The name took on the taste of those unpleasant monikers and caused Rycroft to scowl as he said it. "Blackmoore has no intention of giving up his habits after he marries." Rycroft once again felt his jaw clench as he tried desperately to keep his emotions under regulation. "If I had known of his activities and his attentions, I would not have allowed him in my home or introduced him to your daughter. For that, I apologize."

"I am not convinced you need to apologize, but I will accept it." Mr. Bennet's chin rested on his steepled fingers, and his head tipped to the left as he studied Rycroft for a silent half-minute. "I assume your friend's habits include a woman?"

Rycroft nodded. "An actress with a fondness for gaming."

Mr. Bennet gave a small shrug of his shoulders. "It is my understanding that such affairs are not unusual in the higher circles, of which, I assume, Mr. Blackmoore is part."

The response surprised Rycroft and before he could think better of his response, he replied rather sharply, "Sir, we speak of your daughter."

Mr. Bennet's lips tipped up on the right side first before becoming a full smile. "I am aware of that fact. I was merely wondering about your stance on such things. I take it from your response that you do not approve of Mr. Blackmoore's keeping a mistress?"

"I most certainly do not approve. I will not lie and tell you that I have been a paragon of proper behaviour, but it is my firm belief that a man is to take and keep a wife in good faith. To do otherwise is reprehensible."

"I am glad we are agreed." Mr. Bennet leaned back in his chair. A small smile continued to play at his lips. "You may breathe easy. Mr. Blackmoore's offer was refused out of hand by myself and my daughter. Mary refused to even read his letter." His smile grew as Rycroft's shoulders relaxed in relief. "However, you I would not refuse."

Rycroft's eyes grew wide. "I beg your pardon?" Did Mr. Bennet always give answers that were so unexpected?

Mr. Bennet chuckled. "I see I must speak plainly."

To Rycroft, the statement sounded a great deal like something Mr. Bennet's daughter might say.

"I approve of you," he continued, "and if you wish to court or marry my daughter, you have my blessing." He shifted in his chair a bit. "I would make you work harder for my approval, but I may not have the luxury of time, since I am still not well. Therefore, should anything happen to me before you can convince Mary of your worth and find yourself in need of my blessing, I am giving it now."

Rycroft shook his head. "You barely know me."

Mr. Bennet shrugged. "I know enough. Mary continues to count you as one of her friends, does she not?"

Rycroft's brows drew together. "I believe she does."

"Then I am satisfied." Mr. Bennet winced slightly as he shifted again in his chair. "You do know that a letter containing the information you have shared with me would have sufficed as a proper warning, do you not?"

Rycroft could hear the laughter that lay behind the statement.

"Based on the fact that you chose to deliver the warning in person and not through the post, I assume you would like to see my Mary."

Rycroft drew in a deep breath and released it. It would be foolishness to try to refute such reasoning. Not that he really wished to refute it. It was true. However, he had hoped to ascertain his hope of succeeding with Mary before speaking to her father.

"Yes, sir," he said, "I would like to see Miss Mary, and I thank you for your approval." There. The secret of his heart's desire had been presented.

"So then, you do care for her?"

"A great deal, sir." He stood and paced the length of the room and back to dispel some a few of his nerves.

Mr. Bennet chuckled. "It is an unsettling feeling at first. Sneaks up on a fellow."

Rycroft smiled. "It does indeed."

Mr. Bennet's eyes shimmered. "Love her for who she is."

"I will." He already did, and he did not see that changing. Ever.

"Very good." Mr. Bennet dabbed at his eyes with his handkerchief and gave a shaky chuckle. "Before I become a watering pot, could I ask for your assistance in walking to the sitting room? I find I tire of my books and actually wish to hear the noise of my family, as shocking as that may be."

Lord Rycroft held out his arm to Mr. Bennet, who, once again, had risen with some difficulty.

"My strength has not returned," he said apologetically. "I fear the doctors may be right, and my days are numbered. But as Mary would say..."

"All our days are numbered."

Mr. Bennet chuckled softly. "I see you know her well already."

"Papa, are you to join us?" Miss Kitty, who had just descended the stairs, dipped a curtsey in greeting to Rycroft.

"I am. Is Mary upstairs or in the sitting room?"

"I am here," Mary said, coming from the back of the house. She smiled at Rycroft, who nodded his head instead of bowing. "I knew Mama would wish for tea, since Lord Rycroft is not the only visitor to have arrived. I saw Mr. Bingley's carriage from my window."

"Ah, well, it seems I shall soon discover if I have a place to sleep tonight." Rycroft chuckled.

"Well, my lord, if Bingley will not receive you, Longbourn is not without guest rooms," Mr. Bennet offered. "We would be honoured to do you the service."

"I will bear that in mind." He leaned a bit closer to Mr. Bennet. "In fact, if Bingley's sister becomes too much of a trial, I may call upon your assistance whether there is a room at Netherfield or not."

Mr. Bennet chuckled and then coughed once. "In that case, I think we should arrange ourselves in the sitting room in such a way as to thwart her advances."

"Just so, sir." Rycroft turned to Miss Kitty and Mary. "Will you ladies be of assistance?"

Miss Kitty wrapped her arms around Mary's arm. "We would be delighted, would we not, Mary?"

Mary's cheeks had taken on a light shade of pink that caused Rycroft to wonder if she was irritated by the thought or if she were actually delighted.

"Of course."

The response was quick, as if said without a thought. Then, Rycroft saw her give her sister a small smile that seemed to contain a secret before she continued.

"Perhaps," she said, "Colonel Fitzwilliam could help as well. He is planning to call."

Miss Kitty's eyes grew wide, and she darted an uneasy glance at Rycroft. "That would be lovely."

No, it would not be lovely. Not if the secret smiles and looks passing between Mary and Miss Kitty indicated what he feared – that his cousin had earned the place in Mary's heart that he desired for himself.

Though his heart was sinking, he smiled and agreed before entering the sitting room, where after greeting Mrs. Bennet and her sister and then helping Mr. Bennet to a chair, he took a seat in a grouping of four chairs with Mary on his right.

Mary placed her hand on his arm after he sat down, drawing his attention to her. "I am glad to see you," she whispered.

"Are you as glad to see me as you are to see my cousin?" He tried to keep his tone light and teasing.

Mary's eyes did not leave his. A smile crept to her lips, and she shook her head as if something were amusing.

"My lord," she said, "as hard as it may be to believe, I have missed your taunting. Therefore, I believe I am more glad to see you than your cousin. The colonel is pleasing company, but he is far more polite than I have grown accustomed to in this past week."

Rycroft could not refrain from laughing at that. "I endeavour to be polite, but you are most provoking."

"I? Oh, no, my lord, it is not I who is most provoking." She raised her left eyebrow, and her eyes twinkled. It was an expression that he adored.

"You are too charming by half, Miss Mary," he said dryly.

She tipped her head as if acknowledging a great compliment. "Thank you, my lord."

Miss Kitty coughed lightly and tipped her head toward the door where Richard was entering with the Bingleys.

Mary bit her lip and looked to Rycroft, "Could you draw his attention?"

"Is that what you want?" She had said she was happier to see him than his cousin, but still, Rycroft felt uncertain of the situation.

"It is what we want." She emphasized the word we as she darted a look at Kitty. "Unless you would rather give the chair to Miss Bingley."

"Please." Miss Kitty's petition was soft, while her eyes were imploring, and her cheeks, rosy.

Rycroft smiled as understanding dawned on him. It was not Mary but her sister who wished the company of his cousin. "I would rather not encourage Miss Bingley," he said as he motioned for Richard to join them.

He allowed his hand to brush Mary's arm as her chair was close enough to do so without being obvious. Although he knew his feelings for her, it would not do to let the rest of the room know before he had spoken to Mary.

She gave him a startled, questioning look, so he leaned a bit closer to her and spoke softly. "Miss Bingley has no hope with me, for my heart belongs to another." Once again, he allowed his hand to brush her arm. "I only hope I have a chance of success with the lady."

Mary's eyes grew wide, and she opened her mouth to reply.

Rycroft shook his head. "I fear I have shocked you." He had known he would, but the topic had to be broached. "Please do not answer now. Just consider me."

"Of course."

He held her gaze, searching her eyes for any sign of hope.

"I will," she said when he did not move or reply. "I promise."

A promise from Mary was not empty words. He was satisfied. "Thank you," he said before standing to greet his cousin.

Chapter 20

RYCROFT SETTLED INTO A chair near the fire in Netherfield's drawing room and opened a book. He had made certain to draw the chair away from the others, separating himself, he hoped, from any possible conversations. He did not wish to discuss his reasons for travelling to Hertfordshire any longer, and he knew that Bingley and his sisters, in particular, would not stop their questioning until they had gotten the full story. Apparently, the need to see Mr. Bennet and deliver some news was not reason enough to quell their curiosity. In fact, it seemed that it had only incited it. He sighed as he watched Darcy draw Bingley aside. Bingley listened intently to Darcy and then turned to look at him. Rycroft nodded. He was sure that the most trustworthy of the Bingley siblings now knew that Mary was his true reason for arriving unannounced.

He let his eyes fall to the page of his book, but his mind was not particularly interested in the words that the author had written. It was more pleasantly engaged in contemplating Mary. She had been surprised at first by his declaration, but her actions toward him did not seem to discourage his suit. In fact, she had eagerly agreed to his calling on her tomorrow.

"Sister," Caroline said in an exaggerated whisper. "What we heard today in the village is true."

Louisa gasped softly. "Indeed? Pray, how do you know?"

"Miss Lydia said that a letter was delivered to her sister, and the stable hand told Mrs. Philips that the messenger was paid handsomely to ensure that news of the delivery was shared. It was from a wealthy gentleman in London."

The desire to do bodily harm to Blackmoore rose within Rycroft once again. The blackguard! It was bad enough that he had written to Mary without permission, but to pay to have rumours spread was truly beyond the pale. The man was lucky he was in London and not in Hertfordshire with Rycroft. Of course, venting his displeasure on his friend would only help him feel somewhat better. It would do nothing for Mary, and she was what mattered most in all of this.

"Is there a secret engagement?" Louisa leaned eagerly toward her sister.

Rycroft held his breath as he waited for the reply.

"No." Caroline's tone was one of great disapproval "What kind of lady accepts a letter from a lover without an understanding?"

The anger Rycroft was feeling towards his friend redirected itself to the gossip who had just insinuated that Mary was less than proper.

Louisa sighed. "If you consider how her sister snared Mr. Darcy, you should not be surprised. It seems the Bennet ladies have a lack of scruples." She clucked her tongue and shook her head. "I do not know what Charles is thinking, tying himself to such a family."

That was a step too far. Rycroft snapped his book closed and leveled a very displeased look at Bingley's sisters.

"A lack of scruples?" He gave a short bitter laugh. "The Bennet ladies do not lack scruples, unlike you two scandalmongers who repeat tales as fact even though they were first told by a man paid to tell them!" He shook his head and expelled a deep, growling breath. "Not only do the two of you lack scruples, you quite obviously lack intelligence."

He rose. There was a lot more he would dearly like to say, but it would do nothing more than use up his time and breath. These two were not worth that. "If you will excuse me, I would rather not have my reading disturbed by the babblings of a harpy." And spotting a chair in the opposite corner of the room, he headed toward it.

This chair was closer to Darcy. Whatever conversation he might overhear from this chair was far more likely to not cause him distress.

"I wish he had at least a small measure of your patience," he heard Bingley say to Darcy. "Do I apologize to him or speak to my sisters?"

Darcy chuckled. "I would not wish to speak with your sisters at present. I do not believe I have ever seen them quite so displeased. Rycroft's scolding must have been harsh indeed."

Rycroft smiled with satisfaction. He hoped the Bingley sisters were thoroughly put out with him. He opened his book and peeked at Darcy to see what he was doing.

His cousin was looking toward the side of the room that Rycroft had just left. When Rycroft turned his eyes in that direction, he understood Darcy's look of concern. Elizabeth was seated close enough to Caroline and Louisa to have heard the whole exchange, and she did not look unaffected by it.

Rycroft chided himself for not including Elizabeth in his leaving of Bingley's sisters. He should have offered to escort her away from them. He saw her rise and, out of the corner of his eye, caught the movement of Darcy's head calling his wife to him.

"I believe my wife may be able to be of assistance." Darcy took her hand when she reached him and placed it between his. "Elizabeth, do you know what made my cousin so angry?"

"Gossip," she whispered.

There was a waver in her voice, and Darcy pulled her closer to his side.

She glanced nervously behind her to where Caroline and Louisa sat.

"Do not worry about them," he said softly.

"You did not hear what they said," she replied. "Apparently, I snared you and due to the letter that was sent to Mary, we Bennet ladies are without scruples."

Darcy turned toward the sound of Richard's groan. "You know about this?"

Richard's brows drew together. "You know about it?"

"I know about a letter," he replied cautiously. "Mary did not read it," he continued. "She gave it to her father, and he read it. She did not even consider Blackmoore's offer."

"I do not know about this," Bingley said.

Darcy sighed. "Blackmoore offered a courtship. His plan is to marry her to please his father and keep his inheritance. But," he darted a glance toward Rycroft, "Rycroft learned that Blackmoore has no intention of breaking off his relationship with a particular actress. It is why he is here — to inform Mr. Bennet of Blackmoore's character."

"And, based on what I observed today, to court Miss Mary," Richard said.

Darcy shrugged. "Aye, that, too."

Bingley blew out a breath. "And my sister is displeased and attempting to discredit Miss Mary, but," his brows drew together, "how did she learn about the letter?"

"The messenger was paid to spread the news." Rycroft stood and took a seat next to Richard so he could join the conversation he had been watching.

"And my aunt was most willing to share the information." Elizabeth turned to Rycroft. "Does my sister know about Mr. Blackmoore?"

"No, I only spoke to your father about him."

"Then, I shall call on Mary first thing tomorrow while you gentlemen are off riding."

Darcy shook his head. "I will attend you."

"But my mother will be busy with preparations for the night's dinner."

"And your father will be pleased to hear something other than a female voice."

Elizabeth laughed. "That is very true, so you have my permission to attend me."

"Thank you, my dear," Darcy said. "Would you care to join me, Rycroft?"

He would like nothing better than to join them. Indeed, he almost wished he had taken Mr. Bennet's offer of a room at Longbourn so that he did not have to be away from Mary now. However, he was not at Longbourn, and he had made arrangements with Mary to see her already. Therefore...

"No, no. Miss Mary expects me later, and if I have learned one thing from my mother and your sister, it is that you do not surprise a lady outside of calling hours. It was quite the lengthy diatribe, but there was something in there about proper gowns and hair." He chuckled. "They did not appreciate my theory that such a call was most beneficial since a gentleman should know what he will see each morning."

This earned laughter from all who were gathered, but when it had died, Rycroft became serious once more. "Her reputation..."

"It may be tarnished for a time," Elizabeth said softly.

"And if I call on her or offer for her, do you think it will make it better or worse?" He rubbed his hands nervously in circles on his knees.

Elizabeth smiled at him as if she understood how his nerves were flitting and fluttering about. "My aunt will assume that it was you who sent the letter," she said, "and when Aunt Philips makes an assumption, it is not long before all of Meryton will know."

"So, I should not call on Mary?"

Elizabeth leaned towards him and placed a hand on his. "You should do what your heart tells you. Believe me when I say, fighting it is not worth the battle." She gave his hand a pat. "Mary would not be the first Bennet lady to endure the whispers of Meryton."

She tilted her head to the side and gave him a playful look. "Mr. Bingley is hosting another ball, and he has a very nice library. One rumour is often forgotten when another is begun." This drew a laugh from them all.

"If it becomes necessary," Rycroft said as he rose. "I think I will take my book to bed." He cast a look in Caroline's direction. "The door will be locked and a piece of furniture against it, so if there is an emergency during the night, you will need a couple of stout footmen to help you gain entrance."

Bingley chuckled. "I can have Hurst return to town earlier than planned."

"No," said Rycroft, "I would like her to witness her defeat." He smiled wryly. "I just pray I am successful."

Chapter 21

"AND IT SEEMS HE paid the messenger to spread rumors to force your hand." Elizabeth rubbed Mary's shoulder. "I am sorry that you have to hear this, that he had behaved so abominably to you."

Mary's mouth hung open, and she looked at her sister in disbelief. She could not believe that the intentions of Mr. Blackmoore had been so dishonourable. To play at courting and loving her to please his father was horrid, but knowing he did it while planning to keep up an affair with another woman was despicable! Add to that his scheme to tie her to him against her will, and well, she did not have words for what that made him.

She was once more overwhelmed by the thought that no man who paid her particular attention was doing so because he loved her. She was just a pawn in some game. Was it that she was unlovable? Or was the fault all on the side of the gentlemen she met?

"Are all men so devious?" she asked.

"What do you mean?" Elizabeth asked.

"Do you remember Roger?" Even the mention of his name made Mary's insides quiver with shame over having been so easily led.

Elizabeth nodded. "He seemed quite smitten with you, and at first, I thought you were equally as smitten with him. But then, you seemed to be indifferent."

"I was not indifferent." She had been humiliated and disgusted. That was more than indifferent. "And he was not smitten with me." Mary blew out a breath and fought the tears that gathered. "I thought he was, just as you thought he was. But he was not. One morning, I slipped out to meet him as he asked me to do — it was the first time I had agreed to do so — and I arrived at our meeting place earlier than planned because you know I like to be early rather than late." A tear slid down her cheek. "My habit saved me." She pressed her lips together to steady them before continuing. "I was not the only one who was early. Roger was there..." she blew out another breath, "with someone else. I turned and ran and avoided him as best I could for the remainder of his stay in Hertfordshire."

Elizabeth gathered Mary into her arms. "Oh, Mary, how dreadful. And now, Mr. Blackmoore has done the same." She said it softly as she stroked Mary's hair. "Not all men are dishonourable. Papa, Mr. Darcy, Uncle Gardiner, Colonel Fitzwilliam, Mr. Bingley and..." she pulled back slightly to look into Mary's face, "and Lord Rycroft are all honourable men. They are not perfect since they are as human just as we are, but they are trustworthy and good. And I believe Lord Rycroft is in love with you."

Mary sighed. He had asked her to consider him; therefore, she had to agree with Elizabeth, even if her heart did not know what to do with that information.

"When Lord Rycroft learned about Mr. Blackmoore's intentions two days ago, he immediately came to tell Mr. Darcy and me."

Mary smiled at that. Lord Rycroft was a good man.

"He was so distraught," Elizabeth continued. "I thought he might be ill. And then when he learned about the letter that had been sent to you, he was on his horse and gone before a half hour had passed."

Elizabeth sat for some minutes with her arms wrapped around Mary and her chin resting on top of Mary's head while Mary sniffled and wondered about Lord Rycroft's regard for her.

"Mary," Elizabeth said at last, "how do you feel about Lord Rycroft?"

Mary sighed a long drawn-out sigh that was filled with confusion. "He is agreeable, even if he does vex me at times, and he is kind." She sighed again. "He does not know it, but I have seen him lend a hand to a footman who was struggling to move a piece of furniture. And all of his servants seem content and at ease. And Georgiana adores him and he, her. I believe she could ask for the moon, and he would attempt to get it for her." She tilted her head to see Elizabeth. "Papa seems to approve of him."

"Those are all very good signs," Elizabeth said with a laugh, releasing Mary from her embrace.

Mary crossed the room to get a fresh handkerchief. As she did so, she passed the parcel that Elizabeth had brought.

"Oh," she cried, "my gown! I had nearly forgotten you brought it." The handkerchief was forgotten for the moment as Mary opened the parcel and lifted the dress out with great care. "It is beautiful," she whispered as she held it up in front of her.

"It is," agreed Elizabeth. "The detail is lovely." She ran a finger gently over the small red roses that adorned the neckline and sleeves of the cream coloured material. There were more rose embellishments at the hem and a frothy ruffle that made the dress seem as if it was rising from a cloud. "You shall outshine all in attendance."

"Are you and Jane not attending?"

Elizabeth was glad to hear the teasing tone of Mary's voice. "We are, but this dress is truly exquisite."

"He chose it." Mary's cheeks took on a rosy hue. "I was struggling to make a decision about which dresses to order, and Lord Rycroft took the book from me, flipped through it and marked every dress I should choose and told me which colours for a few."

Elizabeth shook her head in disbelief. "A gentleman chose this dress?"

Mary nodded. "And nearly all of my new wardrobe. His taste is superb. Uncle will like him." She hung the dress carefully in her wardrobe. "He even asked Lord Brownlow's sister for a riding habit for me to wear since he guessed we were close in size." She turned to Elizabeth. "He was right. The habit fit as if it had been made for me."

"You must accept him then if he offers," teased Elizabeth. "A man of such talent must not be refused."

Mary giggled but soon grew serious. "He would be a good match for me. I believe I would be happy."

"You still have not told me how you feel about him."

"That is because I do not know." She wished she did, but she did not.

"But you will accept him?"

Mary shrugged and nodded. "If he offers —"

"He will," interrupted Elizabeth with a smile.

Mary scowled. "If," she emphasized the word, "he offers, I believe I will. It is not too fast, is it? I mean, I have only known him for a very short period of time, and I am not even certain how I feel about him. Maybe I should not."

Elizabeth smiled at Mary's look of confusion. "You look now how I felt in our bedroom at Aunt Gardiner's. Do you remember how fearful I was?"

Mary nodded. How could she not remember how her normally brave to a fault sister was more nervous and fluttery than their mother, and how it had been all because she was being forced to marry Mr. Darcy?

"Who do you think of first in the day? And last before you go to sleep?" Elizabeth chuckled. "From your startled look, I am going to guess it is him."

Mary grimaced but nodded her admission that Elizabeth was correct. Lord Rycroft had filled her thoughts for some time now – and not just when she was awake. He even appeared to torment her in her dreams.

"Then, I shall tell you what Aunt told me. Be brave, my dear sister. Do not let those feelings frighten you, for they will lead to a very happy life for you just as they have for me. Lord Rycroft is a good and honourable man. He is not like the others." She gave Mary another hug. "Now, our mother may have need of us. Although I fear if her nerves are not the end of her, they will be the end of me."

She opened the door. "You know, Mary, it is pleasant being the mistress of your own home instead of the assistant to your mother. It is far less trying to one's nerves."

Mary could image it was more pleasant to see that things were done your own way rather than being directed in how to do things. She followed Elizabeth out of her room.

"You think I love him?" she whispered.

Elizabeth put an arm around Mary's shoulder. "I suspect you might, but it does not matter what I think. What matters is what you think. Do you love him?"

Mary's shoulders lifted and lowered. She might love him. At least, she might love him a little bit. But was that enough? She was not sure. Perhaps she would discover as time passed that her little bit of love was just a passing fancy. Or, she thought as she took another step down the stairs next to Elizabeth, maybe her little bit of love would grow into something similar to what Elizabeth felt for Mr. Darcy. She would not be sad if it did. That was a good thing, was it not?

Yes, yes, it was, she assured herself. If Lord Rycroft offered for her, she would accept. She bit her lip. Most likely.

Chapter 22

RYCROFT SLOWLY PUSHED OPEN the door to the small drawing room behind Mr. Bennet's study and shivered slightly at the coolness of the air that greeted him. He held high the candle Mr. Bennet had given him as he looked around the room. Mary's father had told him that this was often where she sought refuge from the busyness of the house, and today, with guests arriving for a dinner party, Longbourn was bustling. Therefore, she was most likely in this room, or so Mr. Bennet had assured him.

If she was in here, why had she not lit a fire? It was perfectly frigid. He stepped two more steps into the room and surveyed it again.

Ah! There she was in the corner, curled into a ball in a large, winged chair. Her face was peaceful, and her shoulders rose and fell as she breathed slowly and steadily. She was the very picture of serenity. He placed the candle on the table. It must not have been so dark when she first entered, for a candle sat unlit next to her.

"Mary," he called softly as he shook her shoulder gently. "Mary."

Her eyes fluttered open for a moment, and she smiled at him before closing them again. It was a precious expression he hoped to see over and over and over again all his life, but first, he must wake her.

"Mary," he called again. "You must wake."

This time, her eyes snapped open. "Oh," she said as she pulled herself into proper posture. "I did not mean to fall asleep. I only wished a few moments of quiet."

Rycroft chuckled as she immediately checked her hair. "Not a strand out of place," he assured her.

"How did you find me?" she asked. "Has everyone arrived? What time is it?"

He stilled her hands and did not let them go but kept them within his. "Your father told me I could find you here. I came early, which I know is poor form, so do not lecture me." He smiled at the scowl she gave him. "It is yet an hour before the others arrive, and an hour and a half before we dine." He rubbed her fingers with his hands. "Your fingers are so cold. I am surprised you do not catch a chill napping in here."

"The rest of me is quite warm. It is only because my fingers were outside of my coverings that they are cold." She tried to pull her hands out of his. "We should not be in here alone," she said softly. It was not a scold but a gentle reminder.

He adored her love of propriety even when it caused her to scold and lecture him. She demanded great things from him, and he truly desired to meet those demands, for her pleasure was a prize of unspeakable worth.

"We have permission from your father," he said. "Your mother and sisters think I am in your father's study. We are safe." He sat back on his heels where he kneeled beside her chair.

"But someone may come looking for me," she argued.

He shook his head. "Mrs. Darcy will see that they do not."

"And why is that?" Her expression was skeptical and a trifle accusatory.

"I have asked her to see to it." He shifted, trying to make his position more comfortable.

"You have?"

He nodded.

"So, you have purposed to have a private conversation?"

He smiled. "I have, and both Mrs. Darcy and your father approve of it." He hoped that the slight widening of her eyes and the faint pink tinge to her cheeks were signs that she would welcome his further proposal.

She tipped her head to the side and raised her left eyebrow as she smiled at him. "Then, you may wish to sit in a chair instead of the floor, for a chair will be much more comfortable."

"Very true. But I do not wish to be far from you as we speak." He rose from the floor to pull a chair close. "I will not be dismissed too easily." He hoped he was not dismissed at all, but that remained to be seen.

"I would not expect you to ever be dismissed easily," she replied.

He chuckled. "That is a true fact, though if you asked me to leave, I would do so without too much resistance."

She once again looked at him skeptically.

"I am not sure how to begin," he said as he sat down in the chair he had retrieved from before the cold and dark hearth. "I wish to marry you, you see, but to just say so seems rather direct and not at all the thing to do."

Her mouth hung open for a moment before she closed it and gave a small shake of her head. "It is most certainly direct."

"Yes... well..." He tugged nervously at his cravat. "I cannot say I have ever had this conversation with a lady before. I find I am somewhat at a loss." He gave her a wry grin. "Not that I did not spend most of the night and a good portion of the morning thinking about what I should say. However, it seems all my well-thought-out words have flown from me." He took her hand. "I knew them until I entered this room and found you sleeping in this chair. You were so charmingly situated, and I thought how privileged I would be to wake with such beauty beside me should you accept me... and they were gone."

Mary's cheeks were now brilliantly rosy, and she ducked her head. However, she did not try to stop him. It was a small thing that he was going to take as encouragement. He rubbed his thumb across the back of her hand.

"I should have written them down, for I am afraid I am likely to offend you if I speak without preparation."

She giggled. "That bodes very ill for marriage if you must always prepare a speech before conversing with your wife."

He laughed. "I had hoped it might come easier with time and practice." He drew a deep breath and gave her a determined look. "Very well, I shall attempt to make my heart known to you without causing offense, if you will promise to stay in this room and tell me if I have offended you so that I can make my apologies immediately."

"I believe that is a fair arrangement, my lord," she said with a smile.

He shook his head. "I am afraid you must not smile at me, for it will make it far too difficult for me to make a coherent speech." He placed a finger on her eyebrow. "You must definitely not raise that eyebrow, for the expression is far too beguiling."

He tipped his head to the side and studied her for a moment – her expressive eyes, her pretty lips, the straight line of her nose, the curve of her neck where it met her ear. It was all most becoming and utterly distracting. "Perhaps, you should look away."

She shook her head again and laughed. "I have read the papers, my lord, and was under the impression that you were very capable of talking to ladies."

His eyes narrowed. "First, my name is Samuel, not my lord. Second, the ladies you mention, whom I was able to charm to some extent, meant very little to me other than a stolen kiss or a brief moment of pleasure." He looked at his hands which held hers. "It is a life I have left in the past, and a life that was not nearly so debauched as reported."

It was still not as proper as the lady before him would have wanted for her husband, but there was no going back and undoing what was done, now was there? There was only moving forward as he should have always been.

Mary squeezed his hands. "I am sorry. I should not tease. I had hoped —"

He placed a finger on her lips. "I know, and it did help. Please understand that I do not mind the tease. I just need you to know that the man I was, I am no longer." He lifted her hands to his lips and kissed the knuckles on each. "I would never do as Blackmoore planned. I do not take a wife lightly. She will not be merely the mother of my children and a companion at soirees. My wife will be as much a part of me as the air I breathe and the food I eat. She will be the very beating of my heart, for I have promised myself that I would not marry if I were not completely, utterly in love with the lady to whom I present my offer." He lifted her hands to his lips once again. "I have found that lady, and she is you, Mary Bennet. I love you. Most ardently. Would you do me the great honour of being my wife?"

A tear slid silently down her cheeks as she looked up at the ceiling for a moment before returning her gaze to his. His heart nearly stopped beating when he saw the sadness in her eyes. It was as if her heart were broken by his offer. He expelled a breath as if he had been hit in the stomach.

"You do not want me," he whispered.

Her lower lip quivered, and she shook her head. "It is not that." She drew in a ragged breath. "How can I accept you when my feelings are unequal to such love?" She sniffled.

He drew a breath. It was worse than he expected. He had thought she might say it was too soon, but he had never imagined that... "You do not love me?" Had there ever been a more difficult and painful question to ask?

"Not as you love me." She lowered her eyes and squeezed his hands, as if she did not wish for him to pull them away from her. It was as if she was clinging to him even though her words were not asking him to stay by her side forever. A small spark of hope sprang into his heart at her both her confession and her actions.

"But you love me?" If she loved him, there was yet a chance to win her.

Her shoulders rose and fell in a sad shrug. "I do not know."

He managed to extricate one hand from hers so that he could fish out his handkerchief for her. She released her hold on his hands completely and, accepting the handkerchief he offered, dried her tears.

"I had determined I would accept you when I spoke of the possibility with Lizzy, and she assures me that I may indeed love you. However, I am unsure. I have thought myself in love before only to be disappointed. Not that you would ever disappoint me as he did. I know that."

"Blackmoore?" Had she truly loved the scoundrel?

She shook her head. "No, not him. When I was younger." She pressed her lips together and shrugged once more. Her features were etched with the struggle to know one way or another. Her eyes held his, and he could see his future there, even if she could not.

"I could never knowingly cause you pain, nor could I bear your regret."

There would be no regret. He would eventually be the happiest of men as her husband. He would be. There was no other option.

"You love me," he said as he drew her to her feet and into his embrace. "You just need time to recognize it." He kissed her gently on the forehead. "I will marry you, Mary Bennet, for my heart demands it." He held her close for another moment before releasing her and moving to the door, where he stood with his hand on the door handle.

"I shall not importune you any further this evening. We shall talk and eat, and no one shall be the wiser." He crossed the room to her once again when she started dabbing her eyes with his handkerchief. "All will be well," he said as he drew her to him again. "I promise."

She gave him a watery, wavering smile.

"I really do have to leave you."

"I know."

Her lips spoke her understanding, but her eyes spoke of her longing. He gave her forehead one last kiss, reassured her that all would be well one more time, and took his leave.

Chapter 23

THE NEXT DAY, AS calling hours drew near, Mary chose a seat near the window where she could work on her stitching. Mrs. Gardiner and her children sat nearby. Mary smiled as she listened to the lilting voice of her aunt, who was reading a story.

The Gardiners had arrived only moments before the group from Netherfield had last night. They should have arrived a day earlier, but there had been an issue with an order, and Mr. Gardiner could not leave without attending to it.

Mr. Gardiner and her father were tucked cozily in one corner of Longbourn's sitting room with a deck of cards. Jane sat with her mother going over details for the wedding breakfast while Lydia tried to insert herself into the discussion.

Kitty sat next to Mary with a sketch pad on her knees in which she drew yet another gown. This one nipped in below the bust as so many did, but it stayed close to the body all the way down to the waist before flaring out.

"I would like to wear that," Mary said, peeking over Kitty's shoulder. "You should show it to Mrs. Havelston. She may be able to create it."

Kitty darted a look around the room and then leaned closer to Mary. "I am drawing it for her," she whispered. "You cannot tell a soul, but she liked some of my drawings. She saw them when I was with Jane, and she purchased two." She bit her lip. "I have not yet told Papa. Do you think he will be angry?"

"She bought some of your drawings?" Mary was surprised by the revelation, though the fact that Mrs. Havelston liked Kitty's drawings was not shocking news. Kitty had a talent for drawing and fashion. Heaps of it.

Kitty nodded. "She has promised to keep my name a secret, and I have signed them with only a K for Katherine and an M for Marie. I dared not put my last initial."

"That is a wise idea."

"I know that it is not what ladies do," Kitty whispered. "But Mrs. Havelston was so insistent, and uncle seemed to think Papa would not be angry."

"If you are discreet, he may be accepting of the arrangement, but should it become known…" There was some real concern there. Who knew what the gossip mill would do with that detail, especially when it was added to the fact the Lizzy had to marry Mr. Darcy, and that letter that had arrived for Mary.

Kitty bit her lip and nodded. "I know. It may harm my chances of a good match. I shall be careful." She snapped her book closed as the Netherfield party was announced and tucked it between the leg of her chair and the wall before taking out another book that contained drawings of flowers.

Colonel Fitzwilliam crossed the room to take a seat next to Kitty and Mary as he always did on his calls. Mary suspected that it was not only Kitty who enjoyed the other's company. She smiled at the colonel as he took his seat and then looked expectantly toward the door.

She blinked. It was empty.

The colonel must have noticed her look of disappointment, for he immediately said, "Rycroft has gone to London. He was off early this morning, so he should be there by now."

"He left?" She blinked against the tears that sprang to her eyes at the thought.

"Do not fear, Miss Mary. He has promised to return in time for Bingley's ball and wished for me to ask you to reserve two dances for him." He pulled a paper from his pocket. "The supper dance and the final dance of the evening." He showed her the paper where those two dances were listed, and then folded it and returned it to his pocket. "He said he had some pressing business to attend to and that something which he needed had been left behind in error. He suspects that is likely due to his hasty departure."

"And this will take three days?"

Richard shook his head. "A bit longer since one of the days is the Lord's Day. That is why he wished to reserve those dances. He was unsure if he would return in time for any of the earlier ones."

Mary nodded and turned back to her stitching. If only her needle could close the hole that had formed in her heart.

"He thought about leaving you a note, but with the rumours about the letters, he chose to leave his message with me." He glanced at Kitty and his face turned a slight shade of pink. "There was one more thing in his message."

"And what was that?"

"He said he will miss you," he swallowed, "and that I am to remind you," he blew out a breath, "of his love. He said it in a much more flowery fashion, but I told him I refused to say such things to a lady who was not mine."

Mary bit back a smile as she noted the redness of the colonel's ears. "Thank you. I can imagine that was not an easy message to deliver."

He laughed uneasily. "I would rather lose a boxing match," he mumbled.

"It has put my mind at ease, so I truly do appreciate your willingness to carry his message to me."

"Ah, Miss Mary." Caroline slipped into the chair that was supposed to have been for Lord Rycroft. "I imagine you are excited to return to town and begin your season."

"I am." Mary glanced at Caroline warily. It was not like her to be so friendly. "I am particularly looking forward to seeing Georgiana again."

"Will she not be returning to her brother's house?" Caroline's hand rested dramatically at her heart. To what effect, Mary was uncertain.

"I believe she will, but she is a frequent visitor at Rycroft Place."

Caroline shook her head as if seriously concerned about something. "I cannot understand how your father will allow you to remain living at Lord Rycroft's home after..." She gave a little gasp and leaning close, whispered, "It was not Lord Rycroft who wrote the letter, was it?"

Mary pressed her lips together and said nothing.

"I dare say it was not," she continued, "but for your father to leave the care of his daughter to a man who allowed her to become acquainted with a man who is so forward as to write to a lady without an understanding..."

"I will be staying with his mother just as I was before. It is Lady Sophia who –"

"I suppose," Miss Bingley interrupted, "your father is not familiar with how these things go, being from the country and all. Therefore, I am sure he is unaware of Lord Rycroft's reputation."

She looked at Mary with as much contrived concern as Mary guessed could be mustered.

"My father is not ignorant of –"

"Oh!" Miss Bingley's hand flew once again to her heart as dramatically as it had before. "A refusal of a scandalous proposal made by letter could add to your interest. However, I am afraid it may come at a high price." She leaned close once again. "Gentlemen like to bet on almost everything, and there is said to be books at their clubs where they place bets on who will become betrothed to whom or who will be," she dropped her voice to a very quiet whisper, "compromised by whom. I would hate to hear it brandished about that your name had been written in such a book."

"I would not like to hear that myself." Mary's hands tightened on the material in her hands. She had not considered what effect the news about the letter that she had received from Mr. Blackmoore might have when she returned to town. She wondered if she would be looked at by the gentlemen as cold or would they see her as a tease. Neither would be good.

Her discomfort must have been apparent on her face, for Miss Bingley smiled sweetly, if a bit triumphantly, as she added, "I am probably worrying about nothing. Gossip from small towns rarely makes its way into the ton."

"I am sure you are correct." Mary nodded her head but doubted very much that Miss Bingley would keep such a story to herself. She forced her hands to relax their grip on her material and breathed a sigh of relief as Louisa called her sister to her side.

"She is hateful," Kitty said softly. "I would not desire a season if I had to deal with ladies such as her."

"They are not all so unbearable," Colonel Fitzwilliam said dryly. "Some are actually pleasant, but few are very interesting." He sighed. "And I shall soon be expected to select a bride from the lot or accept the one my father selects for me."

"You are not free to choose where you will?" Mary asked. Oh! That was not good for Kitty!

"Would that I were, but my father controls my inheritance and will do his best to use it to force me into an advantageous marriage."

"That is so sad," Kitty said softly.

He smiled at her. "It is."

"You have no means to stand up to him?" Mary asked.

"I shall be cut off if I do." Bitterness coloured his tone.

"Would you be destitute if that were to happen?" Mary tilted her head to the side and studied his face. Worry creased his brow.

"Not destitute but in need of work and with barely enough to support a wife. It would not be a meager existence, but it would be far lower than I would wish for."

"Am I to understand then that you would prefer an unhappy existence with plenty to happiness with far less?" Mary watched his brows furrow as he considered what she had said. "It would be inconvenient, I suppose, to choose a wife without some means to add to your coffers, whether it is to please your father or to ease your life."

He nodded his agreement. "Very inconvenient," he muttered.

"You have your wooden designs," Kitty said hopefully. "They are very beautiful. I am confident many would pay to have such items in their homes, so you would not be in need of work. You would have a profession at the ready."

He smiled. "Very true." His eyebrows raised. "And such work would make me happy."

"It is a very difficult decision to be sure," Mary said softly. She hoped that his decision would not be the one which would break her sister's heart. However, she was practical enough to know that it might.

Beside her, the colonel heaved a great sigh. "It is impossibly difficult," he said.

Mary turned her attention back to her stitching, leaving Kitty to carry the conversation with the colonel. Thoughts of heartbreak for her sister tumbled around her mind along with thoughts about what her own heart wished for. She longed for someone with whom to share these contemplations. She looked at the empty seat beside her. No, she did not long for someone; she longed for him.

Chapter 24

"I HEAR BLACKMOORE WAS unsuccessful with his lady." Endicott took a seat next to Rycroft, where he was seated near a window in a quiet portion of his club the day after he had returned to town from Hertfordshire.

"I hear," Endicott continued, "that she is all but betrothed to some other gentleman. The fellow followed her to her father's home." He drummed his fingers on the arm of his chair. "The name of the chap escapes me."

"Rycroft."

"No, no. I know your name. It is the name of the gentleman who hied off after the chit who was staying with you that I am trying to remember."

Rycroft opened his mouth to reply, but the arrival of Brownlow stopped him.

"I thought you were in Hertfordshire until nearly the new year." Brownlow pulled another chair over so he could join Endicott and Rycroft. "Did your lady send you on your way?"

"Brownlow," Endicott interrupted, "who was it that went after that chit? You know, the chit staying with Rycroft who would not have Blackmoore?" He turned to Rycroft. "Blackmoore is not happy, I will have you know."

"Endicott," Brownlow said dryly, "neither Rycroft nor I care that he is unhappy."

"Nor do I." Endicott gave a shake of his head. "I was merely relating a fact. Now, do you know the gentleman's name?"

Rycroft shook his head. "Endicott," he said, drawing his friend's attention away from Brownlow. "I have been in Hertfordshire, and Miss Mary, the lady," he gave Endicott a pointed look, "who was staying with my mother and me, is from Hertfordshire." He leaned back in his chair and waited for the connections to be made in Endicott's mind.

Brownlow sighed in exasperation. He often had little patience for playing games with Endicott. "It was Rycroft, Endicott. Rycroft went after Miss Bennet. Honestly, you need to keep a notebook with you for recording names. You are the worst for remembering them of anyone I have met."

That was true. Endicott was good at remembering details about the people he met except for the rather important detail of their names.

"Perhaps, I should," Endicott agreed with a shrug. "I suppose I do not need to tell you about it then." He smiled wryly at Rycroft.

"No, you have said enough." Lord Brownlow accepted the cup of tea the footman had brought for him, "However, Rycroft must explain why he is here instead of in Hertfordshire."

"True! I had not thought of that." Endicott propped his elbows on the arms of his chair and clasped his hands in front of him while casting an eager look of anticipation in Rycroft's direction.

The man was far too enthralled with a good story.

"Do you wish to get a notebook to record the details?" Rycroft teased, earning himself a scowl from his tale-loving friend. He turned to Brownlow. "I returned to town to have the marriage papers drawn up."

"You..." Brownlow's brows rose, and his eyes blinked in surprise. "I thought you were only going to stop her from accepting Blackmoore and then perhaps, court her, but you say you have offered for her? Already?"

"I did." Rycroft drew a deep breath and released it slowly. "She has not, however, accepted."

Both men looked at him in confusion.

"Then, why are you having papers drawn up?" Endicott asked.

"That is an excellent question," Brownlow agreed.

Rycroft motioned to a footman and pointed to the cup of tea Brownlow was holding. "Do you remember the details surrounding my cousin's betrothal?" he asked his friends.

Brownlow placed both his cup and saucer on the table to his right. "I do."

"Bingley is having a ball," Rycroft said with a smile. "The night before his wedding, Bingley is having a ball, and I shall be in attendance."

Brownlow shook his head as if trying to make sense of it all. "You would compromise her?" he whispered.

"That is our plan." Rycroft nodded his thanks to the footman for the tea.

"Our plan?" Endicott asked. "Who is helping you?"

Rycroft allowed the warmth of the tea to settle in his stomach before he responded. "Her father, Bingley, Darcy, the soon-to-be Mrs. Bingley, and the delightful Mrs. Darcy." He took another sip of his tea. It had been Elizabeth's idea in a roundabout way. How many times had she suggested that he make use of the library at Netherfield to stage a compromise? Not that he planned to use the library for his scheme. "When next I return to town, it shall be as a happily married man."

"But she refused you." Endicott was obviously still confused. "How can you be happily married to a lady who does not wish to marry you?"

"Ah," Rycroft said, "but she does want to marry me." That was the best part. She loved him. "She just has not yet accepted the fact."

Brownlow laughed and shook his head. "I would not be so complacent if I were you. I would fear that she would be angry."

Rycroft sighed. That was the danger, and it was a very real one. Mary liked propriety, and a compromise, especially as he had planned, was not proper. "I am certain I will have to bear a lecture or two, but I am also certain that the price will be worth the payment." He took the last sip of his tea and placed the empty cup on the table. "I love her, and I will not be without her."

He held out his hand to shake Brownlow's. "I wish to thank you, my friend, for sending me off on that errand those many months ago, for it was on my trip back to town when I met Mary."

He rose to leave but thought better of it and sat back down. "My exile, so skillfully arranged by you, gave me time to consider my life." He shrugged and shook his head. "I did not like what I saw, and so I determined that, on my return, I would not be as I had been. I would do my duty to the title and take on the mantle of responsibility I had shirked for so long."

Brownlow smiled. "And happily, your cousin fell into a compromise and had to marry, which brought your path to cross that of Miss Bennet's."

Rycroft nodded. "Precisely. Although, at the risk of sounding the part of a parson," or a great deal like his Mary, "I would say it was providential. Love is a blessing. I hope you both find it." He chuckled as Brownlow rolled his eyes. "I know, my brain has been addled, and wonderfully so." He rose to leave. "I am in town until the beginning of the week. I would not be averse to some company or a game of cards once or twice."

"Tomorrow morning. Hyde Park," Brownlow called after him. "Foul weather or clear, we ride."

Rycroft gave him a small salute and then gathered his outerwear and headed toward home.

Mary closed the door to the small drawing room behind her father's study quietly, and then, pulled her shawl tight as she crossed
the cold room to her place of refuge from the busyness of the
house. With a sigh of relief, she sank into her favourite chair and
tucked her feet under her skirts.

"A fire would make this room more enjoyable."

Mary jumped at the voice. She had forgotten there was an entrance to the room from her father's study. "Papa, you gave me such
a fright."

He shuffled over to the bell pull and gave it a tug. "I have been
meaning to enjoy this room, and it would not do for me to sit in
here in the cold," he explained to her with a sly smile.

She shook her head. She would have refused the offer of a fire,
and he knew it. He also knew she would not deny him some
warmth. He might be rather feeble in his body, but his mind was
still sharp enough to manoeuver things to be how he wanted them
to be.

Her father took the chair next to her. It was the one in which
Lord Rycroft – Samuel – had sat as he proposed. Mary swiped at
a tear that had escaped her eyes, trying to hide the fact that she was
once again feeling melancholy. She was certain she had spent more
time crying in the past few days than she had in all the years of her
life together.

"Do you miss him?" Her father had not missed the tear.

She bit her lip and nodded.

A servant entered and began to lay the fire while Mr. Bennet
began a discussion of the weather and then of the service that
morning. When the fire was blazing, and the servant had left, he
took Mary's hand. "Speak to me about him. Why did you refuse
him?"

She shrugged. It had seemed the right thing to do at the time, but now? Now, she felt the error of her decision most severely. "He loves me so much, and I was unsure I could return that love."

Her father patted her hand. "And are you still unsure?"

She shook her head. "No. When he left so suddenly, I felt as though my heart has been ripped in two. And when Miss Bingley began her campaign to unsettle me..."

"Ah, yes, I remember you telling me about Miss Bingley and her catty ways."

Her father had found her in here on that day, too.

"I wanted so dearly to talk to him about it, and I knew in that moment, Papa, that he will always be a part of my heart." She wiped at her eyes again. There was no way to stop the tears now that she was allowing her heart to unlatch itself and spill out of her. "I wish he were here now." And if he were here now, she would never let him leave again without her.

"He will return tomorrow, and you may tell him this then," her father assured her. "I am so happy that my girls have found such fine gentlemen who will care for them long after I am gone."

"Shhh, Papa," whispered Mary, "do not speak of such things." She could still not bear with any sort of equanimity the fact that he was so unwell. She still longed for him to be restored to full health.

"But it is true, my dear." Her father's tone was soft and gentle but firm. "I am not well, and I am old. Those two facts do not bode well for a long life. It is the way of things. Life begins and grows and then fades."

"I know, Papa. All our days are numbered, but I am already enough of a watering pot without considering losing you." She drew a ragged breath. "I love you."

"And I, you, my dear. And I, you." He gave her hand a squeeze. "I have not said it enough. Be sure you learn from my error and say it as often as you can to your children." He stood slowly as Mary heard the door to his study open. "I suspect your uncle is looking for some peace from the talk of wedding and ball preparations. Would you mind if we joined you?"

Mary shook her head. "I would love the company, so long as you do not mind a few tears."

Mr. Bennet withdrew his handkerchief from his pocket and placed it on her lap. "I shall send for more if you need them."

She laughed as she picked up the piece of cloth. Her father did not move away from her as she expected him to do. Instead, he stood before her looking gravely serious.

"You will tell him about your change of heart when he returns for Mr. Bingley's ball tomorrow?"

"Yes, Papa, I will."

"Good. Only two more daughters to go and my duty is done." He shuffled toward the adjoining door and called, "Gardiner, come join us."

"Have you a handkerchief?" he added as her uncle entered the room.

"I most certainly do." Uncle Gardiner pulled his handkerchief from his pocket. "Who has need of it? Surely not you."

Mr. Bennet chuckled. "No, not I. I have a daughter and you have a niece who is missing a certain gentleman."

"Ah," her uncle said in an understanding tone. "I know the feeling well. I can remember the times that my love and I were parted." Much to Mary's delight and her emotions' relief, he settled into a chair and began to tell stories of his and his wife's courtship.

Chapter 25

RYCROFT PACED THE SITTING room. He was going to be late. He should have left for Hertfordshire two hours ago, but thanks to a cat and a cup of tea, his papers were not yet ready.

"Your pacing will not make them arrive any sooner." His mother peered up from her work.

"I said I would be there before the supper set, and I shall not be." He dropped into a chair. "Mary will worry." And he would worry about her worrying about him. He despised the idea that he was going to be a source of unease for her and that it was none of his own doing.

"It cannot be helped. She will understand." Lady Sophia turned her eyes back to her work. "Perhaps it will help you regain some amount of calmness to know that the mistress's suite is prepared. I saw to it this morning, and Sarah has moved all of Mary's things into the room." She looked over he glasses at him and smiled. "We are only missing Lady Rycroft."

Rycroft smiled at that, and his mother chuckled at him. But he did not care. Mary would soon be his Lady Rycroft, and that was an excessively agreeable thought.

"Lady Rycroft." Georgiana sighed. "To think Mary will not just be my friend but also my cousin."

"And my daughter," Lady Sophia said. "I have waited a long time to have a daughter." She cast a teasing glance at Rycroft. "However,

I had thought it might take longer for the two of you to come to an understanding."

Rycroft's brows rose at the comment. He knew that his mother, despite her protests to the contrary, was going to play matchmaker for Mary while in town, but he had not thought that she had planned on matching Mary with him.

Lady Sophia chuckled again. "From the moment I met her, I knew Mary was the one for you, my son. A mother knows these things."

"Indeed?" Rycroft said in disbelief. "A lady argues with your son, and you deem her the perfect candidate to marry him?" He shook his head. Of course, his mother probably had thought that very thing. "Does that mean that matching Mary and me was the true reason behind your inviting her to stay with us?"

"No," she replied with a shake of her head for emphasis, "I wished to have her stay with me because I enjoyed her company."

Rycroft, knowing that his mother was relaying only part of the truth with her statement, gave her an amused smile. "Ah. So, it had nothing to do with finding her a husband or me a wife."

Lady Sophia lifted one shoulder in a nonchalant half-shrug. "The fact that I hoped she would marry my son did make the prospect of her company all that much more enjoyable; although, your wayward tongue did give me a fair bit of concern."

He rose to look out the window once again. "As much as I do not wish to condone such scheming, I find I must thank you for your interference."

"And while I am not certain I approve of your methods for securing a wife, I find I am looking forward to the result."

"Does she truly love you?" Georgiana asked.

Rycroft had laid out his plan to give Mary no choice but to marry him to both his mother and his cousin. It was not as if the news of the scandal he planned to cause was not going to reach them. Therefore, he had thought it best to be the source of their information so that they could refute any embellishments that the rumour mill might add to the tantalizing tale.

"She said she could not accept me because she was uncertain she could love me as ardently in return. It is not that she does not love me. She was merely doubtful about the depth of her love for me." Seeing his solicitor mounting the steps, he turned toward his mother with delight. "The marriage papers are here!" He kissed her on the cheek. "I shall bring you back a daughter," he whispered before hurrying from the room as a knock sounded at the door.

Several hours later, Rycroft swung down from his horse and handed the reins to a waiting groomsman before slipping into Netherfield through the servants' entrance. He stopped long enough in the kitchen to charm a few morsels from the cook and then ascended the back stairs.

He paused at the sound of music that filtered through the house to him. Placing the items that he carried on the steps and finding the right door, he pushed it open just a crack so that he could peek inside. He had to rise high up onto his toes to see over the ladies standing near the door, but his effort was rewarded as he saw Mary working her way through the dance. He breathed a sigh of relief as he saw her smiling at something Richard had said. It appeared she was enjoying herself.

A footman slipped through the door, and a maid scurried toward him. Rycroft took one last look and saw Mary looking toward the main entry to the ballroom as she circled away from her partner. He smiled. She was enjoying herself, but not so much that she had forgotten about him. Pleased by the fact, he hurried off to his room. There was not long before the end of the dancing, and he did not wish to attend smelling of horse and the out of doors as he did now.

After a rather cool bath, since the water had been waiting for him for some time, he donned his clothes for the ball. As he stood before the mirror, having his cravat tied, three quick knocks sounded at his door.

"Come," he called.

"It is a relief to see you, Rycroft," Bingley said. "Mr. Bennet is in the library as planned, but I fear you will not have time to meet with him before the final dance." He took a seat.

Rycroft blew out a breath. He had caused plenty of stirs in his life, but this one played heavily on his nerves. Most likely because of his love for the lady who would be unwittingly part of it in a very short amount of time. "He knows about the plan for the dance?"

Rycroft had not had enough time to go to Longbourn, share the details of his plan with Mr. Bennet, and get to town with enough time to secure the papers and license he needed. Therefore, he had left the explanation of what was afoot to Bingley.

"He does."

"And he is amenable to it?" Rycroft cast a concerned look over his shoulder toward Bingley.

"He found it quite diverting. I am to stress to you that it is not proper, but he will not protest. You still have his blessing."

"And Mary? How angry do you expect she will be?" His valet gave a small huff of disapproval, and Rycroft returned to facing the mirror so that his cravat could be given a final straightening.

"I expect she will be somewhat put out, but according to Jane and Elizabeth, she has been out of sorts and anxious for your return." Bingley chuckled. "I am deliriously happy that Caroline is to leave with Hurst tomorrow, for I expect she will be quite unpleasant."

Rycroft laughed. "It is no more than she deserves."

"Most certainly," Bingley agreed with alacrity. "She attempted to unsettle Mary the day you left. Richard told me about it."

Rycroft shook his head and clapped Bingley on the shoulder. "For your sake, I pray she finds a husband this season. I still do not know how either you or Darcy tolerate her."

"She is my sister, and Darcy is too bound by propriety to be anything less than a gentleman." Bingley grinned. "Unless, however, she makes a disparaging remark about Mrs. Darcy or her family. You would be right impressed by the glowers and abrupt words he has given Caroline." Bingley opened the door of Rycroft's room. "You should take the servants' stairs. Mary has not taken her eyes off the door to the ballroom all evening."

"Everything is in place?" Rycroft asked as they hurried down the hallway.

Bingley nodded. "The parson is here. The servants are ready to make arrangements for an extra guest. Jane has informed her mother this evening about the wedding breakfast being in honor of both your wedding and mine, and she has been sworn to secrecy." He chuckled. "That was no easy task."

Rycroft could imagine it was not. Mrs. Bennet was an easily excitable sort of lady.

"Elizabeth had Mary's things packed after the Bennets arrived here this evening," Bingley continued. "She is the only one of our group who expects her sister to accept you tonight."

"You truly are agreeable to sharing your wedding day with me?"

Bingley paused in the servant's hall. "If it is necessary. Both Jane and I are delighted to be of assistance to you and Mary. Elizabeth has assured Jane that it will not be."

"Thank you." Rycroft tapped the packet of papers on his hand. "Have you seen Miss Mary?" he asked a footman who had just stepped into the hall.

"Yes, sir," he replied. "Two doors down. She is very near the door." He bowed and continued on his way to attend to his business.

"I shall inform Mr. Bennet of your arrival and the slight change in plans. Wait about five minutes before entering. I will have him to you before the dancing begins." Bingley did not wait for a reply but trotted down the servant's hall to the door that led to the library.

Rycroft stood outside the door to the ballroom and waited. He paced a few steps forward and back, tapping the papers on his hand as he walked. Finally, he pushed the door open slightly so that he could see her.

As his eyes located her, he saw Mary's fan snap shut and her eyes narrow as she turned toward the group of ladies who were whispering near her. A laugh bubbled up inside of him as he prepared to listen to the lecture she was about to give. She would make a formidable countess. He stepped into the room, unable to resist being at her side for a moment longer.

Chapter 26

MARY TAPPED HER ARM with her fan and watched the door. There were only three dances left, and still he had not arrived. A small twisting began in her stomach and her eyes began to sting as tears gathered in them. Elizabeth nudged her discreetly with her shoulder.

"He will be here," she said.

"But what if something has happened? What if he is hurt? What if he has changed his mind?" She drew a deep breath and expelled it slowly.

Elizabeth slipped an arm around her shoulders. "While an accident is not impossible, it is unlikely. The moon is bright, and I am given to understand he is an excellent horseman. He will be here."

Mary gave her sister a small smile that said she would try to believe what she had been told.

"Miss Mary," Richard said as he bowed upon approaching her, "I believe this is the dance you promised me." He glanced from her worried face to that of Elizabeth's. "That is, if you are willing. I would understand if you chose to sit it out."

Mary shook her head and straightened her posture. "I thank you, Colonel, but I believe a dance is just what is needed to keep my mind occupied." She extended her hand to him and allowed him to lead her onto the floor. As she took her place, she noticed her father being escorted from the room. She glanced anxiously at Jane, who was beside her in the line.

"He is tired, and Mr. Bingley has offered him the use of the library," explained Jane. "You know how Mama did not want him to attend."

"Of course," said Mary. "But he is well?"

Jane nodded. "I believe he has found the evening to be very agreeable."

Mary reached over and gave Jane's hand a squeeze. "Thank you. I find I am more anxious than normal tonight."

"I think you are handling things quite well," Jane assured her as the music began.

As Mary moved through the steps and entered into small conversations with those of her set, her mind did ease, and her eyes looked less frequently toward the door. Soon, she even found herself smiling. If it were not for the dull aching in her heart, she would have found the dance to be thoroughly enjoyable. She curtseyed, thanked Richard, and scooted to the side of the room, taking a place where she could easily see the entry. She watched as the next set of couples lined up.

"From a gentleman from town," a lady to her right said in a rather loud whisper. The comment was followed by a tsking.

Mary closed her eyes. It was not the first whisper she had heard tonight. She thought of doing as she had all evening and moving to a new location, but since this offered the best view of the doorway, she remained.

"You know she was in town staying at the home of a gentleman," the lady paused before adding in a scandalized tone, "It was an unmarried gentleman's home. He is an earl to be sure, but you know how titled men can be." She tittered, and the others joined her.

"I hear he arrived a day after the letter," said another. "He met with her father, and two days later, was gone." She gave a small derisive snort. "I have not seen him this evening, so I believe he must have been refused, just as the gentleman who wrote to her was." Mary heard a fan snap open. "She'll not see him again. I'd not be so particular if I were her."

Mary, her patience wearing thin, snapped her fan closed. "And why is that?" she asked turning toward the group of gossips. "Would you care to explain why I should not be particular in choosing a gentleman to be my husband? Is it my looks? My intelligence? My family? What exactly is my defect?"

The ladies stood silently, their mouths hanging agape.

"Should I not refuse a man who keeps a mistress and is only looking for a proper wife to bear him children? For the man who wrote me is such a man." She took a step closer to the group of ladies. "Or perhaps I should not take time to carefully consider the offer of a good man because I do not wish to accept him unless I can return his affections as ardently as he bestows them?" She crossed her arms and tapped her foot as she waited for a response. Seeing that one was not forthcoming, she sighed. "I would be more particular in my choice of conversational topics if I were you."

"Well said, Miss Mary." Rycroft chuckled. "I was afraid I was the only one to receive such remonstrations — well-deserved remonstrations, I might add." He took her hand and with a sideward glance at the ladies who were watching, lifted it, placing a kiss first on her knuckles and then her palm. A satisfied smile spread across his face as Mary blushed, and the gossips gasped. "I must apologize for being late. There was a mishap with a cup of tea, and my solicitor had to redo a portion of a very important document. I was unable to leave until it was completed." He held up the packet of papers to verify his story both with her and the gossips, who were watching them.

"Ah, Rycroft, at last!"

Mary turned to see Mr. Bingley helping her father toward them.

"I was awaiting you in the library." Her father settled into a chair that stood near the wall. "Go, have your fun. We shall talk after."

Rycroft bowed. "Thank you, sir. It is all here as discussed." He handed the packet to Mr. Bennet. "I still have your approval?"

Mr. Bennet's eyes twinkled with merriment as he gave a nod. "It is not a library, but it shall have to do."

Rycroft chuckled. "But it is a ball."

Mr. Bennet winked. "That it is." He made a shooing motion with his hand and then settled in to look at the documents Rycroft had given him.

Rycroft tucked Mary's hand in the crook of his arm, gave a nod of his head to the gossips, and led Mary onto the dance floor. "My cousin did deliver my message the day I left, did he not?"

"He did." She smiled up at him and said softly, "I have missed you."

"And I, you," he said as they took their places in line between Jane and Bingley and Darcy and Elizabeth. "It was torturous to know I was going to be late and would cause you to worry."

She smiled at him. "I am just glad you have returned."

The first notes of the dance sounded, and she curtseyed to his bow and began the process of working her way through the figures. In sentences broken by the separating and rejoining movements of the dance, he told her about the cat who had upset the tea tray, damaging one page of the document the solicitor had been drafting. She giggled at his recounting. At the end of his story when they once again joined hands, he asked if she wished to know what documents were so important as to have delayed him. She nodded as she circled away from him for a brief moment before rejoining him.

"They are marriage papers," he said as he moved down the center of the line, but instead of releasing her hand and allowing her to circle back to her place, he pulled her into his embrace. "I still intend to marry you, if you will have me." And then, instead of allowing her to reply, he kissed her.

Had she been thinking, she would have been shocked and horrified to be caught in such a scandalously compromising position, but she was not thinking.

"Will you have me?" he whispered when he finally broke away from her.

She nodded and smiled at him. "It seems you have left me no other choice."

He chuckled, but she shook her head when he opened his mouth to speak, and so he remained silent.

She traced the line of his jaw with her finger. "Not because my reputation will be in tatters if I do not, but because my heart will not allow me to refuse. I love you, Samuel Rycroft, and I do not wish to live another moment without you."

He kissed her once more. It was a soft kiss, one that lingered on her lips after he pulled away and left her desiring more. He looked around the room and then back at her. "I brought a special license with me, and I see the parson is here."

Her eyes grew wide. "You wish to marry here? Tonight?"

"I do," he said with a grin. "But, if you prefer, we can wait until tomorrow."

Her brows furrowed. "We cannot marry tomorrow. Jane is getting married tomorrow."

He shrugged. "I do not plan on returning to London without you as my bride." He cocked his head to the side and studied her face, his eyes coming to rest on her lips.

"But such a quick wedding? It just is not done."

"If that were true, Gretna Green would not be the busy place it is." He chuckled as she narrowed her eyes. "Besides, I do believe we have already left the realm of propriety."

She sighed. "Very well. If we are to be completely improper..." She paused and looked at Bingley.

"You are welcome to use my ballroom for your wedding or join us at the church in the morning." He stepped a bit closer and whispered. "You are also welcome to stay here with your husband tonight. Someone can fetch what you need."

She drew a deep breath. "In that case, if the parson is willing, I see no need to delay." She nearly laughed at the look of shock on Rycroft's face. It was quite obviously not the answer he had expected. She cupped his face in her hands. "As I said, I do not wish to live another moment without you, so there really is no other choice." She drew his head down to hers and with a whispered, "I love you," pressed her lips against his.

If she had been thinking, she would have realized that there were preparations being made around her. If she had been thinking, she might have considered that people were whispering, and Miss Bingley was glowering. But she was not thinking.

She was not thinking of the times he would speak without thought or the moments she would lecture. She was not thinking of the fact that every time this dance played, she would be standing up with him, nor was she thinking of how he would insist on ending each of those dances with a kiss. She was not thinking of the soirees she would attend or the ones she would host. Nor was she thinking of his mother, who was anxiously awaiting a daughter, or the friend who was awaiting a new cousin. She was not thinking of the family that would grow around and within her starting this very night.

No, Mary Bennet was not thinking. She was only kissing and loving and embracing what was surely to become her greatest source of happiness. For when one's heart swells as hers had when she had seen him standing behind her, when one's lips have tasted such sweet and consuming love, and when a lady's mind knows that, despite the trials that might come, it will not be at rest without the man whose lips pressed against hers and whose arms surrounded her, there truly was no other choice.

His Inconvenient Choice

CHOICES BOOK 3

The colonel has made his choice. It's Kitty. Not that his father will ever allow the match.

Chapter 1

JANUARY 1, 1812

THE CARRIAGE DOOR CLOSED. It was over. His happy sojourn in Hertfordshire was over. Mr. and Mrs. Bingley were married, as were Lord and Lady Rycroft — their breakfast was nearing its end.

The conveyance in which Colonel Richard Fitzwilliam sat lurched into motion and rolled down Netherfield's drive, moving his person towards town and leaving his heart behind.

He unfolded the small piece of paper that had been tucked into his pocket as he had left the wedding breakfast and shook his head. Two cousins and a friend newly married and all within the space of two weeks was enough to set anyone's world on end. It was also the sort of thing that made Richard contemplate his own future.

As always, such thoughts made breathing become something one had to strain to do. As quietly as he could, Richard drew a slow, deep breath and hoped that with his exhalation the feeling of being crushed would also leave his body.

However, his attempt was only slightly successful. The truth of the matter was that there was no way to remove all the crushing oppression that thoughts of his future brought, for his future could never be so happy as those of his cousins and Bingley. He was not free to choose where he wished. He did not have complete control over his destiny and fortune. His marriage would be one of convenience; his father would see to that.

Not wishing to draw attention to it from the others in the carriage, he looked surreptitiously at the paper in his palm. The drawing there brought a smile to his lips and a pang of regret to his heart. Forget-me-nots graced the lid of a box from which spilled strands of pearls and chains of gold. He refolded the drawing again and slipped it back into his pocket.

If his heart could make his choice for him instead of his father, Kitty Bennet would be his choice. She had stolen his heart while she stood, shivering in the wind, on the street in front of the milliner's shop on Meryton's high street as she had insisted on being introduced to him as Katherine.

Upon further acquaintance, she had proven to be a lady who shared many of his same interests and who made him feel at ease. She expected no more from him than for him to be himself. He did not need to be a military leader or the son of an earl. She cared for none of that.

She had even been interested in his wooden creations — and not as a lady who was trying to make a favourable impression on a gentleman might be. No, Katherine had listened with interest and animation when he had told her about his love of creating with wood. She had even sketched a few designs that he might like to use.

"If you could wait but a year," she had said as they had strolled the perimeter of the ballroom last night, "then your inheritance will be yours."

He had felt her hopefulness and had longed to be able to enter into it with her, but he knew the reality of the situation.

"He will not allow me to be free. He will insist on my marrying before he gives me one farthing more than I have," he had replied.

Her eyes had filled with tears that she had refused to shed, and his heart had broken a bit more at both the thought of a life without her and the knowledge that his father was the source of her pain.

"If I could wait," he had whispered, "I would wait a thousand years for you."

She had smiled sadly at him and said, "And I would wait for you."

He once again ran his gloved finger over the drawing in the pocket of his coat.

"Do not forget me," she had said as she had slipped it into his pocket when he was taking his leave of her.

He knew he would never forget her. He could not. She was burned into his heart forever.

His hand closed around the paper.

"You are looking rather pensive, Colonel," Caroline Bingley said, interrupting his thoughts. "Are they pleasant things that occupy your mind?"

"Not all of them." He turned to look out the window, hoping she would take the action for what it was meant to be – an end to their discussion.

If the weather had not been so foul, he would have refused Hurst's offer to travel with him. Being held captive in a carriage with a lady the likes of Caroline Bingley was not something he wished to do on a day when his heart was not a tattered, mangled mess. Today, the prospect was even less welcome.

"That is a pity," Louisa Hurst said. "I prefer to think on agreeable things whenever possible."

"As do I," Richard said, "but it is not always possible."

"A colonel must have many disagreeable things to consider," Miss Bingley added.

Richard did not turn from his contemplation of the dreary dampness of the day outside the carriage window.

"Indeed, he must," he replied, "and I often do."

Had her fortune been from land rather than trade, Miss Bingley might be of some value to his father. If she had relations in parliament or who were friends of someone who was in parliament, that also would be a mark in her favour, and with those two most important items attached to her name – money from a proper source and some social standing of significance – she might stand a chance of becoming his bride. Not that Richard would ever chose her of his own accord, but his father would.

"However," he continued, "I was not thinking as a colonel just now but rather as a mere man."

Hurst snorted at the comment. "Do leave him be, Caroline."

Hurst was the husband of Miss Bingley's sister and not more than two years Richard's elder. He was also not someone who would meet with Lord Matlock's approval. Oh, his clothes would. For they were always the latest style. His bank account and connections, however, were not as becoming. That is not to say he was poor, but he also was not notably wealthy among the upper circles in town.

"I was only attempting to pass the time in conversation," she replied with a huff. "The light is too poor for anything else."

"I find a quiet nap a most refreshing way to pass a trip," Hurst replied.

"How dull," Miss Bingley grumbled.

"Not at all," Richard countered. "I find I would like to close my eyes. It has been a busy two days."

Hurst nodded. "It has been, and you were out with your men yesterday morning, were you not?"

"I put them through a few drills to test them." Richard turned to his bench mate. "Those who passed my test were allowed to attend the ball last night. Those who did not pass were confined to quarters for the evening."

It had been his plan, and a successful one, to keep Wickham from the ball. He would take every opportunity afforded him by his position while he held it to ensure that Wickham had less enjoyment than he desired. It was one of the few pleasures Richard received from his duty.

"And, I believe, you danced every dance, did you not?" Mrs. Hurst asked.

"All save one." His heart pinched, for that one had been set aside to stroll with Kitty.

"Oh, Hurst, you are right. I do believe a nap must be had. What with an early morning yesterday for the colonel, a night of dancing, and another early start to the day today, he must be very tired." She turned to her sister. "It would be most unkind of us to keep him from his rest."

"I thank you," Richard said with a bow of his head before Miss Bingley could say a word to either agree or disagree with her sister. "I am indeed rather tired," he added as he settled back and closed his eyes.

His fingers once again sought that slip of paper in his pocket. Finding it, he allowed his mind to wander to the lady who had given it to him, and with a deep exhale, he attempted to find some peace in sleep.

Katherine Bennet turned from the window where she had been watching the Hursts' carriage drive away. Her stomach fluttered anxiously, and she wanted to do anything but what she knew she must. There were not many wedding guests remaining, and she knew that both she and the Darcys would leave soon. Then, her opportunity to do what was needed would become nearly impossible, barring a visit to town and Darcy House. She pressed her hand against her stomach, trying to calm the flutters. She could do this. For him, she could do this.

"Mr. Darcy, may I have a word with you?" she said.

"Certainly," her brother-in-law replied with a smile that helped ease her mind the tiniest bit. Still, she could not keep from twisting her fingers together in front of her stomach and biting her lip.

Mr. Darcy's presence always unsettled her. He almost always looked serious. She was sure that he was, at any moment, going to scold her for some foolishness. She knew she had no reason to feel so beyond his sometimes-severe expression, but she did. And what she wished to speak to him about at present was something that could earn her a look of displeasure or more.

She barely resisted the urge to duck her head and hide from him. "I have a little bit of money and expect to receive some more."

She reminded herself that Mr. Darcy was the person who was best be able to advise her about her money and straightened her shoulders before continuing.

"I have sold some dress designs to Mrs. Havelston, and she has requested some more. I have not signed them with my name, and it is to be a secret arrangement." The words rushed from her. "I would like to invest the money she pays me. I know that you can earn money with money, but I do not know how to do it, and I am not a gentleman, which limits me."

He smiled at her. "That sounds like a wise thing to do."

Her brows drew together. "It does?" She had not expected him to commend her for her idea.

"Indeed." He was still smiling at her, so she returned the expression before withdrawing a small velvet pouch from her reticule.

"It is really very little. Just a few pounds. It may not even be enough to invest yet, but I dare not place it in my father's strongbox, for if something happens to him, I do not wish to explain how I came to have this money to Mr. Collins."

Darcy took the bag from her and slipped it into his pocket. "I shall care for it for you. You will keep a record of what you have given me, and I will do the same. Do you know how to do this?"

She pursed her lips and drew her brows together. It was likely similar to keeping a balance for household expenses, but she wasn't sure exactly how it was different. "I will have my father or my uncle show me since I am not entirely certain that I do."

"That sounds like an excellent idea."

That was twice now that he had commended her. It was an extraordinarily wonderful feeling, but she had not presented the whole situation to him.

"Mr. Darcy, could we save some time and trouble if I were to request that my uncle give the money to you?" She twisted her hands again. She could not help it. She was still nervous, though her nerves had shifted from worrying about Mr. Darcy scolding her to someone discovering that she was earning money by selling designs.

"Uncle Gardiner regularly receives payments from Mrs. Havelston for her orders of cloth," she explained, "so no one would suspect she is paying me if she includes my payment with her payment to him. And if he were to meet with you, no one would question the activity."

He tipped his head and looked at her closely but not as if looking to criticize. It was as if he were seeing her for the first time. "You have thought this through very thoroughly."

"I have to. If anyone was to learn that I was earning money..." Her reputation might be damaged and that would reflect poorly on her sisters as well. She could not risk that.

"I understand. It is to be a secret arrangement. I would be happy to have Mr. Gardiner deliver your money to me," Mr. Darcy said. "Do you have a plan in mind for it?"

Oh, how she wished he had not asked that! The tears that had been threatening all morning sprang to her eyes, and her cheeks flushed in embarrassment.

"You do not have to tell me," Mr. Darcy said in a quiet, gentle voice.

She shook her head. "No, you should know since you are helping me." She drew a steadying breath. "I have a foolish notion that will probably be unsuccessful, but your cousin should not be forced to give up what he loves. I thought perhaps... eventually... I could help him find a way to be happy." She shrugged. "If not, then the money can be added to my portion, which will be of assistance to me when I need to set up my own establishment. I do not wish to live solely on the charity of my relations."

"You do not plan to marry?" Darcy asked in surprise.

The tears once again gathered in her eyes, and she blinked against them as she shook her head. "I had hoped to," she said softly as her gaze shifted toward the window and the drive where her father's carriage stood before the door.

"One must not lose hope, Miss Kitty. Circumstances can change."

She drew another a deep breath and released it slowly. Then, she gave him as much of a smile as she could manage. "While I own that it is not an utter impossibility, I think it highly unlikely."

Chapter 2

THE SUN WAS SINKING close to the horizon by the time Richard exited Hurst's carriage and entered Matlock House. He stripped off his greatcoat and handed it, along with his hat, to Mr. Harrison, the butler. Then, he slipped quietly into his mother's sitting room to greet her.

"I am happy to see you safely returned to me," Lady Matlock said as she held him close in a firm embrace. "Will you be staying?" She smoothed the front of his jacket. Then, she took a seat on a settee and motioned for him to join her.

"I have no choice," he said as he sat down next to her. "I do not wish to impose on Darcy or Rycroft as they are settling in with their wives." If he had a choice, he would not be here for more than a few minutes to see her. He would rather avoid his father.

"There is BayLeafe."

He shook his head at the offer. BayLeafe was the small estate just outside of town which was part of the inheritance to come to him through his mother, should his father see fit to give it to him. That estate was no more his home than the grand townhouse in which he sat now. Home should be a place where you felt at ease. That was not Matlock House, nor was it any of his father's other properties.

"Your father is in quite a state, what with both of your cousins marrying outside of what is proper." She reached up and brushed his hair back from his forehead. "He is not all bad, you know. He has been good to me. He is just set in his ways."

"Do you love him?" Richard's voice was soft.

"I suppose I do," she replied. "It is possible to become friends and then more even when you begin as near strangers." She took his hand. "I cannot say I have never wished for more or for another, for I did at first, but now, I cannot imagine my life in any other way."

Richard nodded and placed the small, folded drawing in her hand. "You would have liked her," he said as his mother unfolded the paper.

Where his father blustered, his mother spoke softly. Where his father was arrogant, she demonstrated grace and humility. They were, in many ways, as opposed as darkness and light.

She lay the drawing on her lap and rested a hand on her heart. "It is very well done. Who is she?"

He shook his head and took the paper from her lap. "It matters not, for it shall never be." He rose and went to the window. "She has neither wealth nor significant connections beyond our family."

Lady Matlock came to stand near him. "Is she connected to our family?"

He nodded. "Her sisters are the new Mrs. Darcy and Lady Rycroft." He turned toward her. "And that is not the worst of it. A third sister is the new Mrs. Bingley."

He watched his mother struggle with how to accept this information. He knew she loved him and would wish him only to be happy, but she also held to some of the same ideas regarding marriage as her husband. It was not only his father who wished for him to make a good match.

He tucked the paper in his pocket. "As I said, it matters not, for it shall never be. My heart is of little importance."

Raised voices could be heard coming from somewhere down the hall.

"Your aunt is here," his mother said in answer to his questioning look. "Anne is with her but has taken to her room;, whether it is due to ill health or a need to avoid her mother, I am uncertain."

Just then, Lady Catherine stomped into the sitting room. "He is as unreasonable as ever!"

"I am not being unreasonable," Lord Matlock retorted as he followed his sister into the room. "You are being daft. To accept such connections into the family without some censure? And after Darcy did not marry Anne as we had planned?" He threw his hands up as if unable to fathom the thoughts.

"It would be better for Anne to marry someone with higher connections," Lady Catherine said, "a peer or the son of a peer." Her eyes came to rest on Richard. "Even a second son would do."

Richard attempted to keep his expression neutral, but marry Anne? No, he had no desire to marry Anne.

A sly smile spread slowly across Lord Matlock's face. "That is an idea worthy of contemplation. It would keep all the land holding within the family." He clapped his hands together and rubbed them back and forth. "I shall have my solicitor draw up the arrangement. Shall we have the wedding in two months? I do think that would give enough time to find the colonel a replacement with his unit and ready the necessary items for the release of his inheritance. However, I will have to defer to my solicitor and man of business for advice before we finalize the date." He leveled a hard glare at Richard. "Any objection shall be met with a significant, if not permanent, breach. Do I make myself clear?"

Richard shook his head in disbelief. "Am I no more to you than that? Some hireling to be ordered about?"

"On the contrary," his father said. "You are of great significance, and that is why your future must be secured. If something were to ever happen to your brother, you would need to secure the title with an appropriate heir, one with an acceptable lineage."

Richard's jaw clenched. "Ah, so I am not a hireling but, rather, a well-bred horse in your stable, whose only expectation is to sire the next prize stallion. And, doubtlessly, if I do not, I, like that horse, shall be turned out to work alongside the other workhorses on the estate."

His father's eyes narrowed. "Not on my estates." His voice held more than a little warning.

Richard stepped closer and pulled himself up to his full height, which was two inches taller than his father. "And if you turn me out and something happens to my brother, then where will your precious title fall? Ah, yes, to your brother." The comment caused the reaction he desired. His father took a step back and his face paled slightly.

"Two weeks," Richard said. "I ask for two weeks to consider your offer, my lord."

"What is there to consider?" Lady Catherine asked.

"The value of my life," Richard snarled. He moved toward the door, but his mother's hand on his arm forestalled him.

"Will I see you again?" Her eyes were filled with fear.

"At least once more," he murmured as he kissed her cheek before leaving the room and instructing that his things be readied for a journey.

Richard paused for a moment on the steps of Darcy House before lifting the knocker and allowing it to fall. Footmen waited at the carriage ready to divest the equipage of his belongings as soon as instructed to do so.

"The master and mistress have just arrived. If you will wait here a moment, I shall see if they are home to callers." Daniels held the door open for Richard to enter.

"I do not need to speak with them." Richard cast a glance over his shoulder to the carriage that waited on the street. "I need only to know if I can store my things here until I have a place where they can be sent."

Daniels raised an eyebrow slightly. "If you will wait, the master will see you directly."

Richard sighed. He had hoped that Daniels would simply allow him to leave his things and be gone. He had little desire to speak with anyone. He wandered into the sitting room and took a seat near the window where he could best appreciate the weak winter light before it faded to shadows.

He had only been seated for a moment when Darcy, followed by Elizabeth, entered the room with, what seemed to him, to be more haste than necessary. He sighed again and slowly rose to his feet.

"Why must you store your things at Darcy House?" Darcy asked, ignoring the normal pleasantries of greeting.

"I have nowhere else to put them at present," Richard replied. "I will send for them as soon as I have lodgings."

Darcy motioned to the chair from which Richard had just risen, and Richard obediently sat. It would do him no good to offend the cousin from whom he wished to obtain help.

Darcy unbuttoned his coat before sitting and leaning toward Richard. "The full story, if you will."

Richard scrubbed his face with his hands, settled back in his chair, and related the events that had led to his departure from home.

"Where will you stay?" asked Darcy.

"Not here," Richard replied, hearing the softness of his cousin's question, and knowing that it indicated Darcy's next comments would be to suggest that Richard stay at Darcy House. "It must be some place where my father cannot find me. I must be completely free from him for a fortnight." He blew out a breath. "And it must be what I could afford should I refuse his offer." He ran a hand through his hair. "I must see what my life will be and if I can abide it." He smiled wryly at Darcy. "So, you may not assist me aside from storing my things until I am able to keep them myself."

"Daniels has a sister who works for someone who rents rooms to respectable gentlemen."

Both Darcy and Richard looked at Elizabeth in surprise.

"I like to know about my servants' families," she explained. "We could ask him for the address, and if he knows whether there are any rooms available at this moment. If he does not, he may have recommendations." She smiled at Richard. "You are my family, and as such, I will care for you as far as you will allow me."

He ducked his head slightly, hoping to keep from her the effect that such comforting words had upon him. "I thank you, Mrs. Darcy."

"Elizabeth," she corrected. "Or Lizzy, if you prefer." She rose and gave his shoulder a soft pat. "I will inquire of Daniels while you men discuss whatever might remain to be discussed."

Richard dropped his head into his hands. "I cannot marry her, Darcy. I simply cannot."

"Because she is Anne? Or because your heart belongs to another?"

"Both," came the muffled reply.

Thankfully, Darcy leaned back in his chair and allowed Richard time to collect himself. After a few quiet moments, Richard drew his sleeve across his eyes before raising his head and smiling sheepishly at Darcy. It was rare that he shed tears in front of anyone, even Darcy, but his heart and his life were most likely damaged beyond repair.

"You shall stay the night." There was no question to Darcy's tone, and his countenance, though sympathetic, brooked no objections. "In the morning, you may visit whatever establishment Daniels tells us about, and then, if they are agreeable, you may take up residence there tomorrow or whatever day is mutually agreed upon." He leaned forward again. "You are always welcome here."

Richard nodded. He knew that neither of his cousins would ever turn him away. "But I must make my own way. What kind of man lives on the charity of another when he is able-bodied?"

Darcy slapped Richard's knee. "Just know that I am here." He chuckled. "And if Elizabeth should discover that you have fallen into need and have not informed me, I shall leave it to you to explain yourself."

Chapter 3

THE NEXT MORNING, AFTER a less than restful night of sleep, Richard stood in front of number eight Bartlett's Buildings and checked the slip of paper in his hand once again to make sure he had arrived where he was supposed to be. It was a tidy little lane of houses, which were well-cared for and quite respectable looking. It seemed as if it would be a perfectly acceptable place to live. He raised his hand, rapped on the door, and waited. There was a shuffling inside, and then a friendly looking man with a quick smile and spectacles perched on the end of his nose opened the door.

"Come in. Come in," he said. "It is much too chilly today to be introducing oneself on the street. There is a hook on the wall for your coat and a table for your hat."

Richard thanked him and stepped inside. "I am Colonel Richard Fitzwilliam," he began. "I was given your address by my cousin's butler because he thought you might have a room to let?" He took a quick, sweeping glance around the hall where he stood. It, like the outside of the home, was tidy and well-cared-for. A few pictures and at least one mirror decorated the walls, and a worn, but clean, rug lay under his feet.

The man, who stood waiting for Richard to divest himself of his outerwear, chuckled. "My, my. I must be garnering a significant reputation if butlers are passing on my name." He motioned for

Richard to follow him into a small sitting room off to the right. "Mrs. Wood, this is Colonel Fitzwilliam. Colonel, my wife."

Mrs. Wood put her stitching in her basket and rose to greet Richard. Her smile was as warm and ready as her husband's. She was at least six inches shorter than Mr. Woods and, at least, the same number of years younger.

"A pleasure to meet you, madam," Richard said with a bow.

"The pleasure is mine," she assured him as she returned to her seat and took up her work. "What brings you to our door on this cold January day?" She placed her feet on a foot warmer.

"The colonel said he is in need of accommodations." Mr. Wood motioned to a chair for Richard before taking a seat himself. "He says he was given my name by a butler." He turned to Richard. "Your cousin's butler, was it?"

"Yes. Mr. Daniels."

"Daniels is the butler or the cousin?" Mr. Wood was leaned back comfortably in his chair with his feet propped up on a stool, looking for all the world as if nothing was out of the ordinary and there was not a thing that could disquiet his repose. And yet, there was a liveliness of mind that could be seen in his expression.

"The butler."

"Oh!" Mrs. Wood placed her stitching on the table and became quite interested in the gentleman who had entered her house. "He must be Mrs. Letts's brother. I do believe she said her brother was Mr. Daniels, though she calls him Cyril more than Daniels, of course. Now, if my memory serves me as it should, I believe she said her brother works for Mr. Darcy, a rather wealthy and well-connected gentleman from Derbyshire. Is Mr. Darcy your cousin?"

Richard hesitated a moment before admitting the relationship.

"Oh, do not fear, Colonel; the cost of the room will not increase," she said with a grin. "The connection between you and Mr. Darcy only makes me most delighted to think you might take our room. It can be difficult to judge the quality of a tenant without knowing some of their connections. And Mr. Darcy's connections are good. Indeed, just his relations..." Her eyes grew wide. "Oh, my! Your family name is Fitzwilliam?"

"It is."

"Are you Lord Matlock's son?"

"For the moment, yes." He looked to Mr. Wood, who had yet to ask a single question of him. It appeared that the man preferred to let his wife take charge of the initial parts of the interview for possible new tenants. "I find that my father and I do not see things in the same way. I may only need the room for a fortnight, or I may need it for a much longer period of time."

Mr. Wood nodded thoughtfully. "Career choice or bride choice?"

"A bit of both, I am afraid. I would like to pursue a career in woodcraft and marry where I choose, but my father would see me marry an heiress and become either the manager of an estate or be perfectly idle."

"There is a duty in securing a title, I suppose." Mr. Wood cocked his head to the side. "Although I should think that is more your brother's responsibility than yours." He pulled his hands from his pockets and clapped them on the arm of his chair while lowering his feet from the stool at the same time.

"Come," he said as he rose. "I will show you the apartment, and we can discuss the particulars. I can see that my wife approves of you, and that's all I really need, other than assurance of prompt payment and such."

Richard followed him from the room.

"Has your father chosen a bride for you already?"

"He has."

Mr. Wood opened a door to the left of the hallway. "We dine here. There are two others besides you who live with us."

Richard popped his head into the dining room and looked around. It was well-furnished with a large table with eight chairs and a handsome sideboard along one wall.

Mr. Wood continued to open doors here and there and pointed to items that might interest Richard as he spoke. "My father may not have been an earl, but it sounds as if he was as set in his ways as yours is. Sent me packing when I refused to marry his partner's daughter, he did, and then, he gave my inheritance to my younger brother, who was willing to marry the girl." He chuckled wryly. "My brother was the reason I refused to marry her."

He stopped halfway up the second flight of stairs and turned to look at Richard. "He was in love with Fiona. It did not seem right to marry the lady my brother loved." He shrugged. "However, I would not have married her even if my brother had not been besotted with her, for I had already fallen in love with my Beatrice, and a man should not be separated from his love, even if it is costly." Again, he tipped his head to the side as he looked at Richard before continuing on up the stairs. "You've not already lost your heart, have you?"

"I may have." Oh, he had most certainly lost his heart. There was no *may* about it.

By this time, they had reached the top of the stairs, and Mr. Wood searched through his ring of keys as they walked to the end of the narrow hallway.

"If that is how things stand, you may stay with us for as long as you like, and should you find yourself able to offer for your lady love, I may be of assistance in finding an affordable living arrangement – one that is both comfortable and conducive to raising a family."

He pushed open the door to the room. "It is not large, but it is cozy – stays warm without too much need of a fire in the winter. The window allows for some breeze in the summer, but I'll not lie, it can be a bit stifling at times come July and August."

Mr. Wood was indeed correct; the apartment was cozy, both in atmosphere and size. There was a small sitting area with three chairs and a table pushed to one side, a bedroom with a bed, which looked comfortable enough, and a dressing room with a washstand

and wardrobe. All in all, it was not grand nor elegant. However, it was adequate.

"I have a man," Richard said.

"Many do have a man or a maid – sometimes we have ladies as tenants, though currently, it is all gents. There is a place for your man in the servants' quarters, and he may dine with them. There is an extra charge, of course, to cover particulars." Mr. Wood motioned to the bell pull. "He will be the only one to answer, but a maid will be assigned to clean and collect laundry, and Mrs. Letts, our housekeeper, can be of assistance with whatever else you may need."

Richard turned a full circle and looked at the apartment once again. It was not what he was used to, but it was acceptable, comfortable even. He imagined he would feel at home here within a short time. He nodded and smiled at Mr. Wood. This was right. It was exactly what he needed. "If the price is agreeable, I will take it."

"Excellent." A smile split his face. He waved his arm toward the door, and Richard exited. "I have an agreement and your key in my study. You may take up residence as soon as I have your signature and money." He turned his key in the lock. "You mentioned that you like to work with wood. What kind of things do you make?"

"Boxes are my favourite, but I have also made some furniture." Richard replied as they descended the stairs.

"What kinds of boxes?"

"I have made a variety. My cousin has one in his study for his pen and ink, as well as a tray for collecting correspondence, and most recently, I designed a box for holding jewels for his wife."

Mr. Wood stopped short on the stairs. "I had forgotten that Mr. Darcy got married recently."

A cat that Richard had not seen until now brushed past his legs.

"That is Sally," Mr. Wood said. "She is a good cat, but she's known to upset a teacup now and then. In fact, she nearly caused a catastrophe last week when I was copying some papers." He had begun walking again and glanced over his shoulder. "I do some clerking for a solicitor," he explained.

Richard laughed and shook his head as he wondered what the odds were of this being the same cat which had delayed Rycroft's return to Netherfield. "Were they marriage papers, by any chance?"

"Aye, they were."

"For Lord Rycroft?" Richard asked.

"It is not for me to say," Mr. Wood replied.

"Of course, forgive me. It is just that my cousin was delayed by marriage papers that had to be recopied due to an unfortunate incident involving a cat and tea."

Mr. Wood chuckled. "I would not say that Sally is that particular cat, but I also would not say she is not. No matter where the truth lies in that," he scooped up Sally before opening the door to his study and then sat her back down and closed the door quickly, "she is no longer allowed in my study." He winked at Richard. "Especially when there is tea."

Chapter 4

"WAS IT ACCEPTABLE?" ELIZABETH asked as Richard was removing his hat and coat in the entry at Darcy House.

"It was. It is all very proper-looking, and Mr. and Mrs. Wood are very welcoming people. I felt at ease nearly from the moment I entered their home. Thank you, Daniels."

The butler only nodded in response, though there seemed to be a very pleased look in his eyes.

"You must tell me all about it." Elizabeth slipped her arm through his and led him to the sitting room. "I must be assured that you will indeed be comfortable and well-cared-for, and then, I believe our workshop has missed your presence." She tipped her head and looked up at him with a smile.

He could see why his cousin was so besotted with his wife. She was the very picture of everything bright and caring.

"I am certain the workshop would appreciate a visit from you as often as you would care to call on it," she added.

He chuckled as he took a seat near Darcy. "I shall do my best not to neglect it, but I do not wish to be anywhere my father might think to find me, for I have no desire to endure his arguments. I need to arrive at a conclusion on my own."

"I cannot promise that I will not give you my opinion." Darcy set aside his book.

Richard shook his head. "You do not need to share it. I am sure I can guess." Darcy believed in marrying for love, rather than advantage. He always had. But Darcy's life was far different from Richard's.

"Then, tell me, what is my opinion?"

Richard folded his arms across his chest and studied Darcy. "You think I should follow my heart as you have followed yours. However, I must remind you that my circumstances at present are somewhat less than yours have ever been." He held up a hand when Darcy opened his mouth. "No, I shall not hear of your assistance."

His cousin was a fine manager of all the monies that were in his domain, but he was by no means tight-fisted. Indeed, he was quite generous where there was need, most especially amongst those who were part of his intimate circle.

Darcy closed his mouth and scowled, causing Elizabeth to giggle lightly. "A gentleman's pride, wounded if given help and equally wounded if help is refused. You men are such strange creatures."

"They are strange indeed." Lady Sophia waved Daniels away before he could announce her as she entered the sitting room. "I pray you will pardon my intrusion, but I thought it best to leave my home for a while to give Rycroft and Mary some time to settle into the place." She rolled her eyes as if annoyed by the necessity of leaving her home. Her smile, however, let them all know just how delighted she was to have been inconvenienced to do so by the arrival of her newly married son and his wife.

She placed her hands over Georgiana's ears. "We shall not speak about the compromise," she warned. "Even if Rycroft has given me reason to believe that it was quite spectacular." Her eyes twinkled with amusement.

"That it was," Darcy agreed. "You know she will hear of it." He looked from his aunt to his sister.

Georgiana giggled and pushed her aunt's hands away from her ears. "Much to Mary's chagrin, I have been given a convincing demonstration."

Darcy's eyes narrowed as he looked at his aunt. "Then why place your hands on her ears?"

Lady Sophia shrugged. "It was merely my attempt at making you think I was doing my duty."

Darcy shook his head and chuckled as they all took their various seats. "While I am certain you do not condone such public displays of affection…" He paused to give his aunt a stern look.

"Oh, I do not."

If she had not been doing such a poor job of feigning a serious expression, Richard might have been willing to believe her. As it was, he was only reassured of what he already knew. Lady Sophia liked to skirt the edges of propriety at times.

"I am equally as certain," Darcy continued, "that you cannot help but be delighted with the results."

"Beyond delighted!" Their aunt cried.

Darcy gave his sister a stern look. "Not that the delight outweighs the wrongness of such actions."

Georgiana rolled her eyes as Richard had seen her do many times when her brother was belabouring a point that truly did not need as much attention as Darcy thought it did.

"You have all done an admiral job of instilling the rules of propriety and good sense in me, and experience has taught me caution in keeping them. You have nothing to fear from me. Besides," she said with a playful smile, "it was not Mary who created the scene. I believe the responsibility for that falls to our cousin with some help from you." She picked at a bit of something imaginary on her sleeve. "That is two compromises in which you have been involved, Fitzwilliam."

Darcy groaned while Richard chuckled softly.

"I still do not want you to be forced into a marriage." He took Elizabeth's hand. "Unless, of course, it is for the best and will result in your happiness." He held up a finger indicating he was not finished. "And has been sanctioned by me."

Richard laughed out loud. "Which, I dare say, will never happen as he is loath to allow you to grow up at all, let alone consider courtship and marriage."

"Very true," Lady Sophia agreed. "And that is understandable. However, whether he approves or not, your time will come when such things must be considered." She tapped her finger on her lip as she looked at Richard. "Of course, we shall have to remedy Richard's marital status first."

Richard tried to catch the grimace that such a statement provoked, but he was not fast enough.

"Ah, my brother." His aunt tilted her head to the side and nodded slowly. "He is a problem, and he is not pleased with my son's choice of bride. I have heard it."

"This morning," Georgiana inserted.

"Yes, before breakfast had concluded." Lady Sophia sighed. "He is wrong, of course. He always has been, but he has also always been too stubborn and foolish to see how wrong he is."

Darcy nudged Richard's foot with his own.

"I know," Richard hissed as he pulled his foot out of Darcy's range for tapping. But it did not matter if they all knew that his father was wrong. That would not change what his father did. It never had in the past. Why would it now? Lord Matlock did what Lord Matlock thought was best.

Lady Sophia arched one eyebrow. "Has something happened?"

Richard nodded. "I have a fortnight to choose either marriage to Anne or a significant, if not permanent, breach." Which meant, he would be cut off in all the ways his father could manage to cut him off. There would be no inheritance, and no recognition of him as son. Who knew if his mother would be allowed to see him or not? That was the part with which it was hardest to come to terms.

"Anne! Good heavens!" Lady Sophia could not contain her surprise. "You are staying here then?" It was not so much a question as it was a statement of the only logical thing to be done.

He shook his head. "I have signed an agreement to rent a room at the Bartlett Buildings."

Her brows furrowed.

"I do not wish for my father to be able to call on me, and I would like to see what my life might be like without..." He sighed. "Him."

"It is a respectable area."

Richard was not sure if his aunt truly thought that or was merely trying to support his decision. And then, much more quickly than he had imagined it would happen, her countenance changed from one of worry to one of restrained excitement.

"Two weeks?"

He nodded. A small amount of dread fluttered in his stomach at what might have her excited. He was sure that it included some sort of matchmaking scheme, and although he trusted her more than his father, he had no desire to be matched with anyone, save Kitty.

"Perfect," she said before turning to Georgiana. "Will you play for us?"

The change in conversation seemed to confuse Georgiana, but Richard knew that though the matter was no longer to be discussed, his aunt was not done thinking about it. Hoping to avoid any conversation that might include plans for his future, he rose and said, "As much as I would like to hear your talent, Georgiana, Elizabeth has promised me time in the workshop, and there is a small item I think my new landlord's wife would appreciate." He looked toward Darcy. "If you do not mind."

"My home is your home." Darcy rose and straightened his jacket. "I have a small matter that could use your expertise if you will allow me to accompany you?"

"I would welcome the company." He opened the door to the sitting room and waited for his cousin. From where he was, he watched Darcy gain his wife's attention before giving a tip of his head toward their aunt.

"I shall join you in the music room momentarily, my love."

Elizabeth smiled at him, one eyebrow raising and lowering quickly. "Some tea would be nice."

"I shall inform Mrs. Vernon," Darcy said.

"Will you join us?" Elizabeth asked Richard.

"If my project allows it."

"Have you met my sister, Kitty?" Richard heard Elizabeth ask his aunt as he closed the door.

"If Lady Sophia is scheming, and we all know she is," Darcy said, "she might as well be scheming in an appropriate direction."

"I appreciate the assistance."

"Do you?" Darcy asked with a laugh.

"In this, I do. But I do not want to live on the charity of a relation. Not even if that relation is you."

Darcy clasped his hands behind his back as he led the way to the workshop. "Are you opposed to my hiring your services?"

Apparently, today, it was not just their aunt who was scheming.

Chapter 5

RICHARD KNOCKED ON MR. Wood's study door and only pushed it open when he heard his knock acknowledged and after a quick look for Sally, who sat, swishing her tail and watching him from the far end of the hall. He slipped inside and closed the door quickly.

"I wanted to thank you for allowing me to read your paper." Richard placed the folded newspaper on the desk.

"A necessary luxury." Mr. Wood glanced up from his work. "A man likes to know what is happening in the world." He compared the paper beside him to the one in front of him, then neatly wrote one more word and returned his pen to its holder. "What are you about this afternoon, Colonel? A walk in the park or a visit to the museum?"

Richard laughed. "I shall be walking but not in the park. I had hoped to find some information regarding work that I might be able to do should my tenure at your residence become permanent. I spent yesterday assessing what my expenses would be. They are not above my current funds, even with the room I am renting, but if I intend to advance my place — and I do — I must find additional sources of income."

Mr. Wood rummaged through his drawer. "Ah, there they are."

He pulled out a stack of cards which he flipped through, occasionally stopping to pluck one out and put it to the side. Having exhausted his search of them, he picked up the small pile he had discarded and looked at them once again.

"None of these are too far from here. It should give you a start." He handed them to Richard. "Only one is a furniture maker, the others would do well to carry small boxes for various items in their shops. The jeweler, for instance, might be able to increase his clientele if he were to offer not only the jewels but also the boxes in which to keep them. And the dressmaker might like to have a box such as you gave to my wife for her pins and a larger one for her scissors." He shrugged. "Perhaps if a patron saw the items, they might request where they could get something so nice."

He drummed his fingers on the desk. "It might be of value to you to give a small box to at least one modiste and see what results you achieve." He lifted his pen from its holder as Richard thanked him and rose to leave. "Have you found a place to use as a workshop?"

Richard stopped with his hand on the door. "I have at least one possibility, but, for the present, Darcy has requested that I make use of his until I am better established."

Mr. Wood nodded. "A wise idea. I wish you well, Colonel."

Richard pulled the door open slowly and looked for Sally before slipping out and on his way to visit the places on the cards he held in his hand.

Kitty pressed a hand against the soft package she held on her lap and drew a deep breath before releasing it slowly.

"You will like Mrs. Smith," Mrs. Gardiner assured her.

"I am certain I will if you do." Her aunt had introduced her to Mrs. Havelston, and she liked Mrs. Havelston. She had also not met anyone yet today while calling with her aunt that she did not find to be lovely. Therefore, it stood to reason that any friend of her aunt was likely going to be someone Kitty would like.

"Then, what makes you sigh so?" A kind smile accompanied the question.

The answer to that question was not an easy one to make without tears, but Aunt Gardiner was proving to be all that Jane and Elizabeth had ever said she was – caring, gentle, wise, and so much more. Kitty most certainly could not refuse to answer in some way. So, she said it as simply as she could. "Giving up a dream." She shrugged and turned her face to the window as the Gardiners' carriage stopped in front of number eleven Bartlett's Buildings.

"Mrs. Smith will be happy to receive your linens for the baby, and I would not give up on your dream completely. At least, not yet."

On Jane's advice, Kitty had confided in her aunt about Colonel Fitzwilliam, which, as it turned out, had made asking her uncle to assist with payments from Mrs. Havelston much easier.

Mrs. Gardiner peeked out the window. "I see Mrs. Wood is on her way for a visit as well." She accepted the hand of the coachman to assist her from the carriage. "She will be most impressed with your work. She is quite talented with a needle herself, you know."

Kitty did not know. She had never met Mrs. Smith or Mrs. Wood or many of the other people Mrs. Gardiner had visited today. Of course, she had not often visited their aunt. It was usually Elizabeth or Jane who were requested. But with her three oldest sisters all married, she was next in line, and so her mother and her aunt had decided it would do her good to experience the city and help care for the young Gardiner children.

The baby linens that she was now clutching as she stood beside her aunt were ones she had made and kept in her locked trunk at the end of her bed. They were part of what she had hoped to take with her to her marriage. However, since she would likely never marry and knowing that she did not have time to make anything new for this visit, she had taken them out, for she simply could not visit a new mother such as Mrs. Smith without some item to give her.

"Mrs. Gardiner," the lady whom Kitty guessed was Mrs. Wood greeted as they all arrived in at Mrs. Smith's door at the same time, "it is a delight to see you. What has it been since we last were together?"

"At least a fortnight, I believe," Aunt Gardiner answered.

"How was the wedding breakfast?"

"It ended up that there were two weddings to celebrate."

"Indeed? Was the second a surprise affair?"

Aunt Gardiner chuckled. "To everyone, including the bride. Lord Rycroft managed to talk my niece Mary into marrying him without an ounce of preparation on her part."

The door to number eleven opened.

"She was married at the end of the ball I told you about."

"Oh, my! Married at such an hour?"

"Yes and celebrated the next day after Jane's wedding. She and her earl are returned to town now."

"That sounds like quite the exciting time," a lady who looked to be not older than Jane and whom Kitty assumed was Mrs. Smith said.

"Oh, it was, and that is why I have Kitty with me today instead of Mary as I thought I would have." Aunt Gardiner turned to Kitty. "This is my niece, Kitty. Kitty, this is Mrs. Wood and Mrs. Smith."

Kitty dipped a shallow curtsey. "It is a pleasure to meet you both. I have a gift for your baby." She extended her package to Mrs. Smith.

"What a wonderful surprise!" the lady cried. "I see you have your aunt's good heart."

"And you are such a pretty young lady, too," Mrs. Wood said.

"Thank you." Kitty took a step toward a small bassinette. "May I?" She had always loved children and often sought to spend time with them when Lydia would allow it.

"Oh, you must," Mrs. Wood encouraged.

Kitty took a seat near the bassinette and peered inside. Bright blue eyes blinked as they stared at the ceiling. Tiny feet poked at the blanket that covered them. Kitty sighed as the baby's fist found his mouth.

"He is sweet," she said to Mrs. Smith.

"Such a joy, he is," Mrs. Smith said. "I cannot believe how gracious the good Lord has been in giving Mr. Smith and me such a good boy." Her face beamed with pride as she stroked her son's head. "He looks a lot like his father, does he not, Mrs. Wood?"

"He is a fine image of Mr. Smith," Mrs. Wood agreed. "And if he grows to be half the man the reverend is, we will all be blessed." She was in the process of admiring the items that Kitty had brought. "I am sure I have never seen such fine work from one so young," she muttered.

Kitty blushed. "Thank you. I enjoy sewing."

"You have talent." Mrs. Wood laid the blanket to the side and ran her finger over the tiny flower buds that decorated the corner. "Very pretty."

Kitty thanked her once again and returned her attention to the baby.

"I saw you have a new tenant, Mrs. Wood," Mrs. Smith commented.

"Indeed, we do. I do not think we have ever had a better tenant – at least, not one with the connections he has, but it is not for me to share that. He is with us for at least two weeks, though my husband expects it might be longer." She lowered her voice to a whisper. "He has had a bit of a falling out with his father, but I will not say more than that. You know I am not given to gossip."

She turned to Mrs. Gardiner. "That was he who was just leaving when you arrived. A fine young man he is, very fine. Made me a beautiful box for my needles and thread. I met him one day, and he had the gift for me the next." She laughed. "And then, he apologized that he had not had time to engrave the top — as if I expected it to be decorated!"

Kitty kept her eyes on the baby, daring not to look up as her expression might lead to questions, and she did not wish to answer any questions regarding why such information would cause her eyes to fill with tears and her cheeks to grow rosy. It was silly, really, she told herself. There were surely many young men who could make boxes and engrave them. This could not be Colonel Fitzwilliam. He had a home and when he was not at it, he was with Mr. Darcy. She shook her head just a bit at her foolishness in imagining that he was so near.

Having gathered her thoughts into somewhat of an acceptable arrangement, she cooed at the baby, whose eyes had found her. "You are a very fine young man," she said as she gave his little toes a tap.

"That he is," agreed his mama.

Kitty accepted the cup of tea Mrs. Smith held out to her and took a biscuit from the tray. Then, settling back into her chair, she tried to focus on the conversation around her and not her thoughts of *him* until it was time to leave.

Chapter 6

Upon returning from his calls that day, Richard collected the few items of post that had been delivered to his new address by one of Darcy's servants. It was as he had expected; his father had come that day to Darcy House in search of him.

I have not given him your location, his cousin wrote, *but I have told him that he might reach you by letter through me. It was the best I could think of to placate him. He said your mother was worried, so I attempted to reassure her through him that you were well-cared-for and were not living in some hovel or begging on the streets.*

He chuckled as he imagined the dramatics that his father had employed when pretending to be concerned for his son. His father being worried on his behalf was an extremely unlikely thing.

When questioned about what you were doing, I hope I have not overstepped my bounds in telling him that you are researching your options should you refuse his offer and be cut off. This did cause him to become very solemn and, if I am not mistaken, a bit shaken.

"He must be truly concerned that I will refuse," he said to the letter he held in his hand. "He is only shaken when he thinks his plans are to come to naught." The thought gave him a small amount of pleasure.

My wife sends her best and says to tell you that our workshop has been feeling neglected, and if it would help entice you to come for a visit, she will see to it that a tin of biscuits awaits you. I must warn

you, however, that you will be expected to show yourself to her, so that
she can see you are indeed well.

Do come soon.

F.D.

He would visit his cousin tomorrow, for he needed to make use of the workshop. Richard put the letter to the side and shuffled through the remaining post before checking his watch and readying himself for dinner.

"Good evening, Colonel, was your day a success?" Mr. Wood asked as they settled in for their dinner of stew and bread.

It was a meal that, according to Mrs. Wood, was a staple at number eight Bartlett's Buildings because it was economical, hearty, and easily held for those who were not available to eat at the prescribed time.

"It was. I must thank you once again for your assistance." Richard broke off a piece of his bread and spread a generous amount of butter on it. The meal might be basic, but it was delicious. The Woods' cook was among the best from what he had tasted so far in his short stay.

"The first jeweler was quite interested in my designs and has requested a sample of one. The furniture maker is not taking on new help at this time, but he has my information should he find he has need of assistance on any projects. I have decided to take your advice and have left visiting any modiste shops until I have a pin box to give them, so I will spend the whole of tomorrow, I imagine, in my cousin's workshop."

"Which modistes will you be visiting?" Mrs. Wood asked.

Richard made to reply but before he could, she had set her spoon down and clapped her hands in delight.

"Oh, you must start by visiting Mrs. Havelston. She is simply one of the best in town." She blushed and smiled. "I am a friend, so I might be a small bit partial, however."

Mr. Wood chortled at the comment, but his wife waved away any reply he might have felt compelled to make. "You know..." She leaned forward as if imparting a great secret. "One of her clients has recently become the new Lady Rycroft? It is true. Mrs. Gardiner was telling me just today — when I was visiting Mrs. Smith — about how her niece had recently married Lord Rycroft. It was quite the tale to be sure!" She took a sip from her wine glass.

"Mr. Gardiner, who is also a dear friend," she explained to Richard, "has always supplied Mrs. Havelston with the best quality materials, and her work is outstanding. You would be hard pressed to find better workmanship than what comes from her store. Do you have her card?"

Richard nodded. He had thought her name sounded familiar and so had considered visiting her first. Now, hearing Mrs. Havelston's name linked with that of Mrs. Gardiner, he remembered where he had heard it before. It was the name Kitty had mentioned when she told him that she had sold a design.

"And speaking of quality work." She lay a hand on her husband's arm. "You should see the things that Mrs. Smith received for the baby."

"I am sure I would not appreciate them as you do, my dear," her husband replied with a wink at Richard.

"Oh, to be sure you would not! But even you would be able to appreciate the care taken in their creation."

Mr. Wood sighed. "And would you care to tell me from whom these lovely gifts were received?"

"Oh, I would," she said with delight. "Mrs. Gardiner called, and she had one of her nieces with her. Such a lovely young woman and talented. With a heart of gold, I say, for she had made these things to lay by for when the need arose, and, hearing that she would be visiting Mrs. Smith — a stranger to her — she brought a gown, a cap, and a blanket." Her hand rested on her heart. "Oh, the delicate flowers that she had embroidered on the corner of the blanket." She sighed. "Lovely, just lovely."

Mr. Wood smiled at his wife and then looked toward Richard, whose spoon has stopped halfway to his mouth and was slowly lowering back to his bowl. "Is something amiss, Colonel?"

"Miss Katherine?" he whispered. It had to be her.

Mrs. Wood cocked her head to the side and studied him. "Her aunt called her Kitty. Do you know her?"

He nodded slowly.

Mr. Wood took his wife's hand. "I believe, my dear, that she is the one of whom his father would not approve."

Again, Richard nodded his response. "My cousin is Lord Rycroft," he said after a moment of silence. "And Miss Katherine's sister is his wife."

"Do you mean to tell me that your father does not approve of the new sister of an earl?" The incredulity in Mrs. Wood's voice made Richard's lips curl in a small smile.

"No more than he approves of the earl's wife or Mr. Darcy's wife." Richard sighed. "She is but a lowly gentleman's daughter in his mind. She has no connections and very little money, and is, therefore, unfit to be my wife."

Mrs. Wood huffed. "I thought my husband's father was foolish turning his son out for not accepting a wife when he loved another quite acceptable choice, but I see foolishness is not a respecter of class lines."

Richard chuckled. "Indeed, it is not." Foolish was a very good word for his father.

Mrs. Wood folded her hands in front of her and leaned toward him just a bit, almost as he imagined a mother might her child. "If you refuse your father's choice and chose this life — the life of a tradesman — will you offer for her?"

He wanted to. He truly wanted to, but could he? He shrugged. "She deserves more."

Mrs. Wood shook her head. "In my way of thinking, you are wrong about that. There is no more you or another could give her than for her to be loved completely. To be sure, servants and things make for a comfortable life, but is it a happy life when what you desire is the love of another?" She smiled at him and added, "Your stew grows cold."

Richard scooped up a spoonful of stew and put it in his mouth. Was there truly no more that anyone, even he, could do for Kitty other than to love her? Could he offer for her? He had already determined he would not marry Anne, but in so deciding, he had thought to never marry, for how could he provide for Kitty and any children they might have on a tradesman's income?

Though his mind was deep in contemplation of Kitty and his future, he caught the name Mrs. Gardiner again in the Woods' conversation. He shook his head at his own faulty thinking. Mr. Gardiner was a tradesman, and his family did not suffer for it.

In fact, if Richard looked beyond his current situation to the world that surrounded him, he knew that there were many in trade who had families and many who had amassed great fortunes. How many times had his father complained about just that thing when speaking about Bingley?

He nearly laughed at himself as he realized that Bingley was a perfect example of what could be achieved through the dedicated work of a tradesman. He soaked up the remainder of his broth with the last bit of his bread. He savoured this last morsel as he sat back contentedly in his chair. Tomorrow, he would make a pin box and take it to Mrs. Havelston, and then he would call on the Gardiners. After all, he told himself, it was only polite to call on friends when one knew they were in town.

"Thank you," he said as he rose from the table, "for both the food and the conversation. It was exactly what I needed this evening. I cannot remember the last time that both my body and soul have felt quite so completely well-nourished." He was certain his heart had never felt this light before in his life.

"You are most welcome," Mrs. Wood said.

He turned to her husband. "I believe I will be staying indefinite-ly. No matter the cost, I cannot live with another when my heart belongs to Miss Katherine."

"Will you offer for her?" the man asked. "As I have said before, I can help you find suitable and affordable housing for a family."

The smile that curled Richard's lips started deep within him. "I believe I will. However, I will not marry her until I can provide for her better than I currently can."

"You will be a success. I know the sort who make their way quite well, and you are one of those people, Colonel," Mr. Wood assured him.

"I do hope you are correct. Again, I thank you for the meal and the words of wisdom." He sketched a shallow bow and with hope in his heart, took himself to his room.

Chapter 7

A DAMP, FRIGID GUST of wind made Richard draw his coat more tightly around his neck and duck his head so that his hat and not his face felt the greatest amount of sting from the coldness of the air as he hurried along the street. He had chosen to leave his horse and travel as most did – on foot. He hoped he would be able to keep his horse once he was cut off, but today, he was going to live as if he had no horse. His freedom was worth more than a horse, and for him, that was no small thing to say. He had loved riding from the first time he had been placed on the back of a pony.

"Pardon me," he said as he quickly stepped to the side, narrowly avoiding a collision with a footman who was assisting a lady to her carriage.

"Richard?"

He would know that voice anywhere. It was not just any lady who was returning to her carriage. He stopped and turned back. "Lady Matlock," he greeted his mother with a proper bow. "It is a pleasure to see you."

Her eyebrows rose. "Is it? I had thought you had forgotten about me entirely, since I have heard naught of you for four days."

He gave her a sad smile. "I apologize, but is that not that to which we must grow accustomed?"

She motioned toward the carriage. "Sit with me. Just for a moment. I shall not try to force you to return home with me, but the wind is biting, and it would be far more pleasant to speak if we were out of it."

He saw her shiver and knew he could not refuse her. "I will not tell you where I am staying or precisely how I have been keeping myself," he warned as he offered his hand to help her into the carriage.

"I believe I can tolerate my curiosity not being assuaged for a few minutes of your time, but it does mean that you shall, then, have to listen to me complain about your aunt."

She lifted her feet and put them on a warming box and then smoothed her skirts as Richard climbed into the carriage and took the seat across from her. It was nice to be out of the weather, and it was pleasant, in a bittersweet fashion, to be allowed to sit, perhaps for the final time, on this bench where he had so often sat in his life.

"*That* woman is truly lacking social grace!"

Richard chuckled and listened silently as his mother continued on for a few moments about the demands made on her staff by Lady Catherine and how Anne had spent the whole of her stay thus far in her chambers.

"I am convinced Anne is not at all as ill as she pretends."

Richard had often thought that as well – during nearly every visit he made to Rosings in the spring, truth be told.

"But, then," his mother continued, "I also cannot blame Anne for using the only means available to escape *that* woman. For that reason alone, I would like to see you marry her."

"Are you truly saying that I should marry Anne to save her from her mother?"

"It is not the most horrible of reasons to marry." Her eyes begged him to agree with her.

He shook his head. It was not the most horrible reason. Indeed, it was a far nobler reason than the one his father had presented, but it was still not an acceptable reason – at least, not for him. "She deserves to marry – and to be away from her mother – but I will not be the one to marry her, Mother."

She sighed, and concern etched a deep crevice between her eyebrows.

Richard drew a deep breath and took her hand. He had to tell her the truth of how things were and would be even if he had not reached the end of his two weeks of contemplation time. There was no one he wanted to marry except Miss Katherine Bennet.

"I have made my decision," he began and gave his mother's hand a squeeze when she sucked in a quick breath. "I wish with all my heart that I could marry Anne just so I could remain your son, but I cannot."

Lady Matlock placed her free hand on his cheek. The war of what she thought should be and what she wished for him played on her features. "You are certain?"

He nodded and turned his head to place a kiss on her gloved palm. "I am, and though I shall regret leaving you, I cannot bear to face the regret I would have if I stayed. I love her, Mother."

"More than me?" she asked softly.

He shrugged, unwilling to say the truth and cause his mother's pain, but equally unwilling to say he loved anyone more than he loved Kitty. "With all that I am and have."

"Oh, my son." She stroked his cheek.

"I am sorry, Mother."

"As am I." She leaned forward and placed a kiss on his cheek. "Perhaps your father will relent," she said hopefully.

"You know, as well as I do, that he never relents."

"I must hope." Her lips trembled slightly as she attempted to smile at him.

And he would, too. He turned his head and placed another kiss in his mother's palm.

"I beg your pardon, my lady," her footman said upon opening the door and interrupting the intimate scene, "but there is someone who wishes to speak to you."

"I have to go." Richard moved toward the open door.

"Take care," she said as he climbed out of the coach.

"I shall," he reassured her before turning to leave, but he did not move further. For standing behind the footman, waiting to speak to his mother was Kitty. "Miss Katherine," he managed to say.

She curtseyed deeply. "Colonel Fitzwilliam, my lady." She kept her head bowed slightly as she extended a parcel to Lady Matlock, who had exited the carriage behind Richard. "You left this behind, my lady. I am happy to have found your carriage still here, as it has saved me the trip to your home."

"Miss Katherine, is it?" Lady Matlock looked from Kitty to Richard, who was struggling to look anywhere but at the lady he loved. One of his mother's eyebrows arched in question.

Richard gave her a small smile.

"If you wish, my lady, or Miss Bennet, if you prefer." Kitty lifted her eyes to meet his mother's.

"Tell me, Miss Katherine, do you draw?" she asked as she accepted the package from Kitty.

Kitty looked at her in some confusion. To her, it likely seemed a strange question, but to Richard it was not. His mother was verifying what she suspected. She had seen the picture Kitty had drawn for him.

"I do, my lady."

"I am always curious about the accomplishments of other ladies," his mother said with an air of nonchalance.

She was a practiced actress – one had to be to navigate the *ton* as successfully as she had for years.

"The museum affords great opportunities for sketching," she continued, "though I find I do not enjoy the pastime myself." She lifted the package that Kitty had given her. "However, this is an activity I find particularly enjoyable." She looked at Kitty expectantly, as if she was waiting for Kitty to inquire about what activity it was that she found enjoyable. However, she was to be disappointed, for Kitty did not ask.

"Then, I am doubly glad to have been able to return it to you. It is important that everyone has at least one activity in which they find pleasure." Her eyes darted to Richard for a moment before returning to hold his mother's gaze again.

Was she saying that on his behalf? The thought made his chest swell a trifle with pride at her courage and devotion. How could he ever consider anyone but her as his future? He could not. He would not.

"Indeed." His mother's lips tipped up as if she was pleased by Kitty's response. "Mine is embroidery," she said, answering the question that had not been asked as she lifted the package again. "This is thread for that purpose."

Kitty smiled, and not just politely. It was an expression that radiated her delight at what his mother had said. "I would not like to lose something so precious."

This time, his mother's lips did not just tip up as they had before. This time, they curled into an easy, relaxed, and utterly satisfied smile. He had known his mother would be charmed by Kitty.

"Do you enjoy embroidery?" she asked.

"Very much, my lady. I also enjoy a bit of millinery work, as well as sewing, but please do not ask me to play or sing, for I am afraid those are not among my talents." She pressed her lips together as if stopping herself from speaking and dipped a curtsey. "My aunt is waiting; I must return to her."

"Of course," Lady Matlock said. "Thank you for returning my package to me."

"I am happy to have been of service." She dipped another curtsey, and her eyes turned to Richard for a moment before she returned to the shop.

His mother placed a hand on his arm, and when Kitty had gone back into the shop, said, "You were right. I like her very much, and I can see why you do, too. She is sweet." Then, she entered her carriage and was gone, leaving Richard standing in front of Mrs. Havelston's shop and wondering if he should enter.

Chapter 8

KITTY CLOSED THE DOOR to Mrs. Havelston's dress shop and took a lingering look at Richard through the window. She had not known when she had volunteered to run the package out to the carriage that stood before the shop that the lady whom she was seeking was Lady Matlock. Nor had she expected to see him. She was glad she had even if she had not been able to speak to him.

"Was she still there?" Mrs. Havelston asked, coming from the back of the store.

"She was, and she was most appreciative to have the parcel returned." Kitty slipped off her gloves and bonnet before removing her wrap.

"She liked your drawing, my dear. I am not allowed to make that design, nor am I to show it to anyone, until she has first had a chance to wear it." Mrs. Havelston chuckled. "She paid me well for the privilege, and so I will pass on some of the proceeds to you." She placed her book of patterns back on the counter and returned her measuring tape to the drawer. "I told her I was working with a new designer, and she has made me agree that she is to have the first pick of the new work." She smiled and took Kitty's wrap. "Again, it is a service for which she is willing to pay handsomely."

"I did not know you made dresses for Lady Matlock," Kitty said.

"Oh, yes, I have for a few years now, and when she wears a particular gown that suits her, I often get a few new orders for the same dress in various fashionable colours and fabrics." She raised her brows and smirked. "Not that all the ladies should be wearing the styles that suit Lady Matlock. She is petite with delicate features, so what looks good on her does not look good on those who are... not petite, shall we say?"

Kitty chuckled. She had seen many young ladies follow what they thought was fashionable without a thought about how those style would actually look on them. She took a packet of papers from her aunt, who had offered to hold them while Kitty took the forgotten parcel to Lady Matlock, and handed it to Mrs. Havelston.

"These are my new drawings. Would you like any of them?"

Mrs. Havelston took the packet and began looking through the sketches. "Ah, these are lovely," she said. "And having seen Lady Matlock, would you not agree that they would be perfection on her?" She looked over her glasses at Kitty, who nodded her agreement. "As they would on you. You are very similar in size, I believe." She pursed her lips and frowned. "You are not so tall as she, nor do you bear the results of bearing children, but your features and structure are alike. I would like to make one of your creations for you if you would allow it."

"But you have an agreement with Lady Matlock."

Mrs. Havelston wrinkled her nose in displeasure. "That I do. Perhaps after she has had a chance to wear one?"

Kitty smiled. "Perhaps."

Mrs. Havelston placed the packet of papers under the counter. "Do you wish for me to give you the payment?"

Kitty shook her head as she heard the door open behind her. "We shall proceed as previously discussed." Her eyes must have registered her concern, for Mrs. Havelston only smiled and nodded in response before turning her attention to the newcomer.

"May I be of assistance?" she asked whoever had entered.

"I would like to take a look at your patterns and a sample of your work."

Kitty groaned silently at the sound of Miss Bingley's voice. She had hoped today would be a pleasant excursion, but it appeared it would be one taxing experience after another. It had taken a great deal of determination to greet and speak to Lady Matlock without betraying any particular fondness for her son. Now, she was going to have to endure at least a few words with Caroline Bingley.

No matter how pleasant Kitty tried to be to Miss Bingley, she was always greeted with indifference, if she was so fortunate, or disdain and ridicule, if she was not. She sighed and pasted what she hoped was a pleasant smile on her lips before turning around.

Kitty's smile faltered for one moment as she turned and saw that not only had Miss Bingley entered, but she had done so on the arm of Colonel Fitzwilliam. Although it was only a momentary falter, it was long enough for Miss Bingley to notice and to cause her to smile with satisfaction.

"Miss Kitty," she cooed. It was a grating sound that made the hairs on the back of Kitty's neck stand on end. "It is such a delight to see you." She raised an eyebrow, and her smile grew just a bit. It was obvious to Kitty that she was taking pleasure in the possibility of making her uneasy.

"And you," Kitty replied. "I trust Mr. and Mrs. Hurst are well?"

"Very well, I thank you."

Kitty shifted her eyes to Richard and bit the inside of her cheek to keep from laughing, for the look on his face was the complete opposite of Miss Bingley's. "Colonel Fitzwilliam, I trust you are also well?"

He smiled at her. "I am." He turned to Miss Bingley. "If you will excuse me, I shall not be of any use in looking at patterns and samples." He lifted her hand from his arm. "However, Mrs. Havelston, I would like to speak with you when you have finished with these young ladies. I would not wish to be the cause of their delay in proceeding on to whatever calls they may still have to make."

Caroline's countenance darkened as she looked first at Colonel Fitzwilliam and then Kitty before turning to her friends and Mrs. Havelston.

"I had no idea Lady Matlock frequented your shop," one of Miss Bingley's friends was saying. "Her gowns are delightful."

Kitty smiled as she watched Mrs. Havelston flip open the book of patterns to dresses she thought would suit the ladies before her and then send her assistant scurrying to retrieve three pieces of fabric.

Richard drew Kitty off to the side. "I told them my mother ordered dresses from here. It was the only thing I could think of for why I was standing in front of the modiste shop, staring at the door."

Mrs. Gardiner joined them. "Was there some other reason for it?"

He lowered his voice. "I have a sample of a pin box to give to Mrs. Havelston. My landlord, Mr. Wood, suggested I give a few boxes to various merchants in hopes of creating a demand for my work." He pulled the small box out of the pocket of his greatcoat.

"It is beautiful," Mrs. Gardiner said.

"You are selling your work?" Kitty whispered with a cautious look toward Miss Bingley, whose attention was obviously not fully on what Mrs. Havelston was saying, as her eyes were on Richard.

"I am. There is an explanation for it, of course, but I fear it would be best not to discuss it here." He took the box back from Mrs. Gardiner. "May I call on you tomorrow?"

"Unless you prefer to dine with us this evening," Mrs. Gardiner replied. "We are always delighted to add to our numbers around the table."

"It would be a pleasure," he replied. "I will need the directions and time."

Mrs. Gardiner walked behind the counter and pulled paper and pen from the shelf beneath it.

Miss Bingley gasped slightly at the action.

"Think nothing of it, ma'am," Mrs. Havelston assured her. "Mrs. Gardiner and I have been friends these many years. She is welcome to use whatever she needs."

"Years?" Caroline tone was one of great interest.

"For nearly as long as I have been in town," Mrs. Gardiner said with a smile. She turned her attention to writing down the information Richard needed. As she tucked the supplies back onto the shelf, she bumped Kitty's drawings and sent them scattering on the floor behind the counter.

"Oh," one of Miss Bingley's friends said, "some of those are very nice."

"I am sorry," Mrs. Havelston said, "those are exclusive designs for a particular patron. They are not for general orders just yet."

Kitty's breath caught in her chest when she saw the drawings lying on the floor. She was almost certain that there was nothing on them to connect them to her, but still, she feared that somehow the connection might be made. Her eyes darted to the three ladies who were standing, watching Mrs. Gardiner gathering the sketches.

"Did you draw them yourself?" Caroline turned her attention back to Mrs. Havelston.

"No, but I shall be creating the patterns based on the sketches." She nodded to Mrs. Gardiner and Kitty, who were preparing to leave, then continued her conversation with Miss Bingley about how fortunate she was to occasionally find talented artists willing to share their work with her. "What lady does not wish to have a unique design with which to catch the attention of the other ladies and perhaps a gentleman or two when they arrive at a soiree?"

Kitty could not help but chuckle to herself as she heard Caroline's friends start to chatter about gentlemen and this hideous dress or that divine creation.

"May I see you out?" Richard looked to Mrs. Gardiner imploringly. He had no desire to be held captive in this shop with Caroline and her friends for any longer than was necessary. He would not have entered with them if they had not found him out front staring at the door like a besotted fool.

"Of course, you may, sir." She took his proffered arm and allowed him to escort her out of the shop.

"How long do you think they will be?" He glanced back at the shop.

"At least another quarter hour," Mrs. Gardiner said. "I would be surprised if they do not leave with an appointment to have an order fitted. Mrs. Havelston is a fine saleswoman."

Richard pulled out his watch to mark the time. "Is your carriage near?"

"Just over there." Kitty motioned down the street and then, taking the arm he offered, allowed him to lead her to the carriage and hand both her and her aunt into it.

Richard closed the door and watched as the carriage moved into traffic. He pulled out his watch, looked at the time once again, and pondered what he would do with the remaining time before returning to Mrs. Havelston's shop. The wind tugged at his hat, and he put a hand up to keep it in place. He sighed resignedly, it would be best if he just waited in the shop instead of skulking about on the street and in the cold.

"She's a pretty thing." A man stepped out of the shadows. "I suppose my brother is not fond of such a low connection." The friendly stranger, who was actually no stranger at all, put an arm around Richard's shoulder. They were evenly matched for size. Both were of slightly more than average height with a muscular frame. Of course, the man from the shadows, also known as Admiral Reginald Fitzwilliam, younger brother of Lord Matlock, was older than Richard by at least twenty years.

"No, he is not." Richard shook his head. "You always could find me, even when I did not wish to be found."

The admiral shrugged. "There are very few places I have not tried in an attempt to rid myself of my father and yours." He chuckled. "The sea was the best. Neither of them would step foot on board one of my ships. It was one of the best things about being in the navy."

Richard laughed. "I thought the women in foreign ports were the best."

His uncle clapped him on the shoulder. "I said one of the best, not *the* best. Now, what has you shuffling about this district? Buying a dress for a ball?"

Again, Richard laughed. He had always enjoyed his uncle's company, not that he often had the opportunity to see him as his uncle and his father were rarely on speaking terms. "I am research-ing the option of becoming a tradesman." He pulled the box from his pocket.

His uncle took it and turned it over in his hands. "For pins?"

Richard nodded.

"And would I be correct that your father is the cause of your foray into trade?"

"He is. I have until the end of next week to tell him that I am not going to marry his choice. I expect I will be in need of employment shortly thereafter, as my term in the militia is nearly at an end."

His uncle made a clucking sound as he handed the box back to Richard. "Well, as I said, she is a pretty thing."

"That she is," Richard said with a smile.

His uncle made a sweeping motion with his arm, indicating that they should begin walking. "You can tell me about her while you wait to see my friend Julie, Mrs. Havelston." He shrugged. "I was not as brave as you. I married the sea instead of my father's choice or defying him to marry the woman I loved."

The comment made Richard's left brow arch in interest and question.

"Tell me about your lady first," his uncle replied, "and then when we have time, I will tell you about mine."

Chapter 9

SOMETIME LATER THAT DAY, after the sun was gone and the darkness of night had fallen, Richard stood before the Gardiners' home, waiting to be allowed entry. He did not wait long, for the door was opened nearly before the sound of his knock had faded. Giving his name along with his hat and coat to the servant who greeted him, he again waited, this time in the hall, to be introduced. He took note of his surroundings with an eager eye. This was the home of a well-to-do merchant, and as such, it was the sort of living arrangements he might hope to one day have for himself. It was not Matlock House or even Darcy House, but it was lovely and felt comfortable and welcoming.

"Colonel Fitzwilliam, it is a pleasure to see you, sir. A pleasure." Mr. Gardiner greeted him with a firm handshake and motioned for him to have a seat. "Dinner will be served shortly. May I offer you a drink while you wait? A bit of wine perhaps?"

The man stood beside a dresser that held several bottles of wine and a few glasses. This, too, spoke to Mr. Gardiner's success in business.

"My husband prides himself on his wine selections, Colonel," Mrs. Gardiner said with a laugh. "It would do you well to enjoy it."

"Then I will happily drink whatever you select for me." Richard took a seat near Kitty, who smiled and gave him a brief greeting. He barely refrained from sighing as he settled into the chair next to her. It was heaven to be near her. There was no way he would give this up for any inducement. He would work as long and hard as necessary to be here.

"My wife and niece tell me that you are thinking of stepping down from the first circles of society to join my realm." Mr. Gardiner handed Richard a glass of wine. "I shall refill it for your supper. There is no need to sip like a lady, so to speak," he said with a wink.

Richard took the glass and after a hearty sip began his explanation of his change in position. "My father is very set in the traditional ways of the aristocracy. I am not, and the difference in our opinions seems destined to lead to a parting of ways." Richard lifted his glass. "This is excellent, by the way."

"Thank you. I do try to only stock the best." Mr. Gardiner extended his legs out in front of him and crossed one foot over the other. "I suppose if your plans do not result in a parting of ways between you and your father, it will, at least, bring a lowering of your status through the removal of your inheritance or strictures being placed upon that inheritance."

"Precisely. Though I expect it to be a parting." And an ugly break it would be. It had crossed his mind that he might have to relocate to another city to make his life, depending on how punishing his father decided to be. Of course, Darcy had connections that could be used to sway his father into being merely harsh rather than crushingly cruel.

"It is a shame that parents can be so demanding." Gardiner sighed. "And it is not just in the highest circles that it happens. Bennet faced the same from his father."

"Papa?" Kitty asked in surprise. Apparently, this was a new story to her, just as it was to Richard.

"Aye, your father's father, your grandfather, did not approve of your mother since her father was from trade, and, according to him, any true gentleman does not have ties to trade."

Richard chuckled bitterly at that. "I have heard my father say nearly the same words."

"It is so wrong," Mrs. Gardiner said softly.

"Indeed," her husband replied. "And Bennet thought so, too, and would not hear of breaking off his relationship with your mother, Kitty, and so, the entail on Longbourn was created."

"I did not know that," said Kitty. "I thought it had just always been entailed."

Her uncle shook his head. "No, the entail is a recent thing. It was not a complete removal of your father as heir – your grandfather hated his cousin too much to cut your father off completely. Instead, your grandfather gave your papa a choice, and he chose your mother over an unfettered inheritance." Mr. Gardiner turned back to Richard. "I assume your father wishes you to marry well."

Richard nodded. "That is what he says, although again, our opinions on what that means differ. And so, he has selected a bride for me." He heard Kitty's soft intake of air, but he dared not look at her. "I have until the end of next week to accept or refuse his choice."

"And you are considering refusing?" Mr. Gardiner asked the question of Richard. However, his eyes were on his niece, and concern etched his features. He must know the extent of the wishes that he and Kitty had to be together.

"I am not considering refusing him, sir. I am determined to refuse him."

Mr. Gardiner's eyes shifted back to Richard, and a smile replaced his look of worry. "Am I to assume there is a reason of the feminine variety for this determination?"

As if the man did not know! "There is."

"Well, then." Mr. Gardiner rose to lead them into dinner, and Richard and the ladies followed suit, "we shall have to discuss your plans for your business. I am well-established and would do whatever is needed to assist you if it means the happiness of my niece."

"I beg your pardon, sir?" Had Mr. Gardiner just hinted that he expected a marriage between Richard and Kitty to take place even though Richard had not yet put his offer forward?

"Bennet has told me not to refuse you," Mr. Gardiner said. "I am correct to assume that my niece is your choice, am I not? I assure you it is not an assumption that is based on ignorance, and from what I have seen of you, Colonel, I agree with Bennet. You would make our Kitty a fine husband. That is, you would if she was your choice?" His tone lifted turning the statement into a question.

Richard felt his cheeks grow warm. This was not how he had anticipated the evening to progress. He had expected to discuss his business with Mr. Gardiner over their meal, and then he would discuss Kitty after the meal when they were alone in Mr. Gardiner's study. However, it seemed they had skipped the meal and the solitude of Mr. Gardiner's study and had jumped directly to Richard's offer.

With all eyes turned toward him and his heart beating wildly, he nodded. "You are correct. I would very much like to marry Miss Katherine if she will have me." As he spoke, he felt a small hand slip into his.

Mr. Gardiner smiled at him, nodding to where Kitty stood next to Richard with her hand in his. "I believe you have your answer." He turned to his wife. "We could hold the meal for a few minutes, could we not?"

"At least five," she replied as she followed him out of the room and closed the door.

Richard looked at the door for a moment as he gathered his thoughts before he turned to Kitty. He had prepared a speech before he had left home this evening, but it seemed to have gotten lost on the way to this moment. "I am not romantic —"

"I know." Kitty lifted his hand and brushed her lips against his knuckles.

That did nothing to clear his addled mind. Indeed, it scrambled it further.

"A simple question is all that is required," Kitty prompted.

"But, what about the pretty words that all women wish to hear?"

She shook her head. "I do not need them. I see your love for me in your eyes and the things you do. You have chosen me ahead of family and fortune. There is no need to put it into words."

"I would choose you before I would choose myself." He placed a hand, which had been made rough from working with his men in the militia and the wood he loved, on her cheek. "I do not have the means just yet to support a family," he began.

"But you will." She squeezed the one hand of his that she still held tightly.

He smiled and nodded. He had already known that he would be successful, for the prize he sought was the most precious that could ever be claimed. However, in this moment, he would gladly face whatever trials might come as he established himself as a tradesman twice over just to have her continue to look at him as she did now with such confidence in his abilities. "Yes, I will, and when I do, I would very much like to create that family with you. Will you marry me when I am established?"

A smile lit her face and eyes. "I would like nothing better."

"It will not be a life of ease," he cautioned. For a moment, despite his desire to have her as his wife, he doubted whether he was doing the right thing in asking her to share such a life. His thumb caressed her cheek. "You deserve so much more."

"I love you." She pressed her cheek more firmly against his hand. "I will be happy nowhere else, save at your side."

He knew that he felt the same. It was why he was prepared to defy his father. No matter the money and property he would lose by choosing her, he knew his life would never be so pleasant with those things as it would be with her at his side. Still, he could not resist asking, "You are certain?"

"Yes."

"Then, may I — "

"Yes. You must kiss me."

And he did — soft as a butterfly landing on a delicate flower in a garden, for she was so precious, so treasured. But even though it was a brief, gentle kiss, the emotion that passed to her through it and returned to him as she wrapped her arms firmly around him, pulling him close so that her head could lay on his heart was anything but gentle. It felt strong and unbreakable, and he indulged himself in storing up this feeling until a soft knock at the door drew them apart and sent them on to dinner.

Chapter 10

RICHARD WHISTLED TO HIMSELF as he descended the stairs Monday morning. His time over the past two days with the Gardiners had been extremely pleasant. He and Mr. Gardiner had discussed some possibilities for his business, and he felt encouraged having the support and guidance of a merchant who was so well-established. His smile increased as he remembered the few minutes of privacy that the Gardiners had allowed him with Kitty before he had returned home each time. He poured himself some coffee, and giving a greeting to Mr. Wood, settled into his seat and began to eat. They both ate in silence. Mr. Wood read the paper while Richard contemplated the events of the past two days and the things he planned to accomplish today.

"Oh, my," Mr. Wood said in alarm. "Oh, my." He lowered the paper and looked at Richard, who was just finishing his meal. "You will want to see this. No, no, that is not accurate. You do not want to see this, but you need to." He rose, folding the newspaper as he walked toward Richard. He clapped Richard on the shoulder as he lay it before him. "I am grateful my father was not so scheming as yours." He pointed to the announcement of the engagement of Mr. Richard Fitzwilliam to Miss Anne de Bourgh.

Richard snatched the paper from the table. "No." He shook his head. He could not have read what he just read. His eyes skimmed the words on the page once more. He had read what he thought he had read. "No, it is not true! I am promised to Miss Katherine."

The room felt as if it were making circles around him, and he was aware of the sensation of his breakfast fighting to stay contained in his stomach. How could this have been printed? He still had a week before he had to tell his father of his decision. Unless —

"No, she would not." This simply could not be his mother's doing. She had promised.

He stood with the paper still grasped in his hand. He had to get to Kitty. She needed to know that this was not true. Rushing from the room, he grabbed his hat and coat from the chair near the front door and ran into Darcy as he stepped into the street.

Darcy took note of the paper in Richard's hand and the way his coat was thrown on but not fastened. "I see you have seen it." He placed a hand on Richard's arm. "Take a moment to think before you act."

Richard shook his head and pulled his arm away. "No. There is no time. When Katherine sees this..." His voice trailed off, and he closed his eyes as if it could prevent him from feeling the pain that he knew this announcement would bring to Kitty.

Darcy stepped in front of him. "She will be hurt, but a letter of explanation sent immediately might stem some of the damage."

Richard shook his head again. "She is not at Longbourn. She is in town." If only she were more removed from his father's manipulation. Anger swelled in him at the thought of his father's callousness. How dare he hurt Kitty like this! He would deal with his father later. Presently, he needed to go to Kathrine with all haste.

"With the Gardiners?"

Richard nodded. "I must go." He stepped around Darcy and ran down the street and around the corner just as a carriage was drawing to a stop before number eight Bartlett's Buildings.

Darcy had never seen his cousin in such a fit of agitation, and for a moment, as he watched him running down the street, Darcy considered chasing after him.

"I see I missed him," the new arrival said.

Turning to see who was speaking, Darcy's eyes grew large and his mouth opened just slightly before forming a pleased grin as he recognized his uncle, Admiral Fitzwilliam.

He chuckled at Darcy's expression. "Richard was just as surprised to see me on Saturday." He looked down the street in the direction Richard had taken. "I had hoped to ask him how his evening with his lady had gone. I did try to call on him yesterday, but he was out. I assumed, therefore, that I might be gaining another niece in the near future."

Before Darcy could question his uncle about his statements, Mr. Wood had joined them and was introducing himself.

"I can tell you what you wish to know," Mr. Wood said, "The colonel was successful. He asked his young lady to marry him and was accepted. He has not stopped grinning since that evening, and he was whistling his way into the day until he read that bit in the paper."

"He proposed to Kitty?" Darcy groaned and scrubbed his face.

"And was accepted," Mr. Wood said.

"That adds a wrinkle to this mess," Darcy muttered.

"What bit in the paper?" asked Admiral Fitzwilliam.

Darcy pulled a newspaper from his pocket and handed it to his uncle. He was allowing his uncle a moment to read the announcement when a horse carrying a finely dressed rider came up the road at a fast pace, then slowed, and finally stopped in front of them.

"Darcy, you are not easy to find." Rycroft swung down from his horse. "Uncle Reginald!" He embraced the man and thumped him firmly on the back. "My mother will be delighted to see you." He cocked his head to the side. "You are planning to call on her, are you not?"

"Of course." The admiral laughed. "I dare not slink back to the coast without seeing her."

"Mr. Wood." Rycroft nodded his greeting to the gentleman. "Now, why are we all here?" He folded his arms across his chest and waited for an explanation.

"Colonel Fitzwilliam is my tenant, my lord," Mr. Wood said.

Rycroft's brows rose. "Indeed?"

Darcy nodded. "While you have been otherwise occupied, our cousin's life has been crumbling apart."

"Crashed to the ground this morning," the admiral said.

"Perhaps you would like to use my sitting room for this discussion," Mr. Wood offered.

"Capital idea," the admiral said.

Rycroft led the way, stooping upon entering to scratch the ear of what he called a naughty cat.

"How do you know Mr. Wood so well?" Darcy asked.

"He works with my solicitor as a clerk," Rycroft answered. "Now," he took a seat, "the lovely Mrs. Darcy said that I would find you here and that you were in need of my assistance, Darcy."

"You spoke to my wife?"

Rycroft nodded. "I came to see if you would care to go for a ride, and she greeted me. It seemed most urgent that I find you, so I spared no time in coming here."

Darcy smirked slightly. Despite the seriousness of the matter at hand, he could not resist a small tease. "*Your* wife did not wish to ride with you?"

"She insists on spending time with my mother and *your* sister." He rolled his eyes. "I was instructed by all three that I was not needed for the morning."

Darcy laughed along with his uncle and Mr. Wood.

"Could we return to the subject of Richard?" Rycroft asked in a slightly irritated tone. "What has happened to cause him distress?"

"His father has demanded that Richard marry Anne."

Rycroft's jaw dropped open slightly. "Cousin Anne?"

"Yes," Darcy said. "But, he has decided he will not marry her."

"Which led him to my door in search of accommodations," Mr. Wood added.

Rycroft, with brows drawn together, nodded to each bit of new information as he took it in. "I assume that his father has threatened to cut him off if he does not comply and marry Anne?"

"Precisely," the admiral said. "It is a common tactic with the earls of Matlock, it seems."

Rycroft's head tipped as he gave his uncle a curious look, but instead of pursuing his uncle's comment, which had also piqued Darcy's interest, he asked, "But the breach has not yet occurred, has it?"

Darcy sighed. "Officially, no. But in reality, yes. Richard asked for two weeks to contemplate his future, but his father has not honoured that. The paper." He nodded to his uncle, who handed Rycroft the paper and pointed to the announcement.

Rycroft let out a long slow whistle. "So, Richard has little hope of escaping a marriage of convenience."

"It is worse than that," Darcy said. "You may not have noticed much other than Mary when in Hertfordshire, but our cousin has lost his heart to Kitty."

Rycroft blinked. "I knew there was an admiration on her part and a fondness on his, but has it truly progressed to this?"

Both Darcy and Admiral Fitzwilliam nodded.

"He proposed to her and was accepted evening before last," Mr. Wood said.

Rycroft sank back in his chair. "What do we do?"

That was the question. Lord Matlock would not simply retract his announcement, and they all knew it. Ideas were passed about, discussed, and discarded.

"There is always Gretna Green," Mr. Wood suggested.

"It is not an unworthy option," admitted the admiral, "but what I truly think we need is my sister's help." He looked at Rycroft. "Your mother has always been able to sway our brother. I do not know what she holds against him, but whatever it may be, it is effective. Perhaps it will help Richard out of this mess."

Darcy certainly hoped that Lady Sophia would hold the key to unlocking a happy resolution for Richard and Kitty. The sight of his cousin in such a state as he had been in this morning was not one that was easily forgotten.

"Very well," Rycroft said. "Then, I say we go talk to my mother, and, if that does not work, then we shall cart them off to Gretna Green at midnight." He stood. "I can well imagine Richard's state of mind, as it was not long ago that I was feeling as he is." He looked around the group. "Do we all convene at Rycroft Place, or should one of us go in search of him?"

"He was on foot and seemed to be headed to the merchant district. I would say he is at the Gardiners'," Darcy said. "He needs someone. I will go and bring him to Rycroft place as soon as possible."

"Bring Kitty, too," Rycroft said before turning to their uncle. "Well, Uncle, it seems you are due for a visit to my mother and to meet my wife." He smiled and threw an arm around his uncle's shoulders. "I must caution you that Mary can be a bit rules-minded."

His uncle chuckled as the party moved toward the door. "And she married you?"

"Fortunately, yes." He gave a nod to Mr. Wood. "Thank you, sir, for the use of your sitting room. We will hopefully return your tenant to you in good order." He back turned to the admiral. "I will ride on ahead and warn the ladies that their morning plans are about to be altered." He winked at his uncle. "There is no need for us all to get a lecture." He held up a finger. "But you must never tell Mary I said that. She thinks it shows her in a poor light."

His uncle raised a brow and shook his head. "Is there no hope for you?"

"Very little," said Rycroft with a laugh. "Truly, I do not say such things to just everyone. At least, not any longer."

His uncle groaned. "And she married you?"

"Fortunately, yes." Rycroft swung up onto his horse. "She is the loveliest lady in all of England, if not the world." He clucked to his horse and, with a wave, was off.

"If not the loveliest, at least, the most tolerant and forgiving," muttered his uncle with a shake of his head.

"Excessively forgiving," Darcy agreed with a chuckle. "And she is just what he needed."

"I look forward to meeting both your wives and seeing my other nephew as happily married." He gave Darcy a pointed look. "Go get him, Darcy. He is not going to be another Lord Matlock casualty. Tell him that."

"I will." Darcy wondered at that comment and the one his uncle had made earlier, but now was not the time to discover the story that lay behind them. Right now, his cousin needed him.

Chapter 11

"Miss Bennet."

Kitty stopped, drew a breath, and took a moment to affix a smile to her lips before turning toward Miss Bingley. "Good morning, Miss Bingley."

She looked past her to the two ladies who stood with her. They were the same two ladies who had been with her the other day. Perhaps if she looked at them, Miss Bingley would remember to introduce them to her, although if they were friends of Miss Bingley, perhaps it was better if she did not know who they were.

Miss Bingley caught the direction of Kitty's gaze and with a look that said she was being forced to do something quite disagreeable, she said, "Miss Ivison, Miss Pearce, this is Miss Bennet. She is the sister of my brother's wife."

"Another Bennet?" Miss Ivison cried. "There certainly are a lot of you."

Her comment made all three ladies titter, and Kitty was now certain she did not wish to know any of them. If only there were a polite way to turn and leave them.

"There are five," Miss Bingley said.

"Five?" Miss Ivison's voice dripped with disapproval. "Are you all so *daring* as Lady Rycroft or Mrs. Darcy?"

Kitty did not miss the particular emphasis placed on the word daring. "Not Mrs. Bingley," she replied with a smile. "And I do not think of myself as particularly daring, but I imagine Lydia does."

She spoke in what she thought was a way very similar to Lydia when she was attempting to shock someone into leaving her alone.

"Yes. Well," Miss Bingley said with a cunning look and smile for her friends, "it seems *you* shall have to find a new beau."

"Pardon me? I do not understand your meaning."

"I am speaking about your beau, Colonel Fitzwilliam, being outside your grasp," Miss Bingley said with a flutter of her lashes. "It is in all the papers. Do you not read them?"

"I have not read it today."

"One should always read the society pages if one wishes to be current on all the important news." Miss Ivison made a show of shivering. It was not that cold out this morning, and she was dressed warmly from what Kitty could see. "We should hurry. We have an appointment, after all." Contrary to her words, she made no move to depart from Kitty's presence. "Were you also on your way to the modiste shop again today?"

"I am." A sense of dread began to settle in Kitty's stomach. It was obvious that these ladies were not about to leave her alone. For what purpose she did not know, but she suspected it was not a pleasant reason.

"Do you work there?" Miss Pearce, who had not spoken to this point, tipped her head and studied Kitty.

"No." The sense of dread began to blossom. "My aunt is there. She and Mrs. Havelston are good friends. I was just getting some trim for my bonnet from the milliner." She motioned toward the milliner's shop.

"Hmm," Miss Pearce said. "I thought perhaps you might assist her — recording measurements, gathering material... *drawing patterns.*" She paused and raised a brow as if she knew something that Kitty did not before continuing. "Your mother is from trade, after all, so it must be in your blood."

Kitty was at a loss for how to respond to such a comment.

"Then, I say it is very good that the colonel is safe from her machinations." Miss Ivison gave a small gasp and covered her mouth as if surprised by a thought, but her eyes said she was actually amused and not in the least shocked, as she feigned. "Although, some men do keep mistresses."

Again, all three ladies tittered.

Outrage bubbled inside Kitty. How dare they insinuate that the colonel was so disreputable, or that she was without morals? She straightened her spine and silently drew a breath, tamping down her anger. "If you will excuse me," she said. "I find I have had enough of your insults."

She moved to leave, but Miss Bingley stopped her, putting an arm around Kitty's shoulders and pointing toward Mrs. Havelston's shop. "Look, there he is with his mother. I wonder if Lady Matlock is helping him purchase something particular for his bride."

"His bride?"

"Yes, Miss de Bourgh – his cousin, I believe?" She turned toward her friends who confirmed it.

"It is in all the papers, remember? Oh, no, I had forgotten you have not read it yet." She released Kitty and smiled smugly.

Dread had turned to horror. It could not be true. It just could not be. "If you will excuse me, I must go." Kitty blinked against the tears that threatened to spill from her eyes. It could not be true. It simply could not be, she repeated to herself as she walked as quickly as she could toward Mrs. Havelston's shop. He had promised to marry her. He could not be promised to another. He just could not be.

"Did you tell him?" Richard stepped between his mother and her carriage as she exited the modiste shop. He had been on his way to the Gardiners' when he saw his mother's carriage turning down this street. Likely the driver had been returning to collect her at the end of her appointment.

"Good morning." Lady Matlock attempted to step around him, but he would not allow it. "Have you forgotten all your manners after so few days living with the lower class?"

"It is not a good morning," he growled, "and I wish to know if you are responsible for it or not."

Lady Matlock waved away the footman who had stepped up next to her. "I have no idea of what you speak."

Richard's replying laugh was bitter and cold. "You know very well of what I am speaking. You do not go a day without checking to see who has been engaged to whom. It is nearly as important to you as your first cup of tea." He held the paper out to her. "After I spoke to you the other day, did you tell Father of my decision?"

She pushed the paper away. "I told no one of our meeting. No one." She tugged nervously at a glove. "I did not know that had been submitted until after it was done."

Richard turned from her and threw his hands in the air in disgust. "He could not give me even two weeks?"

"He knew you would not accept." She placed a hand on his back. "We all knew — " She stopped as she saw that they were drawing a crowd.

Richard did not care if the whole world knew his business at present. His life was already in ruins. A public disagreement with his mother would only make his father unhappy, for Richard could not be made any more unhappy than he was. And so, he was going to continue their discussion until he saw who the crowd included. Katherine. She had seen it. He could tell by the pain in her expression she had seen it.

"Is it true?" Kitty stopped in front of Richard. Her lips trembled, and she closed her eyes and tipping her head, gave it a little shake as if trying to clear it. She opened her eyes, and he saw pain and fear mingled in them. "Are you..." She swallowed and shook her head again as she pressed her trembling lips together.

She was trying valiantly to keep from crying. "Are you promised to another?"

Richard placed a hand on her arm, but she drew away. He looked to his mother and then back at her. "I am not, but the papers say I am."

Kitty pulled her lips between her teeth and nodded as a tear slid down her cheek. "If it is in the paper," she said in a quiet trembling voice, "then it is as good as done."

"Katherine..."

She shook her head. "I will not hold you to your promise to me. You must do what is expected."

The tears flowed freely down her cheeks now, and it tore at Richard's heart.

"Is it not enough to cast your child aside?" She looked past Richard to Lady Matlock. "Must you also require he sacrifice his heart?"

She placed a hand on her chest, and visibility drew a breath as if it was a difficult thing to do. Then, she moved that same hand to Richard's arm. "You will always have mine." Her voice was no more than a whisper.

She withdrew her hand and stepped past him toward the shop. Her shoulders sagged as if she were being pressed down. She took one step away from him. Then, another. His hope of a happy future. Everything he held dear was walking away from him. She swayed. Her legs wobbled and –

"Katherine!" Richard shoved past his mother and caught her before she hit the ground but not before her head had made contact with the edge of the doorframe. He looked at Miss Bingley. "Hold the door." He barked out the command as if she were one of his recruits. And just as if she were one of his men, she jumped and did as she was instructed.

"We need cloth, Mrs. Havelston. Quickly." He had seen blood before, many times, but to see the trickle of blood running down Katherine's white face, made his stomach roil.

"You need to sit down, Colonel," Mrs. Gardiner said. "As soon as we have a dressing on her forehead, you may place her in my carriage. It is out front." Her voice was soft and soothing. Her touch on his arm as she led him to a chair was light.

"Oh, my, oh, my," Mrs. Havelston said as she brought some cloth over to where Richard sat with Kitty in his arms and placed it on Kitty's forehead. "She will need a stitch or two, to be sure," she said to Mrs. Gardiner. "What happened?"

His mother stepped forward. "She received some distressing news." She removed Richard's hat and ran her hand through his hair as she had when he was a child, and she was trying to soothe him. She handed the paper, which Richard had dropped, and she had obviously retrieved, to Mrs. Gardiner. "There seems to be a mistaken announcement."

Richard's brow furrowed and his eyes snapped toward her. A mistaken announcement? There was no mistake. It was purposeful – false, but intentionally published. She placed her hand on his shoulder and shrugged. "I am your mother." Her gaze flicked to Kitty. "She is right. I cannot ask you to sacrifice your heart."

"But Father..."

"We will see what can be done," she murmured. "I make no promises other than my support."

Chapter 12

RICHARD SHIFTED KITTY SLIGHTLY in his arms as Mrs. Havelston finished the job, which the door frame had started, of removing Kitty's bonnet. His mother's words were a balm to his wounded heart, but he knew that there was likely little she could do.

"Did she see the paper?" Mrs. Gardiner asked.

"I do not believe she did," Lady Matlock replied slowly as if she was trying to piece together what had happened. "She asked if it was true, but did not seem to know what was said in the paper."

"Then how did she hear?" Mrs. Gardiner tilted her head and looked at the three ladies who stood near the door.

"We have an appointment with Mrs. Havelston," Miss Ivison said.

"Oh, my, I cannot think to keep an appointment at a time like this. Miss Kitty is like family, you see." She looked behind her to her assistant. "Miss Mallory, would you be so kind as to take these ladies' measurements and record their selections? Perhaps one of them could write for you while you work with the others." She added another cloth to the wound on Kitty's forehead. "I would not ask it of my clients," she explained, "but it is the only way I will be able to keep your appointment. However, if you prefer another day, that can be arranged."

Miss Ivison huffed. "You would cancel an appointment for someone like her?"

Mrs. Havelston straightened and turn to face Miss Ivison. "I have already informed you that Miss Kitty is like family."

Miss Ivison shook her head and lifted her chin a bit higher. "She is nothing but a poor country miss who sells you drawings."

"I beg your pardon?" Mrs. Havelston's hands rested on her hips and her features were set in a grim expression of displeasure.

"There was a slip of paper in the pile which scattered the other day that had her name on it." Miss Ivison lifted her chin, a smug look of satisfaction on her face. "She is your new designer." Her tone was mocking. "A gentleman's daughter who has lowered herself to work in trade and hoped to persuade the son of an earl to marry her. I am surprised she did not affect a compromise as her sisters have done to snare their husbands."

If Richard were not holding Kitty, he would remove Miss Ivison from the store!

Mrs. Gardiner gasped and covered her mouth with her hand while Mrs. Havelston's eyes narrowed and with a slight flip of her head, turned away from Miss Ivison indicating they had nothing further about which to speak.

Next to him, Richard's mother inhaled sharply. She looked down at Kitty. "She is your designer?" Gently, she took one of Kitty's hands in hers and smiled softly at Richard. "I do not care if she is," she whispered.

"That I cannot say, my lady," Mrs. Havelston replied. "But what I can say is that these ladies, Miss Mallory, are never to have an appointment with me. Not today, not ever."

Miss Ivison laughed. "I would think twice before denying our business. My father and the fathers of my friends are men of means."

"Your money is not needed. Be on your way." Mrs. Havelston turned back to tending Kitty's wound, which had slowed its bleeding.

"Mrs. Havelston will always have *my* business, and I will continue to refer my friends. I dare say I have more sway than you. It will be too bad that you will not be able to wear any of the exclusive styles Mrs. Havelston creates for me. Of course, I am not sure you could carry them off, so perhaps that is to your benefit."

In that moment, Richard was sure he had never been so proud of his mother as she leveled her most contemptuous look at Miss Bingley and her friends.

With a huff, Miss Ivison, Miss Pearce, and Miss Bingley turned to leave just as the door opened, and Darcy stepped into the shop.

"Hold the door, sir," Mrs. Havelston said. "Colonel, if you will?" She motioned for Richard to carry Kitty out of the shop. "We had best be getting this young lady to her aunt's house."

Kitty groaned and her eyes fluttered open for a moment when Richard stood. "Shh," he said, kissing her gently on the forehead. "All will be well," he whispered. "I have you."

He held her more firmly as he carried her to the carriage and wished with all his heart that his words were actually true. But how could they be? Then, when the carriage door was opened and with a sigh of regret and another kiss to her forehead, he placed her gently next to her aunt. His shoulders sagged as he watched the vehicle move slowly down the road.

"Such theatrics," Miss Ivison said as she passed him, "Swooning over a bit of news. Indeed!"

"Not unlike her sisters in her attempts to find herself in some gentleman's arms," Miss Bingley said.

Richard's hands clenched at his side as he spun toward them. They were utter idiots!

"You boorish, babbling harpies! If Miss Bennet does not recover, I shall personally see to your ruin."

He stepped closer and lowered his voice to a growl. "I promise that there shall not be a place left in polite society which will accept you." He began to turn away, but thought better of it, and added, "And should I hear that you were the cause of her distress, I may ruin you anyway. Therefore, I would advise you to take the first offer of marriage you receive — if you receive any — for it may be your last."

Miss Ivison was, of course, the first to find her voice. "Colonel," she began in a saccharine tone.

"Do. Not." He fixed a glare on her that he knew had frightened many a young officer in his command. "You are no longer welcome to speak to me, and I most certainly do not wish to speak to you." He turned and walked away, leaving the three ladies red-faced with their mouths hanging open. He would have walked right past his cousin and his mother had Darcy not stopped him.

"What happened?" Darcy asked.

"I cannot speak of it just yet. I need to expend some energy, or we shall both suffer from my current state of mind."

Darcy's eyes searched his for a moment before his cousin gave a nod of acceptance. "We are meeting at Rycroft Place."

Richard nodded. "I will be there."

"As soon as possible?"

Again, Richard nodded.

"Are you going to walk the distance?" his mother said. "The wind is cold."

He shrugged. "I may see if I can get a hack along the way."

She sighed. "Where do you board? I can have my carriage meet you there."

He shook his head. "I do not wish for you or anyone my father employs to know."

"I will not tell your father where you are," she said in exasperation.

"It is best if you do not need to keep it from him," Richard said softly. He was already going to be the cause of discord between his parents. He did not need the secret of where he was living to be the reason his mother found her life unbearable.

"Darcy." She turned to him with a look that implored him to do something.

"I know where it is. I will meet you there, Richard."

"Thank you," Lady Matlock said. "I am not as evil as you all might think."

"I do not think you are evil," Richard assured her. "You are too bound by society and my father, but you are not evil."

He turned away and then back. "It was my knowing how good your heart is that made my decision so difficult. It is why I have tolerated my father's demands for as long as I have. I know what you expect of your sons, and I have no desire to disappoint you. That being said, I cannot do what he asks. I simply cannot." He closed his eyes and shook his head. "And now, I do not know how to avoid it."

In all honesty, he wished to sink to the ground and hold his head in his hands. He knew that to break an engagement, whether he had willingly entered it or been duped into it, was no small matter and would not be tolerated by either his father or Lady Catherine. There would be penalties which would have to be paid, penalties which were, no doubt, calculated to make his breaking the engagement an impossibility.

"That is why we are meeting," Darcy said to Richard, with a sidelong glance at Richard's mother. "There must be something that can be done."

Richard shook his head. He wanted to believe there was something, but he knew his father.

"Do I wish to know who is included in this we?" his mother asked.

"Rycroft and his wife, myself and my wife, Lady Sophia, Admiral Fitzwilliam, and Richard."

Lady Matlock's brows rose as he listed the names of Lord Matlock's brother and sister. "So nearly the whole family is against my husband?"

"That is all for the present." There was a steeliness to Darcy's tone.

"There will be more?" Her hand flew to her chest and her eyes grew large.

Richard turned to leave but hesitated. Did it really matter how many more were on his side? Would any of it sway his father?

"Go," Darcy said. "I will come get you."

Richard sketched a shallow bow to his mother and began his walk back to his home at Bartlett's Buildings as Darcy answered his mother's question.

"I may not have a title, Aunt, but I am not without my sphere of influence. I do not know how the others will proceed, but I will do all that is in my power to support Richard. You know he has always been like a brother to me, and he is Georgiana's guardian. I hope you understand that I cannot allow him to be harmed any more than I could allow it to happen to my wife or my sister." He smiled sadly at his aunt. "And whether you and my uncle are happy about the fact or not, Miss Bennet is now my sister."

Lady Matlock sighed. "I have told Richard that I will give him my support where I am able, so, if I can be of assistance, please, let me know."

Darcy looked at her in surprise. "You will support him?"

"He is my son, and I cannot bear to see him in pain as I saw today." She motioned toward Richard's retreating form. "Save for when your mother and father died, my son has not cried since he was ten. At least, not that anyone has seen. However, less than half an hour ago, he sat amongst a group of women with tears in his eyes." She briefly explained all that had happened prior to Darcy's arrival at the modiste shop. "He loves her too greatly. How can I be a party to such hurt?"

Darcy stared at the door to Mrs. Havelston's shop for a moment. His aunt needed to know that her son was not the only one whose love was great. "She sold the designs for him," he said softly. "No one is supposed to know about the arrangement, so I am telling you in strictest confidence." He sighed. He knew that Miss Bingley and her friends would use the information, whether it was true or not, to disparage Kitty.

"What do you mean, she sold them for him? How would her selling designs assist Richard?"

"She spoke to me at Rycroft's wedding breakfast and asked me to invest the money she made from her sales. It was her hope that, someday, she would have enough set aside to help Richard do what he loves, and, perhaps, with any luck, she hoped he might still be free to marry her."

"But that would take years, would it not?" his aunt asked in surprise.

"She knew that." Darcy motioned to Lady Matlock's carriage. "It is time for me to go collect Richard."

She took his proffered arm. "Surely, Miss Bennet would marry, and the plan would come to naught. I cannot believe a husband would allow his wife to continue saving money for another man. No matter how noble the reason."

"She did not plan to marry if she could not marry Richard," he said as he handed his aunt into her carriage.

"But she is so young," Lady Matlock protested.

"And so very much in love," countered Darcy. "So very much in love," he repeated as he closed the door.

Chapter 13

Mrs. Gardiner placed the tray, which she held, on the table next to Kitty's bed and pulled a chair close. The room rested in shadows due to the curtains being drawn. A couple of candles added a bit of light so she could have read if she had felt like it, but honestly, she was too worried about Kitty to be able to concentrate on anything.

The surgeon had come, stitched up the wound, and left, yet Kitty had not woken. She sighed and placed a hand on her niece's cheek. "Kitty. Kitty, dear. I have some broth. You need to wake up."

She brushed her thumb gently along the bruise that was forming just below the corner of Kitty's left eye. The action elicited a soft groan from Kitty but no further response. Mrs. Gardiner removed her hand from her niece's cheek and, taking Kitty's hand, settled back in her chair to watch.

As she watched Kitty, she prayed until the door opened slowly, and Elizabeth and Mary slipped quietly into the room.

"How is she?" Elizabeth asked. "Mr. Darcy told us about her fall."

Her aunt sighed and rose. Kitty's fall was only part of the trouble. She motioned for Mary and Elizabeth to follow her to the opposite side of the room.

"Did he tell you about what happened before she fell?" She spoke in a hushed tone. She did not want to upset Kitty. Those three ladies at Mrs. Havelston's and that article in the paper had done enough of that. While it was true that Kitty was not awake, that did not mean she could not hear what was being said.

"He did."

Mrs. Gardiner glanced over her shoulder toward the bed. "She groans. Her eyes flutter open occasionally, but there is very little other response, save for some tears. I fear the injury to her heart is a far greater concern than the one to her head."

Both Elizabeth and Mary sucked in a quick breath.

"Do you fear that she will not wake?" Mary asked.

"I do." Mrs. Gardiner sighed. A broken heart was a dangerous thing. "If he were to come..."

Elizabeth placed an arm around her aunt's shoulders. "Hers is not the only heart that has been injured. My husband fears to leave his cousin alone. I will ask Fitzwilliam if he thinks Richard should visit. I am not opposed to it."

"Nor am I," Mrs. Gardiner agreed. "Although it will not solve the issue of his announced betrothal."

"It is incomprehensible to me that a father should treat his son so." Mary shook her head. Disgust was clearly etched in her features.

"Indeed, it is," Mrs. Gardiner agreed. "Now, come. I will send for some tea, and we shall have a lovely chat." She took each by the arm and led them back to Kitty's bed.

"Kitty, darling," she said as Elizabeth and Mary found seats on the bed, one on either side of Kitty's feet, "your sisters have come to call, and we are going to have tea. Would you care for some?"

Mrs. Gardiner waited a moment just in case there was a response before continuing. "Very good, I shall have four cups sent up, just in case you change your mind. We would dearly love to share some with you."

"Tell me about your day," Mrs. Gardiner said after she had rung for the tea.

In hushed tones, they began a conversation about the very mundane aspects of life, being very careful to keep the topic something that was either cheery or non-troubling. Tension that could be felt hung around them.

Just as the tea was being delivered by a maid, Kitty began to toss her head as if troubled by a dream.

"It cannot be true," she muttered in a sleepy, slurred voice.

"Katherine," Mary scooted up on the bed until she could smooth Kitty's hair back away from her face. The motion seemed to calm her sister. "Katherine," she continued, "it is true."

Both Mrs. Gardiner and Elizabeth gasped.

"She wants – nay, needs – to hear the truth even if it is unpleasant."

"I am not so certain," Mrs. Gardiner said.

"I know it in my heart." Tears clung to the rims of Mary's eyes.

Mrs. Gardiner gave her a small smile and a nod. Mary was not the sort of sister to hurt a sister unnecessarily. She could be firm and unmoving, but her heart was not hard.

"Colonel Fitzwilliam's father has done a horrible thing in printing that announcement." Mary reached down and lifted one of Kitty's hands to her lips to kiss it. "It is a wrong that must be righted, and my dear, it would help us ever so much if you would wake up so that we could worry together about how to fix this mess." She kissed her sister's hand once again and lifted it to her cheek. "Please. We need you." A tear slid down her cheek and onto her sister's hand.

Kitty's hand flinched slightly, and her eyes opened briefly.

"Are you awake?" Mary asked softly.

Kitty's mind began to lift from where it had been trapped. She nodded her head but just barely. Still, it was enough to make her gasp. Oh! It hurt so much!

"Oh, my dear girl," she heard her aunt's voice near her, stirring her senses even more.

"Kitty."

Was that Elizabeth calling her? Were they all there? She attempted to force her eyes open. Through her lashes, she could make out the forms of two of her sisters and her aunt hovering around her.

It was true. The thought penetrated her foggy thinking, causing her to want to slip away from the reality of it again, but the tears she felt on her hand as it rested against Mary's cheek would not allow her to retreat.

Slowly, she opened her eyes, blinking in the dim light of the candles. "It is true?" she whispered, hoping that it had merely been a bad dream.

"It is," Mary said, "but it is not finished. We must have hope that things will right themselves with a little help."

The door opened, admitting Jane to the room. "Is she well?" she asked.

"No," Kitty answered. "My head hurts. My eye on one side will not fully open, and I feel as if someone is crushing my chest."

"Oh, but you will be well," Mary said. "I shall see to it." She placed Kitty's hand back on the bed. "Can you sit?" she asked.

"I do not know." Kitty shifted and pushed up on her arms. The pain the motion caused was unpleasant, but the spinning in her head was nearly unbearable. "Oh, the room will not stay still." She closed her eyes as she settled back against the head of the bed. "Ah, that is better."

"You do not need to see to drink." Mary wrapped one of Kitty's hands around the cup she held. "I will not let the cup fall, but you must guide it so that I do not pour it all down the front of you."

She took a few sips. The broth was comfortingly warm, but her stomach was not overly pleased to accept it. "I cannot drink more."

"Then, you will not." Mary's words were gentle. "Perhaps you can lie down again?"

That sounded like a wonderful idea, and Elizabeth helped her to do as Mary suggested.

"Has my husband come with you?" Elizabeth asked Jane as she fiddled with Kitty's pillows, making certain that she was as comfortable as possible.

Jane shook her head, but her eyes sparkled. It was rare to see Jane looking so mischievous.

"No, he and my husband have gone to call on Hurst." She joined Mary and Elizabeth on the bed, sitting between them and directly at the end of Kitty's feet. "I dare say we will be rid of Caroline soon." She smiled widely.

"Charles may be all that is amiable and pleasant, but it seems when pushed beyond his limits, he can be quite the opposite." Jane giggled. "Caroline will be married within in a month, or she will be sent to Scarborough and expected to find a husband there."

She sighed. "I know I should not be so happy about it, but she has been terribly hateful to so many of my sisters." She rested a hand on Kitty's foot and gave it a gentle squeeze.

"Well, I, for one, am glad to hear it," Mary said.

Kitty blinked. Her head must be more injured than she thought. Mary had not just said she was happy that Miss Bingley was being sent away, had she?

"Do not look so shocked," Mary continued.

Apparently, Kitty had heard correctly.

"Miss Bingley is only reaping what she has sown, as is right and proper." Mary gave a sharp, decisive nod of her head to emphasize how greatly she believed what she had said.

The action made Kitty smile. "I think it is better than she deserves. She is hateful."

Jane winked at her and then looked at Mary and Elizabeth as if she had the best secret to share. "It is worse than it sounds," she whispered. She leaned forward toward Kitty and the others followed suit.

"I am sure I was not supposed to hear this part, but Charles intends to seek out Mr. Blackmoore." She grinned widely as her sisters gasped. "He ended his conversation about it with 'and I do not care if he has to compromise her to make her agree.'"

"Oh, my!" Mrs. Gardiner cried.

"Indeed," Jane replied happily. "Caroline will not be able to say a word about any other compromises if she falls into one herself."

"If only the same could happen for her friends," Kitty muttered.

Mary and Elizabeth nodded their agreement, and then, at Jane's look of confusion, the three of them took turns telling her all they knew about Miss Ivison and Miss Pearce.

Chapter 14

"ONE PROBLEM IS WELL-IN-HAND," Darcy said upon entering Rycroft's sitting room. He gave his aunt a kiss and nodded his acceptance of a drink from Rycroft. He shot Richard a questioning look.

Richard lifted one shoulder and let it drop in response to the unspoken question. He was not better nor was he any worse.

"Bingley and Hurst are calling on Blackmoore," Darcy continued, "to see if he is still in need of a wife – one with acceptable connections, a tidy fortune, and who will be happy to be a baroness one day, no matter the arrangements at home."

"Will Mr. Blackmoore keep his mistress?"

"Georgiana," Richard said in unison with Darcy and Rycroft.

"I know there are gentlemen who keep them."

"I wish you did not know that." Darcy took a large gulp of his drink.

Richard, on the other hand, was glad that Georgiana was not unaware of such things. But then, he was her cousin and not her doting older brother who struggled to see her as anything other than the sweet younger sister she was.

"And I wish it did not happen," Georgiana replied with a shrug. "I cannot imagine having to abide such an arrangement."

Darcy groaned.

Georgiana smiled at him reassuringly. "There is no need to worry, Fitzwilliam. I have learned many things over the past year about men, and I can promise you that any gentleman who keeps a mistress will not on my list of possible suitors, for I shall not abide such a man. A man who touches another woman shall not touch me."

Darcy squeezed his eyes shut as if in pain. "Could we please speak of something else?" he begged.

"If you wish," Georgiana replied.

Richard could not help the smile that crept onto his lips at the look of relief on Darcy's face to have the topic turn from his sister becoming a lady of marriageable age.

He leaned against the frame of the window and stared out into the darkness that was descending on the city. He peered as far up the street and then down as he could see from his vantage point. Bingley was to see the ladies home from their aunt's house, and Richard knew when they returned, they would have news about Kitty.

He glanced at Darcy, who was still watching him warily.

Once Bingley returned, Richard would convince the others – most especially Darcy – that he was capable of not doing himself harm, and he would be allowed to return to his rented room where he could wallow in his sorrow privately.

He closed his eyes and leaned his head against the frame of the window, attempting to find some peace, but it was no use. No matter how much he tried to think about something, anything, else, he saw Katherine, lips trembling, eyes filled with tears, telling him he had her heart and then, turning away.

"I would like to take a walk." Lady Sophia slipped her arm through his. "I find this room to be rather boisterous." She gave him a meaningful look and motioned toward the door with her head. "There are a great deal more rooms in this house that are far less crowded."

If his aunt wanted to offer a moment of escape from the watchful eyes of his cousins, he was not going to refuse. So, pushing off the window frame, he allowed her to lead him from the room.

"Reginald is correct," she said as they strolled down the hall. "I do have something that may help sway your father from his position. It is in my apartment if you care to see it."

Richard turned toward the grand staircase. "I will take whatever help and hope you can give."

"My brother, your father, has been a selfish creature all his life. You should have seen the airs he would put on when we were young. It is a miracle he lived to ascend to the title." She chuckled. "Reginald may have taken orders when he was first enlisted in the navy, but it was never his lot to be on the receiving end of commands. He was always destined to be the one giving them. So, you can imagine the scuffles that took place when your father had pushed his eldest son and heir role too far."

Richard smiled despite himself. He would have liked to have seen his father on the receiving end of some unpleasantness.

"Catherine was just as bad." She shook her head. "She lorded her position over Anne and me and gave us instruction on things about which she knew little more than we did." She sighed. "And her lectures about propriety were more than sufficient to bore even our tried-and-true governess to tears." She laughed. "Catherine was constantly telling Miss Blair how the lessons were being presented incorrectly. It is a wonder the lady stayed with us all those years. I dare say my mother paid her handsomely not to leave."

She drew her key from her pocket and opened the door to her sitting room. "I was glad that Catherine was married before I had my come out. Anne was not so fortunate. Oh, the trials she endured! Catherine was determined to select a husband for Anne, and, as you can imagine, she was not pleased that Anne chose to fall in love with a mere mister, a very wealthy and well-connected mister, but one who was sadly lacking a title."

She pulled out a drawer of her desk and laid it aside. Then, she bent to look into where the drawer had been and reached to the back. Two clicks and she had a small box in her hand. "One of my many secret treasures," she said with a smile as she handed Richard the box.

Richard took the box and, after examining the detail of it, removed the lid, revealing a golden necklace. He lifted it by its chain, suspending it in front of him until he had placed the box back on the desk. Then, he let the pendant, a heart made of woven and twisted gold, drop into his hand.

"It was my mother's," Lady Sophia explained.

"It is beautiful."

"I hope to one day give it to Mary."

"She would like it."

Lady Sophia nodded. "There is another necklace just like it somewhere in this world."

"Did the jeweler make many?" Richard lifted it again and studied the craftsmanship of the heart. The weaving of the metal reminded him somewhat of a bird cage, but instead of a bird, there was a pearl locked away in the center.

"He made only two, and at my mother's request, he destroyed his mold after the second was cast."

Richard watched the heart twirl at the end of the chain. "This is the necklace she wears in her portrait, is it not?"

"It is." Lady Sophia took the necklace from him. "It was a memento of a lost love. Rare as the pearl, precious as the gold that encircles it. That is what Mother would always say to me when I would play with it as a girl." She lay the necklace gently back in the box. "It is the kind of love she told me to seek and the kind you have found."

She motioned for him to have a seat and then sat beside him on the couch. "My mother was devastated when the necklace went missing from her room. She thought it had been stolen by her maid, and so the maid was dismissed without reference. However, it later appeared in Reginald's room. My brother pled his innocence, but my mother and father were furious with him and sent him away to sea." She shrugged sadly. "My brother, your father, told his father that Reginald had taken the necklace to give to a lover, a woman, he claimed, who was of inferior standing, a shop girl."

"Julie," Richard said softly.

"That is the name I heard." She gave him a quizzical look. "She exists?"

He nodded. "She is now a modiste. You know her as Mrs. Havelston."

Lady Sophia gasped, and her eyes grew wide. "The woman who made Mary's gowns?"

"She is also my mother's modiste," Richard said.

Lady Sophia chuckled wryly and shook her head. "Your father must not be aware of the connection. I cannot imagine him allowing your mother to support that fortune seeking adventurist, I believe that is what my father called her." She patted his hand. "However, that is not what makes this necklace a source of influence."

She stopped and thought for a moment. "Or perhaps it makes it an even greater one." She shook her head. "Reginald had not taken the necklace. It was your father who had taken it to pay a gaming debt. However, when the news of it having been stolen fell on the wrong ears so that the necklace could no longer be used as payment for his debt, and after a rather heated argument between my brothers, the necklace found its way into Reginald's room to be discovered by a maid who was more than a little friendly with your father." She raised an eyebrow and pursed her lips in displeasure.

"So, you know the truth, but Uncle Reginald does not."

"My eldest brother told me he was not above forcing me to marry someone of his choosing by arranging a compromise. And since I was already in love with my Lord Rycroft and hopeful of an offer, I kept his secret." She shrugged. "After I was married, his threat held little weight, but Reginald seemed happy at sea, so I never told him. Perhaps I should have." She shoved the box at Richard as if it were coal that burnt her hand. "I had hoped this would help you, but oh, my, Reginald will be so displeased."

"I think he would understand. It is not as if being cleared of the wrongdoing would have made it possible for him to marry Mrs. Havelston." He opened the box and looked inside once again at the beautiful heart. "You said there were two made. If grandmother had one, what became of the second?"

"She gave the second necklace to a particular groomsman who was not long after dismissed from the stables at Matlock House. That necklace was accompanied by a note explaining its importance to both her and two of her children to act as a protection of sorts for him should he need it. It was her way of keeping her husband from pursuing him any further than having him dismissed from his position."

"Do you mean to tell me that the rumours of an affair are true?"

Lady Sophia nodded.

"But could my grandfather not just take the necklace and note from the man?"

She smiled. "Your grandmother was clever. You see, it was when she suspected she was with child, shortly before she married your grandfather, that she gave the necklace to her lover with the instructions that he hide it and the note in a safe place known only to him and one other. She never told her husband what the memento was that she had given to the man, just that it had been given with a note that could damage the reputation of the child she carried, who was by then thought to be heir to the Earl of Matlock."

"Did no one question the timing of the birth?"

Lady Sophia shook her head. "Your grandmother carried twins, your father and Catherine. It is not uncommon for twins to arrive early. Until she told me the story when she passed the necklace on to me shortly before she died, I had no idea that I did not share a father with my two eldest siblings. I had heard rumours of infidelity and seen some amorous exchanges between her and other gentlemen, but I had thought my father would have thrown her out if it were true that she had borne him another man's child. However, I suspect it was easier to accept them as his own and save his reputation than to send them away, and she had made sure he could not send them away quietly, since she had happily proclaimed her good fortune of being with child to one and all. She was clever."

Richard heartily agreed with that assessment. His grandmother had seemingly thought of everything needed to ensure the security of herself and her children, as well as the safety of her lover. "You do not know what happened to this man?"

"I have no idea what became of him, and if she did, she never spoke a word of it."

"And this," Richard held up the box, "has the potential to cause a rift between brothers and, if the other necklace were found, to bring embarrassment to my father?"

"He could lose his title if Reginald cared to put forth a challenge, which he might."

"But only if the other necklace were ever found?"

"An unlikely event after all these years." Lady Sophia stood and smoothed her skirts. "However, the threat of my telling his brother of the truth of that necklace," she pointed to the box, "has on occasion swayed your father's position."

Richard turned the box over in his hand as he began contemplating how best to use the information he now possessed. It was a decision that would take some time and thought, and so standing, he handed the box back to her. "Tuck it away again until I need it."

She smiled and did as he suggested.

"Shall we go see if Lady Rycroft or Mrs. Darcy have returned with news about your lady?"

His aunt slipped her arm through his after locking her door.

"You shall marry her," she whispered, "even if I have to stuff you both in my carriage and whisk you off to Gretna Green by myself."

Chapter 15

RICHARD PICKED UP THE bottle of port and eyed the glass that sat on the table in his rented room. He had planned to consume much of the bottle last night when he had acquired it from Mr. Wood.

However, knowing Kitty had awakened and that he had some hope of swaying his father's position, coupled with the fact that an excess of drink would muddle his thinking for more than the night, he had refrained. One could not properly plan strategy while one's brain was muddled, after all, and he was not giving up Kitty before exhausting every option either he or his relations could contrive. Therefore, in the end, he has settled for just two smallish glasses of port before casting himself into bed.

Be that as it may...

He removed the cork and poured a measure of the sweet, red wine into the glass — a little bit for fortification for the day that lay ahead might be a good idea. He replaced the stopper and sat himself down to drink and attempt to think of nothing else save the richness of his beverage. What to do about his future could be considered later.

He had done a fair bit of thinking on the subject while he should have been sleeping in the wee hours of the morning, and he had come to the conclusion that he would only use the necklace if... or rather, when... it became necessary, for there would likely would be a point where there would be no other option but to put it forward and reveal the whole secret to the admiral.

Just as he was draining the last drops from the glass, having done a very poor job of not thinking about what lay ahead, there came a stomping on the stairs, followed by a loud knocking at his door.

"Fitzwilliam," Rycroft called. "Open the door! It is of great importance."

Richard opened the door and scowled at his cousin. "Your stomping and shouting are most unsettling for this time of day."

Rycroft pushed his way into the room and began gathering Richard's coat and hat. "To put it bluntly, I do not give a farthing about unsettling your day." He shoved the coat at Richard. "Put it on."

Richard's brows rose. It was unlike his cousin to be so demanding. "What has you in a temper?"

"I should be in bed with my wife, but instead, I have been sent to collect you."

Richard bit back a smile at the look of utter frustration on his cousin's face. "And why must I be collected?"

"I am not exactly sure. I honestly was not listening as I ought to have been." He waved a hand in the air. "It has something to do with the paper and your father. I have never been particularly good at listening to Aunt Catherine when she is in a dither."

"Aunt Catherine?" Richard took his hat from Rycroft.

"Yes." He leveled another less than pleased look at Richard. However, this one was not directed at Richard. The roll of Rycroft's eyes before he began speaking again was the telltale sign that this one was meant for their aunt. "She appeared at my home demanding to see you. Apparently, Darcy's butler is better prepared to handle her, as she did not gain admittance to Darcy House," he grumbled.

"I would not blame your staff too much. She was probably in no mood to be put off by the time she reached your home if she was unsuccessful at Darcy's." And their aunt in a mood was not the sort of woman capable of being refused by many.

"Most likely." Rycroft held the door open for Richard. "If you would be so kind as to hurry. Until I have produced you and our aunt has been satisfied..."

Richard held up a hand. "I know. You do not need to explain." He locked the door and descended the stairs as quickly as he could.

"I see you found him, and in one piece." Mr. Wood met them in the entry with his wife beside him.

"You mustn't begin your day without a bit of food." Mrs. Wood held out a small parcel to Richard. "A bit of cheese and a roll. It's not much, but it should help settle your stomach."

Rycroft stopped mid-step and spun to look at Richard. "Are you unwell?"

"Most of us men are after a few too many drinks," Mr. Wood replied.

"I did not have as many as I had planned."

"That is good to hear. I wish you well." Mr. Wood held the door open for Rycroft and Richard.

"Thank you for the port, and the breakfast," Richard said as he followed his cousin out of number eight Bartlett's Buildings.

Rycroft climbed into his carriage and shook his head. "I was not thinking," he said apologetically. "I am afraid I have forgotten rather quickly the fear of losing one's love. I am sorry."

Richard waved his cousin's words away. He did not wish to speak of his loss. "It is understandable when one has been granted the blessing of happiness."

Rycroft groaned. "That is another thing I should not have mentioned, I suppose."

"I do not wish for you all to treat me with pity," Richard growled.

Rycroft's eyes searched Richard's expression before he nodded and said, "You should eat. Our aunt is difficult enough to endure under good circumstances."

Richard untied the cloth and broke off a bit of the roll. He hoped it did help settle his stomach, for it would be nice to have at least one part of his body feeling settled.

Rycroft waited until he had put the food in his mouth before he spoke. "I was not speaking of pitying you. I was speaking of being considerate. I was not considerate, as I was, in fact, only thinking of myself." He leaned his head back. "However, if you would like to pity me, you may, for I find I am feeling quite sorry for myself and would enjoy the company."

Richard rolled his eyes. He knew that his cousin was not being as selfish as he sounded. As was often the case, Rycroft was attempting to lighten the unease of another by painting himself in an unflattering light.

"If you wish to have someone with whom to share that particular type of misery, I suggest we stop at Darcy's and drag him along. I am afraid I may never be able to join you in such misery, as there is reason to believe that I will never have a wife with whom I wish to lie in bed all day." He broke off another piece of roll. "Ouch!"

"I beg your pardon."

"It was no accident," Richard snapped as he rubbed the shin Rycroft had kicked.

Rycroft shrugged. "Perhaps it was not, but it was well-deserved. You should not speak such lies." He leveled a glare at Richard. "You will marry for love. Has my mother not already said as much?"

Richard nodded. "But it is not settled that it will be." He wanted to believe that the necklace would be enough to purchase what he longed for with all his heart, but he did not trust that his father would not find some way to make it impossible.

"You know my mother. It will be done. Very little will stand in her way... including your father." Rycroft leaned his head against the back of the carriage once again. "Finish your food. Mary will be displeased if she hears I took you away without allowing you to break your fast." His head popped off the wall of the carriage. "And when I call for tea, drink some." He leaned his head back again, a small smile creeping its way onto his lips as he closed his eyes.

Richard gave his head an amused shake. It was good to see his cousin so happy even if it made his own heart ache just a bit more.

"This is your fault!" Lady Catherine jabbed her finger in Richard's face as he entered the drawing room at Rycroft Place.

"It is lovely to see you as well, Aunt," he said wryly before greeting the rest of the occupants of the room.

Lady Catherine huffed. "If you had just agreed to marry Anne, none of this would have happened!" She snatched a newspaper off a chair and flung it at him before plopping, in a rather unladylike fashion, into that chair. "She is ruined. Utterly ruined."

Richard picked up the paper and searched for whatever it was he was supposed to see. Rycroft stood at his shoulder.

"Oh!" Rycroft's tone was one of surprised amusement as he tapped an announcement. "I see our cousin has a mind of her own after all."

Lady Catherine made a thoroughly unladylike sound of displeasure.

Richard laughed as he read what Rycroft had pointed out. "I do not see how this is my fault. I am not the one responsible for the 'grievous error in announcing the betrothal of Colonel Fitzwilliam and Miss de Bourgh,' nor am I the one who placed an advertisement for a husband."

He took a seat across from his aunt. There was a seat next to her. However, after having had his ears tugged and hands swatted many times over the years, he decided the safest option would be to sit where she could not reach him, for he was certain that her disgruntled mien mingled with his equally foul mood would result in sore ears and hands, at a minimum.

He folded the paper and read the announcement once again.

It is with a heavy heart that this paper must inform the public of a grievous error which was made in announcing the betrothal of Colonel Richard Fitzwilliam and Miss Anne de Bourgh. No such agreement exists, nor is it an agreement into which either party is willing to enter. However, Miss de Bourgh, an heiress in her own right, does wish to inform those Christian gentlemen of good reputation and having in their possession a title, as well as solvent and accurate financial reports, that she is willing to accept correspondence and calls with the intent of reaching a marriage arrangement. Please be advised that references and documentation showing an adherence to the above criteria will be required.

Richard chuckled and lay the paper aside. Perhaps his future would not be as difficult to claim as he expected it to be. He allowed a sliver of hope to tentatively take root in his heart.

"Rycroft, did you not promise me a cup of tea?" He crossed one leg over the other.

"Indeed, I did." His cousin gave him a grateful smile. "I am afraid I rushed Richard along to get him here as quickly as possible."

Mary lifted a brow at her husband and then tilted her head and narrowed her eyes slightly before asking, "Have you eaten?" Her question was directed at Richard, but her eyes remained on Rycroft, and a teasing smile graced her lips.

Richard smiled. "I have, thank you."

Chapter 16

"Tea at a time like this? Does no one care that my daughter's reputation is in tatters because of him?" Lady Catherine stabbed the air in Richard's direction.

"As our nephew has said, Sister, this is not his fault. The fault lies squarely on the shoulders of whoever made the erroneous announcement, as well as any party to the original agreement that was made, quite obviously, without the consent of either Anne or Richard." Lady Sophia sighed and shook her head. "While I imagine the larger part of the blame falls to our brother, I cannot help but think the advertisement for a husband is due in large part to the young lady's mother never giving her a proper come out."

The room collectively held its breath as they watched Lady Catherine's face turn a deep shade of red. Her eyes narrowed. Her lips became a tight line.

Lady Sophia calmly tilted her head to the side and waited expectantly for her sister to respond.

"Her health would not allow it. She is of a delicate constitution which would have found the rigours of a season far too overwhelming."

Richard nearly caught his laugh of disbelief – nearly.

"It is true." Lady Catherine turned toward him.

"I apologize, Aunt, but I cannot reconcile a lady of a delicate constitution with a lady who has the temerity to announce her refusal of one marriage offer and in the same breath ask for another."

He accepted a cup of tea from Mary and took a sip. "I find I am quite pleased by her boldness."

Lady Catherine huffed. "You needn't be so pleased. Your father was creating a list of gentlemen with unwed daughters on whom he wished to call when I left."

Richard took a few more sips of his tea and contemplated that piece of news. He had known it would be unlike his father to quit a matter so easily. He looked at Lady Sophia and smiled. "I believe, Aunt, that it is time my father and I had a *particular* discussion."

He cast a sidelong look at his uncle Reginald and waited for Lady Sophia to give him approval. He would not do this without her consent, for he knew that it held the potential to cause a good bit of family strife.

"A splendid idea, Richard," Lady Sophia said. "And I wish to come with you. Samuel, we will use your carriage. Reginald, would you ride with us?"

Richard's eyes must have shown his surprise, for she smiled and added softly when she had risen and was standing beside him, "Your father will be more compliant if we have Reginald in the sitting room."

Richard smiled and shook his head. "You are well-versed in strategy."

She leaned closer. There was a twinkle in her eye. "How do you suppose so many of my young friends have found themselves happily married?" She pulled on her gloves. "Some people play chess. I do not. I have the season."

"What about Anne?" Lady Catherine crossed the room toward them. "What am I to do about Anne?"

Lady Sophia turned toward her sister. "I would make sure tea is served at the interviews and that she is shown to best advantage."

"Interviews?" Lady Catherine said in surprise.

"There will be callers. Anne is an heiress, the daughter of a baronet, and the niece of the Earl of Matlock. One of those things would make her an attractive choice to many gentlemen, but when you combine them, she will have a surfeit of suitors." Taking in her sister's calculating gleam, she added, "I would not, however, try to make the choice for her, since she obviously has a mind of her own and is not afraid to exert her opinions."

"But..." Lady Catherine grabbed Lady Sophia's arm. "But I do not know how to show her to best advantage." Though her voice was soft, barely above a whisper, there was no missing the panic that filled her.

Lady Sophia patted the hand that lay on her arm. "Catherine, that is of your own doing; however, I am not without some compassion for my niece." Her hand stilled but remained on top of Lady Catherine's.

Richard noted the way her brow rose slightly, and her mouth curved into a small smile, and he knew she was preparing some bit of strategy as she stood quietly for a moment.

Finally, she gave her sister's hand another pat and said, "I will help Anne, if, and only if, you help Richard and Miss Bennet."

Lady Catherine's eyes grew wide. "Miss Bennet?"

"Yes, Miss Bennet, the young lady whom Richard would like to marry."

Lady Catherine darted a look at Richard before giving a small shake of her head. "I tried to warn him about Mrs. Bennet. I told him to accept Mrs. Darcy and Lady Rycroft without hesitation, but he would not listen." She tapped her hand over her heart. "Oh my, I feel quite ill."

And she did look it. The colour had drained completely from her face, and her breathing had become noticeable, as if taking in air were a challenge. Richard took her by the arm and led her to a chaise. "A bit of wine," he said to Rycroft.

"Salts," Mary ordered, "then the wine." She took the newspaper from where Richard had discarded it and began to fan Lady Catherine. "My mother suffers from fits of nerves," she explained. "A few moments of quiet, combined with a fan, some salts, and a glass of wine have always been effective."

Richard watched as Mary took charge and soon had his aunt looking decidedly less ill.

"It would be best if she were to return to Matlock House and retire for a rest." Mary directed the comment to Richard and then turned back to Lady Catherine. "However, I am curious to know something, if I may, your ladyship." She waited to receive permission before continuing. "You mentioned that you advised Lord Matlock to accept both my sister and me. Is it because of what my mother said when you visited Longbourn?"

Lady Catherine closed her eyes and began to look faint once again as she nodded.

"Then," Mary's voice was soft, "I would suggest you try again to convince Lord Matlock to accept my family, not for my sake, nor even for the sake of my sister Elizabeth, but for the sakes of Colonel Fitzwilliam and my sister Kitty." She bit her lip as if unsure if she should continue, but after a short pause, she did. "I have seen the necklace. The delicate weaving of the gold is exquisite and not easily forgotten."

Richard felt Lady Sophia's hand grasp his shoulder from where she stood behind him.

Lady Catherine drew a deep breath and moved to stand. "You are quite right, Lady Rycroft. It would be best if that necklace were not seen again."

"Do not move," Admiral Fitzwilliam commanded before she could rise. "Do you mean to tell me that the rumours of my mother having a paramour are true?"

Lady Catherine bowed her head and looked at her hands which were clasped firmly in her lap. "Yes." She peeked up at him. "I did not know of their truth until I attempted to stop Darcy's marriage."

The admiral opened his mouth to speak and then closed it again. He raised his finger as if he were going to make a point and then lowered it. Finally, he gave a curt nod of his head as if he had decided upon something and extended his hand to Lady Catherine.

"We have a meeting with Lord Matlock. One that it seems is long overdue." A smile spread across his face. "Oh, how I shall enjoy this. How often has he lorded his rank over me?" He chuckled. "And to think that all this time, it should have been I who was above him." He tucked her hand into the crook of his arm and patted it. "Do not fear, Sister, as long as he is reasonable, this matter shall stay a family affair."

Lady Catherine huffed. "When has our brother ever been reasonable, Reginald?"

He raised an eyebrow at her comment.

"Oh, he may have favoured me because we were twins, but he did not let me forget that I was not only second born but also female. No matter how loudly I object to anything, he nearly always ignores me."

"Unless," the admiral said, "it is in his best interest to agree."

"Precisely," Lady Catherine agreed with a further huff before beginning a diatribe about her brother, that announcement, and her daughter's future as she exited the sitting room.

"She is well recovered," Richard muttered to Lady Sophia as they followed Lady Catherine from the room.

Lady Sophia sighed and patted his arm. "I fear your father will take a bit more persuasion."

Rycroft accompanied them to the door of the sitting room, but being unwilling to leave Mary alone and not wishing to prolong his guest's departure, he called out his good wishes for their success and watched as his relations left from there. Then, as the door was closed behind the last person, he turned back to Mary.

"Are you well?" he asked as he knelt beside the chair where she sat, looking rather confused.

She shook her head. "I do not understand exactly what has happened. I knew that the necklace and the accompanying note cast doubt on Lady Catherine's legitimacy. That is why I referred to the necklace at all." Her eyes were wide and filled with concern. "I had hoped she would lend her support to my sister. I did not wish to create any larger scandal, I can assure you."

Chuckling, Rycroft rose and pulled her up into his embrace. "My dear Lady Rycroft, it seems you are as proficient at starting scandals as I." He stopped her protest with a kiss. Sighing contentedly as he broke the kiss, he held her for a moment.

"Lady Catherine and Lord Matlock are twins," he said at last, "so your revelation concerning the necklace that my grandmother gave to her lover casts doubt not only on the legitimacy of my aunt but also my uncle. And, if the admiral were to be of the vicious sort — and I assure you he is not — he could challenge his brother's right to inherit."

"Oh." Mary's voice was filled with remorse. "If he does challenge it, what shall become of Lady Matlock and her children?" She pursed her lips and shook her head. "I should not have said anything."

Rycroft tilted her chin so that she was looking at him. "You did nothing wrong," he said firmly. "It is a secret that has been kept too long. Strong words will be hurled, threats will be made, but Lord Matlock will capitulate to whatever demands the admiral makes. And then, all will be well, or at least, as well as can be expected in this family."

"You are certain?"

"As certain as one can be." He kissed her forehead and then the tip of her nose. A rakish smile spread across his face. "I, however, am the rightful heir to my title and as such, have a duty to it." He bent and scooped her into his arms. "It is a duty that I dare not shirk." And despite her protests that it was most improper to be carrying her through the house and up the stairs, he did just that.

Chapter 17

LORD MATLOCK LOOKED UP briefly from his desk as Richard
entered his study. He gave a slight nod and scowl as he waved to
a chair. "I had not thought I would see you for a few more days."

"Did you not?" Richard took a seat.

His uncle Reginald had wished to confront his brother imme-
diately upon entering Matlock House, but after a few words with
Lady Sophia in the carriage, he had agreed to let Richard speak to
Lord Matlock first.

"I am surprised you did not expect me yesterday what with that
announcement in the paper and all." Richard lifted his chin and
peered down his nose slightly at his father the way he might if he
were dealing with one of his recruits. He had determined before
entering the study that he would not act the part of a son, but
rather of a man of rank and position, which he was. It was high
time his father remembered that.

"Yes, well, that has come to naught now, has it not?" His father
placed his pen in its holder. "Foolish girl," he muttered before leaning back in his chair and clasping his hands in front of his stomach.
"I imagine you have come expecting to be free from your duty to
your family since my first choice has not proven to be a good one."
His lips curled in a scowl. "I have begun negotiations for another
acceptable choice." He tapped the stack of correspondence to his
left.

"So Lady Catherine said." However, there would be no others. His Katherine was his choice.

Richard commanded a nonchalant smile to curve his lips as he leaned forward and snatched the pile of letters from off his father's desk. Standing, he made a show of reading the name on the first letter. He did not actually look at the name. It did not matter who the lady fortunate enough to be considered good enough for Lord Matlock's second son was.

"Oh, she will not do at all." He tossed the first envelope into the fire that warmed the room. The page caught and glowed brightly before turning into sparks that rose towards the chimney.

"What are you doing?" his father cried, leaping out of his chair and rushing toward Richard.

"As a matter of fact, none of these will do." Richard tossed the full pile into the flames. He watched as the fire claimed the pages that he had fed it. "I have made my choice, and she is not any of these ladies."

His father's face was red with anger. His mouth hung open, but no sound came out.

Richard walked past him and took a seat once again. "That is why I have come. My decision is made. I am selecting my own bride. Your assistance is not required."

His father whirled toward him. "You will not see a farthing of your inheritance." He stomped over to the bell pull and gave it a firm tug.

His father's response was as expected. Richard calmly crossed one leg over the other and, once again, forced an unconcerned smile to his lips. It was an action which seemed to make Lord Matlock sputter even more about duty and foolish notions and failure. It was a tirade that only ended when the butler opened the door.

"My solicitor. I have need of him at once," Lord Matlock demanded of his butler as he glared at Richard. "Within the hour. I must see him within the hour."

"Yes," Richard agreed, "within the hour would be excellent." Again, he smiled at his father. "If you are through with your ranting, my lord, there is a matter we should discuss before Mr. Fletcher arrives."

Lord Matlock's eyes narrowed. "Very well. What have you to say for yourself?"

"Please have a seat, Father." Richard fidgeted indifferently with his cuff while he waited for him to be seated. "I had an enlightening discussion with Lady Sophia yesterday when I was feeling ..." he paused, "rather melancholy."

Lord Matlock's brows rose. "What did my sister have to say?"

"Do you not wish to know why I was melancholy?"

His father huffed and waved his hand, indicating that Richard should continue with his tale.

"Very well. I shall tell you. It seems that my father did not keep his word. He had promised me a fortnight to come to a decision, but he did not hold true to his part of the bargain." He held up a hand to keep his father from interrupting. "It was shocking to see one's life signed away in an announcement in the paper in such an underhanded and ignoble fashion. However, that was only a portion of my grief."

For the first time since walking into the room, Richard let his emotions rise to the surface and take up residence in his expression. As he leaned forward and rested his elbows on the arm of his chair, he knew his face must be conveying his displeasure well when he saw his father flinch.

"You see, the real trouble lies in the fact that I had already come to a decision and had only two nights prior declared myself to a young lady." He saw his father's eyes grow wide. "I did not wish for your money and property more than I wished for her love," he explained, although he did not know why he attempted to as he heard his father snort in derision.

"Though she knew my lot in life was not going to be one of wealth, she accepted me, so you can imagine how the news of my supposed betrothal to Anne took her by surprise. In fact, her surprise was so great that it caused her to swoon and receive an injury to her head." He drew a deep breath and released it slowly, attempting to contain the anger he felt for his father's role in Kitty's injury. "I understand that she did eventually wake yesterday; however, at the time when I was speaking to my aunt, she had not yet regained her senses."

Lord Matlock affected an air of indifference. "So, a young lady of low birth swooned and hit her head. What is that to me?"

Richard clenched his teeth as his anger struggled to be released with his desire to remain in control of himself. "She is a gentleman's daughter," he snarled at his father.

"Of wealth or title?"

"No," Richard growled, "but she is of good character."

Oh, how easy it would be to turn his back on his father at this moment and to leave in a fit of fury and to stomp and shout as he did so. But to what avail? It was not as if his father would take much notice of it. To his father, all that mattered was position and power, and so, Richard swallowed his fury so he could retain what little power he had.

"Character is of little importance when it comes to position in society, my boy."

Richard gave his father a sweeping look of assessment. "Yes, that is obvious." He did not veil his disgust; however, the tone seemed lost on his father, who merely shifted to a more relaxed position in his chair.

"Now that I have endured your little tale of woe, would you be inclined to tell me what my sister told you?"

Richard smiled, and this was not a forced smile but one of genuine pleasure. Now was the time to see his father begin to feel uneasy. Now was the time to shift the tide in this engagement, and for the mighty Lord Matlock to feel the loss of the precious power he craved.

"No, I would not be so inclined, for I find I would rather tell Admiral Fitzwilliam the tale I heard." He was pleased to see the puzzled and somewhat concerned expression on his father's face. "Lady Sophia showed me grandmother's necklace." His smile grew as his father's eyes widened in understanding. "I see you know the story of your perfidy at my uncle's expense. However, I am led to believe that the admiral does not know it." Though he likely did now since Lady Sophia was going to tell him about the necklace she had secreted away in her apartment. Be that as it may, his father did not need to know that bit of news. "That is a fact that could be easily remedied."

Lord Matlock sank back in his chair, looking decidedly ill-at-ease.

"Did you know that there were two such necklaces?" Richard rose, went to the door, and opened it. "Harrison, please, send my uncle to me," he called to the butler before closing the door once again.

"What are you doing?" Lord Matlock's voice was satisfyingly filled with panic.

"Did you know that there were two necklaces?" Richard repeated as he stood near the door waiting for his uncle's arrival.

"I had heard there might have been."

"There is no might have been about it," Richard replied. "In fact, I know where the second necklace can be found and of, at least, two people who have seen it."

Ah, there. There was terror in his father's eyes, and it was a delicious sight.

"Remember what I know about grandmother's copy of the necklace when you speak with my uncle," Richard cautioned. "I would hate to see our family ruined." He lowered his voice and took three steps toward his father. "I would not hesitate to speak of what I know, if the ruin would only affect you, but I must think of my mother and brother."

The door opened to let the admiral enter, and Richard turned to leave but stopped before his uncle and nodded toward his father. "I have had my say. He is all yours, Admiral. Do as you see fit. I will await you with my mother and aunt."

And with that, he quit the room and walked the length of the hall slowly. He needed a moment to collect his thoughts and calm his mind. There was no need to bring his anger and frustration with him to a room where emotions would likely be strained by the uncertainty of what would come from the meeting between brothers which was just now rumbling to life in Matlock House's study.

Upon reaching the door to the drawing room, he straightened his coat.

"Tea has just arrived, sir," Harrison said.

Richard nodded toward the room. "How are things?"

"It is not for me to notice, sir."

Richard cocked an eyebrow and his head at Harrison's answer. "I am not my father."

"No, sir, you are not."

Richard waited.

"There were raised voices for a bit, but things seemed to have been sorted."

Richard smiled. "I appreciate the information, Harrison. Do not fear; I shall not alert anyone to the fact that you have ears which are in working order."

"Thank you, sir." There was the hint of a smile on the man's face.

Richard clapped him on the shoulder. "Into the fray then," he said as Harrison opened the drawing room's door for him.

Chapter 18

As soon as she saw Richard at the door, his mother rose to pour him a cup of tea. It was as if she had been watching for him rather than paying attention to anything else in the room. "Was your father reasonable?" she asked as she handed him the cup.

He kissed her cheek before accepting the cup. "He never is, but I think he is ready to see reason." He took a sip of tea. "Did you tell the admiral what you knew about grandmother's necklace?" he asked Lady Sophia as he took a seat next to her on the settee next to his mother's favourite chair.

She nodded. "He was understandably angry." She looked at her hands which were folded in her lap. "If I had known..." Her voice trailed off.

Richard placed a hand on hers. "What you knew was not willingly concealed, and you thought him happy."

Her smile was sad. "I know, and he understands that."

"I believe his anger is more toward my husband," Lady Matlock said.

"As it should be," Richard muttered. There was little he felt in regard to his father save for anger and disappointment, but his mother was a different story. For her, he felt love and concern. For her, he had endured his father for years, attempting to please not him but her.

"Are you well, Mother?" He took another sip of his tea before placing it on the table next to him and leaning toward her. "You look a bit worn."

She placed her hand on his cheek as she often did when trying to comfort both herself and him. "It has been a trying two days."

"Indeed," he agreed. He chuckled as Anne came into the room and flopped into a chair with a huff. "I dare say it shall not be any less trying for some time," he whispered to his mother.

"Do sit up." Lady Catherine gave Anne a glare as she crossed the room. "If you insist on finding a husband, you must do it properly, and a proper lady does not fling herself about." Her hands waved wildly in the air as she said it.

Anne pulled herself up in her chair and folded her arms. "I shall have to add that to my list of questions. 'Are you capable of accepting a wife who does not always sit properly when at home?'"

"You shall not ask that."

"Oh, I think I shall."

"I do not know what has become of you. It must be the foul air of the city." Lady Catherine turned toward Lady Matlock. "She is so compliant when at home."

Richard bit his cheek to keep from laughing as Anne rolled her eyes when her mother was not looking.

"I avoid you when at home, Mother, as I had been doing whilst here. However, I will not sit by and allow you to marry me off to some second son." She waved her hand in Richard's direction. "My father was a baronet, and I am his only daughter. I would expect nothing less than..." She pursed her lips and tapped her fingers on the arm of the chair. "Oh, I suppose I could accept someone as low as a knight."

Her mother huffed. "A man with wealth and land is not to be overlooked."

"And which did my cousin here possess?" She crossed her arms and slouched further into her chair.

"He would have had both if he had but listened to his father." Lady Catherine's eyes narrowed. "Sit up."

Richard watched the exchange with interest. He had never heard so many words from his cousin at one time. At Rosings, she always appeared to be weak and in need of solitude. Now, he found himself smiling at her antics as she raised a brow at her mother's command and slowly pulled herself up to a semi-proper position. Then, she tilted her head and smiled as if daring her mother to speak.

"Headstrong, obstinate girl! You will be lucky to capture a fortune hunter with such an attitude. Gentlemen, especially those with a title, desire biddable wives."

Anne pulled herself up to her full height in her chair and turned first to her aunt and then, Richard. "Did Rycroft wish a biddable wife? Do you?" She looked at both expectantly.

Lady Sophia shook her head. "Samuel would not know what to do with an amenable wife. He needs a woman who can challenge him at times." She glanced at her sister. "However, though his wife shares her opinions with him, I have not seen her do so improperly. There is a difference between having your own mind and being a harridan. In fact, Lady Rycroft would be an excellent instructor. She has helped Georgiana greatly."

"Has she?" That was news to Richard.

"Indeed, she has. You would not think such a change could occur in such a short amount of time, but I think you will find your charge a more thoughtful girl for having spent time with Mary." She gave Richard a meaningful look. "There is even that mantle of uncertainty that she wore which has lifted."

"Splendid." Richard nodded as he contemplated the information. He had worried that it would take much longer before Georgiana found her sure footing again after her ordeal.

"She is one of those Bennet girls, is she not?" Lady Matlock asked softly.

Richard nodded. "Mrs. Bingley is the first; Mrs. Darcy is the second; and Lady Rycroft is the third."

She bit her lip in an uncharacteristic show of uncertainty. "I do not know if I should say it, but I was impressed with Miss Bennet the day she returned my parcel. She seemed a proper lady."

Richard smiled. He understood her cautiousness in voicing such an opinion. He was certain it was not one of which his father would approve, and unlike his cousin Anne, his mother was a tractable wife. It was what she had been taught to be. Her husband's opinions came first, and hers fell in line with his. It had always been thus. There had been moments of pause when she had wished to speak for her son. He could see it in her mannerisms, but she had maintained her composure and held her tongue as she thought was fitting a lady of her station.

"I think you would be pleased to meet the Bennets. They are all well versed in the social graces," Lady Sophia told her. "All, that is, save, perhaps, for the youngest." She cast a sidelong glance at Anne and smiled a Lady Matlock. "The youngest seems to be less compliant with society's rules." She turned toward her niece. "She is, however, very young. I dare say she is the same age as Georgiana."

Her comments were not lost on her niece, for Anne's posture straightened. "I would like to meet Lady Rycroft."

"Perhaps next week," Lady Sophia assured her. "She is just newly married, and my son is loath to share her with anyone."

Richard laughed. "No truer words have been spoken. He was none too happy to be fetching me this morning."

Lady Sophia's eyes twinkled with amusement. "He was a bit of a thunder cloud."

A dark, heavy, grumbling thunder cloud, and Richard was about to say as much when his father threw open the door to the drawing room.

"Ah, good. You are still here." He glanced around the room, but his eyes came back to rest on Richard as he pulled in a noticeable breath and straightened his waistcoat before continuing. "My solicitor will have instructions for you about how your inheritance will be handled and suggestions for how to draw up the necessary papers to present to the father of this lady to whom you are betrothed."

Richard blinked. Had he heard that correctly?

"Oh, do not look at me so. I am not fit for Bedlam. I have merely decided it would be best if you married this young lady since you have already proposed the idea to her. A broken betrothal is not something we wish to have in the papers, and the financial consequences are not something I wish to take on. While I am still not complacent with her rank, it shall have to be."

Richard's eyes shifted to the admiral, who wore a satisfied smile.

"It is true. My brother has finally found his sense." Uncle Reginald arched an eyebrow at his brother. "However, his manners have not improved perfectly, it seems."

"Is it not enough that I do what is right? Must I also be happy about it?" Lord Matlock grumbled.

"As long as your dissatisfaction does not cause *any* of my nieces or nephews to be unhappy, I do not care how miserable you are."

Lord Matlock huffed and turned to Anne. "That means you shall also be allowed to choose your husband." He swallowed, and his lips curled as if he had tasted something sour. "He must meet with the approval of your uncle, Admiral Fitzwilliam, and your aunt, Lady Sophia. He does not need to meet the approval of myself or your mother since we were both complicit in the arranging and announcing of your betrothal to Richard."

"And my nephew's commission?" the admiral prompted.

Richard's father closed his eyes tightly and rubbed the furrow between his brows. "If you wish and a suitable replacement can be found to fill your place, I will be willing to see to his generous compensation." He blew out a breath. "Your inheritance –"

"All of it," the admiral inserted, "is yours."

It was true? He as a free man to marry how he wished and without losing anything?

"I can... I can marry Katherine?" Richard stammered. "Without losing my inheritance?"

"Aye," said his uncle said with a smile. "And you may still sell your boxes if you wish. Your father will not stop you."

Richard rose to his feet. "I can truly marry her?"

"Yes." His uncle said with a laugh. "By special license, am I right, *Lord* Matlock?"

Richard did not notice the emphasis placed on his father's title or the small flinch of his father's face. He was far too overcome with his good fortune to be aware of much. He kissed first his mother, then his aunts and cousin before startling his father with a kiss on the cheek.

"Go," his uncle said as he embraced him. "Tell your lady the happy news. It will take days for the papers to be ready. I will make certain you are dealt with fairly."

"Harrison," Richard called, "My hat and coat. Immediately." He paused and turned to his uncle. "Thank you."

"Go," his uncle replied. "Take the carriage. My brother will see to my needs."

Richard took his hat and coat from Harrison. "I can marry her," he told the butler as he rushed out the door with his hat somewhat askew and his coat unbuttoned.

"I can marry her," he called to the coachman as he rushed toward him. "Gracechurch Street as quickly as possible, my good man." He settled into his seat, and with a smile firmly in place on his face, he leaned his head back, closed his eyes, and with a sigh repeated to himself his good fortune. "I can marry her."

Chapter 19

KITTY CLUTCHED THE PACKET of sketches, which she had collected from Mrs. Havelston, tightly to her chest as the large door opened in front of her.

"Miss Katherine Bennet to see his lordship." She tried to keep her voice from showing the fear she felt at coming to a place such as this.

The butler gave her an appraising look. "Is my lord expecting you?"

"No. However, I can assure you that I have rather urgent business that requires his attention." She squared her shoulders and lifted her chin as she had seen Lydia do when asking for things that others might find impossible to even consider receiving.

"Do you have a card?"

Kitty fought the urge to drop her gaze. "I do not. Please, just tell him who is here to call on him." She tried to smile as sweetly at the older gentleman as she could. "And if you do not mind, may I wait inside instead of on the step? The wind is biting, and I promise to move no further than just inside the door while I wait."

He motioned for her to enter, and then, after closing the door and telling her to wait right where she stood, he moved slowly down the hall, pausing once to turn and peer at her again.

It was odd how he had seemed to recognize her name. His scrutiny had been rather unsettling. She should be used to it by now. Everyone, especially her mother, was always weighing her features and accomplishments against those of her sisters, but no matter how often such evaluation happened, she always felt wanting.

That was why she had attempted to emulate her sisters by picking dresses like Jane and flirting like Lydia. She was sure she would not be accepted as plain old Kitty who liked to draw and would rather sit and watch a dance than partake. She smiled to herself. There was probably not one person in all of England who knew she did not relish dancing.

She sighed. Colonel Fitzwilliam would. But then, she had, on Mary's advice, been more herself with him than with any other person.

She fidgeted with her papers. She had spent several hours last night considering her life and her dreams, and she was determined that from this day forward, she would be Katherine Bennet — not Lydia's or Mary's or Elizabeth's or Jane's sister. No, today she would begin being herself with everyone.

She straightened her posture as she saw the butler approaching.

"My lord will see you. If you will follow me."

He turned and Kitty followed, stopping before entering the room to which she had been led to hand her coat and hat to Henriella.

"Miss Bennet." Lord Matlock stood behind his desk and motioned to a chair. "I am expecting my solicitor soon, but if your business is of a quick nature, we can discuss it. I do not, however, see how we can have any business to discuss, what with you being a woman and all."

"I thank you for your time, my lord. I will get as directly to the point as I am able." Kitty smoothed her skirt. She had taken care to wear her best dress today. "I assume that, as any good husband would, you see to the bills acquired by your wife's purchases?" She paused for a moment while he confirmed that he did.

"I will also assume since I have heard that you are often seen with her in public that her appearance as she stands beside you is of great importance. I mean, one cannot be looked upon as a great man with a wife who is wearing last season's styles, now can he?" Again, she waited for his acknowledgement of the fact. She knew from spending so much time with her youngest sister and her aunt Philips that appearance and appealing to one's sense of position and popularity could be used judiciously to achieve the desired end.

She tapped the packet of papers on her lap. "I have with me some designs for dresses that I happen to know your wife adores." She sighed as if the next thing was not something she wished to admit. "I have been considering keeping the sketches for myself instead of selling them to the modiste whose shop your wife frequents. In fact, I stopped by that very shop to collect these just this morning." She closed her eyes for a moment and rubbed near her eye to attempt to dull the throbbing in her head. "Forgive me, I have a slight headache."

Since she had entered the room, Lord Matlock's eyes had been drawn many times to the gash on her forehead, and they were there once again.

"I know it must look a fright," she explained, gingerly touching the scar, "but it is in such a place that I was unable to cover it with my hair." She chuckled softly as if the injury to her head was nothing with which to be overly concerned. "It will only look worse as it heals, I suppose. Bruises are never pretty." She smiled and opened her pack of papers. "But we are not here to discuss my beauty or lack thereof. We are here to talk about my designs."

Lord Matlock blinked and turned his attention away from the wound on her head for a moment. "Why would I be interested in designs?"

"Because, my lord, you have the power to decide if your wife will get to wear my designs or if they will be tucked away or, perhaps, provided to another lady." She flipped through her designs. "She was particularly enamoured with this one." She placed it on his desk. "She would look lovely in it; do you not agree?"

He picked up the sketch and examined it. "How is it that I have this power?"

Kitty's stomach fluttered, and she was unsure if she had the courage to continue. The old Kitty would not, but she was not that girl any longer.

Lord Matlock placed the paper back on the desk. His eyes once again found that gash as he waited for her answer.

Kitty swallowed and lifted her chin determinedly. "You, my lord, have something I want."

His brows rose high. "Do I?"

"You do."

"How did you do it?" He pointed to her forehead. "It is quite ugly," he muttered.

"Some news took me by surprise, my lord."

He tapped his fingers on the desk as his head nodded slowly. "Ah, so you are *that* Miss Bennet."

"I beg your pardon?"

He sighed as if being bothered by an annoying child. "I know who you are and what you want."

She could feel the heat creeping up her neck and onto her cheeks at his dismissive tone. The room was spinning a bit faster than it had been when she walked in.

"You will need to explain." She tried not to let her head lean on her hand, but it was becoming far too difficult to keep it upright between the spinning and the throbbing. Therefore, she allowed herself the luxury of not sitting entirely properly.

"You are to be my daughter. I must say I am impressed by my son's selection. You are lovely and daring, coming here to blackmail me with your sketches. Did you expect to win me over so that I would allow you to marry my son?"

Kitty groaned softly and rubbed her head. "I did not come to win the colonel's hand. I came to win his freedom."

"Freedom? I do not see how he has ever been anything but free."

She straightened herself and folded her hands primly in her lap, attempting to ignore the movement of the objects around her. His lordship was as ignorant as he was arrogant.

"My lord," she began in the most imposing tone she could muster, "if you will forgive me for being so direct, I must disagree. Neither man nor woman can be free when they are controlled by another. If you would but release him from his betrothal to his cousin and allow him to choose his own path..." She swallowed and allowed her gaze to drop. "I will give you my drawings and turn him away, if I must." She blinked at the tears that gathered.

"I am afraid I cannot."

Kitty sucked in a breath. She had failed.

Lord Matlock rose. "My solicitor will be here at any moment, and I am under the impression from others, who are as eager as you to see my son choose his own path, that you and he are to wed, and I am to allow it."

She would have shaken her head to clear the fuzziness that was settling in if she did not know it would hurt so very much. "Is he not to wed Miss de Bourgh?"

"She has withdrawn her consent. Have you not read the papers?" He held up a hand. "Of course, you have not. You are a lady." He scrunched his face slightly as if considering something. "Although my wife does follow the society pages. I am surprised you do not."

Kitty stood slowly. "My uncle rises first and takes the paper with him to his warehouse. I do not see it until the evening, my lord."

"Warehouse?" There was a tinge of horror to his surprised repetition of the word.

"Yes, my lord, my uncle is in trade."

"Indeed?" Lord Matlock did not look pleased to hear such a thing.

"I believe he is what you would call a *cit*, my lord."

Lord Matlock huffed as he came out from behind his desk, moved toward the door where he stood with his hand on the handle, and looked at her with some interest. "You seem well-spoken for the niece of a tradesman."

"My father is a gentleman, sir. Nothing less is acceptable." At least, it was not acceptable to him.

His brows rose and his lips puckered as if he had never considered such a thing before. "Very true," he agreed. "You are fascinating, Miss Bennet. I may find myself actually liking you in time."

She curtsied. "Thank you, my lord. You do me a great honour." Flattery was a fine tool to use when dealing with those who thought so well of themselves.

He straightened just a bit, puffing up a bit like the old rooster at Longbourn did when he was getting ready to crow. "Indeed, I do. You know, I pride myself on honouring those who are of slightly lower standing than myself. I suppose I could extend that to your class as well."

"We would be most appreciative, my lord. Again, I thank you." She clutched her packet of papers to her chest and began to exit through the door he held open.

"One moment, Miss Bennet. About the sketches."

"They shall be returned to Mrs. Havelston when your son is completely free to choose his own path. As I see it, my lord, you refused my offer and countered with one of your own. However, your counteroffer did not include mention of my drawings." She put a hand on the wall to steady herself.

"Now, wait just a moment," he sputtered.

"Do not fret, my lord. You may have overlooked the mention of my designs, but I fully intend to honour my promise to you as soon as Colonel Fitzwilliam is free. It is what anyone of good breeding would do, is it not?"

Lord Matlock looked confused for a moment but then agreed and bid her good day.

"Miss, you are unwell," Henriella said wrapping an arm around Kitty. "Please let Thomas and me take you home."

"No, I have one more stop to make, and then you may take me home and someone can explain to me about what Lord Matlock was speaking." She leaned on her maid as she walked. "Perhaps a short rest in the carriage before the next meeting would be advisable. Do you think we could take a short drive?"

"I will ask Thomas," Henriella said. "La, you are so pale, miss."

"Is there anything I could get for you?" Lord Matlock's butler stood in front of the door. "A small glass of wine perhaps?"

"I thank you, but I do not wish to impose."

"It is no imposition, miss." He snapped his fingers and a footman hurried over. "A bit of wine for the lady." He looked at Kitty. "He will bring it to your carriage. Your maid is correct; you do look pale. It would be best if you found rest soon."

"I thank you, Mr. —"

"Harrison, miss."

"Mr. Harrison, you have been very helpful."

"It has been a pleasure, Miss Bennet." He held the door as the two exited, and when Kitty looked back from the carriage, he was still standing there watching until she was safely inside the vehicle.

Chapter 20

"Miss." Henriella nudged Kitty sometime later, after the Gardiners' carriage had navigated the streets of London from Matlock House to the handsome townhouse in front of which it now stood. "Miss, we are here."

Kitty opened her eyes and stretched. She straightened her hat and smoothed her clothes. "Oh, I feel so much better." It was amazing what a few minutes of rest could do for sore and dizzy head. She rubbed her temples slightly. "It is only a dull ache now. It is not pounding as it was. And the world is standing still as it should be."

"I still think you should go home, miss," said Henriella.

Kitty patted her maid's hands. "I must do this before I lose my nerve or my head heals, and I regain my sense." She laughed lightly in an attempt to ease her nerves. This visit was not going to be any easier to make than the last one had been. Perhaps fortune would favour her and she would be as successful with Miss Bingley as she had been with Lord Matlock.

"Shall I attend you?"

"Yes, please. You may wait either in the room or just outside, but in case my head starts to swoon, I would prefer to have you near."

Henriella nodded and followed her mistress out of the carriage and up the steps to the Hursts' townhouse.

Kitty lifted the knocker and let it fall. Then, she turned slightly to see Henriella, who stood behind her. "I can do this, can I not?"

"You can, miss," Henriella assured her. "And when you have finished, you may go home to a cup of tea and a good sleep."

"Thank you." The promise of rest when this ordeal was done was as good as candy being dangled in front of hungry child. Bless Henriella for knowing the exact right thing to say!

Kitty managed to turn around just before the door opened to allow her entrance. "Miss Bennet to see Miss Bingley," she informed the butler. "A private audience, if possible."

"I shall see if she is home to you."

"Tell her," Kitty added as the butler turned to leave, "that I have something of value to give her."

"Yes, miss."

Kitty shifted from foot to foot. Facing Lord Matlock had been daunting, but seeing Miss Bingley was proving to be even more unnerving. She put it to the fact that she knew naught of Lord Matlock aside from his rigid conformity to social expectations. However, Miss Bingley and her cutting remarks were well-known, and knowing what surely would be hurled at her caused Kitty's stomach to flutter and her hands to twist as she waited.

"She will see you. If you will follow me."

Kitty stood behind the butler while he announced her and then stepped into the room. As she had requested, there was no other person in the room save for Miss Bingley. Kitty dipped a curtsey. "Miss Bingley, thank you for seeing me."

"I have no choice. Should my brother hear that you were here, and I turned you away, I shudder to think of what further strictures he would place upon me." She grimaced at the sight of the gash on Kitty's forehead. "I am sorry you were injured."

Although it sounded rather hollow, Kitty chose to take it as sincere. Today was not the day to dwell in the past. Today was her day to start a new beginning.

"Thank you. I know it looks dreadful." She took a seat and pulled a folded paper from her reticule. "I brought you something." She held the paper out to Miss Bingley. "I have spoken to Mrs. Havelston, and that is an appointment to have measurements taken and a dress made."

Caroline's hands stopped the work of unfolding the note. She looked at Kitty with wide eyes. "I do not understand. Mrs. Havelston said she refused to serve me."

"She did," Kitty agreed. "But, you are family, and I could not let you be cut off from one of the best modistes in England." She smiled.

Caroline shook her head in disbelief.

"Allow me to explain." Kitty folded her hands in her lap and drew a breath. "As you know, I have four sisters. As I am sure is true for you and your sister, I and mine have not always gotten along. There has been fighting. Hats and gloves have been taken. Hair has been pulled. Names have been called. There have been times when I have wished to be an only child because being compared to and teased by my sisters has been a torment." She smiled at Caroline. "Even Jane, as sweet as she is, can be sharp and unyielding."

Caroline's eyebrows rose. "Surely not."

"I assure you it is entirely possible." She looked down at her hands for a moment. "But no matter the grief they have caused, I love them, and every time they offend, I forgive them." She looked up. "It is not easy, but it is necessary. Do you understand?"

Caroline said that she did, and Kitty continued her explanation just to make certain the point had not been missed. "That appointment is my forgiveness. It is not easily given, but it is necessarily done."

"Thank you," murmured Caroline.

"There is one more thing I should like to give you, but for an entirely different reason." Kitty took out a small notebook and a pencil. "As your friends have guessed, I have sold some of my designs to Mrs. Havelston. Those are reserved for Lady Matlock. However, I would like to design a gown for you."

Caroline shook her head and blinked her eyes rapidly to rid them of the tears that threatened. "I do not deserve it," she whispered.

"No, you do not," agreed Kitty. "But I wish to give it you if you will answer a few questions and then listen to an explanation." Kitty opened the notebook. "Oh, and you must not divulge my name as the designer. Do we have an agreement?"

Caroline nodded.

"Very well. I have noticed that you wear dresses at soirees that have small sleeves and a very straight line. Is this the style of gown you would prefer I create?"

"I feel that they make me look taller."

Kitty nodded and wrote that down. "Do you prefer flounces or lace?"

"Lace."

"Light and flowing or more substantial fabrics."

"Light and flowing. It feels nice to have it swishing so easily while dancing."

Kitty smiled. "I agree. It is much more pleasant. Now, colour, what colour do you prefer?"

"Oh, my friends have told me that I look divine in soft orange. They say it highlights the bits of ginger in my hair."

Kitty tilted her head and bit the top of her pencil. Orange was not a dreadful colour on Miss Bingley. However, it was not the best choice. Did she dare to say so? Yes, today, she must dare to do what she believed was right. "I do not agree. The colours are too similar. They blend. I would think that a blue or green would be more flattering. Either of those colours would show the fairness of your complexion and hair to its best advantage."

"You must be mistaken," Miss Bingley said with a smug look. "Miss Ivison assures me that orange is my best colour, and since both she and I have been in society more than you, Miss Bennet, I think we know more of what is accepted than you do."

Kitty lowered her pencil and leaned forward. One did not have to have travelled in any sort of society whatsoever to know which colour flattered which complexion best, and in this, she would not allow herself to be made to feel inferior, especially since what she knew to be true was something which could help the lady in front of her.

"Miss Bingley, I apologize if you find what I am about to say is offensive, but I think it needs to be said. Miss Ivison is wrong, and I would venture to guess she is purposefully that way."

Miss Bingley gasped. "That cannot be true. Miss Ivison is my friend and would not treat me so shabbily as you suggest."

"How does Miss Ivison treat people who have connections to trade?" Kitty leaned back and folded her arms, watching Miss Bingley shift uneasily in her chair. "I believe I know." Kitty touched her forehead and, again, she let Miss Bingley fidget for a moment before continuing. "You have connections to trade, rather direct ones. Why do you suppose she does not shun you?"

"Because I am an educated and refined lady, not some backwater nobody."

Kitty shook her head as a touch of sorrow pricked her heart about the truth of Miss Bingley's reality. "While your education may give you the refinement necessary to traverse the society in which Miss Ivison circulates, that is not what makes her overcome her distaste for all things related to trade. You have both money and a wealthy brother, who until recently was a single man in possession of a fortune. Though he has married, they have not left you because that would lessen their chances of having some important connections, I would imagine."

Miss Bingley's brows knit together, and she shook her head. "No, they are not like that."

"Then, why did they tell you to wear clothes that would not highlight your beauty? I may not have spent time in town, Miss Bingley, but I assure you that there are petty women in the country. One of them is my sister Lydia. She will tell me a dress looks beautiful on me when I know full well it does not. She does it so that the gentlemen will pay her more attention than me." She laughed bitterly. "And you know, I followed her around and listened to her recommendations even though I knew better." She leaned forward once again. "And do you know why?"

Kitty waited, but Miss Bingley stubbornly refused to answer, so Kitty sighed and continued. "Because I wanted what she had. I wanted to have gentlemen flock to me, and while I followed her directives, I was allowed to stand at her side and comfort those she cast off." Kitty shrugged. "Pathetic, is it not? To follow another just to gain a place in society?"

She picked up her pencil once again. "I will not recommend any fabric that will not look lovely on you because you deserve to find your own place in society. It was Mary who told me to be myself if I wished to capture the colonel's heart, and she was right. You will find that Jane, Mary, and Elizabeth put on no airs when capturing their gentlemen, either."

Miss Bingley's eyes narrowed, and she huffed lightly. "Indeed?"

"Most certainly." Kitty closed her eyes and rubbed her head. Why was sitting and talking such a painful task?

"My place in society has already been chosen." Miss Bingley's voice was as pleasant as Lydia's would be when she wished everyone to think whatever she had to say was pleasing instead of disappointing. "I am to wed Mr. Blackmoore. He will have a baronetcy, you know. One day, I shall be Lady Blackmoore."

Kitty continued to rub her temples but opened her eyes. "He also has a mistress, who will spend all your money and leave the estate in ruin."

Miss Bingley gasped.

"Forgive me, but I think you should know. He has taken up with an actress. He needs a proper wife to secure his inheritance." She shrugged. "Mary told me. Lord Rycroft and Mr. Blackmoore are good friends. You should also know that this actress apparently has an appetite for gaming and a pronounced ability to lose. Hence, my concern for your financial future."

Miss Bingley shoved the paper she still held back at Kitty. "First, you tell me my clothes are not right for my colouring, then you insult my friends, and now, you would speak ill of the man I am to marry. I do not need your appointment. I am certain Lady Blackmoore has connections I can use should I wish to switch modistes."

Kitty tucked her hands under her legs. "I will not take it back. You will go to that appointment. I will design you a dress. And if you should wish it, I will do my best to help you get rid of that actress. No lady, no matter the sins they have committed — and you have committed several — deserves such treatment."

Miss Bingley shrugged. "It is the way of society."

"Not all society." Kitty gave an exasperated sigh. Speaking to Miss Bingley was nearly more taxing than talking to Lydia, and since she knew that speaking to Lydia did little good, she rose. "I fear I have overstayed my time."

She held the back of the chair to steady herself just a bit as the room was once again beginning to spin as it had at Matlock House. "My design will be at Mrs. Havelston's by the day on that card. You have only to ask for it. Good day, Miss Bingley." And with a curtsey, Kitty left Miss Bingley standing there still holding the slip of paper.

Chapter 21

KITTY STOOD FOR A moment outside the door to the room she had just been in. Her head hurt, and so did her heart. Every part of her wanted to dissolve into tears out of utter frustration. But she would not.

"I do not know why I tried to be civil. No, not civil, beyond civil — nice, friendly, generous, forgiving even." Kitty grumbled to Henriella as she walked the length of the hall towards the front door of the Hursts' townhouse.

"Miss Bennet," a surprised Mr. Hurst said as he entered his home. "What brings you calling?"

"A fool's mission, apparently." Kitty covered her mouth with her hand. "Forgive me, I spoke without thought."

What she had said was true, but it was not something that needed to be said. She blamed the spinning of her head for her lack of restraint in allowing her disappointment with both Miss Bingley and herself to be put into words. This was why one should not attempt to do business when one was not feeling well. She should have stayed in bed instead of venturing out. However, the things that needed to be done had been rather urgent. Time, she had thought, was of the essence, and therefore, lying abed had not truly been an option.

Mr. Hurst chuckled. "There is nothing to forgive, Miss Bennet. Caroline is rarely sensible, so you must have been here to call on her."

"I was." Kitty swayed just a bit, and Henriella grabbed her elbow. She would not have fallen over – or at least, she did not think she would have – but the assistance was not unwelcome.

"Perhaps you should sit down and rest for a while until you are feeling more steady," Mr. Hurst said. "You will not have to see Caroline. We will make sure it is a nice quiet room. We can even draw the curtains if you would like the room dark. You really should not be out when you are not well."

Kitty held up her hand to silence his litany of recommendations. "I assure you that I will be well just as soon as I return to my aunt's home and have a rest. Truly, as soon as I am in the carriage and able to close my eyes, the world will stop spinning."

"Are you certain?" He did not look convinced, but truly, she could rest in the carriage as easily, if not more so, than she could in one of the rooms here.

"I will be well. Henriella will see to it that I am." It was far better to feel ill in the comfort of familiar surroundings than to be encouraged to be well in strange rooms, even if the person whose rooms one was in was known to a lady. Kitty rubbed her head. Even her own thoughts were presently causing her pain and making her feel somewhat nauseous.

Mr. Hurst gave her one more questioning look and then extended his arm. "In that case, will you, at least, allow me to help you to your carriage and see you safely seated? It really would do my mind a great service and put it somewhat at ease on your behalf."

She could allow him that act of service, especially if it put his mind at ease, so she placed her hand lightly on the sleeve of his impeccably styled jacket and allowed him to guide her out the door, down the steps, and into her uncle's carriage. She did not know him well, but he seemed rather kind for being married to Miss Bingley's sister. She would wonder if it was just Miss Bingley who was unkind, but she knew Mrs. Hurst's tongue was also sharp. Therefore, she almost felt as if she should feel sorry for Mr. Hurst. A kind person would have a dreadfully difficult time living happily with an unkind person, would they not? Maybe that was why Mr. Hurst seemed to often distance himself from his wife and sister-in-law.

All these thoughts tumbled around each other in a clumsy array as Kitty made her way to her seat in the carriage.

"Miss Bennet," Mr. Hurst said as she settled onto the bench. "Why did you call on my sister?"

That was an excellent question, and one that she was feeling quite keenly. Kitty shrugged. It had seemed like such a good idea when she had come up with it, and if she were to think on it more, she would likely discover that, regardless of the outcome, it had been the right thing to do. She was certain Mary would say so.

"I wished to forgive her for all she has done to me and my sisters," Kitty answered, "and I wanted her to have a tangible representation of that forgiveness." She sighed and, beyond logical reason, hoped that Miss Bingley would still accept the dress.

"You did? May I inquire as to what the gift you offered was?"

"I arranged an appointment with the modiste whose shop she was at when the incident," she touched her forehead, "occurred. I have also promised her a dress of my own design, which is something that no one else is to have, save for Lady Matlock."

"And she refused?" Mr. Hurst could not contain his surprise. "She deserves no such treatment I assure you." His tone was censorious. "You are far too generous."

Kitty did not feel like she deserved such praise. "She did not refuse until I overstepped my bounds. I was perhaps a bit too open with her regarding what I know about Mr. Blackmoore and my opinion of her friends."

"Ah." The word was drawn out as if everything was now perfectly clear to Mr. Hurst. "That does sound like Caroline," he said with a nod. "She does value her connections quite highly – too highly in this case. I am sorry for the injury she has caused you and for her apparent ingratitude for your forgiveness. I trust you will be well soon."

"Thank you, Mr. Hurst."

He paused in closing the door. "You will be well?"

"Henriella will see to it that I am, will you not?"

"Of course, miss."

Mr. Hurst drew a noticeable breath and then, with a nod, closed the door and tapped on the side of the vehicle.

Kitty waved to him through the window as the carriage lurched forward. He stood there, watching, until she could not seem him any longer. She had never thought that someone who dressed so fashionably and carried himself with an air of not wishing to be anywhere he was, could be anxious and attentive. Silently, as she rested her head against the back of the carriage, she wondered if it was that attentiveness or just his fortune and fashion sense that had drawn Mrs. Hurst to him.

She closed her eyes. She had done what she had determined she would do upon waking this morning. Unfortunately, not all her plans had ended successfully. At least, the meeting with Lord Matlock had gone better than the one with Miss Bingley.

She popped her head up as something Lord Matlock had said came to mind. "Henriella, do you suppose Thomas would buy a paper for me?" She searched inside her reticule for the amount she would need for the purchase.

Henriella knocked on the roof of the carriage, and soon, they had stopped, and the door opened. "A paper for Miss Bennet," she instructed as she handed the coins Kitty had found to Thomas.

Thomas stared at the money. "But there is not a paper to be purchased here, and it is rather late to be procuring one."

"There must be one boy or another who is desperate to sell what remains of his copies," Henriella returned. "Climb back up on the box and keep a close eye, so that we can stop and purchase the first one you see." Though she was giving commands, there was a pleasantness to her tone, for she was never truly harsh with her brother.

"As you wish," Thomas said. "Miss Bennet, I am sure it will not be too long until I find a paper for you. Or I should say, I hope it is not."

"Thank you, Thomas. All I ask is that you do your best, for I wish to know why Lord Matlock asked if I had read the paper. I really must start reading it in the mornings. If I had, this gash might not be on my head and the world would stand still instead of wobbling about like the colourful jelly at the end of a fine meal."

"I will do my best, miss."

Thomas closed the door, and they continued on their way for some distance before stopping once again.

"Did you find a paper?" Kitty asked when the door opened. "That was very fast – Oh!" she said when she realized that the person at the door was not her uncle's footman but Richard. "I had need of a paper," she explained. "Your father seemed to think it is important that I read it."

"Pardon me, Colonel. I would like to stretch my legs," Henriella said as she moved to exit the carriage. "I will take Thomas with me, miss," she added as Richard helped her from the carriage.

"You might want to look in that direction," Richard said as he pointed to his left.

Once Henriella had scurried off with a call to Thomas to attend her, Richard climbed into the vehicle, took a seat across from Kitty, and closed the door. Then, with a tap on the roof, the carriage began moving.

"Wait! What about Henriella?" Kitty looked out the window in desperation.

"Darcy will see that she and Thomas are returned to the Gardiners'." He moved across to sit next to her.

"Mr. Darcy?" Kitty glanced out the window. "I do not see him."

"I pointed your maid in the direction of his carriage. She will be fine."

"Are you certain? She has taken such good care of me that I would hate for her to be left behind."

"Shhh, my love." He took her hand. "Your maid will be well. I would like to hear about your day. I know that you have been to see my father, and I assume that you are in Mayfair to see Mr. Hurst?"

She shook her head slightly and grimaced. "I came to see Miss Bingley." She closed her eyes and found herself gathered to him with her head pressed against his shoulder.

"I would dearly like to know why, but I do not wish to tax you further. You must be exhausted."

"I am, but if you allow me to rest my head here and speak with my eyes closed, I shall attempt an explanation." And she did. She told him everything from the visit to Mrs. Havelston to the conference with his father and finally, to her call on Miss Bingley.

He stroked her hair as she spoke. The soothing action caused her words to begin to slur as she ended her tale.

"But I do not know why your father wished for me to read the paper or why he insisted that you are to marry me and not Miss de Bourgh."

"Shh," he said as he continued to run his hand along her hair. "There is an explanation, but it would be best if you were rested before I give it. I promise you will know everything as soon as you are rested."

She opened her eyes halfway and smiled at him. She was very fortunate to be loved by such a compassionate man.

He kissed the top of her head. "Just know for now that I will indeed be marrying you and not my cousin Anne."

"You will?" It was not as if she expected him to lie to her, but it was so wonderful a thing that she needed to hear again that it was true.

"I will."

The news made her heart and her lips sigh with delight. He was hers, and she was his.

He kissed her head again. "Rest, my love. All is well," he whispered. "All is well."

Chapter 22

JANUARY 21, 1812

THE SUN PUSHED ITS way over the horizon, etching fingers of colour across the frosted glass of the window and, at long last, giving Kitty permission to rise and stretch. She had lain, snuggled under the warmth of her blankets, for an hour, just waiting for this moment. She knew that now, though her room was chilly, there would be a fire burning in the dining room and her uncle would be there, reading his paper, sipping his tea, and finishing his toast before he left for his warehouse. Now was the perfect time to venture forth from her room. Earlier would not have been.

The anxious fluttering in her stomach, which had greeted her before the sun had, increased as she sat on the side of her bed and looked at the ball gown that hung on her wardrobe door. Tonight, she would be presented to London society as the future Mrs. Richard Fitzwilliam.

She giggled as she rubbed her arms to warm them. It still sounded strange to her to call him Mr. Fitzwilliam instead of Colonel, but at Admiral Fitzwilliam's insistence, a substitute had quickly been found to complete Richard's term in the militia, a situation that pleased Richard but left his father less than happy. Seeing that Lord Matlock was often disgruntled seemed to be the new purpose of Admiral Fitzwilliam's life. As far as Kitty was concerned, her future father-in-law deserved the discomfort. He was, as Mary liked to say, only reaping what he had sown. Truly, Kitty was just glad that her colonel would be able to chart his own future and that she would be able to be at his side whether Lord Matlock found that to his liking or not.

Having done the few things necessary to make herself comfortable and presentable – the rest could be done once the room was warmed and water was not so frigid, Kitty stuffed her feet into her slippers and tied her robe tightly around herself before scooting out the door and down the stairs.

"Your paper." Uncle Gardiner handed her the paper as she entered the room. He had already opened it and folded it to the page that showed the important society happenings, such as engagements. "I see no notice declaring you have broken your agreement with Fitzwilliam. I believe you may rest easy."

She smiled at his tease. But it had been those announcements – the ones about which she did not know until they were sprung upon her – which had started her reading the paper first thing in the morning. Now, however, she did it to be well-versed in all the happenings of town. She was determined that in that area, at least, Miss Bingley and her friends would never again find her wanting.

She scanned the announcements and stopped to read a few of the *on dits* so that she was aware of what was what and who was tied to whom in society. This was important information for venturing forth and not looking like a simpleton from the country. It would also help her know about what Lady Matlock was talking, for Richard's mother did enjoy a tantalizing story.

Then, she flipped the paper around to read the news. This part she read to be well-versed on topics of conversation she might hear between the men of her new family.

"Ladies do not read the news," her uncle said with a chuckle.

"Ladies do read the news," she retorted. She knew Lady Sophia did. "They just refuse to speak about it when gentlemen are around for fear the gentlemen might feel threatened."

Her uncle laughed aloud at that and said, "Well, now, I dare say most of us would not be threatened by an intelligent woman."

"That is not what Mama says," Kitty replied with a smile.

"Ah, it is good to hear arguing and merriment in the room," her aunt said as she entered. "You were so sullen and quiet when you came home with us from Longbourn after Jane's and Mary's weddings. You were certainly not the Kitty I knew." As she took her seat, she held up a hand to stop the protest that Kitty was prepared to make.

"I know, you feel as though you have never really been yourself, and that you were rather an actress trying to find her role; however, you know I disagree."

And strongly! Aunt Gardiner had been very vocal about her opinion on that matter.

"You may have been led to do things or behave certain ways by your sister," her aunt continued, "but I remember you as a young child, and sullen is not a word I would ever use to describe the child you were. You were happy, stubborn, and sweet."

She poured a cup of tea and chuckled as she reached for a roll and added, "There is not a one of you girls who is not stubborn to some degree, but then, most of the women in this family have an obstinate bent, whether they are related through blood or just marriage." She winked at her husband, who grinned.

"I will not argue against that, but I will add that they all have their own wonderful sweetness."

"Well said, my dear," Aunt Gardiner said with a laugh before turning back to Kitty.

"You know," she began as she broke the roll apart and prepared to eat it, "I remember on one of my visits to Longbourn, when you were no more than five, you had found a bird hopping around the yard and were determined to catch it. You giggled and giggled and giggled as you chased it until the whole of the garden was filled with your mirth. But then, you caught it."

She shook her head. "And discovered that the poor creature was hopping because it could not fly. Of course, because you could not bear to see another in pain, even if it was a bird, you insisted that it be cared for. Your father was not so certain that it was necessary to tend to an injured bird." Aunt Gardiner tsked. "Oh my, the tears that fell until your father relented!"

She chuckled softly as she lifted her roll, but before she took a bite, she added, "That is who you are – Katherine Bennet, a pleasant young woman who has great determination and a heart that is as soft and sweet as the fresh cream on this bun."

Mr. Gardiner rose and took the paper back from Kitty. "And I have found it wisest to always agree with everything your aunt says." He winked at her and then kissed his wife's cheek before heading to his warehouse.

It was lovely to hear herself spoken of in such a way. She hoped that she could always be the person her aunt described.

Mrs. Gardiner moved from roll to teacup. "How is your head this morning?"

"I have not had a dizzy spell since," she bit her lip and contemplated how long it had been, "since the day before yesterday." There had not even been more than a small headache yesterday.

"Good. Be sure that you are not too active today if you wish to survive the evening. In fact, a rest this afternoon before you dress would be beneficial. I am sure Mary would be willing to allow for that." She clucked her tongue. "I am still unwilling to forgive your little adventure around town so shortly after your injury." Her brows rose, and she looked over her cup at her niece. "But I think you have learned from the experience, have you not?"

Kitty smiled sheepishly. She remembered well the scolding she had received, first from her aunt and then, from the surgeon, after she had returned from her visit to Miss Bingley's house. "I have been good for more than two weeks, Aunt."

And it was true. She had kept mostly to the house. She had only left the house on short excursions with her aunt to a shop or with Richard for a walk. Even at home her activities had been few. Stitching and drawing had proven to be ones that would make her head throb more quickly than simply sitting and listening, sometimes with eyes closed, to the conversation in the room or to a passage being read.

Thankfully, Richard had been obliging and had called often to keep her company. He was a wonderful conversationalist, and Kitty was never so content as she was when he sat beside her reading to her and holding her hand.

Her aunt's teacup clattered just a bit as it was returned to its saucer, interrupting Kitty's reverie. "Well, see that you continue to be so." It might have been a harsh comment had it not been accompanied by a pat of the hand and a smile.

Kitty and her aunt lapsed into a comfortable silence that was broken only by the occasional comment from her aunt regarding some item that needed attention. There were menus to finalize, an order for the larder that needed review before it was sent, and one of Uncle's shirts that needed a quick mend, amongst other tasks.

When her tea was finished, Kitty rose to go back to her room.

"Will you be ready to go in an hour?" her aunt asked.

They were to spend the day with Mary and her sisters at Rycroft Place before the ball that was planned for that evening.

"I can be," Kitty answered, but then, remembering the comments her aunt had made as they ate, added, "But will that give you time to do what is needed? We can leave later if necessary."

"Oh, my dear, yes. I will have plenty of time, and I have no desire to postpone one bit of this day. I think I am more excited about this ball than you." A smile of pure delight lit her aunt's face. "It is not every tradesman's wife who is invited to Rycroft Place to attend a soiree with people the likes of Lord and Lady Matlock."

Kitty's shoulders drooped just a bit. Lord Matlock was still just as arrogant and rude as she had ever known him to be. The admiral or a mention of the admiral kept him from truly puffing himself up, but he was still excessively pompous. There was little hope that he would not say something about her aunt and uncle's social standing tonight. The thought hurt her heart.

As if reading her mind, Aunt Gardiner waved Kitty away. "I know what people of their station think of me, my dear. It will come as no shock if I am shunned. But to see the splendor of it all…" she sighed. "It will be quite the treat."

She rose and wiped her hands on her apron. "Now, for my first task – to see to the children before I leave them with their nurse for the day." She hurried out of the room. "And then, I shall see to the needs in the kitchen before mending that shirt." This was all tossed over her shoulder as she climbed the stairs.

Kitty laughed at her aunt's exuberance as she followed behind her at a more sedate pace. Although Kitty wished to rush up the stairs to prepare for the day, just as her aunt was doing, there was the hint of a small pain above her eye that lingered and made her refrain. She had no time to nurse her head today because she had been foolish.

Tonight, she would be expected to smile, converse, and dance, at least once, which were all things she could do more easily if her head did not hurt, and she did not want to miss out on any of them. However, more than the pain and fatigue that she knew would accompany any overexertion which would make being charming an excruciating challenge, the thought of missing her chance to dance with Richard made her willing to move slowly and to rest when she would rather not, for the dearness of the reward was well-worth the price.

Chapter 23

"Miss Bennet."

Kitty turned toward the sound of the voice but saw no one. The dancing had begun, and having had her first dance with her betrothed, she was now sitting in a quiet corner, waiting for a cup of lemonade to be brought to her.

"Miss Bennet."

Again, Kitty turned toward the voice. "Miss de Bourgh, I can hear you, but I am afraid I cannot see you."

"Behind the plant."

"Oh." Kitty turned, and there, behind a couple of tall potted plants, was Anne.

"Please, do not look at me."

Kitty turned back around. "Very well, but I shall look foolish speaking to myself, and someone might come to investigate." Anne reminded Kitty a bit of Lydia – she was stubborn as a grumpy old donkey, and rather nonsensical at times – such as now.

"I only wish to know if a certain gentleman is occupied." There was a bit of a rustling from behind Kitty. "You would not believe the number of gentlemen who have come to call, and I have had at least ten requests for a dance this evening."

"That is to be expected when one places an advertisement for a husband and declares herself an heiress." Richard took the seat next to Kitty while looking toward his cousin, who was now only partially concealed by the plants. "You look lovely this evening, Anne. No need to hide."

Kitty laughed at the small growling sound that came from behind her.

"Mr. Blackmoore. Is he occupied?"

"Yes, he has engaged Miss Bingley for a dance."

Anne slipped out from behind the plant. "He has called four times this week, wishing to meet with me. I saw him once and told him he had no hope of gaining my approval."

She flipped open her fan and whispered behind it. "He has taken up with an actress, I hear." She tsked. "And I told him, he would not succeed because of it; however, he seems most determined tonight to lead me off into a dark corner."

She scanned the room. "He would be better off with that Bingley woman. Horrible thing she is. Such a ghastly colour she wears, and her airs... as if she were of a standing to be making any."

"I did not know you knew Miss Bingley," Kitty said in surprise.

Anne shrugged. "I do not know her beyond what I have seen this evening and what my uncle has shared of her family, but that is enough." She turned toward Kitty. "Now, if she were a gentleman's daughter as you are, even if she, like you, were of little standing, her airs could be borne. But as it is..." She shook her head. "She makes a fool of herself."

Richard cleared his throat and gave his cousin a pointed glare.

Anne looked at him in confusion. "Have I said something amiss again?"

He nodded, and Anne sighed loudly.

"My mother really did do me a disservice by not allowing me to venture into society beyond what can be found in Kent. Do tell me what I have said."

Kitty placed a hand on Anne's arm. "A lady, unless she is Miss Bingley or one of her friends, does not point out another lady's lower circumstances. However, I know you were not doing so to be injurious to me, but rather simply stating facts. The same will not be true when speaking to other ladies."

Anne closed her fan and took Kitty's hand. "Oh! I am so very sorry, my dear. I like you, you know. Very much." She giggled. "And not just because doing so holds the potential to irk my mother and uncle, but because I like you."

She scanned the room once more. "My mother appears to be engaged. I think I shall find Lord Rycroft and seek an introduction to the gentleman to whom he is speaking."

"Lord Brownlow is a fine choice," Kitty said with a smile as she saw Anne making her way toward the gentleman.

"Much better than Blackmoore," muttered Richard. "I do hope she stays out of dark corners. I would not think Blackmoore above causing a compromise to attain her money and connections." He chuckled. "It would be entertaining, however, to see him matching wills with my cousin."

Kitty gave his arm a light swat and shook her head in amusement.

"Come." Richard captured the hand that hit him and drew her to her feet. "Let's take a turn of the room." He tucked her hand in the crook of his arm but then, paused to give her a searching look.

"I am well," she assured him. "And I have promised my sisters and aunt, as well as Lord Rycroft and Mr. Darcy, that I will steal away for a rest if I should need it."

Noting how his attention seemed to be captured by her wound, she rubbed his arm under her hand reassuringly. "It hurts a little, but as long as I am not turning circles in a dance, the room stands still." She squeezed one eye closed as it seemed to help lessen the small stabbing pains that affected her less frequently than they had at first. "Perhaps we should just walk the edges of the room that are furthest from the musicians?"

He covered her hand with his. "We could steal away together. Rycroft would not mind lending us the use of his study."

She smiled up at him. "As lovely as that sounds, we cannot. I will not have your father thinking of me as a hoyden. It is enough that my uncle is in trade. I do not wish to give him any more reasons to dislike me."

Richard chuckled. "I think, my dear, that he was quite impressed by your visit. He may even like you already."

Kitty shook her head. "That is doubtful. I attempted to blackmail him into giving you your freedom."

"That would be one way to impress a man like my father. He is not above coercion to attain what he desires." He led her down the edge of the ballroom. "He has mentioned you several times since your visit, and always with a *surprising woman* somewhere in the conversation."

"I do not know if that pleases me or not."

They had reached the end of the room and stood next to the very person about whom they had been speaking.

"Ah, Miss Bennet." Lord Matlock gave her a small bow and what she assumed was a pleased smile, although it was hard to say for sure as it was such a fleeting expression. "I trust you are well this evening."

"I am, thank you, my lord." She curtsied. "You appear to also be well."

He preened just a bit at her comment and smoothed the front of his waistcoat before tugging at it to make the buttons form a straight line. "My wife has insisted that some part of my attire match her dress. It is silly, but I did not wish to displease her." He nodded toward where his wife was talking to a group of ladies that included Lady Catherine. "Is that one of the sketches you showed me?"

Kitty nodded. "It is, my lord. It looks quite lovely on Lady Matlock, and that colour is rather heavenly, do you not think?"

"Oh, indeed. My lady does have an eye for colour. Always has." He looked around the room as if searching for someone. "Your aunt is here?"

Kitty did not miss the slight twitch of his lips as if he had not wished to speak of the subject.

"She is, but you do not have to meet her. She is aware of her low standing and will not be offended." She gave the arm that had tightened under her hand a calming squeeze. "It is enough for her to just be here and to take in the spectacle. In fact, meeting someone of such an elevated position as yourself may prove to be too much for her. I would fear she would never recover from such an honour."

Lord Matlock puffed out his chest just a bit more and smoothed his waistcoat once again, and Richard coughed, likely to cover a laugh from the amusement in his eyes.

"Your uncle is in which livery?"

"He is a Mercer, my lord."

"Ah, a high precedence." Lord Matlock's brows rose, and his lower lip stuck out just a bit as he bobbed his head as if this information pleased him. "If it would not tax your aunt too greatly, I would not be opposed to an introduction."

"You do my family a great honour, my lord." She gave a small curtsey. "However, I must first speak with my sister, Mrs. Darcy." Who was approaching them.

Lord Matlock nodded. "Perhaps after supper?"

"If you wish, my lord." She gave one more small curtsey, which caused him to fleetingly smile that smile of approval, and breathed a sigh of relief as they moved away.

"How do you know how to speak to him in such a fashion?" Richard asked softly when they were well away from his father.

Kitty shrugged. "It is no different than speaking to Aunt Philips and Mrs. Long. They like to feel their importance whether it is real or imagined."

"Why are you speaking about our aunt?" Elizabeth queried as she slid her arm through Kitty's free one.

"Katherine seems to be an expert at dealing with my father," Richard explained, "and I wished to know how she learned such a skill. She said she acquired it from dealing with your aunt." He looked over his shoulder toward where Lord Matlock stood. "My father is still looking well-satisfied with himself."

"So, he is," Elizabeth said with a laugh. "You will have to tell me how you do it. I am certain he will never look so pleased after speaking to me."

"It is not so very hard," Kitty said, "but I will show you if you wish." It was pleasant to think that she had something she could teach Elizabeth. "Do you think it would be possible for us to find a place to rest?" Kitty asked her sister.

"Are you unwell?" Concern etched Richard's face.

"I am a bit tired is all."

"Good," said Elizabeth. "Oh, not that you are tired, but that you wish to rest, for I also would like to find some solitude. However, if I sneak off to the library with my husband alone, tongues will wag more than they already do."

Kitty removed her arm from Richard's and moved toward the library with her sister.

"You gentlemen may join us, of course," Elizabeth said to Darcy with a nod toward Richard. Then she leaned toward her sister and whispered. "I am not well, but no one must know, at least not yet."

"What do you mean?"

"I may be with child."

Kitty's eyes grew large. "Are you certain?"

Elizabeth shook her head. "Not completely, but it appears to be true. You mustn't tell anyone, but I could not keep it to myself any longer, and with your injury requiring that you rest, I had hoped you might aid me by providing me with a reason to rest more frequently."

"Of course, I would be happy to oblige if that is what you wish."

"Are you surprised by my request?"

"Not the request, but by the fact that you told me. You never tell me secrets."

Elizabeth pulled Kitty closer. "I am sorry. I plan to change that."

"You need not apologize. Being surprised does not mean I am not pleased. I am. Very, very pleased." She glanced over her shoulder to make certain the gentlemen were not too close to hear. "When will you tell Mr. Darcy?"

"I have not decided. I would like to share it with him, but if I am wrong..." She bit her lip and did not continue. "I would rather be certain."

Kitty squeezed her arm. "I will not say a word, and I will offer chances to rest whenever you may need them."

"Thank you," Elizabeth said as a footman opened the library door for them. "Now, I do not wish to desert you, but Darcy has insisted that we find a place to read." Her eyebrows waggled just a bit and her cheeks coloured.

Kitty smiled. "I hear poetry is the food of a fine, stout love."

Elizabeth laughed. "I have heard that as well," she said as the two sisters parted.

Kitty took a slow turn around the room admiring the tables and chairs and stopping to feel the fabric of the drapery. "It is all so lovely," she muttered. "The colours and the design complement each other perfectly."

"Lady Sophia has an excellent eye. This was her doing." Richard took her by the arm and led her to an alcove with a comfortable seat. "You said you were in need of a rest, and this looks like just the spot for it," he explained, taking a seat next to her. "We will not have anything this fine. BayLeafe is only a small estate."

"I am quite happy with a modest estate, my love. It is what I have always known." She peeked up at him. "Will you be happy? You could have married for convenience and had something far grander."

He pulled her close. "I am quite happy with my inconvenient choice," he teased as he ran a finger across the scar on her forehead and then cupped her cheek in his hand. "I am not romantic, so I fear my terms of endearment might not always be what one might expect."

She smiled up at him. Although he kept saying that he was not romantic, she knew differently. He may not be given to romantic, flowery, loving words, but when he pulled her slightly closer as they walked the streets of London, when he brought her a box engraved with forget-me-knots for her pencils, and when he rubbed her cheek with his thumb as he did now, his actions spoke in thunderous tones of his love.

"I do not require a romantic," she said, pressing her cheek more firmly into his hand. "I require only you."

"And I, you." He kissed the scar on her forehead. "I love you, Katherine Bennet." He kissed the scar once again. "Two days," he whispered. "Two days and you shall be mine."

"I already am," she replied.

"From the moment we met," he agreed.

His thumb continued to caress her cheek as he tilted his head to study her face. She kissed his thumb as it brushed over her lips, causing him to inhale sharply. Sliding his hand around to the back of her head, he drew her to him for a kiss that was, at first, soft and sweet, speaking of the treasure she was to him. But then, as he drew her even closer, the kiss deepened, showing her his need to have her by his side.

When finally, he broke the kiss and leaned his forehead against hers, he whispered, "You will always be my choice. Before money, before connections, before anyone or anything, it will be you. I will always choose you."

"And I, you," she said as she rested her head on his shoulder and her hand on his heart, a heart that would always be hers. Through happy times and times of sorrow, from meager beginnings to days of plenty, it would beat for her just as hers beat for him.

Theirs was a love that would be spoken of in corners of drawing rooms and behind fans at balls, not for its passion, though there was plenty, nor for its demonstrative nature, though their hands were often joined in public, but for its quiet assurance and its unbreakable bonds. It was a love that would eventually win over even their harshest critic, making Lord Matlock into a doting grandfather.

And Richard, when asked to tell of his good fortune — for he would become as sought after for his wooden creations as his wife would be for her designs — would smile, lift Kitty's hand to his lips, and begin each reply with an "Ah, yes, my inconvenient choice."

Her Heart's Choice

CHOICES BOOK 4

Anne refused Alex's offer of marriage six years ago and is determined to do so again. He, on the other hand, is just as resolved to be accepted.

Prologue

January 9, 1812

Alexander Madoch tossed the newspaper he had been reading on the table and tapped the section he wished his friend Jonathan Lester to read. Then, he picked up a hunk of cheese, popped it into his mouth, and rising from his chair, walked to the window that overlooked the street.

Two horses, wearing the colours of his uncle's stable, carried a pair of finely dressed women toward the beach. The ladies were not alone, however, as a group of young swains followed close behind. He smiled as he watched the positioning of the gentlemen shift, one nudging the other out of the way to get closer to one or the other of the ladies.

"So the little termagant has decided to marry, has she?" Jonathan said, drawing Alex's attention back to the room. "I feel sorry for the chap that has to put up with her."

Alex turned from the window. "That chap shall be me. It seems we must make a trip to London."

"You? After the way she turned you out?" Jonathan shook his head and scowled. "I'd not be chasing after the likes of her again. Begone and good riddance, I would say."

Alex turned back to the window.

A young man was finally riding next to one of the young ladies. They were a good distance off, but still he could see how the young woman turned to the gentleman and slowed to allow him to ride more fully at her side.

He bit his lip and tilted his head as he watched the pair ride away. That was what he had wanted those many years ago: a lady, a particular lady, to ride away with him.

"She was not wrong in her refusal," he said without turning toward his friend.

Jonathan huffed his disagreement.

"The risk truly was too great. I had no guarantee of success." Alex glanced over his shoulder at his friend.

Jonathan pushed the paper away from where it lay in front of him. "You also had no guarantee of failure. As I see it, you had only to increase in your standing. Anyone admitted to your confidence knows how hard you work and how you do not begin a venture unless there is a very promising chance of success."

Alex remained looking out the window. It would do no good to argue the point with his friend, for he had wholeheartedly agreed with such a sentiment at first. In fact, if he allowed himself to consider it, he still felt somewhat bitter over the fact that Anne had not believed enough in his success to accept him.

"I did fall into some wonderful chances that I did not expect." He chuckled slightly as he turned toward his friend. "Would she not be surprised to learn of my connection to Prinny?"

When he had first arrived here, next to the sea, to take up his chosen profession, he had not expected that his uncle would be the one to help Prince George find his Brighton retreat, nor had he expected his uncle to recommend him for the position of manager of the Prince Regent's riding school and stables. His friend had also benefitted from the arrangement, because Alex had engaged him, as quickly as could be done, as his man of business and an assistant in his duties to His Majesty.

"That would put an end to her argument of your lack of connections," Jonathan agreed.

Alex began to nod his agreement but then changed it to a shake. "No." His head shook from side to side with more determination as his thoughts settled firmly into his mind. "No. Miss de Bourgh is not to know of my connections. None of them. Nothing beyond those I have through my uncle."

"Have you taken leave of your senses?" Jonathan's expression matched the disbelief in his words, and Alex could understand why. They both knew that convincing Miss Anne de Bourgh to accept anyone without a known title and fortune – or at the very least connections of the most excellent calibre – was going to be nigh unto impossible. Nigh unto impossible. Not entirely impossible.

Or so he hoped.

"I need her to accept me. Not my money and not my connections. I want her as my wife, but only if she accepts me without any..." His right hand circled in the air as if fluffing something. "... of those accoutrements."

Jonathan pulled the paper back to him. "Did you read this?" He lifted the paper and gave it a shake before scanning to find the announcement. "She has required that all potential suitors have, and I quote 'in their possession a title, as well as solvent and accurate financial reports,' and..." He held up a finger to emphasize his point. His tone dripped with disdain as he continued. "'Please be advised that references and documentation showing adherence to the above criteria will be required.' Exactly how do you propose to gain an audience with *her majesty* when you do not have a title and are unwilling to mention your connections?"

Alex chuckled to himself as he crossed the room and opened the door to call to the butler. Jonathan would not like this answer. Not even the tiniest bit.

Having given instructions to see that all was made ready for his trip, Alex turned, with a smile, to his friend. "How have I always gained an audience where none was extended?"

Jonathan groaned. "No. You cannot mean to make me assist you."

"It is your job."

His friend's eyes closed and after he had expelled a great sigh, he asked, "To whom am I to write about soirees?"

Ah, he knew he could count on Jonathan's cooperation even when he did not want to give it. They were too good of friends for something as monumental as pursuing England's most stubborn heiress and convincing her to capitulate her position to separate them.

"Do you still correspond with Brownlow?" he asked.

"On occasion, but that is a business matter and this..." he waved at the paper as he rose to follow his friend from the room.

"Is a business matter," Alex said to complete Jonathan's thought. "Your job is to see that I make all the proper connections and that all the required meetings are arranged so that I have the best chance of being successful in my enterprises, is it not?"

His friend sighed and shook his head. "Even though I still hold that this is not a matter of business, I shall give you every opportunity I can arrange. However, I will have you know that I am still not in favour of the idea."

That was easily seen – and understandable. A fellow could not have a better friend than Mr. Jonathan Lester. Alex clapped that staid and true friend on the shoulder. "As far as I am concerned, this is the most important undertaking in which you will ever take part. That is, of course, until you find yourself a lady of your own to pursue in earnest."

Jonathan groaned once again as they left the dining room.

Alex stopped abruptly and turned to face his friend. "We must not fail in this endeavour." He placed a hand on each of Jonathan's shoulders. "We simply cannot fail." A twice broken heart might not mend.

His friend nodded in an up-and-down, side-to-side sort of fashion that spoke of how difficult it was to say the words that accompanied the action. "Very well. I can see how important this is to you, and I will do my best to help you secure her. Though I question your sanity, I will do it for you."

"Thank you. That is all that I ask." A smile lit Alex's face. His happy future was just within his grasp – finally. "Now, to tell my uncle that I shall be leaving for town in two days."

As he exited the house, Alex expelled a great puff of breath as the burden of Anne's rejection those six years ago lifted, and his body and mind lightened. In truth, he had not felt such welcome vigour in some time. He had no doubt that the challenge that lay before him would tax him to the end of his patience. She always had. But... He drew a deep, satisfying breath as he walked toward the stables. The prize — ah, the prize for endurance would be satisfying indeed.

Finally, his heart would feel whole.

Chapter 1

JANUARY 21, 1812

As SHE HURRIED ACROSS the ballroom toward her cousin, Anne de Bourgh bit back a small smile at the expression of disapproval Mary, the new Lady Rycroft, gave him when he slid his arm around her waist and tugged her closer to his side.

Samuel – Lord Rycroft – had never been one to hold very firmly to propriety. Anne remembered him often getting into trouble for some sort of mischief every time he visited Rosings when he was young. Of course, he had not visited often, since her mother and his mother, though sisters, could only tolerate each other in small doses that were administered with years, not months, between them.

She sighed.

Her aunt, Lady Sophia, was easy to like. It was her mother, Lady Catherine, who was the challenge.

Not even Anne could tolerate her mother's constant nattering and interference for any length of time. It was why she had feigned illness so often and had hidden in her room. She could not hold back her smile this time. On how many of those occasions had she escaped from her mother by taking to her room and climbing down the trellis? The number was not small!

"You are even more beautiful when you smile." Mr. Blackmoore, the living, breathing annoyance whom Anne had been attempting to avoid all evening, stepped into her path.

Her lips ceased smiling and instead curled as they did when she was forced to take that dreadful concoction her mother had gotten from the apothecary and insisted on giving to her at the first sign of a sniffle. No! That was unfair to the concoction. This gentleman left a far less pleasant taste in one's figurative mouth simply by being. Why could he not understand her refusals? She made no reply as she attempted to step around him.

"Come, Miss de Bourgh," he said, taking her by the elbow, "a dance is about to begin. Will you not join me?"

Anne pulled her arm away from him. "Indeed, I will not. I have told you more than once that I do not wish to make or keep your acquaintance." Again, she endeavoured to step around him only to be prevented.

"Miss de Bourgh, it is just one dance. How can you deny me the pleasure of such lovely company as yourself? Surely, you cannot be so cruel."

Anne crossed her arms and chuckled mirthlessly. "I assure you that I can be." She was her mother's daughter after all, which meant she could be rather immovable, and unpleasantly so, when she chose to be.

"Blackmoore." Lord Rycroft's voice held a warning. The gentlemen, though friends, had not re-established the camaraderie they had shared prior to an incident involving Mary.

"Rycroft." Mr. Blackmoore nodded his head in greeting.

"I did not invite you to this soiree to harass my guests." Rycroft tipped his head to the side and raised a brow. Anne could see the slight clenching of his jaw and knew that he was more than just a little disturbed by the actions of his former friend.

"I was merely asking Miss de Bourgh for a dance."

Rycroft shifted his gaze to Anne. "And does the lady wish for a dance?"

"If she does not, then she shall have to sit out the entire evening." Blackmoore smiled at Anne. It was not a friendly smile but one of cunning and calculation, and exactly the type of smile that Anne despised the most.

"My card is full," she lied.

"Surely not." Blackmoore's hand reached out to take her card, but Anne quickly pulled her hand out of his reach.

"This is not my card, sir. I fear I have left my card in the retiring room. I was just on my way to ask if Lady Rycroft would accompany me to retrieve it."

"Not your card?" Blackmoore's tone spoke of disbelief.

"That is what I said." Anne smiled as her eyes held firmly to his for a moment before she dipped a curtsey and, with an *if you will excuse me*, stepped around Blackmoore and hurried toward Mary, leaving her pursuer to her cousin's care.

She stamped her slippered foot and crossed her arms as she came to stand next to Lady Rycroft. Her mother would be horrified because a lady did not stamp her foot. However, at the moment, as Anne scowled at Mr. Blackmoore, she did not care what a lady did or did not do. "He is without equal," she muttered with her eyes still on Blackmoore.

"Are you well?" Mary asked.

Anne turned her attention to Mary. "I am well, but he is not. There is something seriously wrong with that man's head." Her hand flew to cover her mouth as she realized that Mary was not alone. "Forgive me." Her cheeks flushed crimson. "I struggle to keep my thoughts to myself at times."

Lord Brownlow chuckled. "That is a trait that is not unlike your cousin."

"Indeed," Mary said with a laugh and a gently pointed look that made Anne wish she had cared a trifle more about what a lady did or did not do before she had acted and spoken so freely.

"Lord Brownlow," Mary continued, "this is Miss de Bourgh. Miss de Bourgh, Lord Brownlow."

"A pleasure," Brownlow said with a bow.

"Is it?" Anne said in surprise.

Again, Lord Brownlow chuckled. "It is."

"Then, I thank you," she said with a curtsey before turning to Mary. "I fear my determination to avoid a certain situation requires me to ask you to accompany me to the retiring room." She glanced back toward where Blackmoore and Rycroft still stood conversing.

"As much as I would like to continue talking to Lord Brownlow," she smiled at the gentleman, "I find that doing so puts me at risk of speaking to *him* again," she tipped her head toward Blackmoore, "and I have no desire to do so."

"If you are positive it cannot wait –"

"It cannot. I assure you." The faster she was away from that man, the better.

"Well, then, I shall accompany you. Lord Brownlow, if you will excuse us."

"Certainly, Lady Rycroft, Miss de Bourgh." He nodded to each lady in turn.

Anne began to walk away from him but then stopped and returned. "Do you have a dance that is free?" she asked in a whisper.

"I do," he whispered in reply.

Anne cast a wary eye toward Blackmoore. "Which one?"

"The one after supper remains open."

"That will do," Anne said. "I look forward to dancing with you, and I do apologize for being so forward, sir. However, I may have told *someone* that my card was full, and I must now fill it."

Brownlow chuckled softly. "If you need a second dance, Miss de Bourgh. I have the last of the evening available as well."

Anne sighed, and her shoulders drooped in relief. "That would be most helpful."

"I am pleased to be of assistance." Lord Brownlow shook his head as she scooted away.

Mary took Anne's arm as they left the ballroom. "You do know that ladies are not to ask gentlemen for dances, do you not?"

Anne nodded. "I would not have done so if it had not been necessary." She looked up and down the hall, and, seeing that no one was near and feeling confident that she would not be heard, she continued. "Mr. Blackmoore insists on importuning me at every turn. I could not see a way to avoid dancing with him and still be allowed to dance with others." She smiled sheepishly. "So, I lied." She looked away from the disapproving look that Mary gave her. "I know it is wrong," she said softly, "but I should be able to refuse a man like him without refusing all others."

Mary patted Anne's hand. "I agree that it is not fair."

"If you would rather…" Anne looked up at Mary, who, like Kitty and Elizabeth, had become a dear friend over the past two weeks. "I could plead a headache and borrow a room in which to rest."

Mary shook her head. "There is no need for that. We shall just have to find enough gentlemen to fill your card so that your words no longer remain untrue."

And so, they did. With Mary's help, Anne's card was full before they had returned to the ballroom.

For much of what remained of the first half of the evening, Anne remained near Mary or Lady Sophia, which had been quite the delightful and revealing experience, for she had not realized just how pleasant it could be to sit or stand near someone who did not constantly remind you to straighten your posture or smile more engagingly or less widely or less frequently or more often.

And she had even managed to sit for supper without her mother near! It may not have been a miracle above all miracles, but to Anne it was no small thing. When the meal was over and all exhibitions of talent were completed, Anne once again sought to limit the amount of time she had to spend with her mother.

After one particularly lively dance in the latter half of the evening, Anne, at Lady Sophia's insistence, took a seat not far from an open balcony door. The breeze was refreshing, and Anne closed her eyes and filled her lungs with the deliciously cool air.

Her feet were beginning to hurt, and she was certain her arms would be nearly unusable by morning. She had not realized just how much exertion there was in dancing. It was tiring, but the fatigue was not unwelcome. In fact, she found it exhilarating. She had not enjoyed herself this much since the last time she had sneaked out of her bedroom to ride. Riding had always been a pleasure to Anne, but her mother disapproved of too much exertion and exposure to the elements.

Anne was just beginning to ruminate on the ridiculousness of being confined to one's room to preserve one's health when she heard a familiar and unwelcome name.

"Madoch," Lord Brownlow said, "I feared you were not going to show."

"I do apologize for my tardiness, but I had an unexpected call to which I had to attend. There really was no avoiding it."

Anne cautiously turned to look at the speaker. It could not be *him*. It simply could not be. *He* was not of the gentleman class. She paused and sighed. Perhaps she was lowering him a bit more than he deserved. His father was a gentleman, but he was a second son, that much was true.

Her breath caught in her chest as her eyes found the gentleman standing with Lord Brownlow. "Alex," the name fell from her lips on a sharp exhale. It was him! He was here. How could he be here? Why was he here? Did he not still reside in Brighton? Why was he in town?

Oh, this was not good! He could not see her. He must not see her. Her heart might break a second time if she had to actually speak to him. She glanced from him to the open balcony door and then back to him, before rising from her seat and making her escape.

Chapter 2

THE AIR OUTSIDE THE ballroom was even cooler than the breeze Anne had felt inside, for, out here, there were no throngs of dancing people nor were there scores of candles casting their light and warmth. There were a few torches and lanterns, but not enough to do more than scatter the shadows of the night.

She folded her arms and rubbed the upper parts of them as she looked left and then right. If she remembered correctly, the library was to the right, three windows down, and open. That is the door to the garden had been open when she and Mary had gone looking for her cousins, Darcy and Richard, to fill her dance card. She certainly hoped no one had closed it, for she knew that being both alone and so far away from her chaperone was putting herself at risk, but what was she to do? *He* was in the ballroom, which meant she could not be.

Everything would be as it should be just as soon as she reached the safety of the library. Kitty and Richard had not been seen for a while. So, it stood to reason that Kitty had probably required a rest again since her head was still not quite right after her fall and required her to frequently seek solitude.

Therefore, even if the door was closed, they would let her in, and then, everything would, indeed, be well. With that in mind, Anne began heading for the library as quickly as could be done without looking like a fox fleeing a pack of hounds.

As she went, Anne considered how feigning a head injury might be a handy way to avoid her mother. It was an option she had not yet attempted to this point in her life. It could work, and for an extended amount of time. But then, would the care required to attend to such an injury be too much to bear?

She stopped to consider the option. No, it would not do. Her mother would hover or have a surgeon posted outside her door. That was most certainly not the wished-for result. Chances and new schemes were often worth the attempt but only if they did not lead to her avoiding one untenable situation merely to be cast into another that was far worse. One must always – or most times, at least – consider carefully the ramifications of what one pretended.

Of course, there were moments when there just was not time to ponder every eventuality – such as when a lady's uncle and mother were arranging an unwanted marriage for her or when a lady needed to make a quick exit to avoid a former suitor who still caused her heart to ache whenever she passed a stable of horses.

Still quite lost in her thoughts, she began slowly walking toward the library.

The stables at Rosings had not been nearly as pleasant an escape in the past six years as they had been before the day when she had sent Alex away. It had been the right decision. She knew it was, but that did not make it any less painful – not then, not now.

Footfalls on the stone of the balcony broke into her thoughts, and after giving a glance over her shoulder, she lifted her skirt and made to run the few remaining steps to the library.

However, Mr. Blackmoore was quicker than she and had her by the arm before she could flee.

"Miss de Bourgh, it seems we are meant to marry."

"Marry?" Her heart climbed into her throat as the reality of the situation in which she found herself settled into her startled mind. She twisted and pulled at the arm he held. "I think not!" She could not marry him.

He slid an arm around her and hauled her closer to him. "But we are in a very compromising position, are we not?" He wore that sly smile of his once again. "Such a scandal as this will put to an end any other offers of marriage but mine." He bent his head to kiss her, but she turned her head to the side and pushed at his chest.

"I would rather die an old maid than be married to the devil." She turned her head the opposite direction of his mouth once again and pushed some more.

He chuckled near her ear. "The devil?"

The feeling of his breath on her skin made her shiver in revulsion. She pushed against him again. "Yes, the devil. Who else traps a lady into marriage just so he can keep his mistress and his money?"

"You would be surprised to know how many do just that." His mouth was still near her ear, and he whispered into it before kissing it.

Anne gasped and without thought slapped him. "Libertines, the whole lot of them," she cried. "Unhand me at once," she demanded as she continued to struggle to get away.

"No, not until you have consented to marry me," he growled as his grip on her twisting form tightened.

"I cannot. I will not. I would rather –"

"Darling, I have found your dance card." The voice that broke into Anne's protest was not only a familiar one but also the very one which she had been attempting to avoid by coming out here. Relief at being saved warred with her wish to flee from both him and Mr. Blackmoore.

"It was rather foolish of you to hold it so loosely as to let it fall into the border," Alex continued as he joined her on the balcony.

Mr. Blackmoore's arms fell away from Anne, and she spun from him and nearly straight into her rescuer.

"Thank you, Mr. Madoch." With a trembling hand and a curious look, she took a dance card from him. Whose card it was she did not know.

He smiled at her just as he had always smiled at her. It was an open, unaffected smile, a smile of true delight.

Her lower lip trembled, and she sucked it in between her teeth. No one else in her life had ever smiled at her like he did. It was one of the things that had made it so hard for her to turn him away the last time they had met.

"It took a bit of searching." His voice was calm and reassuring. Oh, if only he was not a second son! "And I fear my shoes may be too soiled to enter the ballroom again, but there it is. A prize by which to remember this night."

She nodded her head in place of saying *thank you*, since speaking would put her in danger of crumbling into a weeping mound of tattered pieces.

He took one of her hands and spoke in a low voice. "Perhaps a few moments in the library would be beneficial. I saw one of your cousins at the window."

Again, she nodded as she clutched desperately at her unruly heart while the way he had always been so kind to her flooded her memory. His small touches. His companionable silence when she did not wish to speak because of some tumult of emotions. His ability to think ahead and avoid any further harm befalling her, even if it meant putting himself at risk.

"I will just make sure that this gentleman has made it back to the ballroom before I join you." His voice rose slightly in question, making his tone match the look in his eyes.

She pulled in a silent breath. "Of course," she managed to say without so much as a tear finding its way to her eye.

Truthfully, she did not wish to see him in the library, or any-where, for that matter, but he had just rendered her a great service and the alternative of being left here with Mr. Blackmoore was, without a doubt, the worse choice. So, she gathered her thoughts and her strength and walked as calmly toward the library door as she could.

When she reached it, she looked back. Alex stood in front of Mr. Blackmoore with his arms crossed. He was shorter than Mr. Blackmoore by at least three inches, and his build was slight as far as gentlemen's figures were judged. However, she knew from watching him work with the horses in the paddock at Rosings that his size belied his strength.

She could hear Alex's rumbling angry tone. It wasn't just his strength that was great. His courage had always seemed to be unconquerable to her. She shook her head. He had always stood as her protector. Her heart sighed while a tear formed in her eye and she blinked it away. If only he had the means and position to meet her qualifications, her search for a husband would be over.

"But he does not," she whispered sadly to herself as she stepped into the library.

Chapter 3

"ANNE?" RICHARD, WHO WAS standing near the library door that opened to the garden, caught her by the arm to prevent her from stumbling as she stepped into the room and directly into him. "What brings you to the library by way of the balcony?" His surprise was mingled with suspicion, and he did not release her arm though she had kept to her feet. Instead, he guided her to where Kitty was sitting. "And without a wrap?" There was censure in the question. "You are positively frozen!"

Anne dutifully took a seat next to Kitty. She knew that when her cousin started using the tone he had just used, there was very little chance of doing otherwise. As sweet and gentle as he could be, there were times, such as now, when he towered over her and spoke with such an air of authority that she knew for certain he was indeed Lord Matlock's son.

"I needed some air," she muttered. "I know it was foolish to go out without my chaperone, but..." Her voice trailed off as she saw him fold his arms and shake his head.

"You were outside in the dark, alone?"

She lifted her chin. "I was. At first. But then, Mr. Blackmoore discovered me, and he would not unhand me until Mr. Madoch appeared." Anne huffed. "The rules of society and propriety are insufferable." She folded her arms and glared back at her cousin, bracing herself for whatever battle she might be starting. She was

not in any frame of mind to be scolded by him. What she had just
endured was punishment enough for her foolishness.

To her surprise, he shrugged. "They are." He took a seat near the
settee where Anne and Kitty were sitting. "Be that as it may, it is
not advisable to ignore those rules unless you are prepared to pay
the price." He took Kitty's hand which was nearest to him in his
own. "And the price can be very high indeed."

"So it can be," Darcy said as he joined them. "Although..." He
pulled his wife close to his side. "There are times when doing so
has produced a most pleasant result."

Anne rolled her eyes. Her cousin spoke, of course, of his being
required to marry his wife – with whom he was utterly besotted –
because of a supposed indiscretion.

"Mr. Blackmoore is not a pleasant result." She shuddered at the
thought of being forced to marry *that* ne'er-do-well.

"And that is why we must follow the rules as closely as we can."
The comment might have been a scold if it had been spoken by
anyone other than Kitty. Her soon-to-be cousin's voice was soft
and reassuring, as if she were merely agreeing with Anne. If she
spent all her life searching, Anne was certain she could never find
another lady so sweet as Kitty to be her friend and relation.

Just as Anne was giving Kitty's hand an appreciative squeeze,
the door, through which Anne had only moments ago entered,
opened.

Alex closed the door as quickly as he could but still, it was not
fast enough to keep a cool breeze from following him into the
room. His eyes scanned the gathered group. He had known that
at least one of Anne's cousins was in the library, but he had not
expected to see quite so many people. He stood for a moment
not knowing exactly what he should say to so many people, all of
whom were looking at him in surprise.

Finally, he stepped forward and bowed. "Alexander Madoch."
An introduction was usually the best way to start in any situation
when one was presenting himself.

"Madoch? Not the same Madoch that used to skulk around Rosings' stables and plague the stable master with questions and suggestions?"

It would be Anne's cousin Darcy who would remember him. How many times had they met in the stables? Darcy was forever escaping the confines of Rosings when he was visiting. From what he understood, Darcy had never gotten on well with Lady Catherine – likely because the lady insisted on him marrying her daughter whether either of the pair wished it or not.

Such a trying household Anne had grown up in! It was quite a deal worse than his own, and yet, he and his father had had their share of disagreements.

Alex bowed his head in acknowledgement of Darcy's statement. "One and the same."

"I have not seen you in years." Darcy stuck his hand out in welcome. "How have you been keeping yourself?"

"He has been working for his uncle in Brighton," Anne supplied as Alex shook Darcy's proffered hand. "Or so I have heard," she added softly when all eyes, including his, turned in her direction.

"Miss de Bourgh is correct. I joined my uncle in Brighton five, or was it six, years ago?" As if he did not know how long it had been since the day when she had refused him.

"Six years ago, November." She pressed her lips together as if she had not meant to answer.

He smiled at her. It was good to know she had not forgotten him.

"I believe you have the right of it. It was six years this past November." He turned his attention back to Darcy. "My uncle owns a stable in Brighton. It is a popular establishment with those who come to visit."

He glanced at Kitty and then Elizabeth. "I am fairly certain I know you two gentlemen as Mr. Darcy and Colonel Fitzwilliam, but I am at a loss as to who these lovely ladies are."

"Forgive me," Darcy said. "This is Mrs. Darcy, and seated next to Anne is Mrs. Darcy's sister, Miss Bennet."

"Soon to be Mrs. Fitzwilliam." Richard smiled proudly. "And I am no longer a colonel but happily a mere mister."

"Congratulations to you both." Alex had, of course, heard from Lord Brownlow, at whose house he and Mr. Lester were staying, the full story of each of the gentlemen's now happy circumstances.

"What brings you to town?" Richard asked.

"Business," he said with a glance toward Anne. She would be most displeased if he were to mention just what sort of business he had in mind, and the thought nearly stopped him from revealing it — nearly. However, he was not one to back down from a challenge. "I am, in fact, here to marry Miss de Bourgh."

Anne's eyes grew wide, and she gasped. "You cannot."

"Oh," he said with a smile, "I think I can." And he was determined to succeed.

"But you are not titled or wealthy," she protested.

He shrugged. "Yes, well, that is what we shall have to discuss at our meeting tomorrow when I call on you."

Anne rose to her feet. Panic filled her eyes. "You are not to call on me. I will not be home to you."

"Not home to a friend? How very odd and rather improper."

Her eyes narrowed as her arms folded in front of her.

Alex turned back to the two gentlemen who were both looking at him with concern. "I assure you, gentlemen, that my intentions are entirely honourable. In fact, it is not the first time I have sought to marry Miss de Bourgh, but she was not ready to..." He glanced at Anne. "How did you put it? Oh, yes, she was not ready to sign her life away at that time." He grimaced slightly at the memory of her cutting remarks about his being wholly unsuitable due to his lack of connections, lack of wealth, and plans for his future.

"However," he continued, "according to the paper, she is now ready, and so, I am here to present my suit."

"You have read her requirements, have you not?" There was a tone to Darcy's voice that spoke to his concern for Madoch's mental faculties.

"Oh, I have. More than once," Alex assured him. "Miss de Bourgh is correct when she says I do not meet all of them." He chose his words carefully so as not to be false but also so that they would not reveal his true standing. If she were to choose him, he was determined it would not be for his wealth or position. "I think you gentlemen would agree that there are more important things than a title and money to consider when choosing a marriage partner."

Anne huffed. "Well, of course, whomever I choose must be pleasant and of good moral character." Again, she pressed her lips together as if she had not meant to speak.

Alex tipped his head to the side and stared at her for a moment, taking the time to learn the little changes that had occurred to her features due to the passage of time. It had not changed her beauty. If anything, it had added to it. Hers was a face he could watch for hours.

"That is true," he said at last, "but I spoke of the heart." He continued to look at her as she bit her lip and schooled her face not to reveal the emotions that shone in her eyes.

"One must not be ruled by one's heart," Anne said softly.

He nodded. "That is where you have always been wrong."

Though the comment was spoken so softly that it was barely heard, he was certain from the silence which followed it that the message of his words was not lost on Anne or the others watching the exchange. His heart lay open before them all, and he knew it. But one did not win what he wanted by avoiding daring attacks. Not that such stratagems were easily done.

He drew a breath and released it. "I have stayed long enough. I just wished to assure myself that Miss de Bourgh was well and had not suffered any ill effects from her encounter with Mr. Black-moore."

"I am well. Thank you."

He studied her face a moment longer. "I am happy to hear it. Until tomorrow," he added with a bow.

"I will not be home," she called after him.

"Then, I will wait for your return."

He smiled as he heard her huff and stamp her foot. He had always loved her indomitable spirit.

"My lady," he said with a bow as he held the door open for Lady Sophia. Then, with one last look at Anne, he made his way toward the ballroom to let Brownlow know he was leaving.

Chapter 4

Lady Sophia sat down next to Anne. "Where have you been?" She wrapped her arms around Anne's shoulders and drew her close. "I have been so worried about you." She pulled back a bit so that she could look at Anne's face. "Do you know how hard it is to keep a step ahead of your mother? Imagine if she had asked me where you were, and I did not know." She pulled Anne close again.

"I should be furious," she said gently as Anne apologized. "Now, tell me what it was that made you seek an escape."

"Mr. Madoch," Anne whispered.

"Mr. Madoch?" She looked from Anne to Darcy and then Richard, who both nodded. "Do I know him?"

"Perhaps," Darcy answered. "He used to spend a good deal of time in Rosings' stables."

Lady Sophia shook her head. "I have not visited Rosings that often, and even if I had, that still does not tell me why my niece disappeared from the ballroom without a word to me or anyone else."

"He is a former friend from years gone by," Anne supplied when her aunt gave her a questioning look. "I saw him and did not wish to speak with him, so I decided to come to the library."

Lady Sophia held up a finger to keep Anne from saying anything else. "Just like that? You left one room and ended up in another without any trouble on the way?"

"That was Madoch who was just leaving as you entered," Richard inserted.

This comment caused Anne's favourite aunt to scowl the tiniest bit and look at her for an explanation. So, after drawing a fortifying breath, she shared her tale about how Mr. Blackmoore had stopped her to press his suit in a most ungentlemanly way until Mr. Madoch had come to her rescue.

"Well, that was quite an adventure." She sighed. "You do realize, do you not, that you may have put yourself in a very precarious position." She glanced at Darcy and Richard. "If Mr. Blackmoore were to make it known that he was in the garden with you..."

Anne's eyes grew wide, and she shook her head. No, no, no! It could not come to that!

Lady Sophia shrugged. "Gossip has power."

Anne's heart hammered a fast rhythm in her chest, and the unpleasant fluttering that the thought of being Mrs. Blackmoore brought to Anne's mind made it impossible for her to remain seated. She paced to the window and back. "I will not marry that man." She turned to her cousins. "He has a mistress, you know."

They both nodded.

"What else can be done?" Lady Sophia asked softly. "A lady's reputation is a fragile thing, and once damaged, it is nearly impossible to restore. However, I suppose we are worrying before it is needed, and I believe you are engaged for the last set of the night, so we should make sure you are there to fulfill your obligation and to be seen." She stood and held her hand out to Anne.

Anne dutifully allowed her aunt to return her to the ballroom, though she had no desire to go there. She was not in a mood to dance. She was not in a mood to be pleasant. She wished to find a corner in an empty room and have a good cry — first, for her stupidity in sneaking out, and then, for the broken bits of her heart, which she had thought were healed until she had seen *him*.

She sighed as she took her place across from Lord Brownlow. If only Alex had not shown himself, she could have married for advantage without the renewal of the pain of sending him away, for she knew that she was going to have to send him away again and that it would be no less painful now than it had been six years ago.

There was no way she could marry him. He was not titled, nor did he have wealth, and without those things, she simply would not marry any man, including him. Her heart's resolve faltered for a moment, and for a few steps of the dance, she considered that perhaps a title was not necessary, as long as there was money enough.

She smiled and replied to the question Lord Brownlow asked, and then, slipped back into her thoughts.

No, a title, indicating a position that made it difficult for others to bend your will to theirs, was an absolute necessity. She had seen the truth of it. It was a non-negotiable requirement, and Alex had neither wealth nor position. Therefore, he was an unacceptable choice, no matter how much her heart might protest the fact. With that decided, she turned her attention more fully to the dance and her partner.

As the dance ended and Anne curtseyed to Lord Brownlow, a lady to her right bumped into her lightly.

"I beg your pardon," the lady said.

Anne nodded her acceptance of the apology and was about to move on when the woman spoke once again. "You are Miss de Bourgh, are you not?"

"I am."

"I am Miss Ivison."

The lady would have taken Anne's arm after introducing herself if Anne had not pulled it away. Such forwardness was never acceptable in Anne's opinion.

"I have heard of you," Miss Ivison continued, stepping close to Anne. "You put an advertisement in the paper for a husband, did you not?" She smiled coyly before looking toward the door as if trying to locate someone. "I wonder how cool it will be in the carriage on the way home. Did you find it cold in the garden? Or did Mr. Blackmoore keep you warm enough?" With a triumphant look, she curtseyed and made to move away, but Anne's hand on her arm stayed her.

"Where have you heard such tall tales? Me? In the garden? With Mr. Blackmoore? Indeed!" She shook her head and chuckled as if the idea were completely preposterous.

Miss Ivison picked Anne's hand up off her arm and let it drop as if she were removing a piece of lint. "I have had the story from Mr. Blackmoore himself." She gave Anne an appraising look. "At least his tastes are better than I had thought. I had heard it rumored that he was considering Miss Bingley." She made a sound of pitying regret before adding. "Caroline is invaluable to me for her connections to soirees such as this, but do consider it. A man of rank marrying a lady from trade?" She chuckled. "Congratulations for preventing such a travesty." Her left eyebrow flicked up, and her lips curled into a smug smile before she left Anne.

Anne was sure her heart had stopped. She stood in shock for a moment and watched Miss Ivison walk away; however, shock did not take long to turn to anger and anger leapt very rapidly to fury as her eyes searched the room for her prey.

Finding whom she sought, she began to cross the room. People were bidding each other good night and filtering out the various doors to the ballroom as she reached her quarry. She stood for a moment behind him, listening to the tale he was telling.

"She was quite willing," he whispered, "had the night not been so cool..."

The gentleman to his left cleared his throat just as Anne tapped Mr. Blackmoore on the shoulder. His eyes grew wide as he turned and saw her.

"Sweetheart," he said smoothly, covering his surprise.

"I am not your sweetheart," Anne replied coolly. "Nor will I ever be the sweetheart of a man who spreads rumours about me."

He chuckled. "They were not rumours, sweetheart."

She stepped closer to him. "Let me repeat myself. I will happily die an old maid before I will ever consider marrying you."

"A ruined old maid," he muttered. "And everyone will know it. I would not toss my offer to the side so cavalierly if I were you, unless, of course, you wish to remove yourself from society in disgrace."

Her eyes narrowed and had she not been so intently focused on the vile man in front of her, she might have noticed the gentleman, who had earlier cleared his throat at her approach, now frantically waving to Lord Rycroft.

"I assure you, sir," she spat the words out as if they were capable of slapping the gentleman, "that, just as I would I never consider a man who keeps a mistress, I would rather live in disgrace than tie myself to a man who throws his money away on card games because he is too stupid to know he is a poor player." She smiled as his eyes grew wide for a moment. "You thought I did not know about your gaming?" She shook her head. "Then your intelligence is even more limited than even I supposed."

She would have continued, but a hand on her arm stopped her.

"Blackmoore." Rycroft's voice was dangerously gruff. "We are done here. Completely."

Anne looked up at her cousin, who was shaking his head in disgust.

"Do not darken my door," Rycroft continued, "and if I arrive at our club while you are there, you shall do yourself a favour by leaving, or I shall have you removed and banned. Do I make myself clear?" He shook his head again. "What were you thinking? I accept you back after the scheme you attempted on my wife, and you return the favour by importuning my cousin? In my home?"

He cast a look around the group of men that stood with Blackmoore. "If you wish to keep my acquaintance, I suggest that whatever tale was told is never repeated."

While Blackmoore's group of friends each hastily nodded their agreement, he turned back to Blackmoore and motioned toward the door. "Go."

Then, before Blackmoore could say a word, he turned, and with Anne's hand on his arm, strode away – quickly, nearly too quickly for Anne to keep pace with him without scampering.

"Do not look back," he cautioned her in a low voice. "The break must be clear." He slowed his pace a bit as they reached the edge of the ballroom. "I am sorry. I should not have invited him. But, I thought, perhaps... What I was hoping for does not signify. I should not have invited him."

Anne shook her head. "It is I who am sorry. Had I not slipped out that door onto the balcony, you would not have had to cut off a friend. I shall scold myself forever for my stupidity."

Rycroft laughed softly. "I do not think that is necessary, and I fear we may argue a long while and never be satisfied with where the blame should fall. It is likely best if we just share it."

She smiled. "That does seem to be the most logical solution."

"Are you well?" he asked quite seriously.

She nodded. "I am. Thank you."

"You are certain?"

She lifted one shoulder and let it drop. "For the moment."

"Then," he said with a smile, "allow me to remedy that and escort you to your mother."

Anne could not help the laugh that escaped her.

She glanced back once at the ballroom as they moved toward the door. It was nearly empty now, save for servants. Her first ball was over, and at present, she was not sure she ever wished to attend another.

Indeed, she wondered if she would ever be invited to another. Perhaps Mr. Blackmoore and his friends would not speak about the rumours, but what about Miss Ivison?

She shook herself slightly. Tomorrow. Tomorrow would be soon enough to worry about such things. At present, all she wanted was a warm bath and a soft bed. Dancing had been enjoyable but taxing, and that, combined with some of the events of the night, had made her body and mind wearier than they had ever been.

Chapter 5

THE MORNING AFTER RYCROFT's ball, in the middle of the time at which making calls on young ladies – even stubborn ones – was acceptable, Alex swung down from his horse in front of Matlock House and handed the reins to a waiting groom. Then, he took a newspaper and a flask of coffee from his saddlebag and made his way to the door.

He lifted his hand to knock on the door when it opened and a gentleman, whom he did not recognize, exited.

"Good luck to you," the man said with a shake of his head.

"Was it a difficult interview?"

His companion merely chuckled and kept walking.

Alex turned back to the door. "Mr. Madoch to see Miss de Bourgh." He held out his card, which the butler refused with a barely perceivable shake of his head.

"Regretfully, it is my unpleasant business to inform you that Miss de Bourgh is not home to you."

Alex tucked his card away. "I expected as much." He bent to sweep the step with his newspaper and then sat down. Glancing over his shoulder, he saw the butler looking perplexed.

"I will just wait here until she returns," Alex said by way of explanation.

"I believe you misunderstand, sir. She is not home to you and will not be home to you."

"Well, that is to be determined, my good man."

"No, she was quite clear in her instructions. You are not to be admitted."

Alex shrugged and unfolded his paper. "And I was clear last evening when I said I would call on her. That is my intent, and I do not plan to be moved from this spot under my own power until I have gained admittance. Now, if you would be so kind as to go inform the ever-so-obstinate Miss de Bourgh that I am here and will remain here until she sees me." He made a shooing motion with his hand and then turned his attention to his paper.

Behind him, the door closed, and he listened carefully to see if he could make out the sound of a couple strong footmen being summoned to remove him from his perch. No such noise was heard, so Alex opened his flask and took a sip of his somewhat cold coffee which had been mixed with a touch of whiskey to give it some warmth – though he knew the alcohol would not, in truth, warm him.

He was halfway through his flask of coffee and just beginning to read a third article from the paper when the door behind him opened.

"Lady Sophia has agreed to see you," the butler announced.

"Not Miss de Bourgh?" Alex pretended to be disappointed. He was, in fact, pleasantly surprised that he would gain entrance to see anyone. He had expected to spend the whole of calling hours on the step at Matlock House if he were not forcibly removed.

While the thought of being given an audience with the lady whom he knew had been appointed as Anne's advisor was pleasing, he was not so trusting as to believe it impossible for Lady Sophia to simply walk him through the house and out the servants' door. Still, he was hopeful that, at least in the few moments that he might have to speak to her, he would be able to present his suit.

"I am afraid not, sir. It seems Miss de Bourgh is still not home to you. However, if you will follow me, Lady Sophia will see you in the music room."

Alex kept his hat in his hand and his paper under his arm as he followed the butler.

"Mr. Madoch to see you, my lady," the butler said, stepping into the music room ahead of Alex.

Lady Sophia thanked him and rose to greet her guest. "A bit of tea, please, Harrison. A warm cup would be much nicer than whatever you have been partaking of from your flask, would it not?"

"Indeed, it would," Alex agreed.

"You may put your coat and hat there," Lady Sophia motioned to a straight-backed wooden chair that sat near the door. "I promise that you shall not be removed from the house without them." She smiled as she made the comment and motioned for him to take a chair near where she had been sitting. "I gather from your presence here today that you have a desire to marry my niece?"

"I do," Alex said as he casually crossed one leg over the other and rested his elbows on the arms of the chair. "However," he continued, "I fear I do not meet all the published requirements."

Lady Sophia's eyes sparkled with intrigue. "You do not?"

He shook his head. "I have no title, and I am a second son."

Lady Sophia nodded slowly. "But your financial papers are well in order?"

He cocked his head to the side and considered for a moment how much he should tell her. She merely returned his look without wavering as he contemplated her trustworthiness. It only took him a fraction of a minute to decide that if both the admiral and Anne trusted her, then, he could also. He let a sly grin tip his lips as he flicked his eyebrows. "Very well in order, my lady, although I do not have them with me, nor will I be presenting them to Miss de Bourgh for inspection until she has accepted my offer. Of course, I tell you this in the strictest confidence."

Lady Sophia's lips twitched with amusement. "You are very confident to be coming to a meeting knowing you are lacking in some areas and refusing to prove you are not in others."

"Foolishly confident?" he questioned. He needed to know her thinking before he revealed too much of himself.

"That remains to be seen." She rose to pour him a cup of tea as the tea service was set up. "However, I think you just may have what is needed to marry my niece." She put her hand on the teapot and looked up at him. "And it is not anything found in your financial reports."

Alex silently sighed in relief as the music room door opened. It seemed that she would be an ally in his quest.

"Ah, Brother, have you had enough of the conversations in the drawing room? We have just begun an interesting one in here."

Alex stood and bowed to Admiral Fitzwilliam.

"Madoch?" the admiral said in surprise. "What brings you to..." He smiled and clapped his hands together once. "Do not tell me. You are also here to marry my niece."

"He is," Lady Sophia said, "and though my acquaintance with him has been of only a few moments, I would second the notion." She smiled as she handed Alex a cup of tea. "As I said before, I believe you will find this better than what you had been drinking." She arched a brow and gave him a stern look.

"It was coffee, my lady, with just a touch of whiskey to give it the illusion of heat." He took a sip from his cup. "This is infinitely better."

"You are not given to drink, are you?" Lady Sophia busied herself once again with pouring a cup of tea, this time for her brother.

"Not Madoch," the admiral assured her. "Others may indulge but not Madoch. This one always has his wits about him. Shrewd as they come, he is."

Alex gave a small nod in acceptance of the praise. "I thank you for the compliment, sir."

"How is your uncle?" The admiral took a seat and settled in as if he were there for a long chat.

"He is well. His foot pains him occasionally, but it is not enough to do more than slow him. He still insists on being at the stables each day."

Admiral Fitzwilliam turned to his sister. "Thank you," he said as he took the cup of tea she offered. "Madoch's uncle runs the finest stable in all of Brighton."

Alex cleared his throat softly.

Admiral Fitzwilliam chuckled. "Perhaps not the finest. Prinny's is possibly better, eh, Madoch?" He winked at Alex.

Lady Sophia's hand, which was reaching for her own cup of tea, stopped mid-stir. "You know the Prince Regent?"

"Know him?" scoffed the admiral. "This boy runs his stables and his riding school. It is said that Prinny does not make a decision regarding a horse without Madoch's approval."

Lady Sophia dropped into her chair, her tea forgotten. "You sway the opinion of His Highness?"

Alex shook his head. "I do not sway it, my lady. When it comes to horse flesh, I form it."

Lady Sophia's mouth hung open for half a moment before she snapped it shut. "You may not have a title, Mr. Madoch, but you most certainly hold position."

He shrugged. "I do, but for how long? The prince may, at any moment, decide that someone else has better sense, and then where will I be?"

The admiral snorted. "On his own estate, breeding and selling horses is where," he muttered. "Do not let him fool you, Sophia. This one has connections aplenty and money to equal them."

"Is this true?" Lady Sophia's eyes danced with delight.

Alex leaned forward in his chair and lowered his voice. "What the admiral says is true; however, Miss de Bourgh is not to know about it." He held his breath, hoping that Lady Sophia and Admiral Fitzwilliam would not ruin his plans to win Anne's heart without revealing the particulars of his situation.

Confusion replaced the delight in Lady Sophia's eyes. "Why ever not? She will refuse to consider you without knowing of your qualifications."

"Because I wish for her to choose me. Not my wealth. Not my connections. Me." He held Lady Sophia's gaze. "I wish for her to follow her heart."

Lady Sophia's eyes grew wide as understanding dawned on her. "You love her? But how?"

Alex released his breath quickly. "My father's estate is in Kent, near Rosings." He paused, not sure how much of his story he should share.

"This family is good at keeping secrets," Lady Sophia encouraged while casting a quick glance at her brother.

"Aye," the admiral agreed, "from the world and each other." He winked at his sister.

"Can you assure me that not a word of my situation will be shared with Miss de Bourgh?"

"Not a word," Lady Sophia agreed.

"Will you allow her to walk away from me if that is her choice?"

Lady Sophia was silent for a moment. "Yes, I will allow it unless in doing so she will be utterly miserable." She shook her head. "I cannot allow that." She smiled reassuringly at him. "Perhaps the knowledge I gain from your tale will assist me in knowing how best to help."

"My sister, the matchmaker," the admiral said as he waved his hand toward his sister with a flourish. "She'll not rest, my boy, until things have been arranged to best advantage."

Alex could not help the chuckle that escaped him. "Very well. Then, I shall tell you."

Chapter 6

"I was not done with my schooling – about halfway through my studies of the law – when I met her." Alex took a sip of his tea. "I had visited several stables in the area surrounding my father's estate. Each time I came home for a visit, I would revisit one or find another to tour for the first time. I never intended to take up the law profession. I had set my mind to the study to help me when it came to writing contracts and conducting deals."

The admiral chuckled. "I told you he was shrewd," he muttered.

"Shh," Lady Sophia scolded. "Tell me about your meeting."

For the next ten minutes, Alex told of his interest in the stables at Rosings and of the young girl of fourteen who had sneaked into those very stables in search of a fast horse, one that was quick enough to cause her troubles to float away on the wind.

In his mind's eye, Alex saw the red rims of Anne's eyes and heard her soft sniffle as the groom readied a steady mare.

"She is not fast enough," the delicate but distraught young miss grumbled.

"She is the only horse you are allowed, miss," the stable master explained. "I'll not risk my position or your life. I dare say I risk

enough by allowing you to ride when your mother is unaware."
He gave Anne a stern look.

Anne huffed. She pulled her arms more tightly around her waist,
as if trying to hold her hurt inside. She stood silently shifting from
foot to foot and watching a cat swish his *tail* back and forth as he
sat perched on a stool.

"Henry will ride with you." The stable master took the reins
from the groom and led the horse out to where the steps had been
put in place to help Anne in mounting the mare.

"Mr. Madoch," he called over his shoulder, "you may also attend
Miss de Bourgh. It will give you the chance you have been wanting
to see our horses in action. I will be interested to hear what you
have to say about their quality when you return."

Anne looked at Alex, who was leaning against the side of the
stable.

"Miss de Bourgh." The stable master stood ready to assist her in
mounting. "That is the younger Mr. Madoch," he explained.

Alex pulled himself straight and bowed.

Anne's brows furrowed. "I know who he is. I have seen him at
church. Why is he here?"

"He has an interest in horses," the stable master continued.

"Does he not have one of his own?" She scowled at him. Clearly,
she did not want him to ride with her.

"I will not trouble you, Miss de Bourgh, unless you wish it." Alex
smiled at her.

"Why are you not at school?" she asked. Her tone was decidedly
displeased.

"I return Monday next," he said, swinging neatly into his seat.

"What are you studying?" Anne asked.

"Law." He was studying it, but he had no desire to pursue it.
His interests were entirely wrapped up in horses, but his father
insisted that he study a proper profession. And so, thinking that
the law might help him in his future dealing with customers and

landowners, he had taken up the study of the law and had excelled enough to please his father.

Anne chewed her lip as if it might help her figure out whatever it was that had caused her distress while Alex rode silently next to her. Silence was not easy to maintain, especially when, from time to time, she would cast a cautious glance at him.

"I had intended to remain silent and merely observe the horses, but after she had looked my direction the fourth time, I spoke. I told her about my love of horses and my plans to one day own my own stable." He smiled. "And so started a friendship. When I was home, I spent more and more time at Rosings. We rode together and discussed all that was both right and wrong in our worlds. She eventually told me that an argument between her parents had sent her to the stables on the day we met." Hers was not an easy life.

"She was just set to be given a season in town the last time I saw her," Alex continued. "She was nineteen, and I was afraid she would be whisked away by some gentleman as soon as she set foot in town." He paused and looked at his hands. "So, I spoke to her about my desire to marry."

Lady Sophia gasped, while the admiral sighed and shook his head. "I take it, since we are here discussing your desire to be her husband today, that the discussion did not go well?"

Alex chuckled bitterly. "To put it gently. I had met with her in the stable as was our wont, and taking her by the hands, I presented my offer..."

⌒╌ℒ╌⌒

"Marry you?" Anne asked in surprise, pulling her hands away from him.

"Yes."

"I cannot marry you." Anne turned her back to him. "In truth, I am not ready to sign my life away to anyone, but you? You are *a second* son with little inheritance. Your father is no one of importance while my father is a baronet and my uncle is *an earl*." She turned back toward him. Her eyes shimmered with unshed tears, and her lips trembled.

He would bet all he would ever own that she was not so un-attached to him as she was attempting to portray. He had always been excellent at reading horses and nearly as good at deciphering people.

"But I will be a man of substance one day, Anne. Earls and even dukes, if not the king himself, will seek me out." He did not plan to be content with some non-descript life. He planned to be the best at what he did. He had to be. His father's opinion mattered to him – nearly as much as the opinion of the lady in front of him did.

She laughed coldly. It was a painfully sharp sound and one that seemed foreign coming from her.

"You?" she scoffed. "You must be mad. People of rank do not seek out people like you. They use them, manipulate them, and cast them aside. I want no part of that!" She clenched her jaw tightly and shrugged. "You are not good enough." She had pressed her lips firmly together, swiped quickly at a tear which had rolled down her cheek, nodded a goodbye, and fled from him.

Alex blew out a breath and sat quietly for a moment at the end of his recitation of the events of that day. The harshness of her refusal had taken him by surprise, and it had torn his heart in pieces. However, he had known then, just as he knew now, that she had loved him, and he was nearly certain she still loved him as much as he loved her. But she was like a scared filly – skittish and wary, with a temper that would flare to protect herself. He only hoped he would be able to convince her that her fears were unfounded if she chose to trust him.

"This is why I must insist that you not tell her of my position," he said, breaking the silence in the room. "I have risen to what she would not believe back then that I could be, and I assure you that my affairs are such that I cannot be cast aside." He straightened a bit. "In fact, it is I who am now able to cast aside if I so choose. My opinions and advice are not given unless I decide they should be shared." He smiled wryly. "Unless, of course, you are the Prince Regent. I find it difficult to put him off very often."

Once again, the room fell silent. Finally, Lady Sophia stood and said, "I shall not share a word." A smile spread across her face and a scheming glint shone in her eyes. "However, that does not mean I will not promote you to her. Are you going to the Hamilton's musicale?"

"I had not thought to," Alex replied.

Lady Sophia shook her head. "Are you going to the Hamilton's musicale?"

Alex nodded slowly. "I am?"

Lady Sophia clapped her hands in delight. "Excellent, so are we."

"I suspect, my boy, that there will be a chair available for you next to my niece," the admiral said with a chuckle.

Lady Sophia shrugged and winked. "I cannot promise, but I would be delighted if you would *happen* join us. This has been such a pleasant interview, in which I learned as much as I could. You are a fine gentleman and worthy of consideration. Financially sound, hardworking, respected, and whatever other descriptors I might find between now and when I speak to Anne."

Alex blinked, somewhat confused by the way in which Lady Sophia was speaking.

The admiral threw an arm around Alex's shoulder. "What do you say we sneak out the back entrance and take a walk so that I can attempt to explain the workings of my sister's mind?"

"That might speed up the process for me," Alex agreed and went to get his hat and coat.

Admiral Fitzwilliam held the door for him to exit. "Firstly, she cannot invite you to join her because if Anne asks, she will be forced to either tell the truth, which she does not wish to have revealed, or lie, which she does not want to do. And before you ask it, no, she is not concealing anything because she never invited you."

Alex glanced at Lady Sophia who tapped her nose, indicating her brother was correct, and then poured herself a fresh cup of tea as the door closed behind Alex and the admiral.

Chapter 7

ANNE CAST A GLANCE at the sitting room door when it opened to allow Lady Sophia entrance. Her eyes wandered to the clock, and she wondered at the length of time of time her aunt had been gone from the room. Had it been more than a quarter hour? She was almost certain it had been. It should not have taken more than a few moments to see that Mr. Madoch was removed from the front of the house and reminded that he was not to put forward a suit. Sadly, he was not a suitable candidate. Perhaps she needed to make those facts plain to her aunt once again.

Yes, she would do just that as soon as she finished with Sir Hugh — she looked at the papers in her lap — Mattingly. She tilted her head to the side. Lady Anne Mattingly. That sounded very acceptable. She turned her attention to Sir Hugh's documents once again.

He was not wealthy beyond measure, but he was solvent and substantially so. She flipped through the papers, looking at his holdings and financial records. Then, she placed them in the stack that was slowly building on the table next to her.

She looked carefully at the gentleman before her. He was not plain. In fact, his face was very like those created from marble by a master sculptor's hand. He held himself with dignity under her scrutiny and merely smiled. That could be a weakness, she noted. He might be far too self-assured to be pleasant. She leaned forward, feigning a need to fix something on her shoe.

"It is such an annoyance when one's slipper catches on one's dress." She had inhaled deeply as she had reached for her foot. He smelled very pleasant. She marked off good hygiene on her mental list. So far, he seemed a very likely candidate.

"Sir Hugh," she said, situating herself back in a proper upright position. "You are a knight, not a baronet, is that correct?"

"It is, indeed, Miss de Bourgh."

"And how did it come to be that you were given the title?" Knighthoods were not inherited, after all.

"There was a matter of some money owed that was forgiven, and as a sign of gratitude, the title was bestowed."

"Do you gamble?" That would be a sad thing, she was beginning to like looking at him and his voice was very pleasant.

"On occasion, but never more than I can afford and always when His Highness demands it."

She raised an eyebrow and contemplated that. "Are you often with the prince?"

"No, no, I have only been invited to play with him a handful of times."

A handful was not so many, but then, to be included in a group so close to the prince did have its merits. It was not as if Sir Hugh had been born to such rank and privilege.

"You say you never wager to excess?" She needed reassurance. Debt was a very easy way for a man, and therefore, his whole family, to fall under the power of another.

"Never. My estate and legacy are far too valuable to risk on an evening's entertainment."

She smiled and relaxed just a bit. He did seem to know the proper answer to give. "And in what other forms of entertainment do you partake? The theatre? Concerts? Riding?"

"I do enjoy an invigorating ride either on horseback or in a curricle and would be most honoured if I were allowed to escort you to the park on a drive."

A drive in the park? Oh, that sounded lovely! He was the first gentleman to ask it of her. But was it wise? Would it raise his expectations too much? There were still things she did not know about him. However, the smile he wore did make the offer hard to resist.

"I think I would like that; however, and you must forgive me for being so forward, there are still two vices about which I must question you."

He chuckled, and Anne suddenly became less concerned with his uprightness and a good deal more eager to drive through the park with him.

"I do not drink to excess," he said. "And I would never consider a mistress after I was married unless my wife made it necessary."

Anne's eyes grew wide, and she blushed at what he implied, which made him smirk. It was a somewhat annoying expression, but it was also quite handsome.

"Do I pass, Miss de Bourgh? May I take you for a drive tomorrow?"

Anne bit her lip and furrowed her brow as if in deep thought. Then after what she deemed was an appropriate length of time for consideration, gave a small nod of her head and extended her hand. "You have succeeded so far as a ride is concerned. We are not yet acquainted well enough to determine if your suit shall succeed above all."

He took her hand and instead of shaking it as she had extended it for him to do, he turned it and placed a kiss gently on her knuckles.

My! Where was one's fan when one needed it?

"Until tomorrow at five, then, Miss de Bourgh," he said as he rose.

"Yes, until then."

Anne tipped her head to the side and allowed her eyes to follow him all the way to the door of the sitting room. He cut quite a stirring figure as he left the room, and since all the other hopeful gentleman had left, she did not bother to check her pleasure at watching him leave.

"He is quite acceptable, I think," she said to Lady Sophia when the front door to Matlock House had closed behind Sir Hugh.

"He is rather attractive," her aunt said from her place of observation to the left of Anne.

Rather attractive was not giving his appearance the credit it was due, but Anne was not certain she should say such, so instead, she picked up his financial reports. "And he is both titled and wealthy."

"He seems practiced." There was a note of caution in her aunt's tone.

"He is two and thirty, Aunt Sophia. I expect a man of such an age has had his share of experience in speaking to a woman." She knew what her aunt was talking about, but she did not want to consider at this moment that the handsome and charming Sir Hugh was anything less than acceptable.

Lady Sophia huffed. "Not as smoothly as he spoke to you. *I* do not trust him, and I think you should take care, but despite my misgivings, I shall allow you to take a drive with him tomorrow. You must remember, however, that it is your uncle and I who have the final word as to whether he is acceptable." She dipped her head to the side and her eyes held Anne's in a demanding stare. "That means that he must impress not only you but us as well."

Anne sighed heavily.

"I love you, Anne," her aunt said softly. "I do not wish for you to be unhappy, and if I fear Sir Hugh will shower you with pretty words now and neglect you later, I will not approve of him. I have seen more of the world than you, my dear. I am not opposed to your seeing it, but I am opposed you being hurt by it."

Anne nodded her understanding. What else could she do when the aunt she loved spoke so fervently about caring for her?

"What did you think of Sir Hugh, Catherine?" Lady Sophia turned toward Anne's mother, who was still in the room but had been only allowed to have a chair in the far corner.

Anne had not wanted her mother hovering. Truth be told, she had not wanted her mother present at all. However, that was a battle she had not felt like engaging in today, and so she had granted her a place in the room from which to watch the proceedings. It had been a good thing, too, after all, when Lady Sophia had been required to deal with Mr. Madoch.

"Oh, he seemed a fine choice. Quite handsome with a charming smile and amiable personality, and do not forget he has a title – minor though it is," her mother effused. "I would not mind him for a son at all."

Anne scowled. Her mother approved of him? That was most definitely a strike against the man.

Lady Catherine rose to look out the window, leaning close to peer at the equipage making its way down the street. "He has a fine carriage and horses. It would make for a comfortable ride to and from Kent and wherever else his estate might be."

"Mother, I am not selecting a driver. I am choosing a husband."

"Oh, yes, yes," Lady Catherine turned back toward Anne. "I know what you are doing, my dear. But you will need an elegant carriage in which to ride. Travel can be a strain and with your ill health…"

"My health is not a concern." She narrowly refrained from adding that her health had never truly been poor. Maladies had come and gone as needed to keep her free from her mother and so she could enjoy her time as she pleased. "I find I have never felt so well in all my life. It must be all the activity and splendour of the season."

Lady Catherine gave a disapproving snort. "If you keep too busy a schedule, you will soon find yourself once again in need of a doctor. I think you would do well to keep to your room for the evening. A long rest would see you certain to impress Sir Hugh on the morrow." She looked around the room and waved her arm in an encompassing motion. "Will there be more of these calls?"

Why could her mother not show a fraction of the care that Lady
Sophia did? It seemed to Anne that her mother was only interested
in having this ordeal of gentleman callers over with and her daughter ensconced in the best carriage one could buy, but then, what
one possessed had always been of most importance to her mother.
Therefore, she should not be surprised by her mother's actions. It
was, after all, the reason she knew that she could not just marry as
she wanted to marry but had to be so careful in her selection of a
husband.

"There will be more calls if more gentlemen come." The sharp
pain Anne felt in her heart coloured her tone. "I shall not just
accept the first seemingly agreeable gentleman and be off to Gretna
Green."

"I should hope not!" Lady Catherine cried. "My heavens! What
a scandal that would be! It is bad enough that you have advertised
for a husband. Were you to hie off to Scotland, there would be no
hope of establishing yourself in polite society." She shook her head.
"I cannot imagine what a gentleman is thinking by presenting
himself to a lady as if he is a sample that needs to be purchased.
Financial concerns should be left to the men. It is the way of
things."

"Yes, Mother." Anne spoke through clenched teeth. She wished
to point out to her mother that having a gentleman present his
assets and credentials was not so different from a lady learning
to dance and sing and perform so that she might be seen as an
acceptable choice, but she knew that would only lead to a long and
protracted argument and a sizeable headache. Neither were things
she wished to endure, so instead she gave her aunt an imploring
look. "Would it not be best if we were to retire to my apartment to
review the particulars of each caller?"

"I think that is an excellent idea." Lady Sophia rose along with
Anne and then followed her from the room.

Chapter 8

"MAY I SEE THE papers you have collected?" Lady Sophia asked Anne as they entered her sitting room.

"Of course." Anne made her way to her favourite settee and, sitting down, removed her slippers. "You were gone for quite some time with Mr. Madoch."

Her aunt looked up from reading the papers and smiled. "He looked cold, so I offered him some tea to ward off any dangers from being chilled. I would not want him to become ill." She returned to her perusal of the financial reports she held.

"Is that all?"

This time her aunt did not lift her eyes from their task as she replied. "We had a lovely conversation along with the tea if that is what you wish to know."

Anne wanted to ask her aunt what they had talked about, but that seemed like it would make her seem more interested in Alex than she should be.

"Your uncle joined us, and then he and Mr. Madoch left together. It seems they know one another – at least in passing – from the time the admiral has spent in various seaside locales. He is quite a lovely young man. It really is too bad that he did not bring any documents like these with him."

Anne laughed. "What would he put on them? That he is a second son with little fortune?"

Her aunt's eyes sparkled with amusement. "Perhaps. He struck me as the very direct sort."

That he was. There was no pretense with Alex. What he said, he did, and what he thought was not hidden any more than it was required to be in certain situations. If only he had a title and a fortune!

"You can place those on this table when you are done," Anne suggested, "and we can sort them into three piles — acceptable and worthy of pursuing, potentially suitable and worthy of a second consideration, and without doubt, never to be considered again."

Lady Sophia held the papers out to her. "I am afraid I am not able to judge your opinion. That being said, the acceptable and those just missing acceptance will need to be reviewed by your uncle and me."

"Yes, I know." Anne rose, took the papers from her aunt, and began sorting. Goodness! There really were not many to put in the first two categories. It seemed it would be much harder to find a husband she would not mind spending the rest of her life with than she had supposed. That was not a very encouraging thought.

"There do not seem to be many of whom you approve," Lady Sophia said as she settled into a chair at the table. "Indeed, it appears that most of your callers were contemptible."

Anne sighed. "They are all so boring." As interesting as a wall in an art gallery without a single painting on or near it.

She pulled herself straight and wagged her head from side to side before standing and speaking in an imitation of a dull gentleman. "Miss de Bourgh, as you can see, my financial reports are in good order." She selected one of the papers from the not-to-be-considered pile and handed it to her aunt. "My father has seen to it that my education is good and the title to which I will ascend is well protected. There shall not be a want of security – not for my estate, not for yourself, and not for our offspring. In fact, my title and my estate have been secure for many years."

She dropped back onto her chair and looked at her aunt in exasperation. "And then they would prattle on about their family's history and the number of sons that had been born and daughters that had been advantageously married. I did not need a history lesson at this meeting, but it seems they thought I did."

She shook her head and returned to sorting. "I tried to stop some of them from proceeding, but it was to no avail. It was like speaking to my mother!" Here she allowed herself a very unladylike growl. There was no way in this world that she would ever consider someone as a husband if they reminded her of her mother!

"And do you know what they did when I asked them about amusements?"

"I am sure I could not say," Lady Sophia replied.

"They had to think for several minutes before they could share an original thought that had not been given to them by their fathers. How does one not know what one likes to do without being told one likes it?"

She placed the last paper in a pile and rose to cross the room "Sir Hugh was the first to offer anything remotely interesting by way of a drive. Not one of the other gentlemen thought to do so. It was as if they did not enjoy speaking to me at all. It was as if meeting me were a mere formality that must be completed."

Lady Sophia chuckled softly as Anne flung herself onto the settee.

"I do not see what is so humorous about it!" she grumbled.

"I find it a trifle amusing that you find *what you requested* to be not at all *what you want*."

Anne sat up. "What do you mean?"

"Your advertisement requested a responsible first-born son – an heir with a fortune, a title, and proper conduct. As usually happens, the more adventurous, and therefore, less dull, heir is a gentleman who is often given to wild ways and excesses which do not lead to financial soundness or particularly virtuous behaviour. Allow me to present Mr. Blackmoore as an excellent example of an undesirable, yet interesting, heir. He is not dull, but he is also not suitable."

That was true. Mr. Blackmoore was not the sort of heir for whom she was looking, but certainly there must be some gentleman somewhere who fit her requirements and was not completely uninteresting. Perhaps —

"Lord Brownlow is not a bore, but he did not present a file. He came merely as a friend." She sighed and draped an arm across her eyes, blocking out the light that was beginning to increase the small pain in her head. "I wish he would have brought his papers. I quite like him, and a lord is better than a sir."

"That it is," Lady Sophia agreed. "Perhaps you should expand your search to include those without a title? It is not the title a gentleman holds that brings the security of a stable home and finances."

"But it brings power," Anne protested. And power was important. "It means that the man in possession of that title has sway over another merely because of his title."

She thought of many of the arguments she had overheard as a child. How many of them had ended with "*but you must remember who my brother is.*" This had always been followed by her father doing whatever it was that he had not wished to do simply because it *would not do* to offend the Earl of Matlock.

She had seen the sadness in his posture and the dimming of the light in his eyes. Her heart had broken for her dear father a little bit more each time she had witnessed it, and she was convinced that it was that constant battering of his pride which had led to his finally succumbing to illness – perhaps not altogether, but in part.

"You are not wrong," her aunt agreed. "A title can give power, but it is not the only thing that can, my dear."

Anne lifted her arm and peeked at her aunt, from whom she received a gentle and understanding smile.

"A lowly man with no title can become quite powerful when he has the one thing that is needed by many — be it money or safety or food," her aunt explained. "And a great man can be controlled by those to whom he owes money. While a man of little feelings for anyone save himself can be powerful due to his cruelty, and a person who possesses knowledge of that which you fear most can sway you with little effort." She shook her head sadly. "My sweet Anne, we cannot guarantee that another will not at some point try to bend us to his will – no matter our standing. Remember what happened in France to those who were of the aristocracy."

Anne shook her head. How was she to find safety and security when so many things threatened? Was it truly impossible?

"Do not look at their title, my dear niece. Look at their character. A man with few worldly possessions but with integrity is better than a king with great wealth and no conscience."

Her smile turned teasing as she rose from where she was sitting. "Do not be alarmed, but I am going to agree with your mother and suggest you have a short rest. We have a musicale to attend, and I would not wish for you to fall asleep during the performance."

She walked over to Anne and held out her hand. "Come. You need a proper rest. Lying here in such a position will only give you a stiff neck and a foul mood."

Anne looked at her aunt's hand for a moment before she took it and rose to her feet. If only all those who held titles were so willing to offer help as Lady Sophia was.

Before allowing her to go to her bedchamber, Lady Sophia drew Anne into her embrace. "I think you are wise to see to your financial future. Very wise. A lady should not blithely dance into her future in that area, but she must also not forget everything else that makes a gentleman a good husband while conducting her analysis of his bank account and holdings. Promise me you will consider what I have said."

Anne squeezed her aunt close and nodded against her shoulder as a tear slipped down her cheek. She could feel the love of her aunt wrapping itself around her mind and heart as tightly as her aunt's arms held her close.

"I will," she promised.

Chapter 9

Anne's uncle, the admiral, stood at the end of a row of chairs while she and her aunt, Lady Sophia, took their seats among the other guests in the Hamiltons' music room.

"These two chairs –" Her uncle indicated the two next to Anne. "Are not to be given away." He raised a brow and gave both Anne and Lady Sophia a hard stare.

To Anne, both the request and the glare were a bit odd. "Of course," she said.

Lady Sophia smiled and made herself comfortable while saying, "Then, be quick, for I will not be held responsible for giving away your seats if a handsome young man or two need them."

"I will not be any longer than is necessary," the admiral said before hurrying away as if he were on a mission to secure the final piece of apple cake on a platter. Her uncle did enjoy a sweet treat, especially cake.

"This is my first musicale of the season." Lady Sophia's excitement at the thought was evident in her tone. "If only you played, it would give you quite the stage from which to draw attention from the gentlemen present."

"I do not like performing," Anne said quickly. "There are too many eyes watching the performer, and most of them are looking to find fault." She shuddered. She had had enough flaws pointed out to her by her mother over the years. She did not need to give strangers an opportunity to do so. "I would not play even if I could."

She turned and took a hasty survey of the room. It was filling quickly. Gentlemen stood around the edges of the it, watching as the ladies and their chaperones arrived — looking, she supposed, for the best choice of listening partner. She laughed to herself and wondered if it was much like this, minus the fine evening clothes, when the gentlemen gathered at Tattersall's.

However, she thought as she took in her surroundings, the furnishings and carpet here must certainly be better than those found at a horse auction.

And my! Was not the room beautifully arranged? Rows of chairs with tufted cream-coloured cushions faced a large, rounded alcove where a pianoforte stood next to a harp. Both instruments had a deep reddish hue and had obviously been carefully polished because they both shone beneath the light of the large chandelier that hung overhead. If one had to embarrass themselves with a performance, Anne was certain there could be no place more beautiful for doing it. She was just glad that she was not among the debutantes that would be called on to entertain.

She was so caught up in looking at the people and splendour of the room that she nearly missed her uncle's return with the friend for whom he had been waiting. She glanced to her left as the admiral took his seat and had just returned her eyes to the painting above the fireplace when her mind grasped who had joined them. Her eyes grew wide at the thought, and her heart thumped loudly beneath the ruffles of her dress.

"Aunt Sophia." She leaned close to her aunt and grasped her arm firmly. "He is in the pile of unacceptable choices."

"No, he is not, my dear. You have not received his portfolio."

Anne glared at her aunt. "For good reason," she muttered.

Her aunt patted the hand that gripped her arm. "Smile and be polite, dear. There are many from the acceptable pile who will be watching. It would do you no good to be thought of as cold and aloof. Besides, Mr. Madoch is a friend of your uncle, and I am sure you would not wish to offend your uncle."

Well, no, she did not want to do that. She loved her uncle far too dearly to wish to offend him, but did she truly have to sit next to Alex to avoid doing so? She leaned toward her aunt once and again and whispered, "Then, may I switch seats with you, so that I do not?"

Lady Sophia laughed and bent to look around her. "It is a pleasure to see you this evening, Mr. Madoch. Is it not, Anne?" She gave her niece a pointed look.

"Indeed, it must be if my aunt says so," Anne replied, turning to greet Alex.

Oh, he was handsome in his blue coat – drat him! And he smelled of cinnamon, mingled with other spices, which only made things worse. He had always smelled of cinnamon. For the longest time after she had refused him, every cup of mulled cider, every spiced cake or biscuit had caused her stomach to knot and clench with regret.

No, no, she told herself, it was not regret. It was... she tapped her finger on her leg trying to think of the best way to describe it to herself so that she would not think of her refusal of him as anything more than what should have happened. He was not acceptable because...

She looked at him as he spoke to her aunt. He did not look like a poor ne'er-do-well. That was unfortunate because if he did, then, she could dismiss him as such. He caught her eye and smiled that smile at her again, just as he had on the balcony of Rycroft Place, and she felt her resolve slip again just as it had then.

He was unacceptable, she reminded herself, because...

Because he is, she concluded. She would spend time later listing the reasons he was to remain off her list of marital candidates. Had he just complimented her?

"I said you look lovely this evening, Miss de Bourgh. That shade of pink has always been well-suited to your complexion."

He *had* complimented her and so sweetly – of all the rotten things for him to do! Gentlemen were not supposed to know if a colour suited your complexion, were they? She narrowed her eyes at the thought. Perhaps he *was* just saying what he thought should be said. That, she thought to herself, was quite acceptable, was it not?

"I have always told her so, myself," her aunt said while using her elbow to give Anne's side a light tap.

It was true. Not only had Aunt Sophia complimented her on her dress, but both Lord and Lady Matlock had as well. She sighed. Alex was not given to pretense. She knew this.

"Thank you, Mr. Madoch."

Her aunt's elbow poked her side again.

"You also look well this evening," she added.

He lifted one shoulder in a faint shrug and gave himself an appraising look. "I do know how to clean up, I suppose."

She rolled her eyes without thinking. He had always had a certain amount of swagger about him. He had never been one to over or understate himself. Well, perhaps he had inflated his value when he claimed that the king would one day look to him for advice, but, beyond that, he been quite accurate in his assessments of his abilities.

"I was not aware that you were a friend of my uncle." At least, she had not been until her aunt had mentioned it earlier.

"To be entirely accurate, the admiral is a friend of my uncle, and I have the good fortune of being my uncle's nephew and that has earned me a coveted spot as a friend of Admiral Fitzwilliam." There was a twinkle in his eye, and the comment received the response Anne was certain it was designed to elicit as the admiral guffawed and slapped Mr. Madoch on the back.

"Do not let him fool you, Anne. He has been as much a friend to me as his uncle has. You cannot find a better man to speak all things horse to you, you know. And even an old sailor like me wants a reliable mount when he is on land. No one knows more about horses than Madoch, and he is always good for a friendly game of some sort — no wagers allowed, however. He is not one to part with his money unnecessarily."

Anne noticed a faint blush creeping above the edge of Alex's cravat. The sight of it surprised her. He was not one to be embarrassed. The tone of his voice in expressing his thanks for the kind words was also new to her. It seemed that he truly cared what her uncle thought of him. This picture clashed with the often-brash persona he had demonstrated when she knew him before. But then, people changed over time, and it had been six years.

"Are you performing?" Alex asked in a whisper as a young lady sat down at the pianoforte and began a short piece which was intended to call them to order. "I know you do not play, but you sing quite well. I have missed the tunes you would sing to the horses. My horse does not enjoy my renditions as much as he did yours."

Anne gave him a small smile but said nothing since the programme was beginning. As Miss Hamilton began to play and sing an Irish air, Anne's thoughts were filled with his words. He had missed her. His words had said it almost as much as his tone. The thought did nothing to comfort her. In fact, it increased that knotting of her stomach caused by something that was *definitely not* regret, although she had yet to decide on what it was.

As the night progressed, young ladies played and sang. Some did so with great enjoyment, glowing in the applause that followed and reluctantly returning to their seats, while others performed as if it was something that was a necessary task but one which held very little, if any, satisfaction. This second group of ladies would take their places quickly and begin with no more than a glance at the audience. Then, as soon as the last note faded, they wasted no time in returning to their chairs. Some performances were delightful while some were truly painful.

By the end of the evening, Anne's cheeks were sore from smiling as she politely clapped for each performance and when she spoke about the weather and this dress and that hat with the various people around her. And all that was mingled with the wonderful, yet torturous, presence of the man next to her, whom she longed for with all her heart, despite telling herself several times that he was not acceptable.

To say she was relieved and delighted when, at last, she was able to exit the Hamiltons' and make her way towards Lady Sophia's coach was stating things mildly. She was, in fact, overjoyed by the prospect of the rest that awaited her in her bed at home. However, her escape to the awaiting bliss was not to be a smooth one, for just as Lady Sophia's carriage had pulled forward and a footman was about to put the steps in place...

"Miss de Bourgh," Sir Hugh said as he approached her, "I had hoped to see you here tonight, but alas, I was delayed and by the time I arrived, the intermission had passed, and, with such a crush of people, it was impossible to make my way to you. I am very glad that I have not missed you entirely."

Anne pulled her tired facial muscles into another smile. It was not that she did not wish to see or speak to Sir Hugh, but she was tired, and her nerves were feeling the effects of the evening. "I am glad you were not disappointed."

Having gained Anne's welcome, Sir Hugh turned to the others in her party, greeting first her aunt and then her uncle.

"Madoch," he said with a tip of his head. "I had heard you were in town."

Chapter 10

"Are you enjoying the season?" Sir Hugh gave Alex what he would call an appraising look, so Alex returned it in kind.

"I have enjoyed the two soirees that I have attended." Alex had no desire to speak with Sir Hugh on the best of days, and he particularly did not wish to speak to him now. Nor did he like the way the man had smiled so fondly while talking to Anne or how Anne had so readily returned his smile.

"Do you know each other?" Anne's eyes blinked rapidly as if the thought of his knowing someone like Sir Hugh was startling to her.

"Oh, indeed," Sir Hugh replied, as if the question were one that had quite the obvious answer, which to most it was – though not to Anne. "Not many a fellow does not know Madoch if he has an interest in horses – and who of the gentry or nobility do not have such an interest? In fact, the horses, which will take us through the park tomorrow on our drive, I purchased on his recommendation, and they are a handsome pair. I think you will easily agree when you see them."

Alex did not miss how Anne's brows furrowed, and he was certain that she was attempting to piece together what she had heard with what she knew of him.

"But Mr. Madoch is in Brighton. Do you often travel to the coast just to learn about which horses to purchase?" Anne asked Sir Hugh.

"I am not always in Brighton, and there is always the mail," Alex replied before Sir Hugh had a chance to utter a word.

"Yes, quite right," Sir Hugh agreed. "I admit that I met Mr. Madock once in Brighton a few years back, but when it came to buying my horses, I merely wrote to him for advice."

Anne tilted her head to the side and looked at Alex with her brows still drawn closely together in confusion. "How can anyone recommend a horse through a letter? Do you not need to see the creatures to know if they are good or not?"

"I had seen them," Alex answered. "And the breeder is reputable. There was no need to doubt that they had been well cared for between when I last saw them and when Sir Hugh sent his inquiry. I had facilitated sales from the seller before with pleasing results."

"Indeed?" Anne's brows rose in surprise. "Were they purchased by your uncle?"

"No. Someone else." He shifted uneasily. While he was pleased that she now knew he was held in high esteem by some, she did not need to know that the horses he now spoke of were numbered among those of the riding school at Brighton. Knowing he was an esteemed businessman would not be enough to make her consider him merely for his position, and he was still determined that she choose him because her heart demanded it, not because he met some ridiculous standard of acceptance.

"Who?"

"Not all the sales I broker are a matter of public record," Alex answered as coolly as he could, hoping that his tone would put an end to this conversation. It was true that not all the sales or purchases in which he had a hand were a matter with which society need be concerned. However, the ones about which he was refusing to talk had been made known publicly.

"Oh, of course." Anne's smile was tight, and Alex cursed the success of his sharp reply.

"Forgive my impertinence," she continued before shivering.

The air was not warm, but Alex wasn't sure if it was the ambient temperature of their surroundings or his reply which had caused the shiver. The Anne he knew was proficient at hiding any sign of weakness.

"Miss de Bourgh, you must not catch a chill." Sir Hugh extended his hand to help her to her carriage.

"Very true," Lady Sophia agreed. "You have a busy schedule of outings and soirees. I would not wish you to miss them on account of standing outside in the night air for too long a period."

Anne hesitated a moment before accepting Sir Hugh's assistance. However, she kept a smile on her lips as she dipped a small parting curtsey to Alex and allowed herself to be escorted to and handed into her carriage. Still, he was going to take that hesitation and the backwards glance in his direction as she entered the carriage as signs that he might eventually find success for his quest.

"You have her confused," the admiral said in a soft voice as he made a show of saying his farewells. "I understand a ride in Hyde Park around five in the evening is the time to see and be seen, or so my sister tells me. I may venture out there myself *tomorrow* to test her theory." He gave Alex a wink and then, chuckling, turned toward the carriage.

Alex shook his head at the admiral's meddling. First, he had flattered Alex in such a way as to tell his niece of Alex's dislike of gambling and his seriousness in considering finances. Now, Admiral Fitzwilliam was suggesting a bit more subterfuge in creating a meeting in the park. He chuckled as he went to find his horse. It seemed Lady Sophia was not the only matchmaker in the family.

"Have you made any inroads?" Jonathan, who had not attended tonight's soiree and who was never anywhere unexpected without a reason, sat on his horse next to where a groom held Alex's.

Alex swung up onto his mount before motioning with his head for his friend to follow him. "Why have you come looking for me?"

"I am curious."

Alex laughed. "No, you are not. You are the least curious person I know. So why?"

"Have you made any progress with Miss de Bourgh?"

"I believe I have. Now, why are you here?

"I heard something."

Alex slowed his horse and drew closer to his friend. "And why is this something of importance to me?" There was no other reason for Jonathan to have tracked him down. It was not as if the fellow was a gossip eager to share tales just for the pleasure of telling the tale.

"It seems that someone has talked the termagant into leaving her lair and going for a ride."

Alex nodded. "I know. Sir Hugh mentioned it this evening."

"You know he cheats."

"Yes, I am aware of that fact. It is why I do not play with him unless I can help it and have money to lose." He sighed. "Why are you telling me things that I already know?"

"He wants her money." Jonathan said it softly and slowly and then just let the idea hang in the air without adding to it.

Alex closed his eyes as the facts fell into place. He had never liked Sir Hugh. Yes, Alex had given him advice about some excellent horses, but that was business. It profited Alex and kept the scoundrel from seeking ways to harass him as he had done with others.

"How?" If anyone knew the plot that was being planned, it would be Jonathan, for he was dreadfully good at being both inconspicuous and attentive.

"That was not agreed upon by the gentlemen I heard. Some think he will force her hand, while others think he will either buy off or spread misinformation about any other suitor who might be a threat. But since they knew of no other suitors, the wager has fallen, for the moment, on his ability to charm her."

It was the answer Alex had expected. Sir Hugh was not only known for making a nuisance of himself among his peers, but he was also a well-practised charmer of the ladies. It was something that Prinny found to be to his benefit. Sir Hugh was sure to attend any function with some pretty lady on his arm and could usually be counted on to lure along at least one or two friends of the lady with whom the prince would flirt while Sir Hugh, through sleight of hand, lined his pockets with the crown's money.

"However," Jonathan continued, "since he has seen you with her this evening, I expect he will do his best to discredit you while he charms her." He drew his horse to a stop and waited for his friend to do the same. "I must ask..."

"Yes," Alex said sharply. "Yes, she is worth the risk."

"You know he will not stop at just trying to lower you in her eyes."

Alex exhaled loudly. "I know." He circled his horse around Jonathan's. "I know that by pursuing her I will risk my position and my future plans, but frankly, neither has any meaning without her."

"You know my opinion, but I am your friend and will stand by you, which is why I did not want you to move ahead blindly."

There truly was no better friend than Jonathan Lester! A smile spread slowly across Alex's face as an idea captured his mind. "Will you also ride beside me?"

Jonathan's eyes narrowed. "I want to say yes, but I would like to know to what I am agreeing before I do so."

"It seems," Alex said lightly, "that five o'clock is a grand time to go riding in Hyde Park." He held his friend's gaze. "Tomorrow," he added in a very serious tone.

Jonathan sighed. "Must we always knock down the hive?"

"Only if we want the honey." Alex nudged his horse to move forward. "And I want the honey, Lester."

Jonathan sighed. "Very well."

Alex heard the resignation in his friend's voice. "You do not have to do this," he said. "I believe the admiral would be happy to ride with me, since it was his suggestion. If it will ease your mind, I will tell you that I do not plan to storm the castle until I am forced to do so. For now, I wish only to make my presence known."

Jonathan shook his head in disbelief. "You have already told her cousins you plan to marry her. You have sat on her step, trying to gain an audience with her, and you are using her aunt and uncle to assist you in your quest. I would say you are already well on your way to storming the castle." He chuckled. "You do typically beat down the front gate rather than waiting for it to be opened for you. You do it quietly and with few casualties, but I fear, my friend, that you are constitutionally incapable of *not* storming the castle."

Alex shrugged. He could not deny it when he looked at it from Jonathan's perspective. Though he had fallen into some fortunate circumstances, he had also quietly beaten down many doors to gain his current position.

Jonathan was still shaking his head. "I cannot believe I am about to say this, and I am not sure I will ever repeat it, so listen carefully, Madoch." He drew a deep breath. "Miss de Bourgh may actually be the best woman for you. She has a backbone; I will give you that — misdirected as it may be." He held up a hand to forestall anything Alex might have to say in reply.

"I do not want to hear it. I just want to get home to my bed. It is best to storm castles when well-rested." He clucked to his horse and was off before Alex had time to more than laugh.

"Not the best woman for me," he called after his friend, "the only one for me."

Chapter 11

ALEX PACED THE LENGTH of the green sitting room at Brownlow's townhouse. Then, he peered through the window before turning and pacing the length in the opposite direction.

"Blasted rain," he muttered for the fourteenth time in the past half hour. There would be no riding in the park and no sitting on the step at Matlock House today. And at present, he did not know where Anne would be this evening. He had hoped to discover that bit of information when he saw her at the park.

"Blasted rain." He inhaled deeply and rapidly and then exhaled just as quickly as he turned to make yet another circuit of the sitting room.

"It is not necessary to wear holes in one's boots before purchasing a new pair," Lord Rycroft said as he entered. "Brownlow will be along soon." He took a seat near the window. "I have recently been made aware of the fact that you are in town to marry my cousin." He tossed his right leg over his left knee.

Alex paused his pacing, tilted his head, and gave Anne's cousin an appraising look. How had the man come to know that information? "That is the plan if the rain ever stops." He turned toward the window at the end of the room.

"Ah, yes, rain will put a damper on outdoor plans such as riding in the park at the fashionable hour, will it not?"

Alex turned back to Rycroft, who raised a brow and steepled his fingers together in front of him while a smile curled his lips. He had definitely been talking to someone and seemed to be entertaining himself quite well by revealing bits and pieces of what he knew.

"How do you know I was planning to ride in the park?"

"My uncle."

Alex sighed in relief. At least it was not from someone who should not know.

Rycroft chuckled. "And my mother. They seem to like you. I cannot imagine there is much more that I need to know about you that my uncle has not already told me. He does not shower praise to earn friends. He only speaks highly of those he deems worthy, and it seems you are worthy." Rycroft shifted slightly in his chair. "I almost feel jealous, for I do not believe I have ever earned such accolades as you have."

Alex shook his head. "I do not know why he feels I deserve them."

"You saved his horse," Jonathan said from the corner and then turned his attention back to his book. "And you are as upstanding as any man ever was, which is one of the reasons so many of us stand with you even when we do not agree with you. You are annoyingly correct." He muttered the last bit in a tone that was very close to a growl.

"Have you met Mr. Lester?" Alex asked Rycroft.

"Not officially, but my uncle could not speak of you without speaking of him. You, Mr. Lester, also seem to hold my uncle's good opinion."

Jonathan inclined his head in acceptance. "That is Madoch's fault," he said with a smile. "As is most of the good fortune I have met in my life." He stood, placed his book on the table, and bowed. "Jonathan Lester, Mr. Madoch's man of business, at your service, my lord."

"Please." Rycroft waved the man back to his chair. "I do not stand on ceremony among friends, and since my uncle has spoken so highly of you both, I intend for us to be friends, unless there is an objection."

"You will get none from me," Alex said as he finally took a seat.

"Which means you will also get no objection from me." Jonathan picked up his book again and ignored the pointed glare that Alex was giving him. "Not that I would have objected if I had been able to form my own opinion."

"Read your book before I sack you," Alex growled.

Jonathan chuckled and opened his book. "That is not possible. I am invaluable, you know."

"Read your book," Alex growled again before turning back to Lord Rycroft. "Would you care for a game?" He motioned to the chess set at the far end of the room. "I admit to being unable to sit unoccupied for any great length of time."

"Especially when there is a plan that is being thwarted by rain," Jonathan added from behind his book.

He sighed. "Especially then."

"You remind me of my cousin Darcy." Rycroft rose from his chair, and Alex followed. "Sitting unoccupied was one thing at which I could best him. Richard and I used to challenge Darcy to a game we called observe or die. It was a bit of a dramatic name, I suppose, since no one actually died, but we were young."

Alex chuckled at the name of the game but could not fault Rycroft and his cousins for it. As a young man, he had preferred to think of his games as more daring than they likely were.

"We would pick a place to sit and an object to observe," Rycroft continued as he took a seat next to the table on which sat the chessboard and pieces. "And then, we would see who could hold their position the longest. I never won — Richard always did — but I also never lost. Darcy was always the first to quit the field, claiming he had something that needed his attention."

Rycroft arranged his pieces on the board. "However, place a book or a tiring pile of estate papers before him, and he will out-sit me every time." He chuckled. "And this is one game in which I hesitate to ever accept his challenge."

"He should play Lester."

"Good, is he?"

Alex nodded. "He can see things a few steps ahead of most people. It is part of what makes him invaluable." He smiled slowly as he placed his last piece. 'I have, however, on occasion, beaten him.'"

Rycroft sighed. "Are you telling me then that I have no hope?"

Alex chuckled. "My mind is a bit busy devising a plan to replace the one that has been washed away by the rain. You stand a very good chance of winning unless I can find my concentration."

Rycroft pulled a paper from his pocket. "Then I likely should not give you this as you may find it helpful in creating a new plan." He handed the note to Alex. "My mother and my wife have agreed that tonight would be an excellent night for dinner and games. Neither of them had any other soiree to attend, and, as you know, it is raining. I must warn you, however, that Anne will be there as will be the Darcys, Richard, Miss Bennet, and the Bingleys." He sighed. "Including Miss Bingley." Rycroft turned to his friend, Brownlow, who had just joined them. "Will you attend, Brownlow?"

"My sister has committed us to another dinner for this evening, and since I expect to be adding the man and his family to my own, I dare not try to alter the plans."

"Oh!" Rycroft sat up as if someone had poked him in the back. "I nearly forgot that my wife's aunt and uncle will be there and her youngest sister, who has just arrived in town to assist Kitty in wedding preparations." He rolled his eyes.

Alex gave him a puzzled look. "That seems a rather normal thing to have a sister help another sister prepare."

Rycroft chuckled. "Miss Bennet has four sisters. One of her sisters is, of course, my wife. Another is Darcy's wife, and the third is Bingley's. Miss Lydia's help is not needed, but I suspect her mother is hoping that she might be thrown in the path of some wealthy gentleman, and wedding clothes seemed as good reason as any to send her to town."

"That seems reasonable to me," Brownlow said from where he stood behind Rycroft, studying the chessboard. "I am sure if I had five daughters to see secured, I would take every opportunity available."

"She is sixteen." Rycroft moved a piece on the board.

Alex whistled softly. "That seems a trifle young to be sending her out into society."

"It is." Rycroft studied the board after Alex had made his first move. "You and Lester will come, will you not?"

Alex nodded. "Yes, and thank you."

"Good."

"I have called for tea in half an hour," Brownlow said. "Until then, I shall let you get on with your game, as I would prefer to follow Mr. Lester's lead and read."

Alex watched Brownlow stop and pick out a book from a shelf near where Lester sat. Then, he turned his eyes back to the chessboard and tried to school his mind into concentrating on the game instead of the good fortune of being able to see Anne that evening.

Two games were begun and finished within the span of time it took for tea to arrive. The first game had not gone well for Alex, but the second had seen him come very close to winning.

Rycroft let out a breath as if relieved of the possibility of a third game as the tea things were being set up.

"I am absolutely certain you would have had me at a distinct disadvantage in another round," he said while placing his pieces back on the board. "Your concentration seemed to return a quarter of the way into that second match." He chuckled. "It was also about the same time that your sole remaining knight was threatened."

Alex picked up the chess piece in question and smiled ruefully. "I do hate to see a horse endangered, and it is my belief that a king should be left with at least one noble steed when he meets his demise."

"That is the key to it," Jonathan said around a mouthful of pastry. "Threaten his knights, and he'll leave his king to save the horses. For him, it is about the horses. It is always about the horses."

He gulped down a bit of tea, seemingly unaware of the glare Alex leveled at him or the chuckles of the other gentlemen. He was not unaware of what was going on around him, of course. Jonathan was rarely oblivious to his surroundings.

"Before you begin threatening to sack me again, Madoch," he said, "I must add that that is precisely what makes you the best at what you do."

"Well said," Brownlow agreed. "I have only heard good of you."

"And that," Alex said dryly, "is another reason why I cannot sack Lester. He has an irritating way of making sure I do not ruin my reputation with a hasty decision. Like I said, he has a knack of seeing things a few steps ahead of most people."

Chapter 12

ALEX LEANED BACK IN his chair next to the small table on which the tea service was laid out and took up his cup.

"I find it difficult to believe that you would do anything in haste." Rycroft directed the statement to Alex. "You seem to be more of the calm and calculating type of gentleman rather than the rush ahead and let things fall where they may sort."

Jonathan snorted. "To a point," he agreed, "but pass that point and all bets are off, gentlemen. He would cut ties with his mother if she crossed him."

"I would not!"

"That is only because she would not cause you to ever have a need to prove me right."

"I say, you two have a very different relationship," Rycroft said. "But my uncle did mention that it was equal parts camaraderie and business."

Alex shook his head. "Truth be told, it is more friendship than business. We are nearly brothers, or, I should say, Lester is more of a brother to me than mine ever was."

"That is because we share a common interest. Your brother knows nothing about horses other than they are needed to drive his carriage and provide a means to escape the house in the morning, and, added to that, he sees your pursuit of them as only a waste of legal training."

That did sum up his brother's opinion about horses quite well and stated the main point of contention between him and his father. Alex's soft chuckle at the apt description was tinged with the bitterness that came with the strained relationship he had with the other men of his family.

"You do not lie," he agreed. "Neither he nor father was pleased when I refused to take up my robes and instead took a position with my uncle." He placed his cup on the table.

From the looks of interest on the faces of his companions, he felt his relationship with Jonathan needed some explanation. "I clerked for a year after my graduation. As was my custom in any area where I found myself, I learned who had the best horses and grooms. One of those grooms happened to have a son who was more interested in learning accounting and bookwork than in learning how to mend a harness. I traded what I knew of the subjects for the opportunity to learn what he did not wish to learn."

"He already knew how to mend a harness." Jonathan's mouth was once again full of pastry.

Alex shrugged. "True, but your father knew things that I did not, and I wanted him to share them with me." He turned toward Rycroft. "Lester's father is, in my opinion, one of the best grooms I have ever met." He smiled. "He is a man of excellence in his field, tucked away in the country, serving a country squire and as happy as any man could ever be."

"Sharing his knowledge with me," Jonathan said, "and gleaning what he could from my father kept Madoch from having to attend many social functions."

That had been quite the boon to the relationship. "I only had to attend one assembly and two or three card parties during the entirety of my term. It annoyed my employer's wife to no end, which pleased him quite well. Of course, when I did attend a soiree, I used the opportunity to meet the gentlemen of the area – that also did not please my employer's wife." He pursed his lips and thought for a moment. "I think I managed to only be required to partner one or two young ladies for a dance. They were lovely, but my heart was not available, and my plans were not to be fulfilled through courting."

"Ah, see, I was right!" Rycroft cried. "Cool and calculating."

"More like driven," Jonathan muttered.

"I find it admirable," Brownlow said. "I wish I had thought of pursuing the breeding and sale of cattle as a means to avoid social events."

Rycroft chuckled. "You are an earl, and I have never seen you at a loss for entertainment at a soiree. And, I feel as though it is my duty in my mother's stead to remind you that, unlike a second son, there is a certain level of expectation on the one to whom an inheritance and title fall."

"Do not," Brownlow grumbled, "begin speaking to me about duty, or I shall toss the lot of you out into the rain."

"It is not so bad," Rycroft said with a smile. "In fact, it can be most delightful to fulfill one's duty."

"We cannot all be so fortunate as you, Rycroft."

"Why not?" Alex looked from one gentleman to the other. Brownlow's was an attitude that had long bothered him. "I see no reason why every man, titled or not, cannot find happiness in marriage. It does not need to be a matter of chance."

"The strictures of society prevent it," Brownlow answered. "It is nearly impossible to get to know a lady. She is told how to speak, what to say, what not to say, how to laugh and bat her eyelashes. It is nothing more than a show. They are all actresses, but their stage is not in a theater: it is in a ballroom or a drawing room."

Alex tipped his head to the side as he considered what Brownlow had said, but he could not – would not – accept it. There had to be a way. "Perhaps you are not looking in the proper places then. It cannot be as hopeless as that."

"You must excuse my friend's opinions, for he still does not attend functions to spend time with ladies," Jonathan inserted before turning his attention to Alex. "I assure you, Madoch, that what Brownlow says is true. You should pay more attention to these things."

"Then I do not see why it must continue in such a fashion." He shook his head. "What gain can there be in being tied to someone whom you deceived into accepting you?"

Jonathan sighed as if they had had this conversation before, which they had, and it was bound to be one they would have again since Lester seemed unwilling to admit that society could and should change.

"It is not a deception," he said. "It is showing oneself to best advantage."

"Presenting perfection is deception," Alex countered. "There is not one person living or dead, save the good Lord himself, who is perfect. Why must one pretend to be such? It will surely only bring disappointment and embarrassment when the truth is discovered. It is much better to simply be yourself." He scowled. "Unless, of course, yourself is entirely unacceptable. Then one might try a bath and some lessons in etiquette," he held up a cautioning finger, "not acting."

A small growl emanated from Jonathan, and Alex could see the storm clouds brewing in his friend's demeanour. It would blow through quickly. He would make his point. Alex would counter it, and then, all would be well. Therefore, he paid no mind to the noise of displeasure and selected a sweet treat from the tray.

"Then, my friend," Jonathan said in a flat but serious tone, "why do you insist on concealing your true value and connections? Are you not lying to try to win Miss de Bourgh's hand?"

"No, I am not."

"How are you not?" Rycroft asked.

"Concealing would mean I am covering up a truth. I am not." A small amount of guilt had begun to form in Alex's mind. It did seem to be a bit less noble now that he heard himself defend it.

"A sin of omission is still a sin," muttered Jonathan.

Alex paused, taking as long as possible to chew the morsel of cake he had just popped into his mouth. Perhaps his friend was correct. Perhaps he was being just as deceitful as the many misses who stood in the ballroom saying only what they were allowed and never straying from the prescribed form of behaviour. He swallowed and took a sip of tea to rinse the stickiness from his palate.

"Not presenting her with my circumstances is necessary," he said.

"So you admit I am right." Jonathan had crossed his arms and was glaring at his friend.

"I maintain that I am concealing nothing." Alex straightened a sleeve. "I am merely not revealing all — and for very good reason. I must know the truth of her heart, and if she knows all, that truth will be clouded."

"How do you suppose she will respond when she discovers that you have not been open with her about your standing?"

She would likely bluster. Alex let out a frustrated breath. Perhaps his plan was not as good as he had thought it was. "Miss de Bourgh has already discounted my success as an impossibility. She would not believe me if I told her."

"Then show her," suggested Jonathan. "Take her to St. James's."

"No!" His frustration pushed him to his feet. "That place is not fit for a proper lady — at least it has not seemed to be when I have been there." He paced the length of the room and returned. "And then, how would I know if she chose me for me and not for my connections?" That issue still remained. "Perhaps I should cut my ties to the place. Then there would be nothing to omit. I would be as she declared me." He scrubbed his face with his hands.

"Perhaps the rain will clear," commented Brownlow causing all eyes to turn toward him. "If the rain clears, then you could go for a ride. Nothing clears the mind more than a lonely jaunt on a horse."

"Not always," Rycroft said before turning the conversation back to the topic. "If you cut ties from His Highness, what will become of you? What do you have to offer my cousin?" He smiled and softened his tone. "Aside from your heart, of course."

Alex drew a breath. "I have a small estate left to me by a distant relation. An entailment," he explained. "It is near Brighton, and I travel to it regularly, but my main residence to this point has been a small house in Brighton. I see no need to rattle around an estate except when needed to see that improvements are begun to aid in the raising of horses... some fence repairs, a new stable, some slight alterations in the planting of crops, that sort of thing."

"And you would take that as your primary residence and livelihood?"

Alex nodded. "I have set aside a substantial sum for future living and would still offer my services in assisting gentlemen to find horses to meet their needs, even if they are not my horses." He smiled at Rycroft's chuckle.

"It is a well-thought-out plan," said Brownlow, "except for one thing. Will you be able to sever your ties to the school at Brighton?"

"Perhaps not completely."

"But we have considered that," Jonathan said with a smile. "We entered the agreement with the prince knowing that, eventually, we might need an escape."

Alex clapped his friend on the shoulder. "As I said, gentlemen, Lester here sees several steps ahead, which makes him invaluable."

The men spent several more moments in conversation regarding horses and plans, hearts and ladies before Brownlow moved to break up the group by citing a need to prepare to accompany his sister to her dinner party.

"I dare say my wife will be wondering what has become of me." Rycroft stood. "Although," he said with a smile, "a few more minutes might earn me a scolding. Perhaps I shall stay."

Brownlow shook his head. "You are incorrigible," he called as he left the room.

"I am not staying," Rycroft called after him. He moved toward the door and then turned back. "Do not tell Anne. Arrange your life as if she has accepted you. Present your financial papers to her if you wish, but do not tell her about your connections. If she discovers them, so be it." He looked levelly at both gentlemen. "I agree with Madoch. Marriage should be based on mutual affection. Do not settle for less." He gave them each a bow of his head and then left.

"Will you present your papers?" Jonathan asked.

"Not yet. If I knew beyond a doubt that she still harboured feelings for me – which I think she does – then I might. I do not wish to live my life wondering if she loved me or my money. I am sorry. I know it is not what you wish to hear, but I have seen one marriage too many where wealth was the only thing that both the husband and wife liked about each other." His had not been an unhappy home when he was growing up, but his parents' strained relationship was not the ideal he sought.

"Shall I write his majesty a letter stating a desire to meet?" Jonathan asked as they climbed the stairs to their guest rooms.

Alex nodded. "It will take time." Gaining an audience with the prince was not easy, although, for those on whom he relied for advice and who were directly involved with his ventures such as the riding school, as Alex was, it was not quite so difficult. Still, his majesty moved only when his majesty deemed it to be suitable.

"Have you ever wondered," Jonathan said as he stood outside his room, "why Miss de Bourgh insists on wealth and position?"

"What do you mean?"

"I know why you insist on a love match and why wealth has been of little value to you beyond seeing that it is accumulated to provide for a family. Your father and mother's marriage is not one for which you wish." He shrugged as he opened the door. "Could it be possible that she has a similar reason?" He stepped into his room and, closing the door, left a gaping Alex standing in the hall, pondering his words.

Chapter 13

WHILE ALEX WAS PACING the drawing room at Lord Brownlow's home, Anne was once again discovering that what she *thought* she wanted was not, in fact, what she wanted.

Since the drawing room was currently free of visitors who were there to see her, she excused herself and took herself down the hall and into the library. Closing the door, she leaned against it and expelled a frustrated breath. There had been half a dozen callers today, and, on paper, all of them appeared to be exactly what she sought. However, just as on the previous day, this set of gentlemen was as exciting as a long and wordy sermon by her mother's parson, and that was not what she wished to endure every day for the rest of her life.

She pushed off the door and ran her fingers along the backs of chairs and tops of tables as she made a circuit of the room. Then, she stood in the middle of library and turned a complete circle. This is what she wanted. A life designed as elegantly as this room and filled with fine things and tales of adventure, nothing extra-ordinary, but small trips, little visits, friends whose very presence filled you with joy. This room felt safe. This room felt full.

The drawing room, on the other hand, though filled with people, had felt empty, and her footing in there had felt as if she were walking on the top rail of a narrow fence – one wrong step and she would plummet into some sort of injury. Every potential suitor who had called since she had placed that ad in the paper were qualified. They had titles. They had wealth. And not all of them were insupportably lacking in countenance or carriage, though a few were rather wanting in one or both areas.

She shook her head. Why, if they were acceptable, did she feel as if they were not? It was most vexing! How was she to choose a suitable husband?

She was so caught up in her contemplations that she jumped at the sound of a soft knock. She turned toward the sound just as the door opened slowly.

"I apologize for disrupting your solitude, Miss de Bourgh." Sir Hugh stepped into the room and left the door slightly ajar but nearly closed. "I saw you go into this room as I entered, and I was afraid you were distressed. Are you well?" He crossed the room and came to stand near her.

"I am. I just needed a few minutes to think." She smiled at him as if her troublesome thoughts had not just turned to consider how his arrival had disturbed the tranquility of the room and to wonder if it was just because he had entered and spoken or if it was something more. "It is a grey and dreary day, is it not?"

"I was sorry to see the rain," he said. "I am afraid our drive will have to be postponed. That is what I came to tell you." He took a step closer. "I was also rather hopeful that in place of our drive, you would allow me to spend a few moments with you doing something – perhaps reading or playing the piano?"

"Do you play?" That would be lovely if he did. She loved to listen to an accomplished pianist whenever she could.

Sir Hugh blinked. "No... well... yes, but just a bit," he stammered.

Well, that was disappointing.

"Then you are far more accomplished than I," she admitted while fixing her eyes on one of the flowers that decorated the rug on which they stood. "I attempted to learn, but to no avail. Playing is not my talent." She glanced up at him and then returned her eyes to the flower. Somehow speaking to a flower was much easier than speaking to the handsome man beside her.

"While I do not play, I can sing. However, I do not perform." She flinched as he placed a hand on her arm and then slid it down to grasp her hand. Not because it was unpleasant. It was not. It was startling.

"I apologize if my desire to spend time with you has made you feel uneasy," he said as he led her to a settee near the window. "It was not my intent, and I do hope you will not fault me for it. I am willing to do whatever you choose."

"Why?" Anne arranged her skirts about her as she took a seat. She found her tingling fingers and fluttering tummy to be unsettling, and so before they could disconcert her any longer, she chose to redirect the conversation and keep her hands safely out of his.

"What do you mean?" He was blinking at her in a startled fashion once again.

"I do not like to play games, Sir Hugh," she said softly. "I find it best to be as direct in my dealings as is acceptable." She tipped her head to the side, furrowed her brows, and pursed her lips for a moment before adding, "Although I seem to not always know where acceptable ends and forward begins."

It was a dreadful thing to be so. It had not been while at Rosings, but here, in town, it did seem to be a rather unhelpful trait. She shook herself slightly from her contemplation of that and continued with what she had intended to tell him.

"I see no reason to make this ordeal anything more than it has to be. I have advertised for a husband. I do not expect a love match, but rather a pleasant business arrangement. I shall serve as hostess and attend to all the duties expected of a wife while my husband will tend to his duty of providing securely for myself and any children. A friendship would be desirable, of course, but I am under no illusion that one must swoon with admiration in the presence of her spouse to have a comfortable and pleasant life."

She folded her hands in her lap as her heart whispered that a marriage could be more, and a fleeting image of Alex passed through her mind. She pushed them both away. That was not a match that was meant to be. It would be unwise. She must focus on the reality of her situation and making as wise a choice as she possibly could. The safety and security of her future depended upon it.

"My desire," she continued, "is not to hear pretty words but to become familiar with you to see if we would suit. You need not pretend to be enamoured of me."

He was blinking at her again. "I do not pretend," he finally said. "I find you pleasing to the eye, and your forthrightness, while I must admit it takes me by surprise, is quite refreshing." His eyes swept over her figure. "Very pleasing," he said with a smile. "It would not be a hardship to fulfill my duties as your husband," he muttered just loudly enough for her to hear as he took her hand once again.

If he had expected her to blush, he was not to be disappointed. How could she not blush? He was being quite improper! However, if he had expected her to quietly turn the conversation, he was to be startled once again. There were things she needed to know.

"You mentioned before that you would not take a mistress after you were married unless it became necessary." Despite the heat flooding her face and the rapid beating of her heart from the anxiety she felt at discussing such an indelicate topic, Anne continued, "I assume that it will become necessary should you find me not satisfying?"

He cleared his throat. It was obviously not what he had expected her to say. "I meant if my wife turned me away."

Her brows furrowed. Having wrested as much information as possible from her governess, a young, widowed woman who found it necessary to support herself, Anne knew about what happened between a man and a woman once married. "But a wife must turn her husband away at times when she is incapable of receiving his attentions."

"I did not speak of indisposition but of refusal when no need for such exists."

She nodded. The words of Mr. Blackmoore on the balcony about how many men kept mistresses still played in her mind. She did not wish for a husband who would take a mistress after they were married, nor did she wish to be betrothed to a man who currently had one. "One more question, and then we shall put this improper topic away. Do you have a mistress now?"

"I do not see how that affects the discussion of our marrying. Whether I do or do not have a mistress now, I shall not once I marry."

She pulled her hand from his. "Then, you do have one?"

"I did not say I did," he retorted.

"Nor," she shot back, "did you say you did not. Therefore, I will assume you do."

She rose to her feet. She knew she should dismiss him as she had Blackmoore, but there was part of her that still wished to see him. It was wrong, she supposed, to allow him to remain merely because he was attractive, but she would give the rightness or wrongness of her decision to allow him to stay more consideration later. For now, she was going to take the opportunity to spend some time with a gentleman doing something other than reviewing financial papers and listening to family histories.

"I must say it is a mark against you," she said, turning to look at him. "Not that you have a mistress, per se – although I do not condone it, of course – but because you attempted to conceal the fact. Deceit is a far more grievous sin." Her heart pricked at the thought of his perfidy. She should not trust him, it seemed to say, but instead of paying heed to its whispering, she took a breath and smiled at Sir Hugh.

"You are not to be discarded for one error, so if you wish to spend an hour with me once my other guests have left, I prefer poetry about nature to the sonnets of Shakespeare. I am certain you will find something suitable on the shelves of this room. Until then, Sir Hugh." She dipped a curtsey and turned to leave, but he caught her hand and, rising, pulled her into his embrace and kissed her quite soundly.

"In case I am dismissed for some other error, I did not wish to leave without a taste of your sweet lips," he explained before kissing her once again. "Delicious," he whispered as he broke the kiss but not his hold on her.

Anne felt as if her legs were about to fail her. Shock and pleasure fought for dominance in her mind. She willed her arms to push away from him, but they would not listen. And so, she remained wrapped in his delightful embrace until a gasp – a familiar, criticizing gasp – caused her formerly unwilling body to move quite forcefully and rapidly away from Sir Hugh.

"Anne!" Her mother stood for a moment looking at her and, then with another less displeased gasp and a small smile, she turned toward the hall and called for her sister and brother.

"Mother!" Anne took Lady Catherine by the arm and attempted to pull her into the library. "It is not necessary to call for my aunt and uncle."

"Is it not?" Lady Catherine fairly sang the question. Looking into the room, she added, "He is an excellent gentleman. So handsome. It was very clever of you to arrange a compromise. Wishing to see me, indeed! I should have known you would never call me for some trivial thing."

Anne was certain her heart had dropped to her toes. "Call you?"

"Yes, yes, Harrison said you wished to see me."

"I never called you." Anne gripped her mother's arm more tightly and once again attempted to pull her into the library. Why would Harrison lie to her mother like that?

"Oh, but you did, and you had left in such a haste that I assumed you were unwell. However, I could not get away from my guests quite as quickly as I would have liked, but then, it seems I was just in time." She looked around Anne to Sir Hugh and sighed happily. "Such a fine-looking son I shall have. You are such a clever girl."

Chapter 14

ANNE'S MOUTH HUNG OPEN as she stared at her babbling, excited mother. This could not be happening. Surely, her mother was not going to force her to marry Sir Hugh, was she?

"I assure you, Mother, that I did not send for you. I was not unwell. I just needed a few moments of quiet and then, Sir Hugh arrived..." Her eyes grew wide, and her thought hung unfinished as she began to grasp what had actually happened. The cad had planned this!

"Yes, he did, did he not?" Lady Catherine's voice was nearly gleeful. "Such a clever girl," she said. "Sophia, Anne is to marry Sir Hugh."

Anne shook her head. "No. I am not!"

"Oh, but why else would you be kissing him?"

"Mother, please," Anne said. "Keep your voice down. Do you wish for everyone to know?" She tugged again on her mother's arm and this time, with the help of her aunt, managed to guide Lady Catherine into the library.

Admiral Fitzwilliam closed the door as Lady Catherine was being seated. "What has you bellowing in such an unladylike fashion, Catherine?" His voice was nearly as severe as the glare he directed at Sir Hugh, who nervously straightened his jacket. "Anne will be marrying no one unless she has my approval."

"You must give it," Lady Catherine said. "He has kissed her, and so he must marry her."

"Do you wish to marry Sir Hugh?" The admiral turned his ferocious gaze from Sir Hugh and directed it more softly at his niece.

"I had thought I might, but no." She shook her head slowly. "No, I do not. He planned this." Her voice wavered as she tried to contain her emotions. How dare he do this to her? How dare he attempt to take her choice from her?

"There you have it, Catherine," the admiral said. "Anne shall not be marrying Sir Hugh."

"But she must!" Lady Catherine cried. "Think of the scandal if she does not."

"How will there be a scandal?" Lady Sophia asked. "No one knows of this outside of this room."

"And they shall never know of it," added the admiral.

Anne shivered slightly at the danger contained in the tone of her uncle's warning, and yet no matter how foreboding his tone, it was comforting. He wished to know her desires and would see that they were fulfilled if he could.

Sir Hugh must have heard the warning, as well, because he lowered his eyes and mumbled his agreement.

Lady Catherine, however, seemed impervious to the tone. Either that or she was just unwilling to comply. Whichever it was, she was not through attempting to see her daughter married. "The door was open. There are servants, and we had guests. It is possible that the tale will be spread, and one cannot control how it might alter in the telling."

"I will not allow the marriage, and Anne cannot marry without my approval. That is the end of it," the admiral said. "Added to that, Anne has not accepted any offer, and as far as I know, none was made. Whatever tale we might encounter must be refuted as a lie." He turned to Sir Hugh. "I suspect your welcome as a suitor has run its course. We shall remain cordial unless you insist it be otherwise. Any unwanted advances toward my niece or whispers about her will be counted as an insistence."

Anne watched the way Sir Hugh's mouth tightened, and his eyes narrowed just a bit before he nodded, gave his agreement, and took his leave.

Lady Catherine threw her hands up in the air. "I begin to wonder if you will ever marry. First, you refuse your cousin and make a spectacle of yourself with an announcement. Now, you allow a gentleman liberties and refuse his suit!" She huffed and flopped back in her seat. "There will not be a proper gentleman in all England who will consider you if you continue as you have."

"Catherine," Admiral Fitzwilliam growled. "Your daughter has taken an unconventional route to finding a husband, but she has done nothing wrong in refusing a man such as Sir Hugh."

"Nothing wrong?" Lady Catherine harrumphed. "He seemed a proper gentleman."

"*Seemed*, I believe, is the correct word," Lady Sophia said softly. "Not all who appear to be proper are." She placed a comforting arm around Anne's shoulders. "It is a disappointment when the truth is discovered; however, we were fortunate to learn of it before connections could not be reversed."

"I would like to go to my room." Anne's head was beginning to throb, and her chest felt tight and painful.

"A rest might help," Lady Sophia agreed. "You are expected at dinner at Rycroft Place this evening. You would not wish to disappoint Lady Rycroft." Her lips curled into a smile as they always did as she said the title.

Anne knew how happy her aunt was to have added Mary to her family. Anne also knew how happy Mary and her cousin were. She attempted to smile in return, but the tightness of her chest kept her from succeeding.

"I will accompany you," Lady Sophia said. "Reginald, please have a bit of something sent up, and Catherine, inform Harrison that Anne is not home to any other callers today."

She paused for a moment before giving her sister a pointed look. "If you love your daughter at all, you will not speak about what happened here with anyone."

"If I love my daughter!" Catherine harumphed. "Of course, I love my daughter."

"Then, you will want what is best for her," the admiral said as he offered her his arm. "Just as we all do," he added with an encouraging smile for Anne before escorting her mother from the room.

Anne followed her uncle and mother from the room and started on her way to her room with Lady Sophia. Her limbs felt as heavy as her heart did.

"Are you well?" her aunt asked as they took the stairs side by side.

Anne nodded and then gave a small shrug. How was one supposed to feel when one had been tricked? Part of her wished to run after Sir Hugh and make him explain why he had done what he had done, while another part longed to forget all that had just happened, climb under her covers on her bed, and begin the day again.

"You are an attractive match," her aunt said as if she knew what Anne had been thinking. "You have both wealth and connections, as well as beauty." She opened the door to Anne's room and entered.

Anne crossed to the window and looked down at the wet street. She saw people moving quickly from house to carriage and servants scurrying on their errands with collars pulled high and hats pulled down against the weather.

"I stood here this morning," she said, not turning from the scene, "and I was upset because I would not be able to go for a drive. I have never been on a drive with a gentleman, you know." She sat on the cushion in the window seat and kicked off her shoes. She pulled her feet up under her skirts but remained positioned in such a way that she could still watch the people below.

"If he had attempted a compromise in public, I would have been forced to marry him." She drew a shaking breath. "I would have found myself precisely where I did not wish to be, unable to do as I wanted because someone had more power than I did." She rested her head against the wall at her back. Weariness pressed down upon her. "How does one remain safe?" Would she always feel as if she was struggling to be seen and heard? Was that just how her life was supposed to be?

Lady Sophia joined Anne at the window. "Safety is never guaranteed."

Anne sighed. "Then, how am I to choose?"

"What did your heart tell you about Sir Hugh? Did it feel safe when in his presence, or was it excited or maybe unsure?"

Anne considered the question and thought of how her heart had told her to dismiss Sir Hugh, but her mind had overruled her heart. If she had but listened. She shook her head at her own foolishness.

"It was unsure. I liked his attention and found him handsome, but I never felt at ease. I thought I might learn to feel so. After all, I had only met him and knew very little about him."

Lady Sophia patted Anne's knee. "Just so. Your heart is an excellent guide if you will listen to it carefully. It is not above being tricked, but there will often be that little worry, hanging at the back of your mind, when your heart desires something it should not. Let it guide you, and then ask for advice. I will always tell you the truth. You know that, do you not?"

"I do." Anne gave her aunt a small smile and then turned her attention to the scene outside her window. There was only one gentleman who had ever made her feel safe, but he was not a wise choice because he had neither wealth nor position enough to not be constantly swayed to do what he might not wish to do by someone like her mother or her uncle, Lord Matlock. If only she could marry where her heart wished. She sighed and attempted to turn her mind away from comparing Sir Hugh and Alex.

However, her thoughts and the silence which reigned in the room were unbroken until a tray containing two small glasses of sherry and a few biscuits arrived.

"Marrying for love alone is not enough," Anne said as she took a sip of sherry and wrinkled her nose. It was not her favourite drink.

"And I believe, unlike your mother or Lady Matlock, that marrying for position alone is also not enough," her aunt countered. "Matrimony is a tricky business."

"It is indeed." Anne ate a biscuit in silence and finished her drink. If there were truly no way to be safe in marriage, then, why marry? Perhaps that was her answer.

"Marriage is not for everyone," she said more to herself than her aunt. "I did not want to always live in my mother's house." She shrugged. "I had hoped to have a home of my own to run, but perhaps it is not to be. Maybe I should return to Rosings and find some work to occupy my time – a charity perhaps?"

Lady Sophia placed her empty glass on the tray and then crossed to Anne and kissed her forehead. "You need a rest. I do not believe you are destined to remain unwed." She cupped her niece's chin and lifted it so that Anne looked up at her. "Let your heart choose," she said gently. "Promise me you will give it a bit more time before returning to Rosings? I would miss you dearly if you left too soon."

Anne could not help but smile. Was it possible to exchange her mother for her aunt? She loved how loved she felt when with Lady Sophia.

"I will not return to Rosings until after I have visited Hertfordshire and have shared in the celebration of my cousin Richard's wedding. However, if I have not found a prospect by then, I shall go home with my mother."

Lady Sophia kissed her on the forehead once again. "You are not giving me very long to help you, but I will do my best." She turned to leave. "Do you wish to sort the papers from today's visit after your rest?"

"Have them placed in my sitting room," Anne replied with a nod.

"Very well. I shall see you at dinner?" There was a slight lift of uncertainty in her voice.

"You will," Anne assured.

"Rest well." Sophia closed the door softly.

Anne climbed onto her bed. She knew it would be more comfortable to undress, but she did not wish to call for her maid. She wished to lie here in her tangled mess of emotions alone and dismiss them in sleep. To that end, she closed her eyes and drew a deep breath of the peaceful, soundless air and released it slowly and repeatedly until, finally, her mind drifted away from the worries of the day and into the land of dreams.

Chapter 15

ANNE TURNED TO THE right and then the left as she stood in front of the mirror. She pulled her shoulders up and back and looked again from side to side. Satisfied with what she saw, she dismissed her maid.

She stood for a few more moments where she was and ran a finger along the gold chain of her necklace as she thought. Her sleep had been refreshing to her body and partially to her mind. The removal of one man, no matter how handsome or charming he might have been, did not mean her search was at an end. There were many more names on papers in the sitting room. Surely one of them might prove to be an appropriate – even wise – choice. It might even be possible for her to speak to her uncle and have the most promising candidates investigated. That way, she could know more about them than what they presented.

"It is a good plan," she said aloud before giving her reflection a nod and turning to leave the room.

That lingering feeling of never being truly safe hung at the edges of her mind as she descended the stairs which she had only hours ago climbed in search of refuge from events that had transpired in the library.

She drew a long breath – one which took two whole steps down the stairs to complete – and instructed herself that with her exhale, she would push all thoughts of duplicitous men from her mind.

"You look lovely." Admiral Fitzwilliam greeted her at the bottom of the stairs with a smile.

"Thank you."

His smile faded. "Your mother has asked to see you before you go, but I have not given her my word that you would. The choice is entirely up to you."

She sighed and considered not seeing her mother, but then, she knew if she did not at least make a brief appearance, her mother would comment on it for days, if not weeks. Sometimes, when it was not too taxing to do so, it was best to just appease Lady Catherine, and Anne knew this was one of those times. "I will say a quick farewell."

And she did. After a few moments of conversation with her mother and Lord and Lady Matlock, Anne was back at her uncle's side and being handed into the carriage.

"Are you looking forward to the celebration?" he asked as she settled into her seat, and he took his. "Sophia mentioned that a special cake has been commissioned for Miss Katherine, although, I am told, it is to be a surprise to her from her sisters. So, we mustn't let on that we know."

Anne wondered what it would be like to have a family of siblings who planned special treats for one another to mark momentous occasions such as a betrothal.

"And Rycroft has invited several friends," her uncle continued, "so that games can be played, and I know that if he has his way, a dance or two will be had. All in all, it promises to be a delightful evening."

Her uncle chuckled. "I still find it amazing that two such opposite people as Rycroft and his lady should make such a good match. That boy could try the nerves of a saint."

"Then perhaps she is an angel and not a saint?" Anne, too, had noticed how very different in personalities Lord and Lady Rycroft were, but it did not seem to hinder their relationship. In fact, it seemed that it aided it as one complemented the other perfectly.

"I am quite anxious to see Lady Rycroft as well as Mrs. Darcy and Miss Katherine."

"Lady Rycroft? Mrs. Darcy? Miss Katherine?" Her uncle's tone was one of surprise. "I thought you called them by their Christian names? I have not missed some important development, have I?"

"No, you have missed nothing. It is just that it is a formal event," she explained. "Besides, I believe you led the conversation by referring to them formally."

He chuckled. "So I did. I suppose it is as you said, the thought of it being a special occasion which is at fault. It is not every day that one gets to celebrate a betrothal of a nephew to a lady as lovely as Kitty." He shifted in his seat. "It is sad that Richard's parents could not attend, but Sophia agreed that it might be best to keep it to the younger set and a couple of old chaperones."

The light was not great in the carriage, but Anne was positive that the comment had been made with a wink.

"I am quite pleased for Richard. He has found a fine wife." Kitty was all that was sweet and good. Theirs would be a happy marriage where neither would put anyone or anything in a position of power over the other. That was what she wanted. What she longed for with every fibre of her being.

"Finally, we Fitzwilliams will have a family that is happy instead of one made up of the fighting factions of my generation and the one which came before." He sighed. "Lord Matlock has done his best to keep things as they were, but thanks to you and your cousins, his ways have been tumbled for a time."

He reached across the carriage and patted her knee. "You do know that my greatest wish for you is that you are just as happy, do you not?"

"I do," she said in a voice that was just above a whisper.

"Then I must express my opinion on a matter." He shifted again in his seat, this time leaning towards her and grasping her hands. "I lost my love a long time ago. I have tried on many occasions to find something, anything, that would fill the void left by her absence. The sea came close, but that is now gone, and the empty place remains." He chuckled wryly. "We remain friends, but she has established her life and seems content, for that I cannot help but be happy."

"Did she marry?" Anne bit her lip after the question left her mouth. She hoped he would not be offended by her curiosity.

He squeezed her hands. "She did. I wish with all that I am that I would have followed my heart. Trust me when I say that there is no greater regret than to have been so close to grasping happiness and having it slip away, never to return. I beg you to consider my error before you make any choice about marriage. Please. Please, promise me this."

There was no mistaking the urgency in her uncle's voice. She could only imagine the grief that lay behind it. She pressed her lips together as the distant memory of searing pain at knowing she had to send her heart's choice away flitted through her mind.

She nodded. "I will consider it." But it would not change what could not be. It could not change it, could it?

"Thank you. I would not be doing my duty to you if I did not ask you to ponder such things, since I know intimately how great the weight of choosing wrongly can be," he said as the carriage drew to a stop in front of Rycroft House.

Again, Anne nodded. What else could she do? Was there anything that she could say to bring comfort other than her promise to do as he had asked?

Mary stood between Rycroft and Kitty, waiting to greet Anne. "I am so happy to see you, Anne. I have been longing for a visit from you, but Lady Sophia tells me you have been very busy with interviews."

"I most certainly have been!" Anne leaned close to Mary and lowered her voice. "However, it has not been enjoyable. All my callers are rather dull, and I would much rather spend time with you and your sisters."

Mary smiled and pulled Anne into an embrace. "Tomorrow, you must join us at the museum."

"I would like that." Anne felt a sigh of relief pass through her at the thought of not having to be subjected to yet another round of uninteresting interviews.

"You have not yet met our sister, Lydia," Kitty said as she took Anne's hand and gave it a gentle squeeze. "I can assure you that our visit will be anything but dull with her along."

Mary chuckled. "She has improved in the last month, but she is still Lydia."

A rather loud giggle was heard from the drawing room.

"That is Lydia," Mary said. "She is rarely quiet. Come."

She wrapped her arm around Anne's, ignoring the look of displeasure from her husband at being displaced by his cousin. That action made Anne laugh softly.

"I will introduce you," Mary said as they moved down the entrance hall. "Everyone else is here, so we are just beginning with some wine in the drawing room while we wait for our meal to be ready."

"Georgiana was allowed to come." Kitty had taken Anne's other arm. "Since we did not wish the men to outnumber the ladies."

"Samuel invited some friends." There was a hint of concern in Mary's voice.

"Yes, my uncle mentioned he had."

"Did he mention names?" Mary asked.

Anne shook her head.

Mary sighed. "There was one whom Samuel did not wish to invite, but things have changed, and it really could not be helped."

Anne stopped walking. They were just outside the door to the drawing room, and she could clearly hear Alex's voice. Alex was counted among her cousin's friends?

"And who might these guests be?" she asked, turning toward Rycroft.

Rycroft glanced at Richard and the admiral as if asking for their support. "Madoch, Lester, Endicott, and Blackmoore." He grimaced at the last name. "He is the one that could not be helped. Please stay."

"All will be well," Mary assured her. "Mr. Blackmoore has offered for Miss Bingley and has been accepted. He has also apologized to Samuel and promises to be on his best behaviour. He knows that his footing is tenuous. Should he be dismissed from this gathering, he might also lose Miss Bingley."

She leaned her head closer to Anne's and lowered her voice. "Mr. Bingley and Mr. Hurst were not pleased to hear of the cut he received, and, were they not so anxious to rid themselves of their sister, I doubt his offer would have found success. However, it has, and we, therefore, must extend a tentative welcome whether we wish to or not."

"My wife is of the *not* ranks," Rycroft whispered.

Anne smiled at that but shook her head. Her body wished to run from the house, but her stubborn nature would not allow it. She also knew that she would place a cloud of disappointment over the party if she did not stay, and so she would. That did not mean she would do so without making her displeasure at the circumstances known. She would not dance around disquieting circumstances again today. She had done that once in the library and that had almost ended in disaster.

"I have had my fill of trying gentlemen today," she said as she glared at Rycroft. "I will stay, but if either Mr. Blackmoore or Mr. Madoch do anything to make me uneasy, I will leave."

"No," her cousin replied firmly, "they will leave. Not you. I promise. I have told Blackmoore as much, and as Mary said, he has given his word, although I am not certain I put much faith in it."

"All will be well," Mary tried to assure once again.

Anne wanted to believe her.

"Rycroft has a pistol, and I am a crack shot," the admiral whispered, causing Anne and the others to laugh. "So, you see, you truly have nothing to fear."

Anne shook her head again and drew a deep breath. "Very well, I shall stay as long as Rycroft's pistols are handy."

Mary tightened her arm around Anne's and gave her one more reassuring smile before they entered the room.

Anne, hoping that she was doing a credible job of looking the part of a self-assured lady, smiled and curtseyed in greeting to all who were gathered. Thankfully, everyone returned to their prior conversations as soon as introductions had been made, and Anne found a seat next to Kitty and tucked out of view of the two gentlemen whom she wished to avoid. There, she occupied herself by observing the occupants of the room and attending half-heartedly to the conversation between Kitty and Elizabeth until dinner was announced.

Chapter 16

Finally, after what felt like an interminable amount of time but was likely no more than a quarter of an hour, dinner was announced, and Anne put her thoughts about troubling men and her future away.

"Oh, la!"

Anne barely refrained from grimacing at Miss Lydia's exclamation of delight.

"Who shall escort me to dinner?" Miss Lydia looked hopefully around the room.

Next to Anne, Kitty groaned, and Elizabeth closed her eyes while Mary, who stood next to Rycroft, gave her youngest sister a decidedly pointed look.

"Please do not subject me to taking her into dinner," Alex begged from behind Anne. "I would much rather converse with a friend."

Anne turned towards him.

"Please."

"Of course." She had opened her mouth to refuse, but when he smiled at her just then, she found her words turning to those of acceptance instead of refusal.

"Thank you." Alex extended his arm to her.

Anne hesitated before taking it. It was required that she take his arm, but she knew that doing so would only make her heart yearn for him more than it already did. "This is only as friends," she reminded herself and him.

He nodded his agreement, but there was something about his eyes that made Anne believe he was not being entirely truthful with her.

"We will sit by one of your cousins, and you shall be perfectly safe," he said.

She began to smile at him in acceptance of his proclamation, for that was what she was sure was expected, but then thought better of it. Since when, she chided herself, had she done something simply because it was expected rather than stating her mind on a subject? "I fear you are not being truthful," she said as they walked.

He shook his head. "I am afraid you are wrong. I have no intentions of placing you in the way of danger."

"Perhaps," she agreed as she took her seat, "but you do not intend for us to be mere friends."

"For this meal, I do." He smiled at her and flicked an eyebrow. "Beyond this evening, you know my wish."

"It shall not be granted."

"That remains to be seen," he replied. "Now, shall we turn the topic before you become distressed, and I am ousted from the house? My stomach has been rumbling for half an hour, and I have no intention of going hungry."

"Very well," she conceded. "Of what do you wish to speak? Your uncle?"

He smiled fondly as he had always done when thinking about his uncle. "My uncle is well, though he has a bit of gout in his foot, which slows him, but his business is thriving. There is nary a soul who is not pleased with his service. After all, his stable boasts nearly the finest horses in Brighton."

She laughed. "If you are trying to sell me on his business, Mr. Madoch, you should be saying that his horses are the finest, not nearly the finest."

He smiled. "Ah, but that I cannot do."

"No," said his friend who was seated next to him. "His Highness would not be best pleased to hear his are not the finest." He lowered his voice to just above a whisper before adding, "Even if they are outshone by Madoch's uncle."

"You remember Mr. Lester, do you not?" Alex asked Anne. "I believe you met him once before."

"I am not certain if I do remember him." Anne studied Mr. Lester's face for a moment. He did look oddly familiar, but she could not place him.

"We went riding six years ago – you, me, and Madoch," Jonathan tipped his head and looked back at her. "I believe it was the day before Madoch and I departed for Brighton."

"That was you?" she asked softly. Her mind recalled him perfectly now. She had slipped from her room to meet Alex for a ride and had found him in the company of a friend.

"It was."

"Forgive me for my lack of memory," she apologized.

"It is understandable. It has been six years, and ours was but a passing acquaintance." Mr. Lester's eyes moved from her face to his plate. "I've not had the opportunity to forget you," he said softly.

She heard the accusation in Mr. Lester's tone and looked at Alex, who shrugged. "I often speak of home, and since you are part of those memories, I fear Lester has heard of you often."

Anne attempted a small smile that she did not feel as she focused on the vegetables on her plate. Such comments were definitely not keeping her safe, no matter how closely she sat to any of her cousins or their wives.

He had spoken of her and thought of her – often. She wondered if it had been as often as she had thought of him and if he had thought of her in a flattering way or a vengeful way. That thought startled her. Perhaps he wished to marry her, not because he still loved her, but because he wished to repay her for shunning him. Perhaps he did not want to marry her at all. Perhaps he wished for her to want to marry him, so that he could toss her aside.

She stabbed a carrot particularly hard. The tines of her fork made a horrid scraping sound on her plate, and her cheeks flushed in embarrassment. She chewed the offending vegetable slowly and thoroughly before attempting to continue any sort of conversation.

Carrot conquered, and embarrassment partially faded, she made a second attempt at small talk. "I would tell you about my uncles, but I believe you already know how they do. Well," she said with a wave of her hand in Darcy's direction and a glance toward Rycroft, "at least the ones who remain."

Her cheeks flushed again. She had not meant for the comment to sound as unfeeling as it did. "I mean to say we have had a great deal of loss in our family over the past six years. Rycroft's father, Darcy's, my own." She hated how her voice always caught whenever she mentioned her father's death. It had been nearly six years. When would it ever become a topic about which she could speak without that feeling of despair gripping her heart as it did?

"I was sorry to hear of your father's passing," Alex said softly.

"Thank you," she whispered and bowed her head so that she could not see the understanding in his eyes. Of course, he knew how dearly she had loved her father, for she had spoken of it to him on more than one occasion.

As Alex watched her fidget with the napkin in her lap and draw several silent deep breaths, he began to reason out her refusal just a bit as a particular conversation came to mind. It was a conversation that had caused her to act then as she was now.

"He wanted to take me to Bath to see the assembly rooms, and I wished for him to take the waters, but my mother will not allow it," she had fumed as they rode the length of a long field near Rosings.

The comment had shocked him. Anne's father had been ill for several months – three, at least. It had not appeared to be anything grave or oversetting but rather a general attitude of malaise.

"Why?" he had asked.

"My uncle requires assistance, and so the money that father had set aside for our journey had to be given to Lord Matlock."

She had fidgeted with the reins in her hands and drawn several deep breaths as quietly as she was now. Then, she had continued.

"Lord Matlock must not be refused. He is an earl after all, and my father is merely a baronet. The will of one comes before and at the expense of the other." She shrugged. "It is just the way things are and always will be."

She had then clucked to her horse and galloped ahead of him, and the topic was at an end. She would not return to it, no matter how many times and in how many ways he had attempted to broach it again.

Alex leaned close to his friend and whispered. "I had not considered, when playing, how a pawn might feel being used at the expense of the more powerful pieces on the board."

Jonathan's brows furrowed.

Alex tipped his head toward Anne, just slightly – not enough to draw anyone's attention but enough to direct his friend's thoughts.

"I was just thinking about how you accused me of protecting my knight above all," he explained, "and I began to consider how the other pieces might view such treatment. The pawns would think nothing of it as that is the way of rank." He shrugged. "Perhaps I might win more games if I treated the pawns as carefully as I did the pieces of rank such as the knight."

Jonathan's brows remained furrowed.

"It is as you said. There is often a reason for every action." He smiled at his friend's continued look of confusion. "I am sure you will see what I mean eventually," he concluded and turned back to his meal.

"Do you play chess?" Anne asked.

Alex nodded. "I do. I do not play well, but I do play. Do you?"

"On occasion."

"My brother is quite good," Miss Darcy interjected. "I have beaten him once, but I think he allowed it." She giggled and leaned forward as she whispered, "Elizabeth is helping me learn, so that he will not need to allow me to win next time."

"And is Mrs. Darcy a good player?" Jonathan asked.

Georgiana smirked. "My brother does much more huffing and shushing when he plays her than when he plays me."

Her three companions chuckled at this.

"I have often thought that the pawns were the bravest," she added. "They march forward into battle with little power to protect themselves, but always with the intent of protecting their king." She shrugged. "I find that brave."

"I had not considered it as such," said Jonathan, "but I would have to agree."

"I would not choose to be a pawn, however," Georgiana replied with a smile. "I am not so very brave."

"And what piece would you be?" Alex asked.

Georgiana pursed her lips and furrowed her brow. "I had not considered it."

"I would be the queen," Anne answered. "She can move as she wants and holds great power. The others will often protect not only the king but the queen as well, and," she lifted her fork as she made her point, "a pawn will march his way across a board, facing danger at every move, just to become a queen."

"I would not like to be the queen," Miss Darcy said softly. "I would not wish such a great responsibility."

"Responsibility? What responsibility?" Anne asked.

"Oh, I believe she has the most responsibility of all the pieces," Miss Darcy declared. "If she is captured, does she not put every other piece in greater danger, including the king?" She blushed. "I like to imagine the king and queen love each other." She made the admission quietly. "I would hate to place any whom I love in danger."

She was quiet for a moment, and her companions waited for her to continue, for she did look as if she had more to say.

"I have changed my mind," she finally said, "I think I would like to be a pawn, bravely defending those she loves – if only I could be so brave."

Alex nodded thoughtfully. He admired Miss Darcy's caring heart that would put herself in a place she did not wish to be to spare another from harm.

"I would still be the knight." He smiled. "Not only would I then get to defend my king and queen with my life, but I would also get to ride a horse while doing so."

His tone may have been light, nearly a laugh, but the intensity with which he looked at Anne was far from light. Silently, he begged her to understand that he knew she longed to be protected and that he was offering himself in her service.

For a moment, she chuckled uneasily while the others laughed with ease, but then, she stopped on a gasp as her eyes met his. Had she understood him? Or was it something else? He opened his mouth to ask her if she was well. However, he never spoke, for as Anne held his gaze, her eyes began to shimmer with unshed tears. His heart broke at the sight of it and continued to crumble as she sadly shook her head, rejecting his offer, before pushing her chair back, rising quickly, and hurrying from the room.

Chapter 17

ANNE FOUND A CORNER in the library and curled into the lonely chair that sat there. The realization that what she had sought for years lay within her reach, if she were not too fearful to grasp, it washed over her and ran down her cheeks in the form of hot tears.

He would love her. He would fight for her. She had seen it in his eyes. If she were honest with herself, which seemed to be what her mind desired to be at this moment, she had known it when he had found her on the balcony not far from this room during the ball. And then, she had been reassured of the fact when he sat on the steps at Matlock House, insisting that he be allowed to see her. Yet, he did not force her into any decision. He did not take from her the right to decide as others had tried to do.

She refused to think further and gave herself over to her tears until sometime later, when a hand gently shook her shoulder. She opened her eyes to find Elizabeth standing next to her.

"Is the chair large enough for two?" Elizabeth asked.

Anne dried her eyes as she straightened and slid over to the left, leaving just enough room for Elizabeth to squeeze in next to her. It was a cozy fit, but not uncomfortable. In fact, it felt quite welcoming to be so snugly situated.

This was one of the things she had enjoyed about getting to know her new cousins and their sisters. There was always an arm to be held, a hug to be given, or a smile to be shared. They were things she had not experienced before and had come to enjoy quite thoroughly.

"This is like when I sit with my sisters sometimes," Elizabeth commented. "Chats, when tucked in so closely, are really the best sort."

She placed a hand on top of Anne's and gave her a questioning look, waiting for a small nod of Anne's head before wrapping her hand around Anne's.

"You are distraught, and I am here to listen. A lady must not bear all her own burdens, or she becomes easily overwhelmed." She paused and leaned just a little closer to Anne as she whispered, "You may tell me yours. I promise I am very good at keeping secrets. Is it Mr. Madoch?"

Anne sighed and nodded but was unable to put her jumbled thoughts into words.

"May I tell you a secret?" Elizabeth smiled at Anne. "I am expecting a child. I have told few about it — only Mary, Kitty, Jane, and now you."

"Not Darcy?" Anne asked in surprise. She was to be told something before Elizabeth told her husband?

Elizabeth shook her head.

A small smile touched Ann's lips. She had been included in a secret with Elizabeth's sisters.

"I will tell Fitzwilliam soon. Perhaps after Kitty's wedding. I do not wish to detract from her day." She shifted a bit in the chair. "I suppose I will not be able to sit so snuggly for much longer."

Anne laughed lightly and agreed.

"I must tell you something else that only a few know." She laughed. "Actually, it was Mary who made me realize it. She is quite wise.

"You see, I became betrothed to my husband against my wishes. I thought him proud and unfeeling. I had heard him say something unflattering about me and allowed it to injure my pride, and when a lady's pride is injured, she is not always wise in her actions, and I was not wise. I listened to gossip about him and looked for things to criticize.

"I begged my father not to force me to accept him. I was certain that my life was doomed to be unhappy. But, I was wrong; very, very wrong. I soon learned that the man I was bound to was not at all the one whom I thought him to be, and though I was loath to admit it, I soon grew to love him."

She sat a bit straighter in the chair and cleared her throat with a little cough. "I am going to ask you some questions that Mary asked me. I do not know your heart or the full story of your acquaintance with Mr. Madoch, but they may help you just the same. You need not speak; a simple nod will suffice."

Anne nodded, and Elizabeth began.

"Is Mr. Madoch an honourable man?"

Anne thought of her interactions with him in the past and the night he had rescued her from Mr. Blackmoore on the balcony and nodded. He was honourable. Very much so.

"Is he solicitous of your feelings?"

Anne nodded quickly. She did not have to contemplate that. He had always – from their first meeting – been considerate of how she felt.

"And he cares for you, does he not?"

Again, Anne nodded. He had said he did six years ago, and even a lady as foolish and stubborn as she was at times could not deny that a man who was willing to face rejection over and over again and yet not force his desires onto her own had to love her.

"Do you fear he will ever treat you ill?"

That was the question, was it not? It was the one thing that had kept her from following where her heart led for the past six years. Anne cocked her head to the side and shook it slowly. "I very much think he is incapable of doing so," she admitted.

Elizabeth lowered her voice. "This is the most important question. Will you be content to be parted from him and given to another?"

Fresh tears sprang to Anne's eyes at the thought. She shook her head. "But he is of little standing," she protested weakly.

Elizabeth wrapped her arms around Anne. "Standing has almost nothing to do with happiness or love," she said softly. She squeezed Anne just a bit more tightly before releasing her and adding, "You must examine your heart and do what it says." She wiggled her way out of the chair. "The gentlemen will be joining us soon in the drawing room. I should be there so that Darcy does not worry." She looked down at Anne. "Will you join us?"

Anne nodded. "In a moment."

"Good, for if you do not, several others will come looking for you."

Anne smiled as Elizabeth left the room. It was comforting to know that there were others who cared about her wellbeing. She stood and walked to the terrace door. It was a cool evening but not too cold, so she pushed the door open and stepped outside. A bit of fresh air might help dry her tears and freshen her face.

"Miss de Bourgh?"

She looked down at the gentleman standing in the garden. "Mr. Blackmoore. Why are you not with the other gentlemen?"

"And why are you not with the other ladies?" he replied.

"I needed some air."

"So did I." He came to stand just below where she was. "I wish to apologize," he said. "I behaved poorly the last time we met."

A snort of laughter escaped Anne. "I should say you did." She tilted her head to the side and raised a brow. "Do you wish for me to believe you are reformed?"

He shook his head. "I am not sure I am reformed, but I am betrothed. It seems it is rather difficult to earn the trust of a lady or her relations when one has acted inappropriately and had his friendship with someone like Rycroft severed or nearly so. Therefore, while you may not believe this, I have decided to take my betrothal with some seriousness. Miss Bingley seems to be my only hope for pleasing my father."

"Is that so?" Anne snorted in laughter again as he chuckled somewhat bitterly.

"Indeed, it is. I have tried calling on others of greater standing, but alas, none seem willing to be home to me."

That seemed proper. In Anne's way of thinking, he was not the sort of gentleman any young lady of value should entertain as a suitor.

"Have you dismissed your mistress?"

He gave one sharp nod. "For now, at least. Whether it stays that way or not has yet to be seen."

Anne shook her head and rolled her eyes. At least, he would not be her problem. "How considerate of you," she said dryly.

He shrugged. "I did say that I might not be reformed."

"In case you were wondering, I will not marry a man with a mistress, nor will I become one." She thought it only wise to make sure he understood her position on such things completely since he did seem to lack a bit of sense about them.

Blackmoore laughed. "I would not even attempt to suggest such a thing. I felt the way Madoch protected you the last time we met, and I have endured his glares all evening." He shook his head as he continued to chuckle. "No, no, he is not someone with whom I wish to tangle. I fear I would not win."

The comment surprised Anne. "I beg your pardon, but I do not understand your meaning. What exactly makes a man who cares for horses someone who must be feared?" Alex was not a small or retiring man, but he was not a brute either. How he could inspire such a reaction in a gentleman who was his superior in rank was beyond her comprehension.

Blackmoore laughed once again. "His connections, my dear, his connections. It is not that he cares for horses but for whose horses he cares."

"His uncle?" The question leapt from her lips and with a tone that spoke of her utter disbelief.

Blackmoore shook his head. "Not unless his uncle is heir to the throne." He gave her a slight bow and walked off toward another open door.

Anne's mouth hung open for some minutes. "No, surely not," she said as she turned toward the open door of the library. "No, he could not be responsible for those horses." She closed the door behind her.

Chapter 18

"ARE YOU WELL?"

Anne jumped at the sound of Rycroft's voice as it snatched her from her contemplation of what Mr. Blackmoore had just told her.

"I may not be now," she scolded as he apologized for having startled her.

"Mr. Madoch has left." Rycroft extended his arm to her. "The drawing room should be safe."

Her heart jumped to a gallop. Alex was gone? "Why did he leave? You did not toss him out, did you?"

"You were speaking to him and then became distraught. What did you think I would do?"

Anne gasped in horror. "Oh, no, he did nothing to upset me. My distress was of my own creation. I have had a rather trying day." She shook her head and gripped his arm tightly. "You must go fetch him back. Oh, I feel dreadful." She held a hand to her forehead.

"I did not send him packing," Rycroft admitted.

"Then why did you say you did?" Anne pulled her arm away from him. "Oh, you are so vexing!" She stamped her foot.

Rycroft smiled. "He left of his own accord – he received a summons or some such thing."

"A summons? What has happened?"

Rycroft sighed. "I knew I would not be good at this, but Mary insisted I speak to you. It seems a horse was injured earlier today, and his expertise was needed. I do not know why it must be him, but then why does Prinny do half the things he does?" Rycroft's eyes grew large, and he clapped his mouth shut quickly.

"So, it is true? He tends to the royal horses?"

Rycroft nodded. "I was not to tell you."

"You did not. Mr. Blackmoore did." She turned toward the terrace door. "Just now, before you startled me, I was speaking to him in the garden." She spun back toward her cousin. "Why was I not to know? Why would he not tell me?"

Rycroft sighed once more. "He did not wish for you to choose him for his position or his wealth, about which I am also not supposed to tell you. However, I will say that it is not an insignificant figure."

Anne blinked, and her mouth dropped open slightly. How much had Alex hidden from her?

"Look." Rycroft took her arm and led her to a chair. "I am sure I will bungle this, but I will at least make an attempt to explain."

He let her take a seat and then paced before her. "When a man loves a woman, he will do nearly anything to secure his happiness, but he would not do it at the expense of hers. Any man of sense who wishes to have a marriage based on affection often waits to see if he has a chance of success – that the lady he loves might care for him – before he acts. Madoch is most certainly a man of sense. Therefore, if Madoch had told you of his standing, you might have selected him based solely on that information, and he would never know if you cared for him or his position. And it is important to men such as Madoch that their wives prefer them above all else."

He sat on the edge of the seat across from her. "Do you understand?"

Anne nodded slowly. "I believe I do, but I have always loved him." And she was certain that Alex knew that.

Rycroft's took her hands. "But not enough," he said softly, "and that is what he wished to know – that you loved him enough to look past his position and accept him as a second son with a small inheritance and a love of horses. Do you understand?"

Anne nodded. Her stomach twisted again with regret – just as it had before she had left the dining room. And just as then, tears once again threatened to fall. It was not that she had not loved him enough, it was that she had allowed her fears to overwhelm that love. She had allowed her heart to be overruled by her head. It was not something she would do again. If only she could see him and tell him.

"Shall I call for the admiral's carriage?" Rycroft was looking at her in concern.

She nodded again. "Yes, please. I find I am not well after all."

Anne held the second of two returned letters in as many weeks. She tore open the seal to the letter that accompanied it and plopped into a chair. Her eyes scanned the brief contents of the missive. Alex was not in Brighton, according to his uncle.

She tossed the letters on the table and rested her head against the back of her chair, desperation began to worm its way up and around her heart. She had called at Lord Brownlow's the day after the dinner at Rycroft's. She had wanted to tell Alex of her change of heart, of her willingness to consider him no matter his circumstances, but he had been gone, without a word, save that he had business.

She sighed and rose to complete the few things she needed to do before she left Matlock House. Her cousin would marry the day after tomorrow, and then, she would return to Rosings and settle into life with her mother. She groaned at the thought. Perhaps she could visit her cousins frequently and avoid spending too much time with Lady Catherine.

Darcy would soon have a child. She could help care for the infant. Was that not what spinster relations did? Surely, Rycroft or Richard would add to the number of new family members soon. And perhaps, since Jane was so obliging, she might be willing to allow Anne to visit and tend to any Bingley offspring. She would hold that as a last hope, however. She had very little desire to spend any length of time with Miss Bingley or Lord Blackmoore.

She glanced at the clock. Half an hour. She had half an hour until she would conclude her one and only short season in town. It had not been completely without enjoyment. She had attended two balls, three musicales, and a dinner party. She had entertained several callers and taken in several of the sites of London.

She tucked a sketch into her book. It was a drawing given to her by Kitty and depicted one of the marbles at the museum. She had enjoyed seeing the lifelikeness of the stone. It still amazed her that so much life could come from something so hard and cold. She sniggered. The coldness of that trip had not been solely due to the stone facades of the marbles. No, Miss Bingley and her friends had been there.

"They like to frequent this display," Kitty had whispered, "but even the statues are unwilling to offer for the likes of them."

Both Anne and Kitty had laughed at the comment and returned to their drawing. Anne was not particularly good at drawing, but Kitty was willing to give her some instruction, and Anne was desirous of spending time with Kitty. They had ignored the other ladies after that. If only Miss Ivison had been so kind and reciprocated the action, but she was not. There was very little that was kind about Miss Ivison.

After making a round of the displays, Miss Ivison had come to admire the marble that Kitty and Anne were drawing. She stood off to the left, but not so far away that her conversation could not be heard by the two who were sketching.

"She has turned away an army of offers as if she is the prize of the season." Miss Pearce had tittered.

"And yet," Miss Ivison had continued, "she will return home in failure, an old maid. Fitting, I should think. Advertising for a husband," she scoffed. "No respectable woman does such a thing."

It had been enough to raise Anne's ire, and ignoring the restraining hand Kitty placed on her arm, she had stood and engaged the woman.

"And you do not advertise for a husband?" She looked at Miss Ivison's hat. "You could not make yourself more conspicuous than you do with that monstrosity on your head. It is like a beacon on the sea shouting to all who pass that danger lies just beyond it." Her gaze lowered. "And, if that neckline is not an advertisement as to what can be had... well." She had flicked an eyebrow and smirked. "Perhaps you should try an advertisement in the Times. I had several well-qualified gentlemen lining up to see me, and yet, even with what paltry goods you have to place on display..." She looked around the room and shook her head. "No one seems to be seeking you out."

She had then turned to Caroline. "I do not like you, but even you should know that this woman was keen to have me accept a most indecent proposal from Lord Blackmoore. And do you know why? Because she believes that a title should stay with those who are born to it rather than being given to those, such as yourself, who are of more lowly birth." She had paused. "You would do well to relieve yourself of such clawing females, but I suspect you are not so clever as to do so. Come, Kitty. I think there must be a more pleasant place to pass our time."

She still giggled at the look of displeasure on Miss Ivison's face. There had been a short conversation, conducted in harsh tones, as Kitty and Anne had walked away. Then, as they reached the door, Anne had looked back to see Miss Bingley and Miss Pearce arm in arm and Miss Ivison standing quite alone. She probably should have felt some pang of remorse or sadness for the lady, but she did not. She had felt rather elated, and she still did.

"Are you ready?" Lady Sophia poked her head around the door.

"Soon," Anne said. "If I could have five minutes, please. I need to do one more thing."

"Very well, but do hurry. Reginald grows restless. Military men do not like to be kept waiting."

Anne smiled at her aunt. It was true. The admiral was a stickler for punctuality, but he would have to wait just a moment. He would also have to adjust his route a small amount – that was also something of which a man like the admiral was not overly fond.

Be that as it may, there was something that really needed doing before she departed London, and to that end, she sat at the desk and opened her writing supplies. She dipped her pen in the ink and then, applying it to paper, began one last very important message.

"It is with an anxious heart that I, Miss de Bourgh, once again apply to the readers of this paper..."

Chapter 19

ALEX TOSSED HIS HAT and coat onto a chair near the table that had been set up for him in his room at the inn where he and Jonathan were staying. Another two days, and they would be back home at his estate where they would start arranging things how they needed to be to start breeding horses that others would travel for days to buy. Then, he'd be sitting at his own table rather than a small one in the corner of a rented room.

He sat down in the chair across from Jonathan and sighed. It had been a busy, but successful, day. Lord Brownlow now owned the hunters he desired, and in the process of advising Brownlow, Alex had come into possession of a fine mare to add to his own stables. She was just now getting settled in the inn's stables and waiting to be ridden home by one of his grooms tomorrow.

His business had gone well and promised to be even better in the future. He should be happy, but that was an emotion he doubted he would ever truly feel again. He had gambled his last chance at happiness two weeks ago with a foolish comment about chess. He closed his eyes and tried to block out the memory of Anne shaking her head with such sorrow in her eyes.

"Are the horses well?" Jonathan asked.

Alex nodded. "They are."

"And Brownlow is gone?"

Another nod. "He is, and he seems quite pleased."

"As he should be. That was a fine pair of horses he purchased."

"I would not have advised him to buy them if they were not – even if he did seem enamoured with them." Alex chuckled at how Brownlow had so easily taken to one of the horses in the pair when it had walked right up to him and poked at the pocket of his coat as if looking for some sort of treat.

Alex took up the piece of linen next to his place setting and placed it on his lap as he prepared to eat. The cook at this particular inn was well-known for his talent, and Alex was looking forward to enjoying it.

"There is a bit in here that you may wish to read." Jonathan folded the newspaper he had been reading so that only one small portion of a page was showing and placed it next to Alex's plate.

He pushed the paper away. "I will read it after I have had my fill."

He scooped a large spoonful of stew from his bowl. He did not wish to be bothered with any news that might spoil his pleasure in enjoying a good meal; still, he was curious about the nature of the article.

"Is it about politics?" he asked before indulging in that first bite of savoury goodness cradled in his spoon.

"No." Jonathan took a slow sip of his ale.

Madoch's brows furrowed as he chewed. "So, then, it is nothing to do with Prinny?" he questioned around the food in his mouth.

"No." Jonathan placed his mug on the table and leaned back in his chair. His plate was already empty because he had begun eating while Alex had stopped to question the stable boy about some item of care for his horses.

Madoch stretched his neck forward a bit as he took another bite. His eyes could just see a bit of the paper. If he had not pushed it so far, he might be able to read it as he ate.

"A society bit?" The words were nearly lost as they mixed with the stew in his mouth. Usually, his manners were better, but when it was just he and Jonathan, he often slipped into a more relaxed and far less formal habit than would be acceptable in polite society.

"You could say that," Jonathan said with a grin. "A wedding announcement might also be a fitting description depending on how *you*," he gave Alex a pointed look, "read it." He took up the paper. "I could read it to you if you wish."

Alex shrugged and broke off a piece of bread to sop up some of the liquid on his plate. "It matters not if I read it or if you do, I suppose."

"Does that mean I should read it?"

Alex nodded.

"You are certain?"

Alex scowled and nodded once again. Why would he not be certain he wished to hear a society announcement? He stopped eating as a reason registered in his mind, and the wonderful taste of stew in his mouth became sodden and dull. There was only one reason why Jonathan would think he did not wish to hear the announcement.

"Has she made a choice?"

Jonathan raised only one brow, and Alex knew that she had. He lowered his spoon, wiped his hands, and took a large gulp of his ale.

"Proceed," he said, steeling himself to hear the dreaded news that Anne would never be his.

"You will not believe her choice." Jonathan made a show of snapping the paper into position to read.

"Just get on with it."

"It is with an anxious heart that I, Miss de Bourgh, once again apply to the readers of this paper." Jonathan glanced up from the paper. "Are you sure you wish for me to continue?"

"Did I not say I did?" Alex barked. This was not like his friend. Jonathan did as instructed and rarely questioned more than once before proceeding.

"It is with an anxious heart that I, Miss de Bourgh, once again apply to the readers of this paper..." Again, Jonathan looked up from the words. "She would be gone to Hertfordshire by now for her cousin's wedding."

"I know," Alex said through clenched teeth.

Jonathan nodded and returned to the page. "It is with –"

Alex snatched the paper away from his friend. "You have read that bit twice already."

He took his time positioning the paper so that it could be easily read. Then, he blew out a great breath before turning his eyes to the words on the page and reading the few lines that were there. His brows furrowed, and he shook his head. Surely, he had not read that correctly. He began again. No. No, it seemed to say what he thought it did.

He handed the paper back to Jonathan. "It might be best if you read it. It seems my mind is playing tricks on me."

Jonathan took the paper from him. "It says exactly what you think, my friend, but I shall read it, without further delay, just to prove to you that it is true."

He cleared his throat and began reading. "It is with an anxious heart that I, Miss de Bourgh, once again apply to the readers of this paper for help in the search for a husband. As you, the reader, may know, I advertised not a month ago for a husband. I have made my selection; however, I fear I have taken too long in reaching my decision, and this gentleman may indeed be lost to me. And so it is with a trembling hand that I place this announcement here for all to see in hopes that one Mr. Alexander Madoch will be among the readers of this fine paper." Jonathan lowered the paper. "We can stay with my father," he said quietly.

Alex stared blankly at his friend for a moment. "She chose me," he said at last, "but why?" He rubbed his neck. "Do you suppose it is because she found out that I cared for the prince's horses?" Brownlow had shared that bit of news with him. Apparently, Blackmoore had told Anne about the connection.

"Ask her."

"Ask her?" That did seem to be the logical thing to do but how? She was in Hertfordshire, and he was not.

Jonathan chuckled softly. "Yes, my friend. Ask her. We leave at first light and will stay with my father. I shall inform the stables and innkeeper of the change." He had risen and was standing at the door before he had finished speaking. "I know I did not approve of her when we started this scheme of yours. However, I have changed my position on the matter and will not allow you to refuse her for any reason." And without waiting for any sort of reply from Alex, he quit the room.

Alex once again applied himself to his meal, which had, remarkably, grown tastier in the time it had sat untended. As he scooped a final spoonful of stew from his plate, he exhaled deeply. His days of eating alone or with only Jonathan were at an end. Finally. Finally. His happiness was within his reach, and as soon as he reached Hertfordshire, he would grasp it and never let go.

He looked at his watch and considered running after his friend to inform him that they would be leaving now. However, the day was growing late, and while he knew the likelihood of his sleeping at all tonight was limited, the horses needed their rest. Perhaps it was best if they left in the morning. It had been a long day, after all, but...

He shook his head. No. They would leave tomorrow. He had waited for Anne for six years already. He was nearly certain he could wait just a little longer. Most likely.

Chapter 20

It had been a long day even though it had only really just begun. Anne had smiled when she was supposed to and had attempted to say all the right things, but her heart, though happy for her cousin and Kitty, was anything but joyous.

It had been two days since she had placed that advertisement in the paper, and she could not help wondering if Alex had seen it and whether the joy she had seen on Kitty's face today would ever be hers.

"You look tired." Lady Sophia came to stand near her in Netherfield's drawing room.

Anne gave a small shrug. "I am, I suppose."

"A bit of air might help. Will you take a walk with me?" Lady Sophia sent a footman scurrying with the request for both her wrap and Anne's as soon as Anne had agreed to take a walk. "It was a lovely wedding breakfast, was it not?"

Anne nodded. "It was beautiful."

"I only have two nieces left to see happy." The look she gave Anne was gentle. "I will see them both happy, will I not?"

Anne shook her head. "I cannot say," she whispered. She pulled her lips into a smile that she did not feel. "However, I will attempt to be happy. If I can spend time with you and my cousins and their wives, I think I can be at least content." She shook her head again. "If I have to spend all my time with my mother, I will be neither content nor happy — although perhaps I will learn to enjoy her company."

"Am I to understand, then, that you will not marry anyone but Mr. Madoch?" It was the third time since entering the carriage yesterday that her aunt had asked that question.

"I will not." Anne took her wrap from her maid and, putting it on, followed her aunt into the garden. It was a bright, crisp day, and the freshness of the air felt good as she drew a deep breath.

"Not even for security or position?" Lady Sophia wound her arm around Anne's and pulled her close as they walked to a bench surrounded by some early blooms and protected by a hedge.

"If I found myself destitute, I might," Anne replied, "but I do not see that happening. I have you, Uncle Reginald, and my cousins, who I know would come to my aid."

Lady Sophia patted Anne's hand. "That we would. But, I must say, this is a great change for you, is it not – to be dependent on others and under their power?"

"None of you would ever harm me." Anne took a seat on the bench. "You love me far too much to allow it."

Lady Sophia smiled but did not sit next to Anne. "We do, and I am glad you have come to realize it."

She turned to look down the path. "Your father loved your mother, you know." She spoke quietly, glancing back at Anne. "He applied to my father three times before his offer was accepted." Her shoulders rose and fell with a great breath. "But there were stipulations placed on the agreement. My brother, your uncle, the current Lord Matlock, was not the best at balancing wants with income. He has since improved, but I would still not trust him with my money."

She took a seat next to Anne. "It is not his strength. My father knew this and used the love your father had for my sister to coerce an agreement of support, should it become necessary, which we all knew was an inevitable event, and you know, of course, how important appearance is to your mother. I can only imagine the begging and threatening that might have taken place if your father had not wished to give my brother what he requested." She took Anne's hand. "My imagination is not wrong in this, is it?"

"No, you are not wrong. There were many loud discussions." Her reply was soft, and Lady Sophia had to bend closer to hear it.

"I am sorry to hear that."

There was a question that had always tugged at Anne's mind and knowing her aunt as well as she did now, she dared to ask it. "Did my mother ever love my father?"

"I do not know, my dear. I certainly never saw it. There was admiration and concern, but nothing of the giving of one's very soul to the other, as I had with my husband." She sighed. "That is where the issue lay – not with rank or fortune, but with a lack of the best kind of love. But I think you understand that now."

"I do," Anne admitted softly. It was just too bad that understanding that fact had come too late.

"I always have."

Anne gasped as Alex stepped around the hedge, and her lips trembled while tears sprang to her eyes at the sight of him.

"A man or woman who loves another completely would not allow harm to come to the one they love, no matter the source."

"It is good to see you, Mr. Madoch," Lady Sophia said as she stood and offered her place next to Anne.

"Be happy," she whispered as she gave Anne's cheek a kiss. And then, she was gone.

"You came," Anne whispered as Alex sat down beside her and took her hand. "I was afraid you would not. I called on you at Lord Brownlow's, and I made my uncle give me the directions for a letter to you."

"You wrote to me?"

Anne nodded and lifted her gaze from their joined hands to his eyes. "Twice. The second letter was returned with an accompanying letter from your uncle explaining that you were not in Brighton and would not be for some time." She bit her lip to keep it from trembling and drew a shuddering breath. "I thought I had lost you. Why did you leave?"

"I had some business to which to attend, and I thought I had bungled my last chance with you." He lifted one hand to her face and stroked her cheek. It was the most comforting thing she had ever felt, for in his gentle touch she could feel his care for her. "Why did you choose me?" he asked.

"I love you," she said without a moment's pause. "I have always loved you."

"Then it was not because of what Mr. Blackmoore told you about my connections?"

Anne's eyes grew wide, and she shook her head vigorously. "I had made my choice before I knew. What he or Rycroft may have told me afterward were of little concern."

"Rycroft?"

"My cousin sought me out after I left the dining room to see if I was well, and he accidentally confirmed what Mr. Blackmoore had said."

Alex tilted his head and studied her face. "I am no longer in charge of the Prince's stables in Brighton."

She blinked. That seemed a sudden change of circumstances. Not that it changed how she felt about him at all. She smiled as she realized with even more certainty than she already held that what he was in the eyes of society could not and would not change how her heart belonged to him. "Have you been sacked? Was the prince angry that you left town so suddenly?"

He chuckled. "No, I, or rather Jonathan, made arrangements for me to step down from my position."

Lightness bubbled up in her heart and tipped her lips into a teasing smile. "So, you will not be sent to the tower or off to some foreign land?"

He pulled her into his embrace. "I will be contentedly managing my own stables on my own estate and providing guidance as needed in Brighton as well as a well-bred horse to the Brighton stables on occasion."

"May I join you?" She looked up at him from where her head rested a bit awkwardly on his shoulder. "Will you have me?"

"You truly do not care that my position has changed and that I might fade completely from Prinny's notice?"

"Not even a little bit." She smiled sheepishly at him. "I have been a fool."

His left brow rose, and he smirked. "I will not disagree. You have been, and I am sure you will continue to be at times."

With a huff, she tried to pull away from him, but he was not letting go.

"Be that as it may," he continued, giving her that smile that made her stomach flip, "you will be my fool, and I will be glad to have you." He released her suddenly and stood, leaving her quite confused. "Come," he said extending his hand. "We have a journey to make."

"A journey?" She placed her hand in his.

"Yes," he said with a smile, "a journey."

"To where?" she asked as he pulled her to her feet and back into his embrace.

"Do you trust me?"

"Completely."

"Good," he said before giving her a most delightful kiss.

"I have waited six years to have you as my wife," he said after he had broken the kiss and held her tightly as his chest rose and fell rapidly at first but then slowed to something closer to normal well before Anne's did.

"I will not wait another moment longer than I must," he continued, and then bending, he scooped her into his arms and hurried through the garden and to the carriage – Rycroft's carriage – that stood waiting on Netherfield's drive.

"What are you doing?" Anne demanded as Alex deposited her inside Rycroft's travelling coach.

"Did I not tell you that we have a journey to go on?" He winked at her as he climbed in and took the seat next to her.

"To where?"

"To Scotland, of course," he said as the door to the carriage closed.

"We are going to Scotland?" Anne was positive that she had heard him correctly, but still the thought was so shocking that it demanded confirmation.

"I will not wait three weeks for banns to be read." The carriage lurched forward. "Nor will I spare the time or expense for a license, so we will be married in Gretna Green by the end of the week." Alex pulled her back against him. "Your things are securely fastened to the roof, as are mine."

"And my maid?" Anne asked.

"Will not be needed." Alex tightened his grip on her so that she could not jump away from him.

"We are not married," she scolded as she settled back against his side after a brief struggle to free herself. To be quite honest, she was not entirely unhappy that her attempt at escape had been thwarted. She rather liked the feeling of being snuggled next to him.

"Ah, but we will be." He grunted slightly when her elbow jabbed him in the side. "Very well, a maid can be secured at each stop."

"And I shall have my own room?"

Alex sighed. "If you insist."

"It is only proper."

Alex laughed. "My dear, what precisely is proper about advertising for a husband, announcing your selection in the paper, and then marrying at Gretna Green?" He looked down at her upturned face and kissed her forehead. "However, if it is what you want, then you shall have it."

She smiled and snuggled just a bit closer to him. "How did you manage all this? The carriage, my things, everything."

He chuckled and the sound rumbled through her in a most wonderful way. "I did not manage any of it. It seems Lady Sophia and the admiral, along with Mr. Lester, have conspired to see us happy. As I understand it, in two days' time, all the papers in London, will carry an announcement of our happy union." He squeezed her close. "You are happy, are you not?"

She nodded. "Very. And you?"

"I am. Though I suspect neither your mother nor your uncle will be too pleased when they discover that announcement in the paper."

She tilted her face to look up at him and brought the hand which was not pinned against his side up to rest on his cheek.

"I love you. I always have, and I always will. But more than that, I know with all that I am that you love me and will always, always protect me. How can I not know that when you are willing to anger the likes of my mother and uncle and quite possibly have to bear their reproach for the rest of your life?"

"I would endure far worse for you." He leaned toward her as if to kiss her but stopped just short of her lips. "Tell me again why you chose me."

She smiled and shook her head. "I did not choose you. My heart did."

No answer could have satisfied him more. His quest to secure her love was complete and the challenge to keep it had begun. He kissed her gently and then, ignoring her protest, lifted her onto his lap and kissed her more fully. As she wrapped her arms around his neck and ran her fingers through the hair that curled above his collar and as the carriage bounced and swayed on its journey, he knew that, no matter the trials that lay ahead, no matter the disagreements that were sure to arise, he could and would find solace in the knowledge that he was and always would be her heart's choice.

Epilogue

Dear Reader,

Happiness is not guaranteed. Indeed, it can be a right fickle emotion. One might find happiness only to have it removed, or one might find contentment which grows into a happiness of incomprehensible measure. It might elude the most deserving, or it might grace one who ill deserves it. Just as it might wax and wane in life, so too it may shift in the land of stories, guided, of course, by the pen of an author who, though following closely the personality of her characters, grants or refuses happiness to one and all.

The happiness or unhappiness of our players has developed in the following fashion:

We shall, of course, begin with the least deserving. Miss Ivison, as she is still called these five years after the close of our story, was never fortunate enough to find a gentleman willing to accept her – despite her fifteen thousand. However, that does not mean she went without notice to those seeking a lady willing to press the edges of propriety in an attempt to lure a partner. And so, she lives in a small house near her father's estate with few friends and a daughter, who will never be fully accepted into polite society, no matter the fact that her father held a title – even if he was only a Sir and not a Lord.

Ah, it is a sad tale for the young child to be sure, for her mother was to wed the man until, at about the same time that his penchant for cheating while playing cards with His Highness was discovered, his love of life began to outweigh his love of her dowry, and he skulked off one night to begin a life of travel. What became of him, no one truly knows, though small stories have occasionally surfaced now and again. None of these stories were flattering, however, but such is the life of a scoundrel.

Miss Pearce fared much better after the day she walked away from Miss Ivison in the museum. She found a pleasant gentleman with whom she could live comfortably and grew to love him dearly.

Miss Bingley was fortunate indeed. She has one son approaching his first birthday and another child to arrive in the summer, as well as a husband who keeps himself occupied with his estate when needed and escorts her to social events throughout the season.

She would tell you her life is perfect, but it's not. Having had her faith in friends severely shaken by Miss Ivison, she has few that she has allowed to become close, and so, she finds herself on occasion feeling quite lonely. Her husband has been a source of good fortune, for though he married her to gain his father's approval, he has come to care for her, and despite everyone's expectations that he would once again take up with a mistress, he has not. Whether that is due to his care for his wife and children or a fear of reprisals from his father or Mr. Bingley and his group of powerful friends and relations, it is hard to say, but no matter the reason, he has remained faithful.

Lord Brownlow has yet to choose a bride and fulfill his duty to his title, but a lovely lady from Hertfordshire, herself rather advanced in her years, has caught his eye. Should he not declare himself soon, Mrs. Darcy, the lady's particular friend, along with her husband and his cousin, Lord Rycroft, has planned a soiree for Charlotte's birthday at the end of the month, and her father has agreed to aid in whatever scheme they might employ to speed the happy conclusion of marriage between the two.

Mr. Collins, who was thwarted in his attempt to mend bridges through marrying a cousin, has found himself in possession of his inheritance while Mr. Bennet yet lives. He has taken up residence at Longbourn where he finds himself called on regularly by Mrs. Long and her nieces, as well as Mrs. King and her daughter, Miss Mary King, who was returned to Hertfordshire not long after the departure of the militia.

However, unless one mother or the other soon makes mention of their purpose in calling, it may be quite some time before Mr. Collins comes to the conclusion himself, and the entail upon Longbourn might indeed be in danger of dying with him.

Mr. Bennet, though he still lives under a heavy shadow of ill health, has, at the insistence of his daughters and sons, taken up residence in Bath. Since arriving in his handsome new home, with much complaining, he has found the waters to be to his liking nearly as much as the library which Mr. and Mrs. Darcy had fitted and filled for him.

Mrs. Bennet has discovered that Bath is near perfection for entertaining and being entertained, and, much to her husband's delight, spends a good deal of time in the company of new friends – and not in his library. The grandeur of their new home plays significantly on her happiness.

"It is like a dream," she often comments. "It is so large that we have to close off a floor when we are by ourselves. We quite rattle around in all that space when we do not have visitors." And then she smiles and adds, "My sons are quite wealthy you know, and such dears to see to our care as they have."

But do not fret; the Bennets are rarely lonely or given a lengthy period of time in which to rattle around. For at least twice a year, each of their daughters, with family in tow, come for a visit. And on many occasions, there is more than just one daughter in residence, as is the case at present.

This May, the Bennets' home is filled to capacity as sisters and cousins and children and aunts and uncles and friends have gathered to celebrate both the birthday of the man to whom so many of them owe their happiness and the marriage of the last Bennet daughter.

"This is quite the happy assembly, is it not?" Sir William asked as he settled into a chair near Mr. Bennet at the far end of the drawing room.

"That it is," Mr. Bennet agreed.

"Papa!" A dark-haired child with a rather serious look on his face and a tear on his cheek darted across to the room to Darcy. In one hand he held a book and in the other a page of that book. "Cousin Elinor ruined my book."

Darcy sighed and scooped his son onto his lap as Anne bit back a giggle and Alex, with a shake of his head, rose to go find his daughter, who was altogether too much like her mother.

"It was not nice," Darcy agreed with his son in an attempt to stop a protracted lecture by the boy from beginning in earnest. "One must treat books with care. However, we must also learn to forgive those who treat us ill."

Lucas scrunched up his face into a scowl, his lower lip protruding in displeasure. "She ruined my book," he grumbled.

"I take it you did not forgive her?" his father said.

Lucas shook his head.

"He pulled her hair," Michael, the eldest of Rycroft's three boys, supplied. "And then she threw a block at Amelia and hit her right on her head." He pointed to the right side of his head above his ear where the second youngest of the Bingley girls had been hit. "Amelia cried, of course." He rolled his eyes. "And then Elinor's papa came, but she is hiding." He smiled. "He'll not find her." There was a hint of pride in his voice. "Frederick helped her hide, and he is almost as good as me at hiding."

Rycroft snapped his fingers and motioned for Michael to come stand before him. "Where has your brother hidden your cousin?"

Michael's shoulders lifted and fell. "I do not know. They ran out of the nursery, and I did not follow them. I followed Lucas."

"You are certain you do not know?"

Michael shook his head, causing his sandy-coloured curls to bounce.

"Were there any other mishaps of which we," he motioned around the group of adults, "should know?"

Michael tilted his head to the side and thought for a moment. "The babies are sleeping," he said holding up three fingers to indicate his youngest brother, the Bingleys' youngest daughter, and Kitty's youngest son.

"The girls are drawing flowers." Three more fingers popped up. One for Lucas' sister and the other two for the remaining Bingley children. "And Theodore is building a castle with blocks, although he is rather angry at Elinor for interfering with his plans. I think he might send her to the tower."

Richard sighed. "You will tell me if he does send her to the tower, will you not, so that I can free her?"

Michael smiled and bobbed his head up and down.

"Immediately," Rycroft said.

The smile faded from his son's face. "Must I?"

"Yes. Will you?"

The lad's shoulders slumped dejectedly. "Yes."

"Very well, then, you are dismissed, young man." Rycroft scruffed up the child's hair and winked at him. "You have done your mother proud with your tale bearing."

Lady Rycroft coughed softly.

Her husband merely smiled at her.

The admiral, who was also seated with Mr. Bennet and Sir William, chuckled. "They are a lively lot, but I would expect no less, considering their parents."

"Indeed," Mr. Bennet agreed. "Despite their quirks, they are all quite perfect."

"No truer words have been spoken," the admiral said. "And I am sure that the Lesters and Endicotts will be adding to the number in due time."

"The gentlemen arrive tomorrow, and my wife is beside herself with excitement," Mr. Bennet said. "The other wedding breakfasts were all at Netherfield, so this is the first she will have the pleasure of hosting in our home." He shook his head. "Add to that the fact that Lydia is sharing her day with Georgiana, and you can imagine the delight which has effused from her on a daily basis for the past month and a fortnight."

Sir William chuckled.

"I am not truly complaining, for it is well within her rights to be excited as her final daughter will be happily situated," Mr. Bennet added with a smile. He could not fault his wife for her excitement, since he shared it with her. Each of his daughters would be married and happily so. Not one had married for convenience. They had each found a love match of good character and financial standing.

"My sister is just as delighted to see her last niece happy," added the admiral. "I had feared it would not happen, but it has, thanks to Darcy."

It had been a long two seasons for Georgiana. She had found her heart quite gone before the first had even begun. A gentleman had unwittingly captured her fancy at a brief meeting over a meal at Rycroft Place five years ago, but not being out, she pined secretly for him until just before her debut when she spoke of it to her aunt.

From there, strategies were made, house parties planned, soirees attended, all with the intent of securing her happiness with the gentleman. It was not easily done, however, as the gentleman attended social events only sporadically.

Finally, after Georgiana had refused the fifth offer of marriage from as many eligible gentlemen, Darcy was made aware of the desires his sister's heart. A rather direct letter to the gentleman later, and Mr. Lester appeared at Darcy House to court the young lady whom he had found fascinating but feared was too far above him.

Lydia's story had been less filled with longing. She had happily made her debut next to Georgiana under the watchful eye of Mrs. Darcy and Mrs. Bingley and had been called on by several gentlemen, yet none truly captured her heart. She spoke of it often to a particular gentleman with whom she often found herself thrown together since he was Rycroft's friend. And he, in turn, spoke to her of his reluctance to marry for anything less than the deepest of affection. Their friendship grew and then quite unexpectedly shifted to something more, and now, Lydia found herself betrothed to her friend, the one man at whom she never batted an eyelash and with whom she had never acted a part.

So it was that a week later, both young ladies stood in this very drawing room, repeating their vows and tying their hearts forever to the men whom they loved, before sitting down to a sumptuous wedding breakfast.

"I have a gift for my lovely bride." Jonathan rose as his announcement drew the attention of the rest of the wedding guests. He extended a hand to Georgiana and helped her to her feet. Then, he took a small pouch from his pocket and from it shook out a necklace.

"This is a symbol of love, both past and present – once for lovers long ago, and now for my love for you. As the pearl is locked away within this heart never to be removed, so your love is woven deeply into the fabric of my very being, never to be removed." He stepped behind her and fastened the necklace around her neck. "It belonged to my grandfather."

"It is lovely." Georgiana sighed as she held up the golden heart, woven in such a fashion as to look like it was a delicate cage for the pearl locked inside.

Mrs. Bennet's eyes grew wide at the sight of it. "It looks just like the one my father showed me," she whispered to Lady Lucas, who was on her left.

"It is the very same," Lady Lucas replied. "Mr. Lester's father came to work for Sir William's brother, and his father, Mr. Lester's grandfather, left that necklace as an inheritance to his son. It seems it has now been passed down to the grandson." She sighed. "And there is such a story behind it."

"Indeed, there is!" Mrs. Bennet smiled at her friend and grasped Lady Lucas' arm excitedly. "Passed down to the grandson, who has now given it to the granddaughter of Lady Matlock." She whispered but so excitedly that it was not as soft as it should have been. Thankfully, all who were gathered were family.

Lady Sophia nodded and smiled at Mrs. Bennet's comment. "Finally, the second necklace has come home," she said looking at her brother.

Several pairs of questioning eyes turned towards her as she dashed a tear from her cheek. "There is a story," she began. "It is a story of choices and unequal marriages and eventual happily ever afters." She held up a cautionary finger. "However, it must remain within our family..."

If you enjoyed this book, be sure to let others know by leaving a review.

＊

Want to know when other Leenie books will be available? You can always know what's new with my books by joining one of my reader communities

leeniebrown.com/subscribe

＊

Turn the page to read an excerpt of another one of Leenie's books.

Two Days Before Christmas Excerpt

Now that you have come to the end of the Choices series, please, allow me to suggest my Darcy Family Holiday's series to you as a possible next read. This series starts with some scheming by Darcy's sister to give him the best Christmas present ever. Below is a portion of the first chapter of book 1, Two Days Before Christmas.

Georgiana Darcy peered out her bedroom window to see who had come to call and was causing the flurry of activity in the halls. Her eyes grew wide as she saw her brother step down from his travelling coach and give some directives to a footman — likely about his trunk or possibly requesting tea. Those were the things he most often thought of first when arriving home from a trip. Her brows furrowed, and her lips pinched into a displeased pucker. Her brother was not supposed to be here in town. He was supposed to be in Hertfordshire with Mr. Bingley, learning how to be something other than unpleasant.

Honestly! It was her heart that had been broken by that cad Wickham, not his! Hers was mending, but his? She shook her head. If only she could do something to prove to him that, though she had been hurt — and grievously so –, her heart was no longer affected. In fact, she had recently begun to think that it had never actually been touched at all. She had not been in love with Wickham. She was nearly convinced of that fact. She had been in love with the idea of being loved, adored, and cherished by a handsome man. That she had not been and feared she might never be was what still caused a pinching pain in her heart. Her companion, Mrs. Annesley, assured her it was a foolish notion to judge every gentleman by the actions of one, but it seemed prudent to Georgiana to be cautious, just in case. She had been too trusting. No one could tell her otherwise. However, just because she needed to learn a lesson in prudence, did not mean her brother needed to continue to suffer. He had done precisely as he should. Her pain was not his doing. The fact that he still tormented himself with guilt was what made it nearly impossible for her to lay her own, well-deserved, shame aside.

She had spoken in confidence about such things to Mr. Bingley before he and her brother had departed for Netherfield, Mr. Bingley's new estate. He had promised he would do his best to see her brother engaged in activities that would bring him distraction if not pleasure. She had been so hopeful that Mr. Bingley had been successful, for Fitzwilliam's letters had been light in tone, sharing stories of the various people he had met and wishing he was free of the attentions of one particular person, Caroline Bingley. Added to that, yesterday, Mr. Bingley had called to inform her that her brother had done the most unusual thing by dancing with a Miss Elizabeth — the same Miss Elizabeth that had featured in more than one of Fitzwilliam's missives.

Why he was home when things had seemed so promising, she was uncertain. She grabbed a wrap for her shoulders and slipped her feet into her slippers.

"Your brother has returned," Mrs. Annesley said as Georgiana met her in the corridor.

"I saw his carriage," Georgiana replied. "It is very unexpected."

"It is," Mrs. Annesley agreed. "Do you wish for me to attend you?"

Georgiana shook her head.

Mrs. Annesley glanced down the stairs. "You will tell me how he is, will you not?" There was a note of worry in her whispered question.

As far as Georgiana was concerned, hiring Mrs. Annesley to be her companion was the best gift Fitzwilliam had ever given her. Mrs. Annesley's heart was far softer than her angular features and austere manner of dress suggested. She was also aware of far more than the spectacles that perched on her nose while she read and stitched might indicate.

"Of course, I will," Georgiana assured her.

A twinkle shone in the lady's eye. "Then be quick."

Georgiana giggled as she descended the stairs. Mrs. Annesley was quiet and reserved, as was proper for one in her position, but she was also curious and lively when she and Georgiana were alone. Reaching the bottom of the stairs, Georgiana stopped and waited patiently as her brother removed his outerwear and apologized to Mr. Wright, his butler, for the unexpected change in plans.

Seeing her, he greeted her first with a smile and then, open arms, which she ran into without a second's pause.

"I have missed you," he murmured against her hair before releasing her.

"You did not return on my account, did you?" Georgiana wrapped her arm around his.

"May I not wish to see my sister?"

His avoidance of her question was not a good sign. Such a tactic always meant he did not wish to discuss his reasons for something.

"You may wish to see her, but you should not do so at the expense of breaking your word to a friend." She felt his arm flinch.

"Mr. Bingley called on me yesterday. He seemed eager to return to Hertfordshire." Again, his arm flinched.

"He may return anytime he wishes."

Her brows drew together. Her brother's tone was so flat, so uncaring — so very unlike him. "I assume Miss Bingley and the Hursts accompanied you back to town?"

"They did."

She lifted a brow and gave him an assessing look. "You know Mr. Bingley will never persuade Caroline away from town so close to the season. It was a struggle to get her to go with him at Michaelmas."

He shrugged? The only response she was going to receive to such a comment was a shrug?

"He will be disappointed," Georgiana said softly.

"That cannot be helped."

Georgiana's heart sank at Darcy's words. Mr. Bingley had been so eager to return to Netherfield and a particular lady. In fact, he had mentioned taking his mother's fede ring with him when he returned. Not returning would do more than disappoint Mr. Bingley; it would likely break his heart and the heart of the lady he had left behind.

"Now, as delighted as I am to see you," her brother continued, "I am desirous of a long soak in a hot tub of water." He gave her a tight smile. "To wash away the chatter of Miss Bingley."

He had not remembered to ask her if she was well. That was also odd. For the last several months, he had asked her that question at least three times a day and always upon returning from a time away. She released his arm but only to allow her hand to slide down and grasp his. "Fitzwilliam?" She waited until he looked up at her instead of at their joined hands before continuing. "Are you well?"

His eyes left hers and looked down the hall toward his room as he nodded. "I will be," he said as he lifted her hand and kissed her fingers. "I will be."

Georgiana pulled her lip between her teeth as she watched him walk down the hall to his room. His shoulders were not as square as they normally were, and he ran his hand through his hair which was something he only did when thoroughly overwhelmed by a situation. He was not well. Something was most certainly wrong.

Georgiana gasped as a reason for her brother's melancholy came to mind. Unwilling to entertain the troubling thought for hours before she spoke to her brother again, she hurried down the hall and knocked firmly on his door. Then she waited. There was some shuffling in the room, but none that sounded as if a person were approaching the door, so she knocked again. This time she rapt so loudly that she was positive at least one knuckle would bear a bruise from the action.

However, her sore knuckles had produced the desired effect since her brother, minus his coat and cravat, opened his door.

"She has not trapped you, has she?" Georgiana demanded.

Her brother's brows drew together in question. "I beg your pardon?"

"Caroline Bingley. She has not finally succeeded in trapping you into marriage while her brother was gone, has she?" Georgiana's heart raced with trepidation. Caroline Bingley was not the sort of lady she wished to have as a sister, nor did she think her brother would ever be happy married to such a person. Caroline was not horrid, but she was not gentle or lively or particularly witty. She was just not the sort of lady Georgiana knew her brother needed for a wife.

Thankfully, shock suffused her brother's face as he blurted an emphatic no.

"You are not marrying her?" Georgiana asked again just to be certain of his answer.

"No, Georgie, I am not marrying anyone." The light in his eyes faded as he said it.

In spite of her concern for the sadness in his tone and expression, Georgiana smiled at him. "One day you will," she said hopefully.

"Perhaps one day," he replied without so much as a hint of conviction that it was true.

Oh, he was in a deplorable state of mind, and Georgiana was quite certain she knew why.

"Was there anything else?" he asked as he turned to close his door.

Georgiana shook her head. "Not at the moment."

"Then, I shall see you at dinner."

Georgiana stared at his closed door. "Perhaps, nothing," she muttered. "You will marry one day, and you will be happy," she declared to the door, "even if I must see to it myself." Having settled the matter with her brother's closed door, she turned and went in search of Mrs. Annesley. Undoubtedly, her companion would have some advice as to how to help Fitzwilliam.

More Books by Leenie

You can find all of Leenie's books at this link

bit.ly/LeenieBBooks
where you can explore the collections below

❦

Dash of Darcy and Companions Collection

Marrying Elizabeth Series

Sweet Possibilities and Sweet Extras

Willow Hall Romances

The Choices Series

Darcy Family Holidays

Darcy and... An Austen-Inspired Collection

Teatime Tales (Sweet Austen-inspired Novelettes)

Other Pens

Touches of Austen

Nature's Fury and Delights (Sweet Regency Novelettes)

About Leenie

Leenie Brown has always been a girl with an active imagination, which, while growing up, was both an asset, providing many hours of fun as she played out stories, and a liability, when her older sister and aunt would tell her frightening tales. At one time, they had her convinced Dracula lived in the trunk at the end of the bed she slept in when visiting her grandparents!

Although it has been years since she cowered in her bed in her grandparents' basement, she still has an imagination which occasionally runs away with her, and she feeds it now as she did then — by reading!

Her heroes, when growing up, were authors, and the worlds they painted with words were (and still are) her favourite playgrounds! Now, as an adult, she spends much of her time in the Regency world, playing with the characters from her favourite Jane Austen novels and those of her own creation.

When she is not traipsing down a trail in an attempt to keep up with her imagination, Leenie resides in the beautiful province of Nova Scotia with her two sons and her very own Mr. Brown (a wonderful mix of all the best of Darcy, Bingley, and Edmund with a healthy dose of the teasing Mr. Tilney and just a dash of the scolding Mr. Knightley).

Connect with Leenie in one of her reader communities or on social media. Find links to all of those on her website at bit.ly/connect-with-leenie

www.ingramcontent.com/pod-product-compliance
Lightning Source LLC
Chambersburg PA
CBHW020604040726
47498CB00003B/635